Suddenly the faint touch of Green's thoughts was gone. I spun around, but too late: Green was disappearing up the stairwell. Clutched in his hand was a small briefcase.

With a shout, I went after him. But his lead was too big, and he was already diving into the front seat of his car. With a squeal of tires he took off into the night. Seconds later I was behind him, gunning my old Chevy for all it was worth.

The sense of terrified urgency wrapped suffocatingly around me. Clearly, Green had lied about being able to make a portable mind shield. Bitterly, I wondered what else he'd lied about . . . and whether I'd ever get a chance to warn the others. With the shield going full blast in Green's car, I couldn't reach another telepath. More than once I tried to drift back out of range, hoping to at least let Colleen or Calvin know what had happened, but each time Green spotted the maneuver and matched it.

Finally, sometime in the small hours of the morning, Green pulled over to the side of the road. I pulled up behind him, got out and walked toward him. "All right, Green, it's all over," I told him. "Let's have the shield and whatever else you stole."

"Before you do anything hasty," he said, "I suggest you look at the sign up there."

Frowning, I glanced at a dimly lit sign by the highway. It announced eleven miles to Chillicothe. *Eleven miles?*

I felt the blood draining from my face. "Yes," Green nodded. "She's within the twenty-mile limit. If I flip this switch, you'll both be dead instantly."

Colleen, I thought. *What have I done?*

Baen Books By Timothy Zahn

Cascade Point
Cobras Two
A Coming of Age
Deadman Switch
Distant Friends
Time Bomb and Zahndry Others
Triplet
Spinneret
Warhorse

DISTANT FRIENDS

And Others

TIMOTHY ZAHN

BAEN BOOKS

DISTANT FRIENDS ... AND OTHERS

The following stories were first published in *Analog* magazine and are copyright © by Davis Publications, Inc.:
"Red Thoughts at Morning" (April 1981), "Dark Thoughts at Noon" (December 1982), "Pawn's Gambit" (March 1982), "The Evidence of Things Not Seen" (June 1986), "Expanded Charter" (September 1983), and "Final Solution" (March 1982).

"The Peaceful Man" was first published in *The Magazine of Fantasy and Science Fiction* (September 1982) and is copyright © by Mercury Press, Inc. "Guardian Angel" first appeared in *Far Frontiers VII* (December 1986) and is copyright © by Timothy Zahn.

A Baen Books Original

Baen Publishing Enterprises
P.O. Box 1403
Riverdale, N.Y. 10471

ISBN: 0-671-72131-3

Cover art by David Mattingly

First printing, August 1992

Distributed by
SIMON & SCHUSTER
1230 Avenue of the Americas
New York, N.Y. 10020

Printed in the United States of America

CONTENTS

DISTANT
FRIENDS

RED THOUGHTS AT MORNING

It had been one of those long, frustrating days, the kind that makes you feel like the dish rag at a greasy spoon, and I wasn't in any shape for the headline that jumped out at me as I opened my *Des Moines Register* that evening: TELEPATH KILLED IN HIJACKING.

I stood there, just inside my apartment door, rainwater running off my coat onto the rug, and read the first few paragraphs. Amos Potter, of Eureka, California, had been on a commuter flight from San Francisco to Los Angeles when three men at the other end of the plane produced guns and a bomb and demanded to go to Cuba. The pilot had obediently changed course, but had had to set down in Las Vegas for fuel. Police and FBI men had stormed the plane, killing all three hijackers and wounding four passengers. Amos hadn't been found until it was all over: he'd been stabbed in the heart with one of the galley's steak knives and left in one of the lavatories.

Tears welled up in my eyes and I tossed the paper aside. I'd never met Amos, of course; never even been within two hundred miles of him. But he'd been a sort of elder statesman to the rest of us, the embodiment of easy dignity and high moral character, and it was largely because of him that we had won any tolerance at all from the world.

I made my way to my couch and collapsed onto it. *Colleen,* I called.

Yes, Dale. She must have been expecting my call. *I've seen the news, darling.*

Why didn't you call and tell me? The news at noon mentioned the hijacking, but I didn't know Amos was aboard. Or . . . any of the rest of it.

Maybe I should have called you. Her thoughts wrapped soothingly around my pain, the telepathic equivalent of taking me in her arms. *But I knew you were going to have a rough day, and I didn't want to dump this on top of you at the same time. Did that go all right?*

More or less, I told her. *Both sides spent the whole day arguing legal details before the judge. I got to sit there and listen to them discuss my abilities and ethics as if I wasn't there. When I wasn't being insulted I was being bored. Hardly seems important now, though, does it?*

I know, she agreed soberly. *Did you know Amos well?*

Not really. I felt her smile, and couldn't help smiling myself. It was truly the sort of answer a telepath would give: only when you don't know how complex human beings really are do you lightly state that you "know" someone. *I couldn't reach him in Eureka, of course, but he used to come to Pittsburgh or Louisville once or twice a year, and I always talked with him for a few hours then.*

Me too. I used to feel a bit isolated up here in Regina; you remember how I used to fly to Salt Lake City a couple of times a year just to talk with him. I'm going to miss him.

Yeah. We all are.

For a few minutes we sat silently, maintaining contact

without words, Colleen's presence had a warm, comforting texture to it, and slowly the tensions of the day began to fade. Finally, I stirred. *Have you discussed arrangements with any of the others yet?*

A little. I talked to Gordon in Spokane, and he thought the only fair way was to let all of us draw straws to see who'd get to go to Eureka and attend the funeral.

No, I shook my head, *it should be between those who knew Amos best. That would be Gordy and Nelson, I guess.*

Colleen shifted uncomfortably. *Do you think it would be wise to let Nelson go? I mean . . . you know how he gets sometimes.*

Oh, he'd be all right, I assured her. *He was only mildly paranoid to begin with, and living in San Diego's been good for him. Every time Amos went down to Los Angeles he improved a little; some of Amos's calmness had to rub off at that distance.*

All right. She was willing to concede the point. *Do you want me to suggest that to Gordon?*

If you would. I thought for a second. With Amos gone, Gordy was out of touch with everyone except Colleen. *I'll call Calvin in Pueblo and have him relay the message to Nelson.*

You feel up to that?

I smiled. *Yes. Thanks for always being there when I need you, Colleen.*

Thank you, she said quietly, and I knew then that she'd received as much comfort from me as she'd given.

I love you, Colleen.

I love you, Dale. Good-by.

We broke contact. I'd loved Colleen for nearly three years now, and she'd loved me even longer. And the knowledge that we would never meet each other was a dull ache permanently lodged in my throat.

What a stinking world.

Sighing, I got to my feet and headed for the kitchen to see about some supper.

* * *

I slept poorly that night, and was back at the Des Moines courthouse at nine sharp the next morning for another day of arguments. In one sense the question before the court was straightforward: the judge had simply to decide whether or not my testimony as a telepath could be admitted as evidence in a robbery case. In practice, however, the legal issues and ramifications surrounding the whole concept formed a jungle that made the Amazon basin look like the pampas. My mood this morning wasn't helping a bit, either; it was dominated by depression, fatigue, and some unknown beast nagging at the back of my mind, and all I wanted to do was to crawl back into bed. I wished to heaven I'd never let the D.A. talk me into this.

Today, for the umpteenth time, Urban, the public defender, wanted to hear about my range. "Think of it as listening to someone whispering," I told him once more. "Within two or three feet I can't help but hear someone's thoughts. Farther away, up to about twenty or twenty-five feet, I can choose whether or not to listen; beyond that, I can't hear at all."

"Except with your fellow telepaths, of course," Urban said briskly, as if I needed reminding.

"The defendant isn't a telepath," I pointed out as patiently as possible.

"Of course not. Now, you referred to this as akin to hearing whispers. We all know how easy it is to misunderstand whispers sometimes—"

"The analogy referred to range, not accuracy," I interrupted. "If I can hear the thoughts at all I hear them clearly. Always."

He started to ask something else—and right then, for no particular reason, the crucial question hit me like a Trident missile.

How the hell do you unexpectedly stab a telepath?

It *had* to have been unexpected; the lavatory door had been unlocked and the paper hadn't mentioned any signs of a struggle. But that was impossible; given the circumstances. Amos was most certainly reading out to his full range. So why hadn't he seen the killer coming?

Urban had finished his question by the time I made up my mind. "Excuse me," I said, pulling out my handkerchief and pretending to clear my sinuses. I didn't want to just go glassy-eyed on them, after all; I've learned that sort of thing can be disconcerting to people. But safely hidden behind the handkerchief, I could make my contact. *Calvin? Calvin, are you there? Calvin?*

Right here, Dale, came the calm thought. *You sound agitated.*

I'm getting there, I agreed. *Listen, you've got the location log this quarter, right? Can you clear me to Las Vegas tonight? It's important.*

From Des Moines? That was Calvin—no unnecessary questions asked. *Any direct flight would bring you too close to Pueblo, but I could move out of town for a few hours if necessary.*

No, it's not worth that. Besides, I doubt there's a direct flight, anyway.

Then if you go via Denver or Salt Lake we should be all right.

Great. I'll make some reservations and get back to you as soon as I know my schedule.

All right. Oh—and you'll have to be out of there by six tomorrow evening. Gordy's flying down to escort Amos back to Eureka.

Yeah, okay.

Calvin was getting curious. *I trust you'll tell me what all this is about sometime.*

Sure, but later. I've got to go now.

Talk to you later.

I slid my handkerchief back in my pocket. Already I felt better. "Now, what was that question again, Mr. Urban?"

I got through the rest of the morning without any real trouble. During lunch break I called a travel agent and he worked out a pair of connecting flights that would get me into Las Vegas by ten. That was later than I'd wanted, but my option was to wait until after Gordy had come and gone. This way I'd have at least most of tomorrow before I had to leave town.

The judge and lawyers weren't happy about my announcement that I was taking a few days off, but they accepted it with the grace of reasonable men who have no real choice in the matter. By seven-thirty that evening I was on the first leg of my flight . . . and by eight we were circling Denver, just a hundred miles from Calvin's home in Pueblo.

It's a strange sort of sensation, and more than a little scary the first time you experience it. Even a hundred miles apart, Calvin and I were now close enough that it was no longer possible to block our surface thoughts from each other: to tune each other out, so to speak. It's the same thing that happens when a telepath and human are only two or three feet apart, but with the extra complication that it's a true two-way communication. If the plane now suddenly turned due south and Calvin and I got even closer . . . but that wasn't something I wanted to think about.

Of course, as long as you didn't panic, the effortless communication provided by a close approach was a good opportunity to talk. Cavin and I spent quite some time doing just that, discussing life in general and ourselves and our fellow telepaths in particular. But he couldn't hide his curiosity about my sudden trip, just as I couldn't hide my somewhat perverse decision to make him bring up the subject first.

Calvin cracked first. *All right, you win,* he said at last. *You're not going to Vegas just to say good-by to Amos—I can tell that much. So?*

You're right. I explained as best I could the questions I had about Amos's death—not an easy task, since a lot of my feelings hadn't really made it to verbal level yet.

He mulled at the problem for a bit after I finished, his thoughts an orderly flow of questions, possibility, and logic. *Interesting,* he said. *I agree; something here doesn't ring quite true. I don't know, though. Suppose one of the hijackers recognized Amos, decided to kill him to cover their trail, and threatened to kill some of the other passengers too unless Amos went quietly? He was nobler than the rest of us put together, and I could see him giving in under those circumstances.*

Maybe, I said slowly. *But I still don't like it.*

I can tell, Calvin came back dryly. *You're broadcasting uneasiness over two states. Look, I doubt that there's anything sinister going on here, but I agree it ought to be checked out right away. Let me know if I can help, okay?*

You'll be the first I call, I assured him.

Good. Oh, one other thing you may not have heard about yet: the question's been making the rounds today as to whether or not we should ban commercial air travel by our members.

I thought we settled that issue years ago.

We did, but it's getting another look. If there's going to be a resurgence of hijackings, the margin of safety's going to be all fouled up, and it may be smart to stick with trains or private planes for a while. Suppose, for instance, Amos's plane had been diverted to Pueblo or Des Moines instead of Vegas.

We both shuddered. *Yeah,* I agreed soberly. *But I think the risks can be minimized.*

Yeah, well, I'm not going to debate it with you now. Just think about it, and we'll all discuss it together in a week or so.

Okay. I'd better enjoy this trip, I thought glumly—it might be the last I could take for a while.

Fine. Well, you seem pretty tired, so I think we should break now. I'll talk to you later, Dale.

I glanced out the window in mild surprise. Our layover was over, and we were once again airborne. Beneath the plane the ground was dark; Denver was far behind us. The close approach was over. *Good night, Calvin,* I said, and broke contact.

I dozed the rest of the trip, trying to ignore the peculiar looks and even more peculiar thoughts the stewardess kept sending my way.

* * *

Sometime during the middle of the night I decided I hated Las Vegas, and that first impression was solidified the next morning during my taxi ride to police headquarters. It wasn't just the high proportion of the criminal element roaming the streets: every city has some of that. Rather, it was the greed, goldlust, and despair I could sense all around me. This was a frantic town, a city founded on hedonism and life's more transient gains, and it simultaneously angered and depressed me. It seemed grossly unfair that Amos Potter, a man who had loved the quiet outdoors and had spent his life helping others, should have had to die here.

But the police, at least, were courteous and helpful, and I was routed to the proper officer with a minimum of delay. He was a squat, muscular man with a swarthy complexion and the unlikely but circumstantially appropriate name of Lieutenant James Bond.

"Honest," he insisted as he gave me a quick handshake. "What can I do for you?"

"My name's Dale Ravenhall," I told him. "I wanted to ask a few questions about the recent death of Amos Potter."

He recognized my name and drew back almost imperceptibly. "I see. I'm sorry about Mr. Potter. Was he a good friend of yours?"

"We are, by necessity, a somewhat tight-knit group," I said. "Are you the one who found Amos on the plane?"

He shook his head. "One of the SWAT team discovered the body." His mind flashed the man's name—Sergeant Tom Avery—which I filed away for future reference. "I was called in right away to head that part of the investigation."

"Were there any signs of a struggle? The newspapers didn't mention any."

"No, there weren't, and that's something I don't understand. You people are supposed to read minds at a pretty good distance, right? So why didn't Mr. Potter lock the door?"

I scowled. "I don't know. That's one of the things that bothers me about this."

"What are the others?"

"The lack of struggle, for one," I said, sensing even as I ticked off my list that he had many of the same questions. "The use of one of the galley knives for the murder when they had guns. How come they were clever enough to smuggle those guns aboard in the first place, and yet got themselves killed on their first stop."

"You missed two important ones," Bond said. "Why did they pick a puddle-jumping commuter plane from San Francisco, of all places, to hijack to Cuba? And why didn't Mr. Potter contact one of you people before he died?"

I frowned. That last hadn't occurred to me. "I don't know. I was too far away myself at that time, but maybe he *did* talk to one of the others. I can check on that right now, if you'd like."

Bond had never watched a telepath in action and wasn't sure he wanted to start now. But professional considerations outweighed any squeamishness. "Go ahead; I'd like to know."

From my close-approach contact with Calvin last night I already knew Amos hadn't contacted him before his death. Gordy was a long shot; I tried briefly to get him, but the distance was a shade too great. That left only one possibility. *Nelson? Are you there, Nelson?*

Yes, of course, Dale. What is it?

If Colleen's mental texture was one of warmth and love, and Calvin's one of calmness, Nelson's always struck me as predominantly nervous. *I was just in the neighborhood and thought I'd say hi.*

In the neighborhood?

Las Vegas. Light conversation was often lost on Nelson. *Listen, Nelson, I've been trying to track down some questions about Amos's death.*

What sort of questions?

Oh, just some loose ends. Nelson's nervousness was contagious, and I didn't want to prolong the contact.

Besides, Lieutenant Bond was waiting. *I wondered if Amos had had a chance to contact you before the end.*

No, he said, almost too quickly. *But I might have been out of range.*

Where were you?

I flew down to Baja for a couple of days. His tone said it was none of my business where he and his Piper Comanche had gone. *I was flying back when the news came.*

Okay, just wanted to check. You doing okay?

Save your sympathy, Dale. I'm fine.

Right. I'll be talking to you later.

Bond nodded when I relayed the conversation. "That was Nelson Follstadt, right? Do you think you can believe him?"

I bristled. "Of course. Why would he lie?"

He shrugged. "I hear he has some psychological problems."

"Well . . . yes, he does, but he's improved a lot lately. And he's been away from the other telepath for nearly ten years, so there's no place to go but up."

"Come again? What other telepath?"

This wasn't really the time for a lecture, but Bond truly didn't understand. And I've always tried to avoid littering my path with mysterious statements and obscure hints. "Oh, well, you've probably heard that telepaths can't get too close to each other. That's because the contact gets stronger with decreasing distance, and the two personalities begin to meld into one. At about twenty miles apart—theoretically—the strain becomes too great and both telepaths go permanently insane."

Neither Bond's face nor his thoughts were very pleasant. "Is that what happened to Nelson Folstadt?"

"Fortunately, no. The telepathic ability grows with age, and it's only as you get into the teens that it becomes strong enough for any risk of insanity to show up. Nelson just happened to grow up in the same city with another fledgling telepath, and before they were identified and split up the small effects had gradually built up into a mild paranoia. But, as I said, Nelson's improving."

"What about the other telepath?"

"He committed suicide six years ago." One of our group's worst failures, I reminded myself bitterly.

"Oh." Bond was silent for a moment, wondering if he should ask his next question. I let him take his time. "There's one other thing I've been wondering about," he finally said. "I've heard rumors that you people can . . . well, force normal humans to do what you want. Is that true? And if so, why didn't Mr. Potter stop the hijacking?"

"It's true, in about the same way the CIA and certain religious cults can impose their will on people. It would take almost continuous contact between telepath and subject for several days straight to accomplish it, though. Amos couldn't possibly have done anything in the time he had."

"Hmm. Okay, I'm surprised the CIA hasn't shanghaied you, though. You sound like you'd be handy to have around."

"Some of us have been tested by various agencies. There are drugs that are faster and easier to use. Look, we're getting off the subject. Is there anything else you can tell me about Amos's death or about the hijacking in general?"

"Sorry." He shook his head. "You've got all the obvious facts; the others will have to wait for the lab work. If you'll give me your number, I'll get in touch when I know something more."

"I'd appreciate that." I wrote my Des Moines number on a card and, for good measure, added Calvin's. "I may be moving around in the next few days, but Calvin Wolfe here will be able to relay any messages."

"Fine." He gave me a thoughtful look. "Nelson Follstadt's closer, you know. Don't you trust him?"

"Sure I do. I just—well, Calvin's a closer friend."

"Yeah. Well, thanks for stopping by, Mr. Ravenhall. I'll be in touch."

"Thanks." I shook his hand again and left.

His last question bothered me all the way back to the hotel. Why *hadn't* I given him Nelson's number? —

Especially since Nelson was closer to Eureka, where I had already more or less decided to go next. Was there something about that last contact I'd had with him that had bothered me? Certainly, Nelson had been nervous, but that was normal for him . . . wasn't it? I was beginning to regret having broken off the contact so quickly. My chance was now gone for further questioning; if I called back with the same questions I was likely to stir up Nelson's quiescent paranoia, and I couldn't take that just now.

I glanced at my watch. It was nearly noon. Flopping onto my back on the bed, I closed my eyes. *Calvin? Yo, Calvin?*

Hello, Dale. Learned anything interesting?

Yes and no. I've found the cop in charge of the investigation has some of the same questions I do, but he doesn't have the answers either. Is Gordy still due in here at six, and when is he heading over to Eureka?

Yes, and tomorrow morning.

I need a favor. Would you ask him to delay either leg of his trip by twenty-four hours?

Well . . . I suppose I could ask him. Why?

I'd like to go up to Eureka myself and look around. No particular reason, I added, anticipating his next question. *I'd heard Amos had suspended his psychotherapy practice and was working on something special. I'd like to check it out.*

I can save you some trouble, if that's all you want. According to Gordy, Amos was trying to build some kind of electronic gadget for locating new telepaths.

My jaw dropped. *You're kidding. I hadn't heard a whisper about that. I didn't even know it was theoretically possible.*

Me neither, to both comments, until Gordy told me last night. Apparently Amos didn't want it spread around, in case things fell through.

Now that I thought about it, I remembered Amos had earned a master's in electrical engineering before switching to psychology. *How far had he gotten?*

Gordy didn't know. He was planning to try to find out when he went up there.

I pondered. *Calvin, I'd still like to go to Eureka tonight.*

Okay, I'll try to work things out with Gordy. If not, you two'll be in contact range within a few hours and can hash it over between yourselves.

Thanks. One other thing. I hesitated. *Nelson told me he was in Baja when Amos died. Is that true?*

Calvin was silent for a moment, and I could sense his surprise. Accusing another telepath, even implicitly, of lying was serious business. *As a matter of fact, I don't know. Nelson is a bit of a maverick sometimes, and I'm pretty sure he occasionally takes his Comanche out for a short spin without telling anyone. I think he resents having his movements watched so closely, especially when he doesn't think it necessary.*

I grunted. That was just great. *Maybe I should give him personal notice that I'm heading to Eureka. I'll talk to you later, Calvin. Thanks for your help.*

Sure. Good hunting.

For a moment I just lay there, thinking. Then I rolled over, snared the phone, and placed a call to the airport.

I got into Eureka at eight that evening and rented a car for the drive out to Amos's home. I'd never been there before, but Gordy had given me detailed directions earlier in the day and I found the unpretentious little ranch house without difficulty. Mrs. Lederman, Amos's long-time housekeeper, was waiting there for me; with typical foresight, Calvin had phoned to tell her I was coming.

"I'm pleased to meet you, Mr. Ravenhall," she said when I had identified myself. "Please excuse the mess; I haven't felt much like cleaning today."

"It looks fine," I assured her. Her plump, middle-aged face had lost most of the signs of recent crying; the scars in her psyche would take much longer to heal. I didn't intend to pry, but the texture of her surface thoughts made it obvious that she had loved Amos deeply. I wondered how he had felt about her, and the thought inevitably turned my mind toward Colleen. . . . Wrenching hard, I forced myself back to business. "Mrs. Lederman, did Amos say or do anything unusual before he left? Anything that might imply he was worried or suspicious about something?"

She shook her head. "I've been thinking about it ever since Mr. Wolfe called from Colorado this afternoon and I can't come up with anything. Amos seemed a bit preoccupied when he returned from Los Angeles about two weeks ago, but that cleared up quickly and he went back to work on his telepath finder—I expect you've heard of that by now."

"Yes. Who besides you knew he was working on it?"

"Gordy Sears, of course," she said. "I think he was Amos's closest friend. And I believe Mr. Follstadt knew about it, too."

"Nelson?" That made sense, I suppose. One main use of the gadget would probably be to locate young telepaths before any accidental psychic damage occurred, and knowing such a thing was in the works might ease any fears Nelson had about being hurt like that again. "Would you let me see where Amos worked?"

"If you'd like," she shrugged, and I caught something about a mountain retreat from her mind. "But most of his electronics work was done at his cabin in the Sierra. It was more peaceful there, he used to tell me; nobody else *thinking* nearby."

She led me down the hall to Amos's workroom, and I poked around there for a few minutes without finding anything interesting. "Can you tell me how to get to his cabin?"

"Well . . . it was sort of private, but I guess it'd be okay now. But it'd take five or six hours to get there. You ever driven mountains at night?"

"Enough to know I don't want to try it in an unfamiliar area. I'll head out in the morning. If you'll give me those directions, I'll go now and get out of your way."

"No need for that," she shook her head. "I've made up the guest room for you."

"Oh. Thanks very much, but I don't think I ought to stay."

"It's no trouble. I'm leaving in a few minutes, anyway, and you'll have the place to yourself. Amos was always hospitable, Mr. Ravenhall," she added, as I opened my mouth to refuse again. "I know he would have wanted you to stay here."

What could I say to that?

She gave me a quick guided tour of the premises to show me where everything was, and then left, locking the front door behind her. I watched her car disappear down the road and then, moved by an obscure impulse, returned to Amos's workroom.

Off in one corner of the room was a small writing desk almost buried under neat piles of paper and correspondence. I'd ignored it the last time I came through, but now I went over and gazed down at it. A proper investigation should include a search of Amos's papers ... but I had no right to pry like that. Besides, if I found something significant, would I even know it? I still didn't really know what I was looking for. Resolutely, I started to turn away ... and as I did, the return address on one of the envelopes caught my eye. It was that of a Las Vegas casino.

Frowning, I picked up the letter. It was unopened, postmarked the day before Amos's death. Feeling guilty, I opened it.

The message was very brief:

Dear Mr. Potter,

Thank you for your note of the 4th. We are quite interested in your proposal, and would very much like to discuss it in person with you. Please let us know when it would be convenient for us to fly you down for a meeting.

It was signed by one of the biggest names in Las Vegas.

I reread the letter twice without making any more sense of it. What was Amos doing getting mixed up with

Vegas casino owners? What kind of offer was he making?
And was it pure coincidence that Amos had subsequently
died in that very city?

Some of those questions might be answered if I could
find the carbon of Amos's original letter, but a two-hour
search convinced me that it wasn't anywhere in the
house. Unless Amos had destroyed it or Mrs. Lederman
had taken it away, there was only one other place it was
likely to be. More than ever, now, I wanted to get to
Amos's mountain retreat.

I was rudely awakened from a restless dream by an
insistent knocking at the base of my mind, and it took
me a second to realize that I was being contacted. *Yes?*

It was Gordy. *Dale, are you all right?*

Sure. I sneaked a look at my watch. Four thirty, and
I was lying fully clothed on Amos's guest room bed. *Why
do you ask?*

*When you hadn't checked in by midnight Calvin and
I started getting worried. We thought something might
have happened to you.*

Just fatigue, I assured him. *I'm sorry, though; I had
intended to contact you last night. I guess I was more bushed
than I thought. Listen, I may have something interesting
here. Did you know Amos had a cabin in the Sierra?*

Yes, but I don't know where it is.

I do. I repeated the location Mrs. Lederman had given
me. *I understand he did most of the work on his telepath
finder up there; I'm going to go see how far he got with the
gadget. And to check on something unexpected that's just
cropped up.* I described the contents of the letter I'd found.

What do you think it means? a new voice asked.

I jumped. *Calvin? Damn, but you startled me—I
didn't know you were listening in. Come to think of it,
how come you're within range?*

Because I'm in Salt Lake City, he explained. *I flew
here last night to give Gordy a hand in raising you. Now,
what about this letter?*

*I haven't the foggiest. But I think it might be
important.*

Maybe, Gordy said cautiously. *I gather you'd like me to stay here in Vegas until you're finished with everything?*

If you would. I think it would make things simpler if I didn't have to keep track of where you were going to be. Another day or two at the most.

Okay. Nelson will calm down eventually, I suppose. How's that?

You didn't know? No, I guess not. He was going to fly up to Eureka after I left to attend Amos's funeral. He was furious that we were delaying things so that you could go running around robbing Amos of his last shred of dignity.

That last was a direct quote, Calvin added.

I winced. *Yeah. I'm sorry. But I still think it's got to be done.*

We're not blaming you, Dale, Calvin said. *Just finish up as quickly as possible, okay?*

Will do, I promised. *Look, I'd better let you two go. I'll contact you when I get to the cabin. Honest.*

Gordy chuckled. *Okay. See you.*

I stared out the window at the predawn darkness for a full minute. Further sleep would be impossible; something in the back of my mind was urging speed. Swinging my legs over the edge of the bed, I located my shoes and headed to the kitchen for a fast breakfast.

Half an hour later I was driving towards the rising sun.

I'd half-expected Amos's cabin to be some rude shack on the side of a mountain, and was therefore vaguely surprised to find a quite modern-looking structure, complete with phone and power lines snaking their way down the mountain. With the key Mrs. Lederman had left me, I let myself in. The interior was as modern as the Eureka house, but not nearly as tidy; Mrs. Lederman probably didn't get up here very often. It was basically a single room, efficiency style, almost a third of which was taken up by a long work table holding about a ton of electronic equipment. In the center of the work table was Amos's telepath finder.

There was no doubt as to what it was. Clearly

homemade, it consisted of a metal box the size of a portable tape player with a pivoting direction pointer protected by a plastic dome mounted on top. There were only two switches: on/off and general/tare. *Calvin? Gordy? Anyone home?*

Right here, Calvin answered. *Where are you, Dale?*

At Amos's cabin. I've found the telepath finder.

You made good time, Gordy grunted, sleep-cobwebs still evident in his mind. *I'd forgotten they'd been up much of the night trying to contact me. What's it look like?*

I described it for them. *That's it?* Calvin asked. *No range meter or anything like that?*

Nope. Maybe Amos planned to work on one next. Of course, you could always get range by triangulation.

Right. Have you tried it yet?

No. I wanted you two here when I did. Any ideas what this general/tare thing is?

There was a pause. *A tare is a deduction of the container's weight when weighing something*, Gordy said. *Maybe that eliminates the operator's effect.*

That makes sense, I agreed. *Okay, brace yourselves. Here goes.*

With the second switch set at "general" I reached out and flipped the device on. Instantly, the needle on top swiveled around and came to a stop pointing at my belt buckle. I took a couple of steps to the right; the needle followed me. *Seems to work*, I told the others. *Now I'll try it on "tare."* I flipped the second switch and waited.

Nothing. The needle moved a fraction toward the west, but was still pointing at me when it stopped. I flipped the switch back and forth a couple of times, but the needle refused to move farther than a few degrees. *This part isn't working.*

You sure? Gordy asked.

Yeah. I'm standing on the finder's north side, so if it edits me out it should swing around to point south-east, where you two and Nelson are. It certainly shouldn't point north by west. I turned it off. We can worry about this later. I'm going to see if I can find that carbon.

One corner of the work table was piled with papers. Leafing through the whole stack would take only minutes; as it happened, my search was considerably shorter. *I've found it.*

Read it to us, Calvin said.

I skipped Amos's identification of himself and his list of credentials. The interesting part was in the second paragraph:

> It has recently come to my attention that one of our group has been making periodic visits to your area for the purpose of "gambling"—I use quotation marks because, for him, certain games will not be governed by chance. No names need be mentioned; I do not intend to aid you in catching or prosecuting him, but merely wish this unfair practice to stop. My efforts to dissuade him have failed, so as a last resort I am offering you a deterrent in the form of a telepath finder. . . .

Gambling? Gordy seemed shocked. *Who of us would do something like that? That's just crazy.*

I think we all came up with the same name simultaneously. Calvin was the first to admit it. *If Amos was right, there's only one of us who has really convenient access to Vegas, who can sneak in and out without too much risk of close-approach problems.*

I sighed. *You mean Nelson?*

DAMN YOU ALL! WHY CAN'T ANY OF YOU MIND YOUR OWN BUSINESS?

All three of us jumped violently. It was Nelson's voice, but so convulsed with fury as to make it almost unrecognizable. *Hey, Nelson, take it easy,* I said. *We didn't know you were listening in.*

Of course not. You'd much rather plot my destruction in private, wouldn't you? You and that holier-than-thou Amos. Well, I warned him!

Something was wrong here. Even given Nelson's

strong emotion, his contact shouldn't be this strong. *Nelson, where are you?* I asked carefully.

You! he all but spat. *It's your fault. You couldn't let Amos die in peace. You couldn't let well enough alone. Now you're going to get what he got.*

Damn you, Nelson! Gordy suddenly interjected. *You killed him, didn't you? Amos caught you sneaking into Vegas, so you conditioned those thugs to hijack the plane and kill him!*

It was his own fault, Nelson shot back. *It was none of his damn business how I make my money. I had to do it—can't you see that?*

He'd gone from angry to pleading in the space of a single sentence, and I didn't like it a bit. Was he starting to crack up?

You'd like that, wouldn't you? Well, if I go, you're going with me!

And that shook me clear down to my toes. It had come up so quickly and so unexpectedly that I hadn't noticed: Nelson and I were in close-approach contact.

Nelson was only a hundred miles away!

And getting closer, he mocked me. *I know where you are, too; I listened to you give the directions to your pals this morning. I'll be overhead before you know it.*

Nelson, are you nuts? Gordy cut in. *You'll kill both of you.*

And why not? You're all out to destroy me anyway. I might as well take one of you with me. I've got nothing to lose now.

Dale, get out of there, Calvin ordered. *You've got to try and get away from him.*

I took three steps toward the door and froze. *Get away where? I don't know what direction he's coming from!*

Nelson laughed. His thoughts were getting progressively louder, and it was becoming harder and harder to hear Gordy and Calvin over the noise. Calvin had to virtually shout his next message. *Use the telepath finder. Maybe it really is working.*

I sprang over to the table, snatched up the box, and flipped the switch. In "tare" mode it once again pointed north by west—and stayed there even when I moved out of the way. Instead of coming straight up from San Diego, Nelson had circled around and was bearing down on me from the north. Clutching the box like a talisman, I ran outside to the car.

And then the nightmare began.

There was no way I could outrun Nelson, and we both knew it. His Piper Comanche had a cruising speed of at least a hundred eighty miles an hour and could travel in a straight line, while I had to stay on winding mountain roads at a quarter of his speed. If I could have gone at right angles to his path, let him overshoot me, I might have had a chance. But it was already too late for that sort of trick. Nelson had complete access to my surface thoughts, and there was no way for me to make any plans without his knowledge.

You see? It's useless to struggle. Give up; it'll be easier on both of us.

I gritted my teeth and drove on, trying in vain to shut out the increasing pressure slowly crushing my mind. A curve came up, too fast. I tapped on the brake, managed to negotiate the turn without losing too much speed. Every fiber of my being was screaming for me to get away, but I had no intention of driving off a cliff for Nelson's convenience. Wiping my palms, one at a time, on my pants, I tried to think.

I was completely cut off from Calvin and Gordy now— the close approach had been blocking any other contact practically from the minute I left the cabin. They would know enough to call the police, of course, but there was little chance the cops could help me. It would be less than an hour before Nelson closed to the twenty-mile gap that would ensure mental disintegration for both of us. The Air Force? They could act swiftly, but they'd first have to be persuaded to get involved. And in a completely non-military situation like this, the chances of that were essentially zero.

A reddish haze, more felt than seen, was growing at the edge of my mind. *Nelson, why are you doing this to us? It can't gain you anything.*

*You've all worked against me: you, Amos, Calvin—
everybody. You've robbed me of the money and power I
could have had—that I deserved. But at least I command
my own death. And before that I'm going to make you
fear me. You are afraid, aren't you, Dale?*

He knew I was. For himself, Nelson felt no fear: only
pain, anger, and morbid satisfaction. His death wish
wrapped around me, tinging the reddish haze with black.
Blinking back tears of agony, I kept going.

I don't know how long I drove, or how many close
calls I had with the many cliffs I passed. Indeed, I hardly
even noticed the road any more; I drove by sheer reflex.
As inexorably as the tide, Nelson's mind slowly washed
over mine. Our thoughts, memories, and emotions inter-
twined, becoming bent and altered by the force of the
collision. I saw his decision to kill Amos, and his condi-
tioning of an airline attendant and three drifters to set
up and execute the hijacking. I watched the agony of
Amos's death, and knew that he'd realized, too late, what
was happening. Nelson's current plan was laid bare; how
he'd tried to beat me to the cabin and destroy both the
telepath finder and the evidence of his gambling. I felt
his lust for power, his anger and frustrations—at himself,
me, the world—his self-doubts ... and all this was
becoming part of me. I was slowly being lost in this thing,
this Dale/Nelson creature which was being created; and
the knowledge that Nelson was similarly being swallowed
up only added to my terror.

And all too soon, I saw the end approaching.

I mean that literally, for in a very real sense whatever
there was that was still Dale Ravenhall was now occu-
pying two separate bodies. I could actually see both the
road ahead of me and the more majestic view from Nelson's Comanche. I could feel the plane's vibration, touch
two different steering wheels ... and I knew the agony
would soon be over.

Yes, soon we'll be dead. Was that my thought or Nelson's? Not that the distinction mattered much any more.
I paused for a moment to look through Nelson's eyes, to
gaze at the mountains I would never see again ... and,

suddenly, a sharp left-hand curve around a cliff loomed ahead.

I gasped, and Nelson's death wish within me fragmented as a surge of survival instinct snapped a portion of my mind out of the growing chaos. Stomping hard on the brake, I wrenched the wheel hard to the left; and as the squeal of tires filled my ears, I saw I had overcorrected. The side of the mountain rushed at me, and I leaned back, bracing for the crash.

The world exploded with a ghastly crash and everything went black.

I woke up slowly, painfully, and with a sense of complete disorientation; but what I noticed first was the silence. It was just me again, Dale Ravenhall, and the other presence was gone. Was I dead?

He's awake.

I cringed involuntarily as the thought touched my mind. The other knew it immediately and hastened to reassure me. *It's all right, Dale, it's all right. It's just me, Colleen. You remember me?*

I swallowed hard and, timidly, reached out. *Is that really you, Colleen?*

It's really me. And Gordon and Calvin are here, too, if you feel like talking to them.

How're you feeling? Gordy asked.

Better, I answered. I was starting to wake up now, and memories were coming back. *Where am I?*

Sacramento, Calvin told me. *They airlifted you there after you crashed your car. You were pretty lucky; minor injuries only.*

Yeah. I was dreading the next question, but I had to ask it. *What happened back there? How did I escape?*

Nelson crashed. Went into a dive somehow and ran smack into a mountain. The experts think he must have turned and come down too fast; there's no evidence of mechanical failure.

I nodded within myself. In those last seconds I'd been in the Comanche's cockpit as well as in my own car—and in the latter I'd turned left, hit the leftmost pedal, and pushed on the wheel. Apparently, I'd done the same in the plane. But I couldn't tell the others what had happened. Not yet.

Calvin was speaking again. *You've been under sedation for the last three days while a handful of top psychiatrists did some tests. They say you've got all the symptoms of dissociative hysteria, but that you have a good chance of recovering with proper care and some hard work.*

Unbidden, tears formed in my eyes, and I clenched my teeth to keep them back. *Maybe. But who's going to come out of this recovery? Dale Ravenhall? Or a Dale/Nelson mixture?*

There was a pause. *We don't know, exactly,* Colleen said gently. *But whatever changes have been forced on you, you're still Dale Ravenhall. Hang onto that thought, that reality. You're still our friend, and we'll stick by you and give you all the help we can.*

Even if I turn out to be partly Nelson?

We would have done the same for Nelson, Calvin said. *He was one of us, too. Try not to hate him, Dale.*

I don't hate him for me. But I won't soon forgive him for killing Amos the same way he tried to kill me.

What do you mean, the same way?

I sighed. I wanted so badly to just forget all this. But they had a right to know. *Nelson wasn't in Baja when Amos was killed. He was in Las Vegas.*

But that's where his conditioned hijackers took the plane. Colleen sounded confused.

Which is exactly what he wanted. Don't you see? Picture Amos rushing helplessly toward a fatal contact with Nelson, who is pretending he is there just by chance. You all know how noble and selfless Amos was. What would he do in that situation?

There was a long pause, the texture of which changed from puzzled to horrified to very sad. *He would have committed suicide rather than let them both die,* Calvin said at last. *That's what happened, isn't it?*

I nodded wearily, and Colleen must have sensed my fatigue. *I think we'd better go now and let Dale get some rest*, she said. *Dale, we'll be here as long as you are, so just call whenever you want to talk. Okay?*

Sure. Thank you—all of you.

Take care, Dale. We'll talk to you later.

I turned my head to the side against my pillow. Sleep was pulling at me, and I welcomed the temporary oblivion it would bring. *I am Dale Ravenhall*, I said to myself and to the universe around me. *You hear me? I am Dale Ravenhall. I am Dale Ravenhall. . . .*

I was saying it right up to the moment I fell asleep. Down deep, I knew it wasn't completely true.

DARK THOUGHTS AT NOON

Like a crazed hawk the Piper Comanche dives at me through the red mist. I am flying her; desperately, I grip the wheel, trying to keep the car's screeching tires on the road winding through the mountains. Agony clouds my vision, permeates every fiber of my being. In the distance I hear a bell ring. Ask not for whom the bell rings . . . no, that's not right, but I can't remember how it should be. Beneath me the road sweeps past/the toy-like mountains crawl past. I am Dale Ravenhall/I am Nelson Follstadt/I am Dale/I am Nelson—pain pain pain. The bell rings again—

And as quickly as it began, the daymare was over. I was back in my house on the outskirts of Des Moines, trembling slightly with reaction. Downstairs, the front doorbell rang.

I took a deep breath and got up from the desk chair where I'd been sitting, feeling my shirt stick to my back as I did so. I headed out of the room, and was halfway down the stairs when the call came.

Dale, are you all right?

It was Colleen, of course; she's usually the only one who can tell when I've hit one of my daymares. *Sure, Colleen,* I assured her. *It wasn't too bad this time.*

At a hundred thirty-odd miles away in Chillicothe, Missouri, she was still far enough away from me to edit the thoughts I sent her, but even so the fib was a waste of time. *Oh, Dale,* she sighed, and I instantly felt like a heel as warmth and strength flowed from her, chasing away the final bits of the vision's darkness. *It'll get better, darling—it has to. Do you want to tell me about it?*

Not really. I'd found out months ago that talking about the daymares didn't do anything to eliminate them. *Look, honey, there's someone at the door. I'll call you back when I'm free.*

All right, if you're sure you're all right. I love you.

I love you, too.

We broke contact, and I felt the usual frustration well up inside me. Frustration at my daymares, at Colleen's quiet refusal to return to her beloved Saskatchewan as long as I still needed her close by; but most of all, frustration at the universe's uncaring decree that had kept us apart all our lives. And once more I swore I was going to find a way around that law, no matter what it cost me.

I continued down the stairs, and as I reached the front hall I caught the first wisps of thought from those waiting outside my door. There were two of them, one of whom I recognized almost immediately from the texture of his surface thoughts. The other was a stranger, but knowing Rob Peterson had brought him here made his business obvious. Reaching the door, I opened it wide. "Come in, Rob; Mr.—ah—Green," I said, pulling Ted Green's name from Rob's thoughts.

Green blinked, and I felt him reflexively shrink back as he realized what I'd just done. Rob just grinned and strolled on in; after four months of working for me he'd long since gotten used to telepathic shortcuts. With only a brief hesitation and a measuring look at me Green followed. Pretending I hadn't noticed, I closed the door behind them, then led the way to the living room. We sat down, and I got right down to business.

"First of all," I said, addressing Green, "what has Rob told you about my project?"

"Nothing, really." He shrugged. He'd taken the farthest chair from me that courtesy permitted, and while he wasn't quite out of range there, the thoughts I could get were barely surface ones. But Rob was closer, and his thoughts verified Green's words. "He told me you needed something electronic built, and that I'd be working with the most intriguing bit of gadgetry I'd ever see." He smiled shyly. "How could I pass up a come-on like that?"

It was right then that I decided I didn't like Ted Green. The shy smile was pure affectation, completely out of sync with the cool, calculating mind I'd already glimpsed there. That sort of gambit used by that sort of person, I've found, is usually an attempt at emotional manipulation, a practice I detest. "How indeed," I said shortly. "Before I tell you more, I want it clearly understood that this information is strictly confidential, and that whether you take the job or not you'll keep it to yourself."

"I understand."

"All right." I pursed my lips, mentally preparing myself. I didn't want another daymare now. "Have you ever heard of Amos Potter?"

"Sure," was the prompt reply. "He was a telepath from California—worked as a psychologist, I think. He died last April during a plane hijacking, stabbed by one of the hijackers. Seems to me that was just a few days before your own accident, wasn't it?"

I forced a nod. Amos hadn't been killed by the hijackers, but had been forced into suicide by a megalomaniac Nelson Follstadt; and my "accident," as he called it, was Nelson's attempt to do the same to me. But there was no point in telling Green how much of the story the official version had left out. "Amos also had a master's degree in electrical engineering, and he left us an interesting device: a black box that locates telepaths."

Green blinked with surprise, threw a glance at Rob. "I'll be da—sorry. How does it work?"

I gestured to Rob. "We don't know yet," he said. "Most of the electronics are perfectly straightforward, but there are two components that Amos apparently made himself. They're the heart of the finder—and we still don't know how they work."

"Interesting," Green murmured. He looked at me. "May I see them?"

"Sure. The workroom's in the basement; the stairs are around that way."

I let Rob lead the way downstairs, bringing up the rear myself. Green, I noticed with grim amusement, practically walked on Rob's heels in an effort to stay as far away from me as possible.

I'd only lived in the house for about five months, having moved in just after my return from California with the telepath finder, and the basement thus hadn't had nearly enough time to fill up with ordinary homeowners' junk. That was just as well, because with the workbench and electronic gear Rob had brought in the place was already pretty crowded. In the center of the table, wired to an oscilloscope, was a crab-apple-sized lump of metal.

"That's one of them," Rob said, pointing it out. "We've got seven—Amos left us eight but I ruined one getting it open."

Green stepped over to the table and carefully picked up the sphere. "Heavy," he grunted. "What'd you find inside?"

"A couple of commercial IC chips, an inductor coil he apparently wound himself, and some components that unfortunately were connected somehow to the inside of the shell and which I ruined when I cut it open. But we've got lots of data on its characteristics."

Rob pulled over a fat lab notebook and within ten seconds the two of them were embroiled in a technical discussion about six miles over my head. I didn't even bother to try and follow it; I was more interested in learning as much about Green as I reasonably could. Moving to within two or three feet would have given me complete access to both his surface thoughts and a lot of the stuff underneath, but he was keeping me in the corner of his eye, and I didn't want to push him too hard. So instead I kept my distance and worked on picking up the high points of his personality.

He wasn't going to be as easy to get along with as Rob had been; that much was obvious right from the start. Along with his manipulative tendencies, Green had more than his fair share of egotism, ambition, and something I took to be contempt for people he considered inferior to himself. But he seemed smart enough, if the speed at which he assimilated Rob's pages of numbers and graphs was any indication, and Rob at least seemed to think he could be trusted to keep my secret. If he was willing to work for the pittance I could afford to pay, I decided at last, the job was his. His personality I could live with or stay clear of.

After a while Rob ran out of words, and Green turned back to me. "I think I understand," he said. "These kernel things apparently act as antennas for whatever it is you guys broadcast, covering a broad enough spectrum to pick up all of you and plot a resultant. I gather that it works; so what do you need me for?"

"I want you to use those—kernels," I said, adopting his term for Amos's gadgets, "to design and build something entirely different. You'd be working mainly for the challenge of it, though; I can't afford to pay you much."

"Which is why you wanted another grad student instead of hiring a real EE," Green nodded. His tone was noncommital, but I could tell he was already hooked.

"More or less. Having known Rob for the past four years helped, too. All right. What I want is a device that'll block my telepathic ability."

Green frowned. "You mean like something to make the broadcast directional?"

"No—something to kill it altogether, the way a copper shell around a radio transmitter will absorb the signal."

"But why would you want—" He broke off, having answered his own question with impressive speed and accuracy, even given that my long-distance romance with

Colleen was reasonably well known. "Temporary blocking, I assume?"

"Right." Though there were times I'd wished to be rid of the damn talent permanently. "When do you want to start?"

"I haven't said yet I'd take the job," he said, a bit testily. I hadn't been wrong earlier; he didn't much like having his mind read.

Rob, as usual, saw the humorous side of his friend's reaction and chuckled. Green flashed him an annoyed look, then managed a wry smile. "Right—I don't *have* to say things like that here, do I? Okay. How about if I come in Saturday morning—say around eight-thirty?"

"Sounds fine. I'll see you then."

I leaned against the front door for a minute after I let them out, feeling the contacts fade as they walked to the street and Green's car. I knew I should be happy I'd found a replacement for Rob so quickly; it was only a week ago that he'd realized how much preparation his upcoming prelims were going to take. And yet, despite Green's apparent qualifications, there was something about him that made me uneasy. There'd been something going on beneath the level I could read, something . . . *sinister* was far too harsh a word; maybe *opportunistic* fitted the sense of the feeling better. I probably should insist on a deeper probe into Green's mind before I let him examine Amos's devices further, a part of me realized. But my pragmatic side quickly scotched that idea. As long as he made me a telepathy shield it was a matter of supreme indifference to me what kind of schemes his ambitious little mind might be hatching.

Sighing, I pushed away from the door and headed back to the living room. Patience is a virtue, I told myself firmly. Flopping down on the couch, I put it carefully out of my mind and reached out. *Colleen?*

I'm here, Dale, her answer came immediately.

We talked for a long time, and the afternoon shadows were cutting sharply across my minuscule lawn by the time we broke contact. Spending time with Colleen invariably improved my mood, and I was sorely tempted to ignore my psychologist's standing order and pretend the latest daymare simply hadn't happened. But reason eventually prevailed. Hauling the vision out of my memory, I went over it with a fine-tooth comb. By the time I finished I was depressed again, a mood I'd had to put up with a lot lately—Nelson had always been the melancholy sort.

If only I'd had a telepath shield five months ago. . . .

Whatever other qualities Green might or might not have possessed, I had to give him full credit for punctuality; he arrived on Saturday at eight-twenty-five sharp. I took him downstairs and spent nearly half an hour showing him where all the equipment and supplies were. He still tended to shy away from close contact with me, but since his personality hadn't changed markedly in the past two days such avoidance was mutually agreeable.

"So what are you going to do first?" I asked when I'd finished the grand tour.

"Double-check some of Rob's numbers," he said, pulling an ancient wave generator over toward the center of the table. "I want to see if flipping polarity on any of the kernel's bias terminals will affect the output the way he said it does."

I pulled a chair over to the far end of the work bench and sat down, resisting the urge to suggest that would be a waste of time. He already thought I was too impatient. "What will that tell you?" I asked instead, trying to sound merely curious.

"It'll tell me if energy is disappearing into the thing—if so, it may be acting as a transmitter instead of a receiver. Your shield might consist of one or more of these things blasting out an interference signal."

"Wouldn't it be easier to absorb the telepathic signals instead?" I suggested. "Then you could use them as receivers, the way they're designed."

"It might be," he said. "But I want to know my possible options before I start."

He returned to his work, his mind filling up with technical thoughts . . . but even so he couldn't hide the fact that his last statement had been at best a half truth. He had another reason for wanting to do this experiment, a reason I couldn't quite pick up at the distance I was at.

I thought about it for several minutes in silence. Two days ago I'd been willing to let Green do anything he wanted as long as he got me a shield, but now I was having second thoughts. After all, the telepath finder was Amos's final legacy to all the rest of us, and I had a certain amount of responsibility to make sure it wasn't ruined.

I puzzled at the question for a minute, then came to a conclusion. Leaning back against the wall, I sent out a call. *Calvin? Are you there, Calvin?*

Who's that—Dale? Calvin answered, a bit groggily.

I grimaced; I'd forgotten Saturday was Calvin's only morning to sleep in and that it was only a little after eight Pueblo time. *Yeah. Sorry, I didn't mean to wake you. I'll call back later.*

No, that's all right, he assured me. *I got to bed at a reasonable hour last night. What's on your mind?*

I wondered if Gordy had finished going through all of Amos's things, both at Eureka and at his mountain cabin. Specifically, I wanted to know if he found anything else relating to the telepath finder—notes, schematics; that sort of thing.

Um . . . you got me. I can call and ask, if you'd like.

I would, but you can wait until later. Whether he was in Eureka or at home in Spokane, Gordy would be on Pacific Time, and I had no desire to be the one responsible for waking him up this early.

Okay. Calvin hesitated. *I talked to Colleen yesterday. She said you'd had another daymare.*

Yes. It wasn't too bad, though.

Calvin didn't buy that any more than Colleen had. *Uh-huh. Any changes in the vision? Content, texture, length—anything?*

I sighed. *Not really,* I admitted, *unless you want to count the fact that my doorbell got incorporated into it. Aside from that it was just a straight replaying of*

Nelson's attempt to kill both of us. And before you try to think up a euphemistic way to ask, yes, I still get some of it from Nelson's point of view.

He was silent for a long moment, but it wasn't hard to guess what he was thinking. Among the candle flickers of ordinary humans, we telepaths stand out like carbon-arc searchlights, the strength of our mental broadcast and sensitivity enabling us to communicate over hundreds of miles. But the price for this unique companionship is a heavy one: at anything less than a hundred miles apart the contact is strong enough to be painful, and at a theoretical distance of twenty miles both personalities would disintegrate totally under the strain. Nelson and I had been close to that limit when he finally took a wrong turn and crashed the plane he was chasing me with into a mountain. I'd survived the encounter . . . but not unscathed. The Dale Ravenhall I'd once been had been bent and altered by the force of the mental collision, changed into something that was part Dale and part Nelson. Permanently? No one knew. But the fact that some of each daymare still came heavily flavored with Nelson's memories was ominously suggestive.

Well, Calvin said at last, *it's only been five months, after all. A lot of simpler psychological problems take longer than that to heal.*

I snorted. *Thanks a whole bunch.*

Sorry, he said quickly, and I grimaced. In earlier days he would have recognized that kind of statement as the banter it was. Now, he was bending over backwards to avoid stepping on any toes, real or otherwise. Nelson had been the touchy sort.

It's okay, I reassured him. *I know you were trying to be encouraging. Uh . . . you don't have any plans to travel east in the near future, do you?*

I could come over any time. Why?—do you need some close-approach contact?

Not really. I wasn't ready yet to have all my surface thoughts open to another person, good friend or not. *I just thought maybe you'd be willing to stay in Minneapolis*

*or Dubuque or somewhere for a week or two and let
Colleen get back to Regina for a while.*

*That could probably be arranged. Are her friends in
Chillicothe getting tired of her company, or is she just
homesick?*

*No to the former; probably to the latter. Not that she'll
admit it, of course—she takes her baby-sitting duties
seriously.*

*Uh-huh. Well, look—I'll talk to her and check the loca-
tion log to make sure I wouldn't be flying in on top of
anyone else and then get back to you. Okay?*

*Sure. Thanks; I really appreciate it. And don't forget
to check with Gordy about any other telepath locater
stuff.*

Right. Talk to you later.

I came out of the contact and glanced around the
room, reorienting myself. Everything was as I remembered it ... except that Green was gazing sideways at
me from the work bench, his expression wary. "It's okay,"
I assured him. "I'm not going to faint or anything."

"I know," he said. "Who were you talking to?"

"Uh—Calvin Wolfe."

"Pueblo, Colorado; right?"

"Yes." Frowning slightly, I touched his thoughts. What
I found surprised me. "You've been reading up on us
lately, haven't you?"

Again, there was that little flicker of resentment that
seemed to come whenever I demonstrated my telepathic
ability on him. "For a couple of days, yeah. I wanted to
know what I was getting myself into. It must be nice to
be able to talk to someone that far away so easily."

"You can do almost as well by telephone," I told him
shortly, "and without the disadvantages we've got."

He shrugged. "Not much of a disadvantage. All you
have to do is stay out of each other's way. Big deal."

If I'd been a violent man I probably would've hit him.
Instead, I suddenly felt a need to get far away from such
stupidity. "I'll be upstairs if you need me," I told him
with as much civility as I could manage. Without waiting
for a response, I left.

*   *   *

The call I was expecting came about eight hours later, after Green had gone home for the day; and to my mild surprise it was Gordy himself who made it. *Gordy, where are you?* was my first question.

On a plane somewhere near Billings, Montana, I believe, he said. *I'm on my way to Minneapolis; going to be doing some work there for the next couple of weeks.*

Such fortuitous timing, I told him. *Calvin couldn't get away?*

Even eight hundred miles away I could sense his embarrassment. *You make it sound like we're all conspiring to put one over on you,* he protested. *We're your friends, Dale.*

Yeah, I know. Feeling like a heel was becoming a full-time job here lately. *What's the word on Amos's things?*

I've gone through everything from top to bottom and back again. No notes, no plans, no schematics, no extra equipment other than what you've already got. Either he deliberately destroyed all the documentation or the design of the finder was so obvious to him that he could just sit down and cobble one together. Sorry.

Me too. I thought about the implications of that. From Rob's struggles with the kernels I found it hard to believe they'd been *that* easy to make. Had Amos foreseen other applications for his invention, applications he perhaps hadn't cared for?

My telepath shield, for example?

Gordy broke into my musings. *Look, Dale, don't you think it's about time you let the rest of us in on what you're doing with all that stuff?*

My first impulse was to tell him that they'd find out when I was good and ready and not a solitary second sooner. But that was clearly Nelson talking. *I don't know,* I said instead. *I'm trying to make something new out of the things Amos developed for his finder. If it works—well, it'll benefit all of us. Let's leave it at that for now.*

Gordy was silent for a long moment. *You know, Dale, it's possible to play these things too close to the chest. If we'd known that Amos had caught Nelson making quiet*

*trips to Las Vegas we might have implicated him in
Amos's death before he had the chance to try to kill you.
You could be running the same kind of risk here.*

I'm being careful, I told him stubbornly. My doubts
about Green rose unbidden before my eyes; ruthlessly, I
crushed them down. *I just don't want to raise any false
hopes, that's all.*

All right, he said after another pause. *But be careful,
okay?*

Sure. Enjoy your flight, and I'll talk to you later.

Yeah. Take care.

I sat where I was for a long time afterwards, my book
lying ignored on my lap. Once again I felt torn between
my natural desire for caution and my almost suffocating
urgency to possess a telepath shield. Colleen was practically within my grasp—how could I permit anything to
get in the way of that? Besides, what earthly use would
a telepath shield—or anything else Green could make in
my basement—be to a normal person? A defense against
the highly unlikely possibility of one of us eavesdropping
on a private conversation? Ridiculous, when thirty feet
of distance would achieve the same end. No—I *had* to
be reading Green wrong . . . and I didn't need to be
reminded that Nelson had had a strong touch of
paranoia.

Nevertheless, that evening I went out and bought a
burglar alarm, and by the time I went to bed I had it
rigged so that anyone entering or leaving my basement
would trigger a light and quiet buzzer in my second-floor
study. Now, whenever Green tried to leave I would know
in time to get within telepathy range of him before he
got out of the house. A rather simple precaution, to be
sure—but then, I wasn't really expecting any trouble.

The days lengthened into weeks, as days have a way
of doing, and progress on the shield remained depressingly
slow. Green's idea about reversing the biases hadn't
panned out, and he'd been forced to seek out new approaches. Fortunately, he didn't get discouraged as easily
as I might have, his failures merely spurring him to

stronger efforts. He began to spend more and more time at my house, sometimes arriving while I was still eating dinner and not leaving until after midnight. What made his single-mindedness all the more astonishing was the fact that he still felt acutely uncomfortable around me, avoiding close contact and sometimes even going so far as to fill his mind with technical thoughts to try to forget I was within range. Apparently he was simply the type who enjoyed a challenge for its own sake.

I had a couple more daymares during that period, too, one of them while Colleen was back in Regina. Fortunately, Gordy was still in Minneapolis at the time and helped me get through those first few shaky minutes afterward. I'd wanted him to keep quiet about it, but he insisted that Colleen had a right to know, and the upshot was that she was back down at her Chillicothe listening post within twelve hours. I was pretty upset with her for interrupting her R and R, and I think it was probably that mood that triggered the milder daymare a day later. It was really little more than an aftershock, but it was enough for Colleen; after that, she wouldn't have left me again if the whole midwestern United States had caught on fire. Gordy, too, found reason after reason to stretch out his Minneapolis visit, and when he finally left, Calvin found a plausible excuse to spend some time in Dubuque.

What with all this companionship therapy taking up a lot of my attention, it was early October before I finally noticed something was off-kilter.

It began with an afternoon call from Rob Peterson, who was trying to get hold of Green and thought he might be with me. During the course of the conversation I discovered Green hadn't shown up at any of his classes for nearly a month, a figure that coincided uncomfortably well with the first of his six-to-midnight sessions in my basement. When I asked him about it later, Green admitted he'd been neglecting his schoolwork, but claimed he'd be able to catch up once he finished my shield. As usual, he stayed right at the edge of my range, so I wasn't able to confirm that he was telling the truth; and not wanting a scene I let him go back to work without further cross-examination. I soothed my conscience by reminding myself that he was a grown man, perfectly capable of deciding how to use his time.

But the whole thing seemed funny somehow—I couldn't reconcile this sudden neglect of his studies with the ambitious and calculating personality I'd already glimpsed in him. It bothered me; and gradually I began staying on the first floor whenever Green was in the house, where I could pick up his surface thoughts as he worked in the basement. He knew, of course—my footsteps would have been audible above him—and I could sense an almost frantic note in his attempts to cram his thoughts with technical details of his work. But enough got through. More than enough . . .

I waited until I was sure, and then I confronted him with it.

"You've had it for two weeks now, haven't you?" I said, anger struggling for supremacy with other emotions I was afraid to accept. "You know how to make a telepath shield."

"I don't *know* if I do," he protested. Hunched over the workbench, a soldering iron still gripped in his hand, he watched me with slightly narrowed eyes, as a rabbit might a fox. "I've never tested it."

Hairsplitting; but it *was* a genuine lack of certainty, and that had been enough to fool me for nearly a week. Belatedly, I wondered if perhaps I'd gotten the rabbit and fox roles reversed. "Well, let's not waste any more time. Turn it on."

"All right." Standing up, he went to the far end of the bench. A bulky, three-level breadboard assembly rested there, built into a framework that looked like it'd been made out of leftover angle iron. Three of Amos's kernels glittered among the tangle of electronic components. Plugging the device's cord into an outlet, Green flipped a switch and vanished.

It took a fraction of a second for my eyes to register the fact that Green was, in fact, still standing there in front of me, that it was only his mind that had disappeared from my perception. I must have looked as flabbergasted as I felt, because Green's lip twitched in a smile of sorts. "Like it?" he asked.

"I—yes," I managed. "How does it work?"

"Best guess is that it creates a sort of dead zone where telepathic signals get absorbed. I don't know for sure, though."

"I told you that was the approach to take," I said, feeling a little light-headed. "Will it block other telepaths, too? We project a lot more strongly than you do."

He shrugged. "Try calling someone."

I did; and because I was afraid of false hopes I tried for a solid three minutes. But at the end of that time I was convinced. *Colleen* . . . With an effort I dragged my mind back to Earth. One more important question still needed an answer. "All right. Now tell me what you've been doing these past two weeks, while you were supposedly working on the shield."

He radiated innocence. "I *have* been working on it— I've been trying to make a more practical model." He indicated the breadboards. "You see, this one is big and heavy, with an effective range of probably no more than a hundred feet, and it requires one-twenty line current. I think I can make one that would run off a battery and have almost half a mile of range—and the whole thing fitting inside a briefcase. Another—oh, month or so— and I should have it."

It was a good idea, intellectually, I had to admit that. But all of my hopes and dreams had suddenly become reality and I knew I didn't have the patience to wait another day, let alone an entire month. "Thanks, but no. This one will do fine."

He blinked, and I got the impression that my answer had surprised him. "But . . . I'm not finished here, Mr. Ravenhall. I mean, I promised to build you a practical telepath shield. *This* thing's hardly practical."

"It's practical enough for me," I said, frowning. Goosebumps were beginning to form on my suspicions—he had no business fighting that hard for a two-dollar-an-hour job.

"Before we continue, what say we make things more interesting and turn off the shield?"

He made no effort to reach for the switch. "That's not necessary," he sighed. "I *was* bending the truth a little. I've already been trying to design an entirely different gadget using those kernels, and I was afraid you'd send me away permanently once I'd finished the shield."

"What sort of gadget?"

"A mechanical mind reader."

"A *what?*"

"Well, why not? The kernels clearly pick up telepathic signals. Why shouldn't the signals be interpretable, by a small computer, say?"

I opened my mouth, closed it again as the potential repercussions of such a gadget echoed like heavy thunder through my mind. By necessity, each of us who'd had this gift/burden dropped on us had long ago thought out the consequences of misusing our power. The potential for blackmail, espionage of all kinds, or just simple invasion of privacy—I was personally convinced it was only our extremely limited number and the fact that we were thus easy to keep track of that had kept us from being locked up or killed outright. A mechanical device, presumably infinitely reproducible, would open up that entire can of worms, permanently. "Forget it," I said, finding my voice at last. "Thanks for the shield; I'll give you your final pay before you leave." I turned to go back upstairs.

"Wait a minute," Green snapped. "I *can't* forget it, just like that. This thing'll be a gold mine if I can get it to work. I've put a hell of a lot of work into it—I can't quit now."

"A gold mine for whom? You and a select clientele of professional spies?"

"It doesn't have to be that way," he protested. "Psychologists, for instance—mind readers would be a tremendous help in their work. Rescue teams could locate survivors in earthquakes or collapsed buildings. Doctors—"

"What about bank robbers? Or terrorists? Or even

nosy neighbors?" I shook my head. "What am I arguing for? The subject is closed."

Green expelled his breath in a long, hissing sigh, and his expression seemed to harden in some undefinable way. "I'll have to collect my tools," he said stiffly.

I hesitated, then nodded. "All right. I'll be upstairs writing your check."

I didn't head up right away, though, but crossed instead to the dim corner where the fusebox was. The telepath shield I'd coveted for so long had abruptly become something that could be used against me, and I had no intention of letting Green leave here under its protection—I wanted to know whether he'd really given up or had something else up his sleeve. One of the peculiarities of this house was that the basement lights were all on one circuit and the outlets on another. Finding the proper fuse I pulled it . . . and across the basement, just barely within range, I felt Green's thoughts reappear. Simultaneously, drowning out that faint voice, came a frantic duet.

Dale! Are you there, Dale; can you answer?

Here I am, I said hastily. *What's all the fuss?*

Oh, thank heaven. Colleen's thoughts were shaking with emotion. *We thought something terrible had happened. Calvin and I have been trying to contact you for nearly five minutes.*

Another daymare? Calvin asked, trying to sound calmer than he really was. I didn't blame him; a daymare that had lasted that long would have been a real doozy.

No; this was something good for a change. I told them about the telepath shield, trying to recapture my earlier enthusiasm for the device. But that glimpse into Green's ambitions had dampened things considerably, and I was barely able to keep my report on the positive side of neutral.

Calvin, at least, saw the potential hazards immediately. *Do you think it's wise to let this Green character run around loose?* he asked when I'd finished. *If he can make a telepath shield who knows what else he can do?*

There shouldn't be any problem, I assured him. *Amos's*

special gadgets are the key, and he doesn't know how to make them. I'm sure of that, but I'll double-check before I let him leave.

I don't know, Colleen mused. *I don't trust him. He sounded—oh, too ambitious, I suppose.*

My own thoughts skidded to a halt. *Wait a second. When did you talk to him?*

Last week. She sounded surprised. *He got my number here from my Regina answering service. Said he was calibrating Amos's finder and needed to know where I was. I assumed you knew.*

I frowned . . . and at that exact instant both Colleen and Calvin vanished from my mind.

It was so unexpected that I wasted a good ten seconds trying to reestablish contact before I noticed that the faint touch of Green's thoughts was also gone and finally realized what was happening. I spun around, but too late: Green's legs were just disappearing up the stairwell. Clutched in one hand was something that looked like a small briefcase.

With a shout, I went after him. But his lead was too big, and by the time I ran out my front door he was already diving into the front seat of his car. With a squeal of tires he took off into the night. Seconds later I was tearing down the street behind him, gunning my old Chevy for all it was worth.

And the chase was on.

At first I thought it would be over quickly. I caught up to him with almost ridiculous ease, as if his car was in even worse shape than mine. But as we cleared the edge of town his lead began to open up slowly, and by the time he turned south on I-35 he was staying a comfortable quarter-mile ahead of me.

For me the drive was like an inside-out version of that horrible race through the California mountains. The road here was flat, and I was the pursuer instead of the pursued; but the same sense of terrified urgency was wrapped suffocatingly around me. Clearly, Green had lied about the portable shield—and I, the great telepath Dale Ravenhall, so caught up in my own selfish desires, had let him get by with it. Bitterly, I wondered what else he'd lied about . . . and whether I'd ever get a chance to warn the others. His strategy seemed clear: by forcing me into a chase like the one in California he was trying to trigger a daymare, one that would undoubtedly be fatal even given the sparse traffic and relatively straight road. And with the shield going full blast in Green's car it would be a very lonely death. More than once I tried to drift back out of range, hoping to at least let Colleen or Calvin know what had happened; but each time Green spotted the maneuver and matched it. I wondered what he would do if I stopped completely, to either call Colleen or phone the police. But I didn't dare try it. If I let him out of my sight I knew I'd never see the shield or the rest of Amos's kernels again. Grimly, concentrating on Green's taillights, I fought down the panic bubbling in my throat and kept going.

I don't know how long the chase lasted; my mind was too busy damning my shortsighted stupidity and fighting off potential daymares to think about time. Green got off the interstate at Osceola, heading east on 34. He didn't stay on the road long, though, turning south again on 65. Twenty-odd miles later he picked up a county road heading west, and from that point on I was thoroughly lost. I dimly remember that we were on some road labeled B when we crossed over into Missouri, but all the rest were just anonymous two- and four-lane roads, passing through or near sleeping towns with names like Wooodland, Davis City, Saline, and Modena.

And finally, sometime in the small hours of the morning, Green pulled over to the side of the road and stopped.

I pulled up behind him, feeling a cold sense of satisfaction. He hadn't given me a daymare and hadn't lost me among the country roads of two states, and had now bowed to the inevitable. He was outside the car now, the briefcase he'd taken from my house held across his chest like a shield. I got out, too, and walked toward him, watching for concealed weapons. "All right, Green, it's all over," I told him. "Let's have the shield and whatever else you stole."

In the headlights I saw him shake his head minutely. "Before you do anything hasty," he said, his voice strangely tense, "I suggest you look at the sign up there."

Frowning, I glanced over his shoulder. Highway 65 was cutting across the landscape directly ahead; a dimly lit sign along its side announced eleven miles to Chillicothe.

Chillicothe?

I felt the blood draining from my face as I refocused on Green. "Yes," he nodded. "She's within the twenty-mile limit. If I flip this switch you'll both be dead instantly."

The big toggle switch sticking out of the briefcase looked the size of a baseball bat under his hand. There was no way for him to miss it if I jumped him . . . and looking at his eyes I knew he was half expecting me to try just that. "All right, let's both relax," I suggested through stiff lips. "What do you want?"

"For starters, I want you and Colleen Isaac together. There's no point taking both cars; we'll go in mine. I hope you know where she's staying—all I've got is her phone number. You'll drive, of course."

"Of course," I said mechanically. *Colleen*, I thought. *What have I done?*

There was no answer.

She was waiting outside her motel room door when we pulled up, her expression drawn but controlled. I got out of the car and walked up to her. For a moment we gazed into each other's eyes. Then, almost of their own volition, our hands sought each other and gripped tightly . . . and a moment later she was in my arms. "It's all right," I whispered to her, trying to project confidence I didn't feel, and to hide the disappointment that—despite the danger we were in—I *did* feel. I'd had such romantic dreams about this moment, dreams that would now be forever poisoned in my memory.

Behind us, Green cleared his throat. "We'd better get

moving," he said, sounding almost apologetic. "Both of you in the front seat, please."

"Just a second," I objected, turning halfway around but keeping one arm around Colleen. "Doesn't she at least get to bring a change of clothes?"

"She didn't seem surprised to see us," he countered. "That means she was expecting us. The police may be on their way right now."

"I wasn't expecting you." Collen's voice was slightly higher-pitched then I'd expected it to be and had a slight accent. But it was steady enough. "We assumed you were using your telepath shield to stop Dale from talking with us, but I didn't suspect you were here until I was also cut off a minute before you arrived. I didn't call the police."

"But one of your friends might have," Green growled, showing signs of agitation. "Grab your purse and let's go!"

He didn't relax again until we were five miles out of Chillicothe, heading east on 36. I held Colleen's hand as I drove, though whether for her comfort or my own I wasn't entirely sure. Strangely enough, she seemed the calmest of all of us, and was the one who finally broke the brittle silence. "You know, Ted, this really can't gain you anything," she said, turning her head to the side so that Green could hear her. "By now every telepath on the continent knows about you and your machine."

"That's fine with me," Green grunted. "I'm going to need cooperation from all of you, anyway, so there's no reason to keep it secret. Except from the police, maybe. I hope no one's been stupid enough to call them."

"What is it you want?"

"An electronic telepath," I told her. "And he apparently wants us to sit around and watch him make one."

"I wish it were that easy," Green said. "But it's not. I figure I'll need at least ten kernels to make it, and even then it'll only be a one-way mind reading device—I can't get the damn kernels to transmit anything to speak of."

In spite of the danger, I felt a wolfish smile crease my face. "Ten kernels, huh? And you've only got four left—

you left three in the shield in my basement. So you're licked even before you start."

"No!" His exclamation was so unexpected I jumped, nearly swerving out of my lane. "I can figure it out—could have figured it out. But you weren't going to let me." He paused, and in the mirror I could see him fighting for self-control ... and it was then that I suddenly realized he was as scared as I was. He'd clearly been spinning some high-flying hopes for this particular rainbow, and my adamant opposition had apparently goaded him into an act of desperation that he wasn't really ready for. Now, he was beginning to see just how deep the hole was he was digging himself into.

Colleen must have sensed that, too. "Ted, you don't have to do this," she said. "Let Dale take me back to my motel and then leave him with the shield, and it'll be over. There won't be any charges or other repercussions, I promise."

"What about my mind reader?"

Colleen hesitated. "I'm sorry, but I'm afraid we can't permit Amos's invention to be used in that way."

"Then forget it."

"Green—" I began.

"Shut up," he said. "I have to think."

His ruminations took the better part of an hour, during which time he had me change roads twice. I kept my eye on him in the mirror, hoping he would fall asleep. But he remained almost preternaturally alert the whole time.

Finally, he seemed to come to a conclusion. "Ravenhall, 63 ought to be coming up pretty soon," he said. "Take it north."

"Where are you taking us?" Colleen asked.

"Back to Iowa. I know a little resort near Rathbun Lake where you can rent cabins. We can stay there for a while."

"Taking us across a state line is a federal offense," I pointed out to him.

"How do you figure? I'm not kidnapping you. If you want, you can both get out right here."

I didn't bother to reply.

What with the circuitous route Green made me drive we didn't arrive at the resort until after eight in the morning. My secret hope, that the place might be closed until spring, was quickly dashed; either the warmest October in thirty years had induced them to stay open past their usual closing date or else they catered to the kind of hikers and fishermen who ignore the weather anyway. Green left us alone in the car while he went in the office to register. I tried to think of a plan—any plan—while he was gone. But it was no use. I'd been driving all night, much of it at the edge of nervous prostration, and my mind was simply too fatigued to function. Even as I drove up the gravel road to our cabin I felt my consciousness beginning to waver, and I just barely remember staggering through the front door with Colleen holding tightly onto my arm. Somehow, I assume, she got me to the bed.

I came up out of the darkness slowly and unwillingly, glad to escape the nightmares that had harassed my sleep but dimly aware that something worse was waiting for me in the real world. I opened my eyes to an unfamiliar ceiling, and even before Colleen spoke it had all come back.

"How are you feeling?"

I turned my head. She was sitting in a chair next to the bed, light from the window behind her filtering through her hair in a half halo effect. "Groggy," I told her. "How long did I sleep?"

"Almost ten hours. I didn't see any point in waking you."

I looked at my watch. Six-oh-five. My stomach growled a reminder that I'd missed a couple of meals. "Did you sleep at all? And where's Green?"

"Yes, I took a couple of short naps. Your friend's out in the living room."

"He's no friend of mine." I turned my head the other way and realized for the first time that the cabin wasn't the simple one-room design I'd expected. Colleen and I were in a small bedroom that took up maybe a third of the cabin's total floor space. The door that sat between us and Green looked solid enough, but it opened inward and had no lock that I could see. I wondered how Green thought he could keep us in here.

"Don't try the door," Colleen said, as if she'd somehow penetrated the shield and had heard my unspoken question. "He has the switch on his telepath shield fastened to it with a piece of string. He sealed the window, too."

I hesitated halfway through the act of rolling out of bed, then continued the motion and got to my feet. Walking around the end of the bed, I went to the window behind Colleen. He'd sealed it, all right; a dozen nails and screws had been driven through the wooden sash and into the frame.

Behind me Colleen's chair creaked, and a moment later her hand tentatively touched my arm. "Dale . . . what does he want with us?"

There was no point studying the window any further; it was clear that without a screwdriver and claw hammer I would never get the thing open. Turning around, I faced Colleen, taking her hands in mine. "You heard him—he wants a mechanical mind reader. I gather he thinks we can help him make one."

"How? Does one of us have something he needs?"

I shook my head. "I don't know." It was odd, a disconnected part of my brain thought, how small a part of its target a camera could really capture. I had hundreds of photos and videotapes of Colleen, but not a single one of them had done her justice. Even tired, hungry, and with a horrible death crouching like a leopard over her shoulder, there was a vivaciousness about her that the films had never really showed. I'd known her energetic joy of life through her thoughts, of course; but to see it reflected in her face was an entirely new and delightful experience. If we died now, I would have had at least that much.

If we died now. The thought short-circuited my rising romantic mood and brought me back to Earth. There were a dozen questions that urgently needed answering.

Giving Colleen's hands a squeeze, I let go and walked back around to the door. "Green?" I called through the panel. "You awake out there?"

"Come on out," was the immediate response. "The door's safe to use."

I opened it and stepped into the main part of the cabin, noting in passing that Green's bobby-trap string was not tied to the doorknob but to another nail driven into the door at knee level. Green was sitting on a small couch across the room, a glowing lamp at his shoulder. On his lap, the switch close to hand, was the telepath shield.

"I thought you weren't ever going to wake up," Green commented. "There're some hamburgers in the sack on the table—you can heat them up in that one-quart oven over there. Cokes are in the fridge."

I was too hungry to bother with the oven. Colleen, with a lower tolerance for American fast food, took her burgers and headed for the cabin's tiny kitchen. Green waited until we were settled at the table before speaking again. "I've been making a list of the equipment I figure I'm going to need," he told us, holding up a piece of paper clearly torn from a second hamburger bag. "I figure that with a small x-ray machine I can figure out how everything is put together inside one of these kernels. If not, there are a couple of other things I can try. A good computer would be helpful in designing the mind reader's circuitry, and since I'll probably need one anyway to interpret the telepathic signals we might as well get that, too."

"Just where do you expect to get the money for all of this?" I asked around a mouthful of food. "If you're expecting the rest of the telepathic community to fork it over, you can forget it. None of us has the resources you're talking about."

"You fly all over the country whenever you want to, don't you?" he scoffed. "That isn't exactly cheap."

"Most of us have small stipends from universities that are studying us," Colleen explained to him. "The amounts aren't nearly enough to supply you with x-ray machines and computers, though."

Green's mouth twitched. "Well . . . then I guess you'll have to earn the money some other way."

"Such as?" I asked. Most businesses, I've found, aren't all that enthusiastic about having telepaths on the payroll.

"I suppose industrial espionage would be the most profitable," he said, watching me closely.

If he was looking for a reaction, he wasn't disappointed. Some bread crumbs, tried to go down the wrong way, and it took me half a minute to cough them out. "Forget it," I snarled when I could talk again. "If you think we're going to do *that*—"

Colleen cut me off with a hand on my arm. "Ted, we can't do that," she said, her voice calm and reasonable. "We're all rather well known; certainly the security departments of any major corporation would recognize us instantly."

"Then you'll have to hit key employees at off hours," Green said stubbornly. "Or else wear disguises. I *need* that equipment—don't you understand?"

"And what about us?" Colleen asked. "Don't you see what involving us in crime would do to the trust we've built up between ourselves and the general populace? We can't survive without that good will, Ted."

"I'm sorry. I really am. But it's not my fault." He shifted his gaze to me, where it became more of a glare. "If *he* hadn't been all noble and virtuous and had let me keep going, none of this would have happened."

"Oh, sure—blame it on me," I growled. "Why not blame your parents, society, and the planet Jupiter while you're at it?"

He ignored me. "I want to know how to contact Calvin Wolfe—I know he's a friend of yours and his Pueblo phone's unlisted. I also want something I can say to him that'll prove you two are with me."

My mind raced. Was there some way I could slip in a clue as to where we were? Rathbun, reservoir, lake—I couldn't think of any way to code any of those words so that Green would miss it. I'd never been here before, so referring to a past visit was out. Distance from Des Moines? I hadn't the foggiest idea. I was still trying to come up with something when Colleen gave him Calvin's number and unconsciously undercut my effort. "Just give him your name," she told Green. "He knows who you are."

"Okay." He stood up and gestured toward the door. "We'll have to find a phone booth to make the call from; I don't want anyone tracing us here."

It was an hour before we got back to the cabin, Green having taken us halfway to Ottumwa to get the distance he wanted. We were left in the car while he made the call, and he wouldn't tell us anything about it afterward except that Calvin had agreed to take up the matter with the rest of our group.

"Do you think that's the truth?" Colleen asked me when we were locked again in the relative privacy of our room.

"Probably," I told her. Outside the window the evening had faded into night, and the lights from two or three other cabins could be dimly seen through the trees. Too far away to see a signal, even if I could think of some way to send one without tipping off Green. "Calvin would agree to anything at this stage to gain time." Pulling the shade, I turned on the light and sat down on the bed next to Colleen. The light switch had gone on with a loud click; no quiet SOS possible with that. "I just hope we don't get some gung-ho SWAT team bursting in with M-16s blazing."

"I doubt if there's any danger of that," she sighed. "We'd already decided to keep the authorities out of this when the shield cut me off."

I nodded; I'd rather hoped they'd seen things that way. At the moment no one but us knew it was even possible to build an electronic mind reader. If the word ever got out, chances were *someone* would eventually figure out how to do it. "Good. I guess. Anything else happen while I was out of touch?"

"Yes, but nothing that'll help us here." She shifted position to stretch out on the bed, closing her eyes against the overhead light. "I called your friend Robert Peterson on the phone and asked him to go over to your house and see what was wrong. He called me back on your phone with the news that your car was gone and your house lit and unlocked. Calvin wanted to know whether there was anything there that could be a telepath shield. Robert said there was a heavy monstrosity in the basement that had three of Amos's devices wired into it, but that he couldn't tell what it was without more study."

"Yeah. How *do* you test a telepath shield?"

"Obviously, with a telepath. Gordon was going to catch the next plane to Des Moines, and Scott will most likely come up from New Orleans now that I've also disappeared. He was anxious to get involved and has always rather liked me." She opened her eyes briefly. "Something I just thought of: could Robert modify Amos's telepath finder to locate a *lack* of telepathic signals?"

"Like this shield?" I shrugged. "I don't know, but I doubt it. We had to take apart the finder to get parts for the shields; Rob would have to rebuild as well as redesign it. And, anyway, he hadn't gotten much into design work when Green took over." A fresh wave of shame and anger washed over me. "I should've waited until Rob was available again," I muttered.

Colleen was silent for so long I began to think she'd fallen asleep. Turning off the light I lay down beside her, hating both Green and myself and wondering if I was tired enough to escape into sleep myself for a few hours. Then Colleen stirred. "Dale . . . why did you do it?"

It took me a moment to understand what she was asking. "For us," I told her. "I wanted to be able to see and hold you, to share more than just my thoughts with you. I—when I say it like that it sounds pretty selfish, doesn't it?"

"A little," she admitted. "More like Nelson Follstadt than Dale Ravenhall."

I sighed, closing my eyes in an effort to block the sudden tears forming there. Nelson again—always it was Nelson. Was I never going to be free of him? Or were my motivations and judgment going to be forever skewed by what he'd done to me in the California mountains? It was like carrying my own personal ghost along with me, someone to fowl up everything I did, someone—

Someone to blame.

The thought leaped out at me with almost physical force. Was I using my psychological injury as a scapegoat, a convenient excuse whenever anything went wrong? I didn't really believe it—certainly didn't *want* to believe it. But the possibility was there . . . and blaming other people *had* been one of Nelson's most annoying traits.

And I'd just argued myself in a circle. I never argued in circles. Or, rather, Dale Ravenhall never had. . . .

Colleen's arm slid over my chest, breaking through the spiral of fear and self-pity. "It's all right, Dale," she said soothingly. "We'll get out of this somehow."

For a long time she held me tightly, as if comforting a child. Gradually, my black depression began to lighten; and as it did so my need for her changed, both in nature and urgency. Her response, whether from love, fear, or a combination of both, was so strong it surprised me . . . but within seconds surprise and all other emotions were crowded out by the passion exploding within me.

For the three years since I'd fallen in love with Colleen this moment had formed the basis of virtually all my fantasies . . . and yet, now that it was here, the act was tinged with an unexpected sense of frustration. It wasn't just the circumstances, or the presence of Green on the other side of the door, but rather the missing dimension that even the casual sex of my younger years had had. For the first time in my life I was cut off from the thoughts and emotions of my partner, forced to rely on the subtle physical cues I'd never really bothered to learn. I botched it—botched it badly—and though she didn't say anything I knew she was disappointed. I tried to apologize, but I couldn't find the words, and had to settle for holding her close until she fell asleep.

I stared at the shadows of tree branches swaying across the window shade for at least an hour after that, tired but not really sleepy. With time, I knew, I could learn to be a better lover to her—but time was the least certain commodity in our world just now. I wondered how long it would take Green to get the money and equipment he wanted . . . and I wondered how long the batteries powering the shield would last.

Eventually, I fell asleep.

We both woke fairly early the next morning. That turned out to be a mistake, because the day quickly became one long study in boredom. Green had slipped out before we woke and had brought back donuts and coffee and the necessary ingredients for sandwiches. That last was a disappointment; I'd hoped for the chance to break the window and escape when he left to buy lunch. But as usual, he was one move ahead of me.

To his credit, he also brought back a couple of decks of cards and three paperbacks of the sort found on grocery store book racks. But neither Colleen nor I were great shakes as card players; and I, at least, was too wrapped up in my own real troubles to have any patience with someone else's fictional ones. Besides, the covers of the books strongly suggested they contained a fair amount of sex and/or romance, and after the fiasco of the previous night I knew I wouldn't be able to handle that.

So instead of reading I spent some time going over our room, searching for something I could use as a tool or weapon. It was a small room, though, and it wasn't even eleven o'clock before I gave up.

Mostly, Colleen and I talked.

There wasn't much about each other we didn't already know, of course; but good friends can always find something interesting to talk about. We discussed world topics, history—one of Colleen's pet interests—and our fellow telepaths, and reminisced a good deal about the five years we'd known each other. By a kind of unspoken agreement we avoided talking about our current situation, but the very fact we were using spoken words at all was a continual reminder of what was happening. I could feel a tenseness in Colleen's body as we lay side by side on the bed, and my own attempts at conversation were blunted by my preoccupation with the problem of finding a way out of this mess I'd created.

The damnable thing about it was that, barring some slip on Green's part, I couldn't think of a single way either to escape or to get the telepath shield away from him. And the more I thought about it the more I realized that we didn't even have the threat of official retribution to hold over his head if he flipped that switch—he could probably claim that I'd been so delighted with my new shield that I'd set up this little informal honeymoon trip with Colleen and that I'd dragged him along to take care of the electronics, which had unfortunately failed. With us gone it would basically be his word against Calvin's, and if Green had been smart he wouldn't have said anything to Calvin that actually involved the words *ransom* or *blackmail*. The bad thing about such a scenario was that, once he had what he wanted, Green might feel he had to kill us to maintain the charade.

Nelson had tried once to kill me. Now, it seemed, his ghost had given itself a second chance. I only wished Colleen hadn't been the means it had chosen—but, then again, her inclusion might have been deliberate. Nelson had hated all of us.

Sometime in the middle of the afternoon Colleen and I made love again, at her request, and for a while I was able to forget the danger we were in. Perhaps if I'd been paying closer attention to her I would have noticed the tension had left her muscles by then, leaving behind an almost unnatural calmness, and perhaps I would have wondered what that meant. Perhaps; but probably not. I'm not very good at reading physical cues.

Evening came, and Green again was too smart to leave us alone while he went for food. Apparently he'd become convinced that the police really hadn't been called in, and so he piled us into the car and we went out to a restaurant together. His new-found confidence went only so far, of course; the place he chose was a dark, intimate one with high-backed booths, where our chances of being recognized by anyone were minimal.

I'd expected dinner to be a strained affair; but while it was so for me the others seemed surprisingly relaxed. Colleen kept Green talking, both about himself and his ambitions. If I'd paid closer attention to the conversation I might have learned why succeeding with his mind reader project was so important to him. But my full attention was on the briefcase sitting upright on the seat next to him, and on the arm resting casually on top of it. Even when cutting his steak his left hand never moved far enough away from the switch for me to risk any action. I hardly tasted my own food, and felt almost resentful that Colleen so obviously enjoyed the expensive filet mignon she'd ordered.

The ride back to the cabin was quiet. Colleen huddled close to me the whole time, her hand stroking my thigh in a way more suggestive of fear and loneliness than of passion. Her friendly chatter in the restaurant, I guessed, must have been an act to put Green at ease, and now that I'd been unable to take advantage of the trick an emotional letdown was setting in. I wished that I hadn't been so quick to shoot down her suggestion that Rob might be able to gimmick together a telepath shield locater; at least that would have left her some small hope to cling to.

I parked out front as usual and we went into the cabin, Green with his damn briefcase keeping well back. Colleen turned on the light and we headed toward the bedroom; but as Green closed the cabin door behind us she touched my arm and stopped, turning to face him.

"Well, go on in," Green said, as I followed Colleen's lead and turned around. Green had stopped just inside the door, his expression more puzzled than wary. Not that he needed to worry; we were a good fifteen feet away from him, and even with the shield hanging loosely in his hand we both knew I couldn't possibly get to the switch before he did.

But Colleen didn't move. "No,'" she said calmly. "We can't let you continue with your plans, Ted. An electronic mind reader would bring chaos upon a world that already is sorely lacking in privacy—surely you recognize that.

Do you care so little about other people that you would do something like this to them?"

"Oh, come on," he growled, clearly not in the mood for an argument. "You're blowing this way out of proportion. Only the wealthy and powerful are going to be able to afford mind readers—and they're only going to use them on each other. Besides, once I've sold enough mind readers I'll be marketing these telepath shields anyway. You'll have the status quo back before you know it."

I stared at him—the man was even more cold-bloodedly mercenary than I'd realized.

Colleen shook her head slowly, and for the first time I noticed her face was unnaturally pale. "No. We can't allow it."

"You can't stop me," Green said flatly.

"Yes, I can." Colleen paused, and I heard the faint sound of tires on gravel outside as one of the other campers returned for the evening ... and without warning Colleen screamed.

It was a piercing, mind-curdling scream, so loud and so unexpected that for a second it literally locked my muscles in place. Across the room Green jerked violently, nearly dropping the briefcase; but before either of us could do anything more the scream cut off as abruptly as it had begun—

And Colleen was holding a knife hara-kiri fashion to her stomach.

For just an instant there was a deathly stillness in the room. I don't know how Green looked in that first second; my full disbelieving attention was riveted on Colleen. The knife, still greasy from the steak she'd been cutting with it half an hour previously, glinted with a horrible light from between her hands. Her eyes seemed black in contrast as they stared unblinkingly at Green.

"The game's over, one way or another," she said, her words soft and rapid, but with an iron cast to them. "You will set down that case and step away from it, or I will kill myself. I expect you understand."

With an effort I shifted my gaze to Green. He understood, all right; his face had gone a pasty white. If

Colleen died before he could hit the switch his power over me would be gone . . . and I would kill him. "It won't work," he half croaked, half whispered. "You can't die fast enough. Your brain will live too long."

"Perhaps." Colleen's voice was still glacially calm. "But many people will have heard my scream, and some of them could be coming in the door at any time. You won't be able to pass our deaths off as strokes or heart attacks, not with a knife in me. And even if you manage to get away, you've left fingerprints all over this room." Outside, a car door slammed. "Here they come," Colleen said. "Decide, Ted. Now."

Green growled something deep in his throat, but I hardly heard him. Nausea was trying to turn my stomach inside out, and I fought desperately against the white spots forming before my eyes. But it was no use. The parallel was too close: Amos, too, had died of a self-inflicted knife wound in defense of someone else. The scene in front of me shimmered and faded . . . and the daymare began.

Amos, you're coming too close; it's beginning to hurt.

I can't stop, Nelson. My plane's been hijacked.

You have to stop. You have to! It hurts, it hurts.

You're going to let her die, aren't you, Dale? She's going to die, just like Amos did.

No! I shouted, and even as I stood in the middle of it I felt the vision quiver. This wasn't the usual pattern . . . and with sudden clarity I saw that Nelson's death-wish within me had overreached itself. These were *Nelson's* memories, not mine, given to me in distorted form during our close approach five months ago. They had no basis of reality in my own mind to draw strength from. Illusions only . . . and with all the force I could gather I hit them with the strongest reality I had.

I AM DALE RAVENHALL! I screamed to Nelson's ghost.

And with a shudder the vision shattered.

I'd apparently been gone only a second or two, because the tableau was just as I'd left it. Running footsteps were audible outside, and Green half turned toward the door, his face contorted with indecision. His hand twitched—and I moved.

With my left hand I slapped Colleen's right elbow forward, knocking the knife point away from her body, and with my right I plucked the weapon from her loosened grip. Green looked back at the motion—and with a yelp ducked as I hurled the knife toward him with all my strength.

It bounced butt-end first off his shoulder, throwing him off-balance for a second. But it wasn't enough, and I wasn't more than a third of the way to him when his scrambling hand got to the switch. He froze for a single heartbeat, panic etched across his white face . . . and then he flipped it.

And nothing happened.

My charge ground to a halt as confusion slowed my muscles. The agony I'd expected—the red haze of pain as two minds crashed together—it simply wasn't there. I looked around, half afraid I was the only one unaffected, that I would see Colleen stretched on the floor in death; but she, too, merely looked bewildered. I turned back to Green, and as I did so the footsteps outside ceased and the door was unceremoniously slammed open. Two men charged in: Rob Peterson and a big blond man I'd never seen before . . . or rather, never seen except in photos.

"Are you two all right?" Gordy asked anxiously, looking back and forth between Colleen and me.

And finally I understood.

"It was plain dumb luck that we spotted you leaving that restaurant back in Moravia, or whatever that town was named," Gordy said, shaking his head. "We'd figured you to be a good five miles farther west, and when we cut through the edge of your shield I thought you'd passed us, heading for points unknown, and that we were going to have to start all over again. It's a good thing Rob recognized Green's car."

I nodded, feeling the tension drain slowly out through my arms as I held Colleen tightly to my side, and let my gaze wander. Green was sitting on the ground by Gordy's rented van; in the dim light streaming from the cabin's windows he looked like someone who'd just been condemned to purgatory. Rob, sitting cross-legged inside the van to take maximum advantage of the dome light, was doing a quick check of the wiring in Green's stolen telepath shield and fitting it with fresh batteries. And behind him, tied down securely in the van's cargo area, was the bulky shield Green had first demonstrated for me down in my basement. Chugging quietly beside it was the gasoline generator that supplied its power.

"Only two days," Colleen murmured. "It seemed much longer, somehow."

"To us, too," Gordy agreed. "If I never see another field of corn stubble I'll be perfectly happy."

I sighed. "Okay, I give up. You didn't just quarter the whole state until you found us, and I don't see anything that could possibly be a telepath shield locater in here. So how'd you do it?"

"With the best locaters you could possibly use for the job: two telepaths." Gordy glanced down at Green with what looked like rather cold satisfaction. "Green here made the mistake of telling Calvin that his gadget had a half-mile range, and once I got to Des Moines a little experimentation with the model he'd left behind showed us that the shield absorbs *all* telepathic signals trying to pass through it, whether or not the sender is actually within the field. By then Scott was in Chillicothe, so we had him stay put while Rob and I drove a hundred-mile-radius circle around him. We were just lucky that you'd gone to ground inside that range—we would have had to start all over again with a new circle otherwise."

"All set," Rob reported, hopping down from his perch and handing me the briefcase. "I've rewired around the switch, too, so don't worry about bumping it."

Gingerly, I took it. "What now?"

Gordy answered immediately; clearly, he'd already thought this through. "Rob and I will take Green away in his car while you drive Colleen back to Chillicothe in the van—you'll have both shields that way. I'll call Scott as soon as I'm clear here, so he'll be out of the way by the time you get there. After you drop her off, you can bring the van and shields back to Des Moines. I guess Rob or somebody will have to go retrieve your car later."

"Where will you be?" I asked him.

He hesitated, glancing at Green. "I'll be in the Dubuque area for a couple of days, I think," he said softly. "Even without access to Amos's devices Green knows too much about telepath shields. I don't think we should take the chance."

Beside me, I felt Colleen shiver. It had been done before, I knew; Nelson had used cult-style brainwashing techniques to condition the men who'd hijacked Amos's plane. With the insights and feedback telepathic contact permitted, the process wouldn't take Gordy more than three or four days. Looking at Green's grim expression, I realized that he'd already figured out what we would have to do. I almost felt sorry for him, but decided to save my sympathy for Gordy instead. "I suppose you're right," I said. "Do whatever you have to."

The three of them left a few minutes later. Standing together by the van, Colleen and I watched their tail-lights disappear among the trees. The sound of crunching gravel had been swallowed up by the rustling of leaves before she spoke. "We really don't have to leave here right away, you know," she pointed out. "Now that Green's gone, perhaps we could stay here for a few days."

"And try to repair the damage that's been done to my dreams?" I shook my head. "No. It's too late for that."

"I'm sorry." Her murmur was barely audible.

"Don't be," I said quickly. "It wasn't your fault. It's just that . . . we were like two cardboard cutouts in there. All of what makes you *you* was missing."

The words were hopelessly inadequate, and I knew it; but even as I groped for better ones I felt her nod. "I know," she said, and there was no mistaking the note of relief in her voice. "Your telepath shield made us normal people for two days . . . but we can't *be* normal people; not really. Maybe with enough time and effort we could learn some of the techniques, but it wouldn't be the same. I think perhaps we've been spoiled by our ability, even while taking it for granted. Even if the machines could somehow be made foolproof ..." She shook her head.

"I understand." I sighed. "I'm sorry, Colleen—sorry for everything. It seems sometimes like everything I've done the past five months has gone wrong."

"Oh, I don't know," she said, attempting a light-hearted tone. "You saved my life a few minutes ago, when you took my knife away."

I snorted. "Even there I didn't have any choice. I couldn't let you die like that. It was how Amos died ... how Nelson killed him."

She shuddered. "I guess we'd better go," she said, her voice dark again.

I nodded silently and we climbed into the van. It was strange, I thought, how dreams so seldom live up to their expectations. I'd wanted to be able to hold Colleen, to talk to her, and—*yes, admit it*—to make love to her. Now, all I could think about was getting a hundred miles away from her as fast as I could ... so that we could be together again.

I was tired of being alone.

BLACK THOUGHTS AT
MIDNIGHT

One by one, the last few cars and trucks vanished from the interstate, disappearing down exits to their homes, or—in the case of the trucks—pulled off into rest stop parking lots or entrance ramp shoulders by their drivers for a few hours of sleep. By midnight, new headlights were showing up only once every ten or fifteen minutes, in either direction. By one o'clock, even those stragglers were gone.

And I was alone. Alone, with a lopsided island of rolling pavement in my van's misaligned headlights the only barrier between me and the darkness outside.

I had forgotten, or perhaps never fully known, just how dark the night was.

An absence of light, my educated mind told me; nothing more or less than that. But that was a civilized definition, created by civilized city dwellers for whom darkness was merely not enough light to read by. Out here, driving through North Dakota under a starless November sky,

67

things were far different. The night had a life and a reality of its own; a malevolent life, stirring ancient fears deep within me. Beyond the range of my headlights the world ceased to exist; to my left, I could all but visualize ethereal hands pressing blackly against the side window.

Half an hour yet to the Canadian border. Border crossing formalities, time unknown, particularly if they decided to give me grief over the bulky apparatus strapped down behind my seat. Six more hours after that to Regina.

Seven hours, plus or minus. Seven hours before I could get to Colleen.

I shouldn't have thought her name—*Dale?* her thought brushed sleepily across my mind.

I clenched my teeth. Damn it all—I'd woken her up. *It's all right, Colleen,* I told her, burying my own tension as best I could and working hard at being soothing. If she came fully awake again—*It's all right. Go back to sleep.*

I held my breath; but even as the first flickers of pain began to show through her fogged mind the codeine-laced medicine she'd taken three hours ago glazed it over again. *Okay,* she said, already slipping back down. The word faded into vague, non-verbal sensations, then disappeared entirely.

I took a careful breath, hearing my teeth rattle together with the strain as I did so. Seven more hours to go. Seven more hours of utter helplessness, piled on top of two weeks' worth of steadily growing fears and frustrations. Fears, frustrations, and questions . . . and the horrifying revelation that had driven me onto this road eleven hours ago.

She'll make it, Dale.

I gritted my teeth. *Damn it all, Calvin—no one invited you to listen in.*

He didn't reply, but just stayed there, quietly radiating calm and patience and strength . . . and my anger evaporated, leaving me feeling like a rat. As he no doubt knew I would. *I'm sorry,* I apologized grudgingly. *I know you're just trying to help.*

I didn't notice until after I'd said them how easily my words could be construed as a backhanded insult. I hadn't meant them to come out that way, or at least I didn't think I had. It hardly mattered, though, not with Calvin Wolfe. Even when he noticed insults, he had the kind of overdeveloped patience and secure self-image that let him shrug such things off without even thinking about it.

As he did now. *That's okay*, he assured me, the patience and calm and strength undiminished. *I know you've been under a lot of pressure lately. Where are you?*

I tried to remember the towns that had been on the last exit sign, but it was a futile effort. I'd passed far too many exit signs since leaving Des Moines. *Thirty-odd miles south of Canada.*

You're making good time, he said, and I caught just a hint of uneasy disapproval as he made a quick estimate of the speed I'd been doing. *About due for another break, aren't you?*

I snorted gently to myself. *Who are you, my mother?*

Some of the patience cracked, just a little. *Come on, Dale—you're not going to do Colleen and her migraines any good at all if you conk out at the wheel doing seventy.*

I gritted my teeth, fighting against the swirling emotions with me. He was right, of course; I wouldn't do them any good that way. Not Colleen, not her headaches, not—*I won't fall asleep*, I growled, pushing the thought aside and reaching down for the two-liter bottle of cola wedged beside my seat. Working the cap off one-handed, I took a good swig. *If you're worried about it, you always can tell me stories to keep me awake.*

The patience cracked a little further. *Instead of that*, he countered, *why don't you tell me one? Like, for instance, just what exactly is wrong with Colleen?*

You know what's wrong, I said, the words coming out with the easy glibness of two weeks' practice. *She's suddenly started developing migraine headaches. The doctors don't know yet what's causing them.*

But she *knows*. It was a statement, not a question, without a whisper of doubt behind the words. *And so do you.*

I could have denied it—*had* denied it, in fact, several times in the past twelve hours, vehemently and with a fair imitation of wounded dignity. But it was the Nelson part of me that was the consummate liar . . . and after eleven hours on the road, that part was as weary as the rest of me. *You're right,* I conceded. *She figured it out yesterday evening, and I—well, sort of bullied her into telling me this morning.*

And you responded by loading the telepath shields into a rented van and charging hell-for-leather to her rescue.

A decision that had been less than popular among my fellow telepaths. Every one of the five with whom I shared normal communication had told me in so many words that going to Regina to hold Colleen's hand was a noble but essentially useless gesture. My stock reply had been perhaps unnecessarily blunt. *Colleen and I discussed it between ourselves,* I told Calvin shortly. *What's going on is our own personal business. Period.*

Is it? he countered. *Is it really?*

There was something in his tone. Something that told me he had figured it out. *Calvin. Please—just let it alone.*

I can't do that, Dale, he said, almost gently. *This is going to impact on all of us.* He hesitated. *Colleen's pregnant, isn't she?*

I sighed. *Yes.*

There was a short silence, and even through my fatigue and worry I found it blackly amusing to watch the three different directions Calvin's thoughts went skittering off in. On one hand were the mainly scientific questions of dominant versus recessive genes, and what the odds were that the child Colleen was carrying might not have been a telepath at all. Beneath that line of thought was another, more worried set as he considered what would happen to both of them as the fetus continued to develop, putting dangerous close-approach pressure on both minds.

And buried almost invisibly behind both of those was

the *really* worrisome question: whether I had known the woman I loved had been sleeping with another man. How I was feeling about the whole thing, whether what I was really doing was charging to Regina to confront her with it. . . .

You misunderstand, Calvin, I told him. *It's my child Colleen's pregnant with.*

Close-approach distance—the distance at which two telepaths had surface-thought communications with each other whether they wanted it or not—was supposed to be around a hundred miles. Off-hand, I couldn't remember if any of us had ever close-approached a sleeping person before, but with my own fatigue already tugging at my eyes—and with Colleen's mental patterns being heavily damped by the codeine—it didn't seem like a good time to experiment. As Calvin had pointed out, wrapping my van around a tree wouldn't do anyone any good.

So, just outside Brandon—maybe two hundred crow-wise miles from Regina—I pulled off the road, revved up the portable generator in the rear of the van, and switched on both of the telepath shields.

And a portion of my world went black.

It was an eerie and decidedly scary feeling, made all the worse by the lonely darkness around me. Ever since my early teens, when my telepathy had first begun to develop, there'd been a sort of permanent haze of thought-clutter that added an unobtrusive background to every waking minute. Most of it came from normals out beyond my twenty-foot sensitivity range, and I'd long since gotten so used to it that I had to stop and concentrate before I could even hear it. But with the shields on, all that was gone.

Three of us—Colleen, Gordy Sears, and I—had spent varying amounts of time in the shield a month earlier, and we had yet to come up with an adequate verbal description of the experience. *The gap where a tooth used to be* had been Colleen's best attempt; *growing up next to a waterfall and then going deaf* had been Gordy's.

What I remembered most was being with Colleen . . . and at the same time, not being with her. Everything that I loved about her—her kindness, her patience, her sense of humor—everything that made her the woman she was had been hidden from me, hidden behind expressions and gestures and vocal tones that I'd never learned how to read. It had been the most acutely lonely experience of my entire life.

And now here I was heading back into that loneliness again. The loneliness, and the risk of horrible death if both shields should somehow fail at the same time.

Perhaps Calvin was right to be worried. Perhaps the ghost of Nelson Follstadt I carried within me was still trying to kill Colleen and me.

Maybe this time it would succeed.

I reached Colleen's house a little after eight in the morning; and had just about decided to break down the door when she finally answered the bell.

My first look at her as she fumbled with the storm door latch was a shock. Her face was pale and drawn, with lines etched into the skin that hadn't been there five weeks ago, and her shoulders seemed rounded with fatigue.

And then the storm door came open, and she was in my arms. "Dale," she said into my shoulder. Her body trembled against me; and yet, even as I winced at the tiredness and memory of pain in her voice, I could tell that the pain itself was gone. The telepath shields, blocking the deadly searchlight-strength blazes of our two minds, had also wiped out Colleen's headaches.

We got in out of the doorway—it was just above freezing outside and all Colleen was wearing was a thin robe—and she led me to the living room. "You made good time," she said, sinking onto a well-worn couch and rubbing at her eyes.

"I was inspired," I told her, carefully setting down the briefcase containing the portable telepath shield before collapsing next to her. At the outskirts of Regina, with the end of the long road in sight, I'd experienced a small adrenaline rush, but most of that had already faded away. "How are you feeling?" I asked, slipping my arm around her shoulders and holding her against me.

"Better than I have in weeks." She sighed. "My head hurts a little, but I think it's just left-over muscle tension. Nothing like the migraines." She paused, as if listening. "It's so quiet."

I looked down at her, a shiver running up my back. "You don't mean . . . you weren't getting any actual *thoughts* from the baby, were you?"

She shook her head, her hair swishing across my nose and cheek with the movement. "Oh, no. I just meant . . . you know. Outside."

The background thought-clutter. "Yeah," I nodded understanding. And it wasn't just the clutter that was gone; so too was the effortless communication with the rest of our group. A communication and friendship that all of us had grown accustomed to—for most of us, the only real friendships we had. Slowly, it was starting to percolate through my numbed brain just how much Colleen was going to have to give up here. "I'll be right here with you," I assured her. "The whole eight months, if you need me."

"I know," she said, and yawned.

I yawned, too. "We'd better get you back to bed before we both collapse right here," I said. Gathering my strength, I stood up and took her hands. "Come on; let's go."

She was practically sleepwalking by the time I got her to her bedroom. My original plan had been to go back outside and unload the other, bulkier telepath shield from the van before sacking out myself; but seeing Colleen stretched across the bed was too much for me. There would be plenty of time for such details, I told myself as I took off my shoes, after I'd caught up a little on my sleep.

It was four-thirty in the afternoon when I finally awoke, reasonably rested but with that stiff feeling I always get when I sleep in my clothes. Colleen didn't stir as I eased carefully out of bed and tiptoed out of the room. In the living room I put on my shoes and coat and headed out to check the van.

The gasoline generator had run out of fuel while we slept, shutting down current to the floor-model telepath shield that had been running off of it. The shield itself was probably still operating—Rob Peterson had installed a battery backup system just two weeks ago—but the silent generator still gave me an uncomfortable feeling in the pit of my stomach. Our limited experiments with the backup had showed that even fully charged batteries faded in a matter of hours, as opposed to the seven to ten days of power a similar pack provided to the more efficient portable model sitting inside by the couch.

Not that we could afford to trust either shield by itself, which was why I'd brought both of them with me. Later this evening I would manhandle the larger model into Colleen's house and plug it into regular line current. But with sundown only another half hour away I decided I might as well hold off until full darkness, when any nosy neighbors who happened to be watching would have less to see.

It took only a minute to drive outside the house shield's half-mile range and pull over to the curb. Switching off the ignition, I stretched back against the cold van seat, and for a moment just listened to the background thought-clutter that once again filled the corners of my mind. Gordy's old inadequate image of living by a water-fall flicked to mind. . . .

Dale?

With an effort, I forced my mind from the quiet exhilaration of just being normal again. *I'm here, Gordy,* I acknowledged.

You all right? Calvin's thought joined in. *We've been trying to reach you all day.*

I'm fine, I told him. *Sorry, about that—I lay down for a short nap that stretched out a bit.*

Yeah, we thought that might be it, Gordy said.

Not that it stopped us from worrying, Calvin added dryly. *Do remind Colleen to turn her phone back on when you get back to the house, too.* He paused, and I could sense him brace himself. *So . . . how is she doing?*

The pain's gone, I told them. *When I left a few minutes ago she was still sleeping like a baby.*

Ah. Gordy's reaction to the simile was brief and low-key, but it was enough to confirm that Calvin had filled him in. As I'd rather expected he would. *It was a close-approach problem, then,* he added.

You expected otherwise? I countered mildly.

Not really. Gordy hesitated. *We didn't tell anyone else, by the way. We thought that timing should be up to you and Colleen.*

Though such considerations hadn't stopped Calvin from spilling the beans to Gordy. . . . Shaking my head sharply, I cut the thought off. Calvin, Gordy, and I were the only ones of our group Colleen could regularly reach from Regina. It was only fair that her best friends be let in on what had happened, and to hell with Nelson's paranoic tendencies. *Thanks, I appreciate that,* I said. *I take it, then, that you think we should tell everyone?*

I don't see how you can avoid it, Calvin said. *Colleen's going to have to stay in the telepath shield for the next eight months, minimum, and someone's bound to notice in all that time that she's disappeared from sight.*

Besides, why would you want to keep something like this secret? Gordy added. *The first child born to anyone in our group, let alone to two of us? It ought to be something to cheer about.*

I grimaced. *And what about the telepath shield? Should we cheer about that, too?*

There was a slight pause, and I felt Gordy's enthusiasm deflate a bit. *Ouch,* he said.

At the very least, I agreed with perhaps an unnecessary touch of sarcasm. *Word leaks out about that and we're going to be right back where we were with Ted Green last month.*

They thought about that for a long moment. *Maybe we can still keep it private knowledge within the group,* Calvin offered doubtfully. *Colleen doesn't have any real commitments she can't bow out of for the next few months, does she?*

Her doctor knows she's having headaches, I pointed out. *If she's at all competent she isn't going to drop it just because Colleen says everything's all better now.*

There was another moment of silence. *We'll think of something,* Gordy said at last. *For the moment the main job is to keep Colleen and the baby healthy. Is there anything we can do to help?*

Not that I can think of, I told them. *If I come up with anything, I'll let you know.*

Okay, Calvin said. *You think we ought to set up some regularly scheduled contact time when you'll be outside the shield?*

Maybe later we'll need to do something like that, I said. *For now, I don't think it's necessary. I'll have to leave in a couple of days, anyway, if I'm going to get the van back to Des Moines before the rental period runs out.*

You want me to fly in to stay with her while you're gone? Gordy offered.

A brief surge of jealousy flashed through me before I could suppress it. Absurd, of course—Gordy was nothing more to Colleen than a good friend. *Let me see how she's doing when she wakes up,* I suggested. *If she feels like she'd like company, I'll let you know.*

Unless you'd rather I not even offer . . . ?

So he'd caught the flicker of emotion. *No, of course not,* I said, feeling my face flushing with embarrassment. *Sorry—Nelson must have taken over for a minute.*

There was a short, awkward silence, and I realized my apology had made things worse instead of better. Neither Gordy nor Calvin had made any secret lately of the fact that they thought my close-approach with Nelson had become altogether too convenient a catch-all excuse for me. *Sure, Dale,* Gordy said at last. *Anyway, let me know what she says.*

Right. Well, I suppose I'd better get back. See if she's woken up yet and find an out-of-the-way corner to hook the big shield up in.

Okay, we'll leave you to it, Calvin said. *Take care of her, Dale, and keep in touch. Maybe on your drive back to Iowa we can hold a round table on just how we're going to keep all of this quiet.*

And who all we're going to keep it quiet from, Gordy added. *Say hi to Colleen for us, okay?*

Sure, I said, turning the van's ignition key again. *And don't worry about it. We've got plenty of time to come up with a workable plan.*

And I really believed that as I broke contact and turned around to head back to Colleen's. Really believed that we had weeks—even months—to come up with a good story.

If I'd only known that I had, instead, exactly four minutes. . . .

I saw the flashing red lights two blocks away; but it wasn't until I got past a camper parked on the wrong side of the street that I realized the ambulance was pulled up directly in front of Colleen's house.

I bounced the van half up on the curb right behind it and scrambled out, banging my shin on the door in the process. I hardly noticed, my full attention on trying to see into the slightly ajar ambulance doors. There was no one inside, which meant she was still in the house. Racing across the lawn, I threw open the front door and dashed into the living room. "Colleen?" I called.

"Over here," her voice said from my right. Skidding to a halt, I turned to find her sitting calmly on the couch, a stethoscope-armed woman seated beside her and a group of three men standing in a loose circle around her.

All of them, at the moment, looking at me. And doing nothing else.

"What's going on?" I asked when I got my voice back.

"This is Dr. DuBois," Colleen told me, indicating the woman beside her. "She tells me—" she swallowed— "that I may have lost my baby."

I stared at Colleen, then at the doctor, then back at Colleen. "I don't understand," I said. "What—I mean how—?"

I was interrupted by a loud beep and a flurry of unintelligible speech from one of the paramedics' belts. "Doctor ... ?" he asked, pulling the radio from its holder.

DuBois nodded, a strangely hard set to her mouth. "Yes, you might as well go ahead," she told him. "There's no emergency here now."

He nodded, acknowledging the call with some kind of number code as he and the other two men brushed past me and left. I closed the door behind them and watched as they hurried across the lawn, my thoughts a swirling mass of utter confusion. Only hours earlier I would have sworn the baby was perfectly fine; and now *this.* . . . "How?" I asked the doctor again.

DuBois opened her mouth; but it was Colleen who answered. "Because the headaches have stopped," Colleen answered for her.

I frowned at her, saw the tight look in her eyes. As if she was pleading silently with me to understand. . . .

And abruptly, I did. Somehow, probably through all the tests Colleen had been taking, DuBois had discovered she was pregnant and realized where the migraines were coming from. But with the headaches now stopped—and with no way to know about the telepath shield—she had come to the only conclusion possible, that one of the two conflicting minds had ceased to exist.

Relief washed over me. Relief that the baby was not, in fact dead; relief that now we didn't have to think up some story about the migraines to get the doctor off Colleen's back.

All of that assuming, of course, that DuBois was indeed thinking the same way I was. "You mean that the headaches were because—?" I asked, trying to draw her out.

DuBois nodded, the eerie hint of flashing red fading from her face as the ambulance outside drove off. "Because Colleen and her baby were far closer together than two telepaths can safely be," she explained. She looked at Colleen. "Is this—?"

"He's a good friend," Colleen told her. "He understands about telepaths."

Dubois nodded and turned back to me. "Then you must understand that both of them were in great danger," she said gently. "In fact, that's why I brought an ambulance here this evening, to get Colleen to the hospital for an emergency abortion. As it happened—" she shrugged slightly—"in this case Nature provided her own solution."

I shivered, memories of my own close-approach with Nelson flashing to mind. DuBois saw, misunderstood. "Don't worry—I'm sure Colleen will be all right," she assured me. "We'll make sure tomorrow. Unless—?" She looked back at Colleen, eyebrows raised.

Colleen shook her head. "Tomorrow will be early enough. I'd rather not start a full examination right now."

"Okay." DuBois reached over to squeeze Colleen's hand, then stood up. "I'll see you tomorrow morning, then—ten sharp. But don't hesitate to call before then if you have any problems."

She pulled her stethoscope off her neck and dropped it into her bag. Picking up her coat, she got into it as she walked to the door. I opened it for her, she nodded her thanks—

And suddenly her eyes widened, and her mouth fell open, and the whole thing went straight to hell. "You're Dale Ravenhall," she breathed, staring at my face as if seeing a ghost. "You're one of—" She spun to look at Colleen, twisted back to stare at me. "You can't *be* here."

On the couch behind her, Colleen had gone white. Her mouth worked soundlessly, her eyes wide with helpless horror . . . and beside her, nestled coyly against the couch where I'd first put it down, the briefcase containing the telepath shield seemed as large and obvious as if I'd parked an elephant there.

DuBois mustn't find out about it. At all costs, she mustn't find out.

She was still staring at me. Swallowing hard, I closed the door and took a careful breath. "What I'm about to say," I told her, "is something you must promise to keep to yourself. I mean *absolutely* to yourself. Is that clear, Doctor?"

She hesitated a fraction of a second, then nodded. "I promise," she said gravely.

I nodded back, wishing to heaven I wasn't in the middle of the telepath shield. If she was lying through her teeth, I'd never know it. "All right. You can test for this tomorrow, but my guess is that the baby is still fine. What seems to have happened is that both he and Colleen have totally lost their telepathic abilities."

Behind DuBois, Colleen nearly fell off the couch. "It seems to be a side-effect of the pregnancy," I rushed on before she could blurt something that would pop the bubble. "A safety mechanism, I guess; otherwise, like you said, a telepath couldn't possibly live through a pregnancy."

DuBois nodded slowly. "I see," she said thoughtfully. "Strange, indeed."

"Not all *that* strange," I argued, digging desperately for half-remembered facts as I fought to create something reasonable-sounding on the run. "I mean, a woman's digestive system shuts down during labor, doesn't it?"

"Yes, but that's hardly comparable," DuBois shook her head, turning to look at Colleen. "This is more like a controlled stroke, or possibly something like hysterical amnesia. Either way, it implies that some part of her brain has completely shut down." She looked back at me, her eyes shining with sudden excitement. "Yes. And if so, it means we should finally be able to discover where exactly in the brain the telepathic talent originates."

Even with the cool air leaking in from the front door beside me, I felt sweat beginning to collect on my forehead. "I really don't think this is the time to put Colleen through a whole battery of tests," I suggested cautiously.

"Why not?" DuBois countered, turning back to Colleen. "Don't you see what this might mean, Colleen?—after years of warm-air speculation, we could be on the edge of finally learning what makes you tick. Learning how and where the telepathy comes from— maybe figuring out how to turn it on and off at will—"

"And what will all this testing do to my baby?" Colleen asked quietly.

A lot of doctors would probably have popped off with a brusque or even patronizing dismissal of the question. To DuBois's credit, she didn't. "It should be safe enough," she said instead. "There's no way to guarantee that, unfortunately, not with a fetus with the abilities this one clearly has. But medical science has had a lot of experience with non-intrusive testing over the past couple of decades, and I think the chances of danger will be extremely small."

Colleen looked past her at me, her eyes pleading. "But if there's even a *small* chance he'll be hurt. . . ."

We discussed and argued and bargained with DuBois for over an hour. In the end, we gave in.

You told her what?

I clenched my teeth. *Will you for God's sake settle down, Gordy?* I said. *It's no big deal.*

I'm so glad you're more relaxed about life these days, he came back acidly. *I don't suppose you've by any chance considered the possible consequences of this stupid lie of yours?*

So what was I supposed to do, tell her about the shield?

Why not? She could probably have been trusted with the secret.

"Probably" isn't good enough, I insisted. *And I'm sorry if the lie wasn't up to your usual standards. Next time I have to come up with one on the spur of the moment I'll ask for sealed bids.*

Gordy's comeback would probably have been a juicy one, but Calvin cut in before he could speak. *All right, everyone relax*, he said in that calmly authoritative tone of his. *What's done is done. Let's concentrate on figuring out how this is going to affect Colleen.*

How it's going to affect her is that she's going to get hauled off to the hospital tomorrow, Gordy said blackly. *What are you planning to do, Dale, walk her back and forth between testing rooms lugging the shield?*

I turned to peer out the van's side window at the brightly lit building beside me, my breath making a patch of frost on the glass as I did so. *As it happens, I'm sitting outside the hospital right now,* I told them. *As long as I park reasonably close in tomorrow the shield should have no trouble covering the whole building.*

That's fine for tomorrow, Calvin pointed out. *What happens when they find out that none of her brain cells have in fact closed up shop? Is DuBois the type who'll push for more tests?*

Like at the Mayo Clinic or somewhere equally far out of town? Gordy added before I could answer. *Blast it all, Dale—you should have just told DuBois that you weren't you.*

It wouldn't have helped any, I insisted. Actually, that approach hadn't occurred to me until it was too late— our faces had been splashed on the world's TV screens enough times over the years that I'd never even considered trying to bluff my way out. But I'd had plenty of time since then to realize why it wouldn't have worked anyway. *She was already busy scheduling Colleen in for tests when the shoe dropped. Or were you thinking that during all that she might miss the fact that Colleen was still carrying a live fetus?*

She might have concluded that the baby's telepathic abilities had burned out, Calvin pointed out. *But I suppose that would simply have called for a different set of tests. I'm afraid Dale's probably right, Gordy; the minute the doctor commandeered that ambulance, anything he or Colleen could say or do would only have bought us a temporary reprieve.*

Thank you, I said, passing over the point that the only "us" really involved here were Colleen and me and the baby. *And as for season tickets to the Mayo Clinic, we've already been through that with DuBois. This is going to be a one-day, single-shot study marathon; guaranteed, end of argument. They get all the data they need tomorrow or they're out of luck.*

And if DuBois starts pushing anyway? Gordy persisted. *I know the type, Dale—you let her get her nose inside the tent and she's going to want all the way in.*

Her nose was in the tent the minute Colleen went to her for help with the migraines, Calvin said heavily. *No way to keep this from getting out, I don't suppose?*

I shrugged, the movement making my coat squeak against the van's seatback. *We can try, but I'm not optimistic. DuBois will want to publish anything she finds, of course, but we've probably got a few weeks or months before that hits the journals. More likely the simple fact of Colleen's pregnancy will leak through one of the people who help do the testing tomorrow.*

Any way you can identify the ones most likely to talk and maybe—I don't know—persuade them not to or something?

With my head inside the telepath shield?

I sensed Calvin's quick flash of annoyed embarrassment. *Oh. Right.*

For a moment there was silence. *I guess there's really nothing else we can do at the moment,* Calvin said at last. Reluctantly.

Not really, I agreed. *Before I forget, Colleen said that you might as well start passing the word to the rest of the group. Probably ought to wait until morning—there's no reason to wake people up for this.*

We'll do that, Calvin promised. *How is Colleen holding up?*

I hissed between my teeth. I would have given almost anything to have said she was doing well; or doing badly, or doing medium. But the simple truth was—*I don't know,* I had to tell them, hearing the undertone of frustration behind the words. *I'm . . . not very good at reading her.*

Another brief moment of silence, an awkward one this time. *You'll get better at it,* Gordy assured me. *Just give yourself time.*

I grimaced. Time. It was, indeed, one thing we were likely to have plenty of. *Right. Well . . . I'll talk to you both tomorrow.*

*　　*　　*

Colleen had a roaring fire going in the fireplace, and was sitting at the far end of the couch staring at it, when I returned from my reconnoiter and long-range discussion group. "Well?" she asked, not turning as I closed the door behind me.

"They're not exactly turning cartwheels," I admitted, shrugging off my coat and draping it over the nearest chair. "But they don't see what else we could have done."

"Except maybe telling Dr. DuBois the truth in the first place."

I winced. I'd defended my decision to lie about the shield—defended it successfully, too—in front of Calvin and Gordy. But defending it in front of Colleen was another matter entirely. "I'm sorry," I said. "I really think things would have been worse if we'd told her about the shield, but—well, I know it stepped on your sensibilities, and I'm sorry for that."

She nodded, still gazing into the fire . . . and belatedly the warning bells began tinkling in the back of my mind. "Colleen?" I asked, moving up beside her. "You all right?"

She still didn't look up . . . but from my new perspective I could now see the tear stains on her cheeks. "Colleen?"

"It's so lonely," she whispered. "So lonely, Dale. When you left to talk with the others . . . I've never been alone before. Not like this."

I sat down beside her and slid my arm around her shoulders. Her body trembled against mine. "It'll be okay," I said soothingly. Even I could hear how fatuous the words sounded. "It'll be okay. I'll stay with you as long as you want me to."

She sighed; a deep, shuddering breath. "I'm not going to make it, Dale. Not eight whole months—not like this."

"You'll make it, Colleen." More fatuous words. "You'll make it because you're not the type to give up. And because it has to be done."

"Does it? Does it really?"

I felt an icy shiver run up my back. "What alternative is there?"

She didn't answer . . . but then, she didn't have to. DuBois had already talked about the alternative. "Do you want to have an abortion?" I asked her in a low voice.

"What, kill the only child ever conceived by two telepaths?" A sound that was half laugh, half sob, escaped her lips. "What would the group say?"

"They'd understand," I told her. "Besides, now that we've got the telepath shield this can be done again. If anyone wants it done."

For a long minute the only sound in the room was the crackling of the fire. "What happens after the baby is born?" Colleen asked at last. "I can't stay in the shield for eighteen years."

"I know." That much, at least, was obvious. "We'd have to put him up for adoption. Scott's got a lot of connections with lawyers in the New Orleans area, and Lisa knows everyone important from Philadelphia to the Canadian border. We'll have them quietly get the wheels grinding."

She didn't say anything, just shifted beside me and brought her hand up to rest on her abdomen. "I don't know. None of the options . . . I just don't know."

"Me, too," I told her. "Look, we don't have to make any major decisions tonight. Let's just get you through DuBois's marathon of tests tomorrow and see how you feel then. All right?"

"Sure." She stared at the fire for a minute, then sighed. "It's funny, you know. When I was a little girl I dreamed about being a mother—played house with my dolls for hours at a time. Then I hit puberty, and all the strange sounds I'd been hearing all my life sharpened into words, and I found out what I was . . . and I knew I'd never be able to have children. The dream died slowly, kicking and screaming all the way. But finally I had to accept it."

I thought about my own hopeless love for Colleen all these years, and the way the telepath shield had suddenly made it possible. And what had happened afterward. "Sometimes dreams like that find a way to come back to life," I told her. "Though not always quite the way you envisioned them."

She sniffed, twice, and abruptly I realized she was crying again. "I'm scared, Dale," she said between silent sobs. "I'm scared that I'll hate the baby for what I'll have to go through for her. Or else that I . . . won't be able to give her up."

There were things I could have said. Soothing things, words of comfort and assurance and trust, none of which would have done the slightest good whatsoever. And so I did the only other thing I could think of to do.

I wrapped my arms around her and held her tightly against me, and listened helplessly as she cried.

Along with Nelson's paranoia and general lack of honesty, I had also picked up some of his boundless confidence; but by morning my own natural caution had reasserted itself, and we wound up fudging a bit on my original plans. Instead of both of us driving together to the hospital, we took separate vehicles: Colleen in her own car with the portable telepath shield in the trunk, me in the van with the larger line-current model and gasoline generator chugging away in back. It meant I had to stay with the van most of the day, lest the generator's puffing exhaust line poking out the back doors attracted unwelcome attention, but even that was probably a blessing in disguise. Much as I hated abandoning Colleen to DuBois's gauntlet of tests without being there to hold her hand, I'd begun to wonder if it would perhaps be more than a little foolhardy to parade together all day among dozens of hospital staff and patients. As long as DuBois was the only one who knew about Colleen's "lost" telepathic powers—and as long as she didn't break her promise to keep that knowledge confidential—there was a chance of stuffing the lie back into its bottle with a minimum of embarrassment. The minute someone else recognized me, that chance would be gone.

The middle of December in Regina is hardly the time or the place to be sitting outside in a van for hours on end, but it turned out not to be as bad as I'd feared.

The weather, I gathered, had been somewhat warmer than usual for that time of year, and with the generator churning out a modicum of heat behind me and the blazing sunlight turning the van's dark-blue interior into a wraparound radiator, the temperature stayed reasonably tolerable.

Reasonably tolerable is still considerably short of warm, though, and my teeth were beginning to chatter when, six hours after our arrival, Colleen finally drove her car up beside me and gave me a tired nod. I nodded back and started the van, and twenty minutes later we were home.

"How'd it go?" I asked her, taking off my heavy boots and standing on one of the floor heating grates. My toes tingled unpleasantly with returning sensation.

"Nothing I haven't had before," she sighed, dropping into a chair at the kitchen table and closing her eyes. "Sort of a repeat performance of all the tests we went through when we were first identified as telepaths. Plus a couple of encores they've dreamed up since then."

Those tests were nearly a decade in the past, but I still remembered them. Vividly. "The full spin cycle, in other words."

"Something like that." She opened her eyes. "I don't know about you, but they didn't let me have any lunch and I'm starved. How's your cooking?"

"Tolerable," I told her, "but all my best meals take at least an hour from scratch to fork. You up to waiting that long?"

She made a face. "Not really."

I nodded and reached for my boots. "Me, neither. What's your preference in fast food?"

She gave me directions to a chicken place and I headed back out to the van ... and it was as I was preparing to pull out of the driveway that I first noticed the man sitting in the parked car down the street.

Waiting for someone to join him from one of the houses, I decided; but even so, I watched in the mirror as I headed down the street, half expecting him to pull

out behind me. He didn't, and after the first wave of
foolishness passed I forgot about him.

Until, that is, fifteen minutes later when I returned
with the chicken and saw him still sitting there.

Perhaps if I hadn't just spent six hours sitting in a van
in the middle of a Saskatchewan winter that wouldn't
have struck me as quite so odd. But I had; and it did.
Enough so that I made sure to lock up the van before I
went inside, and immediately after eating went back out
to bring the line-current telepath shield into the house.
The sun was starting to go down by then, its heating
effects long gone, but the man was still sitting in the car,
a black silhouette against the pink clouds to the west.

By the time I had the shield inside and started searching for a good place to plug it in, Colleen had retired to
her bedroom with a book. By the time it was ensconced
in a corner of her back bedroom study and plugged in,
the book was on the floor and she was sound asleep.
Those two weeks of migraines were still taking their toll,
I reflected, and a full day of medical tests certainly hadn't
helped. Turning off her bedside reading lamp, I covered
her with a quilt and bedspread and tiptoed out, closing
the door behind me.

Two minutes later, wrapped up again in coat and scarf,
I slipped quietly out the back door and padded through
the half-frozen mud in the back yard around to the side
of the house. Flitting between the house and detached
garage, I came up to the side of my van and peered
cautiously around it.

The watcher in the car was still there. Crouching
against the van, partially obscured from his view by a
section of hedge, I watched my breath make clouds of
pale white and tried to figure out what to do. Under
other circumstances, it wouldn't have been a problem—
with a sensing range for normals that was just under
twenty-five feet, I would have had no trouble sneaking
up close enough to find out who he was and what he
was doing here. But with two telepath shields blasting
away behind me, that was out of the question.

I was still trying to come up with a plan when he came

up with one for me. From his direction I heard the faint sound of an engine being started, and a moment later his headlights came on and he pulled away from the curb to head leisurely down the street. Fifteen seconds later, I was on his trail.

He drove sedately, heading in toward the center of the city, without any sign of nervousness or awareness of my presence that I could detect. Which was just as well, given that everything I knew about tailing a car had come from watching TV cop shows. I tried to hang back in the waning rush-hour traffic, more worried about being noticed than I was of losing him, and waited impatiently for us to reach the edge of the telepath shield's half-mile range.

It came, as usual, suddenly. One moment, nothing; the next, the background of mental sound filled the back corners of my mind. *Calvin? Gordy?* I called.

Right here, Calvin came back immediately.

Me, too, Gordy added. *So; how'd Colleen's tests—?*

Later, I cut him off. *I've got a problem.*

I gave them a thumbnail sketch of my situation, and for a minute they were both silent. *Could be he's just a reporter,* Calvin suggested slowly.

That would be bad enough, I reminded him. Ahead, my quarry turned right at a small cross street. *It would mean that someone at the hospital leaked the news about Colleen's pregnancy.*

In which case you'd better just turn east and keep going, Gordy said tartly. *You let a reporter get a clear look at you and that cock-and-bull story about Colleen losing her telepathy will start its long slide down the tubes.*

Unless he already has seen me, I pointed out grimly, reaching the corner and turning to follow. Hard to tell, not knowing the town, but it seemed to me we were heading back out of the main entertainment sections. *In which case running does nothing but leave Colleen here to face the wolves alone.*

Gordy considered that. *So you follow him outside the shield's range and find out?* he said doubtfully. *Seems risky, especially if he hasn't recognized you yet.*

If I set things up right he won't have a chance in hell of spotting me, I reminded him. *All I need is a crowded restaurant or bar or something—*

And what if he's not a reporter? Calvin put in.

My thought broke off in mid-sentence. There was an ominous darkness in Calvin's tone. *What do you mean? Who else could he be?*

Calvin seemed to hesitate. *What if it's Ted Green?*

I felt my mouth go dry. *But that's impossible,* I managed. *Isn't it?*

It most certainly is, Gordy said, his voice allowing for no argument. *Everything Green knew about the shield was blocked. Permanently.*

But maybe—

I said permanently, *Calvin,* Gordy all but snarled. There was anger in his tone. Anger at the implication he hadn't done the job right—

Anger with a clear haze of pain beneath it. When it was all over and we'd questioned him about it he'd shrugged off Green's brainwashing as merely distasteful and tiring. Now, for the first time, I was getting a glimpse of just how thoroughly he'd played down the horror and sheer dirtiness of the experience. Briefly, shamefully, I wondered if I'd ever thanked him properly for his sacrifice.

But now wasn't the time for such things. *Could it be a friend of Green's, then?* I suggested. *Someone who knew he'd been working for me and put two and two together afterward?*

It would have to be damn good addition, Gordy grunted. But he said it thoughtfully, not defensively, and there was a growing uneasiness behind it. *But I don't suppose there's any point in taking chances. I'll give Colleen a call and have her call the police.*

They're going to need a reason to pick him up, Gordy, Calvin cautioned him.

I'm not worried about him, Gordy said shortly, and I sensed him scooping his phone off the hook. *This particular guy can't do anything with Dale sitting there on his tail. But he might not be working alone.*

My heart seemed to seize up inside my chest. I hadn't even thought about that . . . and I'd left Colleen alone, asleep and helpless. *Gordy—*

Shut up—it's ringing.

I shut up, and for a moment I drove in silence, listening to the sort of faraway echo effect that always comes of listening in while another telepath speaks aloud. Gordy gave Colleen a quick summary of what we thought or suspected and told her to call the police and tell them she'd spotted someone skulking around the neighborhood. I could hear the worry in her echo-effect voice, and for a long minute wondered if I should just turn around and get back to her. But even as I heard Gordy hang up—*Uh-oh . . .* I said.

What is it? Calvin asked sharply.

My cue, I think. A block ahead, my quarry had turned into a pocket-sized parking lot. Pulling smoothly to the curb, I killed my lights and watched as he got out and headed across the street. He disappeared into a building with a garish neon sign in the window—somebody's night club, it was called, I couldn't quite read the name from the angle I was at. *This is it,* I announced, opening the van's door and stepping down. It was quiet—strangely quiet—with only a few cars moving anywhere within my sight and no pedestrians at all. The skin on the back of my neck tingled; swallowing, I headed for the building. *I get the distinct feeling I'm not in the better part of town,* I told Calvin and Gordy, trying not to let my sudden nervousness show through.

It was a wasted effort. *Dale, maybe we'd better call this off,* Calvin said. *Who knows what you might be walking into there?*

He's probably not a reporter if he's in a place like that, Gordy added. *And if he's something shady, you sure as anything don't want to confront him.*

It was a sentiment I could wholeheartedly agree with. But even as I weighed the pros and cons in my own mind, my feet kept on walking. . . .

Dale?

Quiet a minute—I'm listening. I took another few steps

toward the night club, the action putting me within listening range of another handful of the bar's patrons; and it was immediately clear that my darkest fears had been for nothing. *It's all right,* I told them, letting out a quiet sigh of relief. *There's nothing particularly sinister here. A little off-beat, but it seems safe enough. I'm going in.*

I opened the door and pushed my way in through the blast of warm, smoky air that swept out past me, and gave the place a quick once-over. It was more or less what I'd expected from my telepathic assessment of the clientele: dim lighting, unimaginative decor, and a fairly loud music soundtrack playing in the background. I was, however, a bit surprised by the young women dancing on the raised stage in the center of the room.

I think it's euphemistically referred to as exotic dancing, Gordy told me, and through the heavy tension in his tone I caught just a glimpse of amusement at my surprise.

Right. Anyway, it explained the curious sense I'd had coming in, an aloof sort of lust. It was, I decided, probably difficult to get really worked up, even by a semi-nude dancer, in a large room with a bunch of other men.

And there were a fair number of men there, considering the early hour. Most were sitting on stools pulled up against the stage area, but a handful of tables and booths further out were occupied, as well. All eyes were on the dancers, which was fine with me: my quarry would never see me coming. Piece of cake.

Unless he spotted you following him, Calvin warned. *Be careful.*

Sure. As casually as possible, I sauntered away from the door, eyes darting for likely prospects as I sorted through the cacophony of thoughts surrounding me. It wasn't quite as bad as trying to follow a conversation at a crowded party, fortunately, since looking directly at a person usually sharpened that particular mental voice. I walked slowly past the near side of the stage, shifted direction slightly toward the tables and the booths—

I'd been wrong. There was one pair of eyes most emphatically not on the gyrating women. A pair of eyes locked solidly on my own. . . .

Oh, my God.

What? Calvin and Gordy demanded together.

My mouth had gone dry. *There's a murderer here,* I told them. *John Talbot Myers, wanted in Toronto for three killings during a bank robbery.* For a brief second I thought about trying to escape; but it was instantly clear that even trying it would be suicidal. From his back booth, Myers had seen me walking slowly around as if looking for someone, and was already half convinced that I was either a cop or an informer. His thoughts were edging toward lethal, and I caught a reference to a gun—

Get out of there, Calvin snapped. *Now.*

Too late, I gritted. Too late to run, too late to pretend I hadn't noticed him; too late for anything.

Except. . . .

I'm going to talk to him, I told the others. *One of you better call the Regina police and tell them he's here. I hope they believe you.*

Dale—

Quiet. Moving as casually as possible, I walked over toward Myers's booth. Nelson, I thought dimly, don't fail me now.

Myers watched me approach, and it seemed to me that I could see in his face the trapped-animal sense that I was hearing from his mind. A dozen wild plans fought for supremacy amid his swirling emotion, all of them involving the gun in his pocket; and as I slid silently into the booth across from him I realized with a start that the weapon was no longer in his pocket but was pointed at me under the table.

But I had a weapon, too, one he couldn't possibly know about. Less than three feet away from him now, I was finally close enough to dig beneath the surface thoughts for things he wasn't thinking about directly.

Heart pounding in my ears, my hands folded lightly together on top of the table, I probed furiously for something I could use.

And found it. "Well," I said at last, trying to keep my voice brusque and quiet at the same time. "About time you showed yourself. You have any idea how many places I've been in and out of looking for you?"

It was not what Myers had expected me to say, and for a moment surprise flashed across his mind. But only for a moment. "I think," he said, softly, "that you have me confused with someone else."

"Give it a rest, John," I said coldly. "Unless you've decided you don't want us to help you, that is."

His face didn't change. "And just who is this 'us'?"

I sighed theatrically, probing hard. I needed to tailor my story to the basics of Myers's situation, and while I had a handle on the framework, I still lacked several crucial details. But with a properly phrased question— and a little luck—Myers would supply me with what I needed. "What do you mean, who are we?" I demanded, letting a little scorn creep into my voice. "Who the hell knows you're here in Regina?"

"Why don't you tell me," he challenged. He was smart, all right, or at least smart enough to know that you didn't volunteer information like that to a stranger . . . and totally unaware that in thinking the answer to my question he'd done exactly that.

"Alan Thomas, of course," I said with an air of forced patience, suppressing a shiver as I picked up a short profile of the man from Myers's mind. Thomas was an old colleague from Myers's youth, heavily into Regina's criminal underside and as twisted as Myers himself. "He asked me to help get you out of here."

"Did he, now." Myers still wasn't ready to take me at face value, but the uncertainties were starting to creep in. "Describe him for me."

I could have done so easily, of course: awaiting my answer, Myers had what amounted to a full-color portrait of Thomas hovering in the front of his mind. But along with the portrait came the seeds of an easier way.

"Why don't I just give you the name 'John Alexander' instead."

If a mind could heave a sigh of relief, Myers's would have done so. "John Alexander" was the name that Thomas was going to have false identity cards made up in to facilitate Myers's escape from Canada. "So why didn't Alan come himself?" he grunted, and I heard a faint click as he put the safety back on his pistol. "For that matter, what the hell was he doing, letting you in on this?"

"Because the plan's gone to hell," I told him. *Calvin?*

Right here. I'm on the phone with the Regina police now.

I'm going to try and set Myers up for them. Listen in and cue them in on the story.

Got it.

"You've picked up a tail," I continued aloud to Myers. "RCMP. He's in here right now, watching you."

Myers swore gently. "Where?"

"Over there, watching the show by the stage." It was a safe enough fingering; there were over fifteen men there. "We figure he's either waiting for confirmation of who you are, or else already has reinforcements on the way."

Myers's eyes and thoughts had gone icy. "Let's get going, then," he said, his voice gently vicious. "I'll go first; you deal with him when he follows."

I shook my head minutely. "No need. Alan's come up with a better way to lose him." I smiled sardonically. "We'll simply, right here in front of him, have you arrested."

For a moment his acceptance of me vanished, and I held my breath. And then he got it. "Oh, that's cute," he said, and I sensed a genuine if hard-edged humor at the whole idea. "Real cute. Uniformed cops, squad car, the whole works?"

"Depends on what Alan can get hold of," I told him, letting myself breathe again. "May have to go with plainclothes types and an unmarked car." Dimly, I sensed Calvin relaying the plan to the police, and I sent up a quick prayer that they'd go along with it. If they didn't, there would be a gunfight for sure. "But either way, very convincing."

Myers's eyes swept the stage, too casually. "What if he follows us or wants to ride along?"

"No problem," I assured him, probing again. Thomas had a lot of quiet contacts, one of whom—"One of Alan's people at Mountie HQ ran a profile on the guy, and he's apparently been slapped down more than once for trying to hog credit he didn't deserve and stepping on local toes in the process. The boys who're coming have been briefed, and they'll just tell him to go take a hike if he tries to muscle his way in."

They're on their way, Dale, Calvin interjected into my thoughts. *They say you're a damn fool for getting involved instead of calling them directly, but they're willing to go along with it.*

Good. Tell them to just go ahead and come straight in—Myers isn't altogether crazy about the plan, but he buys it and he won't offer any resistance.

I'll tell them. They'll be there in maybe three minutes.

Which meant I had to move now if I wanted to avoid being picked up in the net and lose whatever chance I had left of keeping my presence in Regina a secret. "Okay," I said, glancing at my watch. "They'll be here any minute. I'm going over there—" I nodded across the room—"where I can keep an eye on our Mountie friend."

Myers frowned. "Why? He's already seen you with me."

"That's the point," I agreed. "It means that after they take you out, he's got to choose which of us to follow. If it's me—no problem, I know how to lose him. If it's you—" I gave him a tight smile—"then I'll be behind him. Making sure he doesn't follow you very far."

Again Myers's eyes flicked over the men at the stage, and I caught him wondering why we were going to all this effort if I was going to take the Mountie out anyway. "I hope I don't have to do that, of course," I added. "Better all around if he just thinks the cops have beaten him to the punch and doesn't figure out what really happened for a couple of days. Nothing heats up a chase like taking out a Mountie."

Myers nodded agreement, and I knew beyond a doubt that I had him. I'd told him things only he and his ally Thomas should have known, had presented him with a plan that he found reasonable and even amusing, and had short-circuited all of his worries, almost before they were fully formed, by echoing his own thoughts back at him.

I nodded to him and left; and I was seated casually across the room when the four plainclothesmen came in.

I held my breath ... but it went as smoothly and beautifully as could be. They came over to Myers, underplaying it exactly as fake cops following my script might be expected to do; nothing to disturb the men watching the show, but more than enough for an undercover Mountie to notice. Myers submitted to them without argument or fuss, acting to probably the best of his ability like a man pretending he actually was being arrested. One of the cops went so far as to give him a reassuring wink as the cuffs went on, and after that Myers would have gone all the way to the police station with them.

Which, of course, he was going to. I wondered briefly what his reaction was going to be, decided my imagination wasn't up to it. *They got him?* Gordy asked, his tone tight.

Just taking him out the door, I told him. *Like I said, a piece of cake.*

Glad to hear it. The hairs on the back of my neck pricked up; there was none of the limp relief I was feeling in his voice. *Then you'd better get back to Colleen. Right away.*

For the second time in fifteen minutes my heart seized up. *What's happened?* I demanded, on my feet and heading for the door. *Is she all right?*

She's fine, he said. *And it may not mean anything at all ... but she just called to say that the police did indeed spot a prowler when they came by a few minutes ago.*

*   *   *

It was just as well that most of Regina's police were busy with Myers at the moment, because I broke most of the city's traffic laws getting back to Colleen's house. Every window was ablaze with light when I skidded roughly into the driveway—she must have turned on every switch in the whole house.

I'd taken her spare key along with me, but it proved unnecessary; I was still fumbling it out of my pocket when I heard the deadbolt being unlocked from the inside. A moment later I was inside, and Colleen was trembling in my arms.

Trembling hard. "What happened?" I asked, my eyes sweeping the room for signs of trouble. Nothing seemed to be out of place. "Did you see somebody?"

She shook her head. "No," she said, voice muffled in my chest. "I just—when Gordon called—and then the police came by and said someone was out there—" She took a shuddering breath. "I'm sorry, Dale. I'm acting like a child afraid of the dark."

"It's all right," I soothed her, feeling like a jerk. I knew she was still getting used to being isolated in the telepath shield, after all. If I hadn't left her all alone while I played private eye. . . .

The shield.

She must have felt me stiffen. "What is it?" she asked, pulling away to look at me.

"Come on," I said, taking her hand and heading toward the back bedroom. Calvin's speculations that Ted Green was involved with all this rose up before my eyes, and I found myself gritting my teeth as I pushed open the bedroom door.

Anticlimax. The telepath shield was right where I'd left it, humming sedately to itself. The portable shield—? I had another flash of dread, then remembered that it had spent the day in Colleen's car trunk and that it was still out there. For a moment I considered going out and bringing it in, but decided it was safe enough where it was. I reached for the light switch—

And paused. On the carpet halfway to the shield, some

trick of lighting angle making it visible, was a small glob of mud.

Mud from my shoes, was my first hopeful thought, from earlier this evening when I brought it in. But between the driveway and the walk and the steps I'd been on concrete the whole distance.

But there was plenty of mud just outside the back door.

It took only a few minutes of searching with angled flashlight beams to find the rest of the trail, a trail that did indeed lead straight to the back door.

"He could have killed us," Colleen whispered, trembling against me again. I didn't blame her; I was trembling some myself. "If he'd taken it—"

"I doubt he meant to," I hastened to reassure her. I didn't doubt it at all; the chances were at least even that he'd intended doing exactly that, but had been scared off by the noise of Gordy's phone call. "Did the police get a good look at him?"

"I don't know, but I doubt it." She pointed toward the back of the house. "They said he disappeared back toward the Abbotts' house—that's the white one two houses down—and that they tried to cut him off but couldn't find him. They said they'd put an extra car in the neighborhood, but that there wasn't much else they could do."

Ten years ago, I reflected sourly, when we were still big news, the Regina police department would probably have fallen all over itself trying to protect her, and like as not we'd have wound up with a ring of armed guards around the house. But all the many and varied expectations of how telepaths would make the world a better place had gradually faded away, and with the rosy glow had gone our celebrity status.

Though of course it was only our relative obscurity these days which had allowed me to sneak unheralded into Regina in the first place. The universe, I reflected, contained no unmixed blessings.

"Well, I guess that'll have to do for tonight," I told Colleen as I double-locked the door and steered her back toward the bedroom. Despite obvious efforts to the contrary, she was already starting to sag with her earlier fatigue. "But tomorrow we'll do something more useful."

She nodded, either too tired to think about asking what I had in mind or else too tired to care. I helped her into bed, turned off the light, and tiptoed out. For the next few minutes I made a circuit of the house, making sure all the windows were locked and setting various jars and other breakable glassware onto the sills, the best impromptu burglar alarm I could think of. And wondered exactly what we were going to do when morning came.

Or more precisely, wondered exactly where we were going to go.

Colleen wouldn't like it, and I wasn't looking forward to telling her she would have to leave the city she loved, possibly for eight months, possibly longer. But I no longer saw any choice in the matter. Clearly, someone had recognized me and subsequently deduced the existence of the telepath shield, and now that somebody had seen the thing up close. If he decided to steal it, then the child Colleen was carrying was dead . . . because as long as she was pregnant, Colleen's life depended on having two functioning shields, one acting as backup to the other; and with one of them gone an abortion would be the only safe course of action. The migraines of the past month were abundant proof that as the fetus developed its close-approach pressures would continue to increase, almost certainly reaching lethal levels long before Colleen was ready to deliver.

And I was not going to risk losing Colleen. Period.

I finished my rounds, turning off lights as I went, and trudged back through the dark to the bedroom. By noon tomorrow we'd be gone, I decided as I lay in bed listening to the unfamiliar creaks and groans of a strange house in an unfamiliar neighborhood. We'd take the morning to throw some essentials into suitcases, and by noon we'd be on the road.

Eventually, despite the noises, my own fatigue caught up with me, and as I drifted to sleep I wondered distantly if perhaps I might be getting a little *too* paranoid.

I was not, in fact, paranoid enough. By noon tomorrow it was far too late.

It was nine-thirty the next morning, and I was still trying to persuade Colleen of the necessity of running, when the knock came on the front door.

For a frozen moment we just stared at each other. The knock came again; rising from the kitchen table, I moved quietly to the door. "Who is it?" I called.

The voice that answered was urbane and calm and educated. And very sure of itself. "The fact that you have to ask that question, Mr. Ravenhall," he said, "tells me all I need to know. Please open the door."

I heard a footstep as Colleen came up behind me. "Dale?—what is it?"

"Trouble," I hissed back. For a moment I hesitated; but there really wasn't anything to be gained by keeping him out. Mind scrabbling hard to come up with a new story to spin, I undid the locks and opened the door.

There were two men standing there. One, obviously the man who'd spoken, was balding and late-middle-aged, heavily wrapped up in an expensive coat and an almost visible air of authority. The second, standing a pace behind him, was much younger, with a coolness to his eyes that made me shiver. "I think you have me confused with someone else—" I began; but practically before I'd started into my spiel the middle-aged man pulled open the storm door and walked calmly in past me, the other right behind him. So much for that approach.

"Miss Isaac." The spokesman nodded to Colleen. "Please—both of you—sit down."

"Perhaps you'd like to state your business first," I said in my best imitation of hauteur.

Almost lazily, the older man turned and studied me. "Please sit down," he repeated, emphasizing each word just noticeably.

Silently, I stepped to Colleen's side and sat us down on the couch. My first hope, that we were dealing with overeager reporters, was gone now without a trace. Our visitor chose a chair facing us and eased himself smoothly into it, his younger companion remaining standing behind him. "Now, then," he said briskly, looking back and forth between Colleen and me. "I expect it'll save time and histrionics all around if I begin by telling you what I know. First: I know that you, Miss Isaac, are pregnant; possibly by Mr. Ravenhall here, though I'm not absolutely certain of that. Second: the child is itself telepathic—or perhaps potentially telepathic would be a better term; it certainly isn't doing any real mind-reading at this stage of its development. Third: the only way you and the fetus can stand being this close together is because you have a device plugged into the wall back there that somehow temporarily damps out your telepathic power, which is of course also the only reason Mr. Ravenhall can be here in this room with you. Now, does that pretty well cover it?"

I felt cold all over, the lie I was struggling to create dying still-born. Or most of it, anyway. "Pretty well," I said calmly. "Except that the machine's effects aren't temporary. They're permanent."

He smiled indulgently. "Really. And you'd like me to also believe that your powers of persuasion are such that you could simply talk a killer like John Talbot Myers into giving himself up."

I glanced at the man standing silently over him, the taste of defeat in my mouth. "So it was you I was following?" He nodded once, still silent, and I shifted my eyes back to the other. "How did you arrange for Myers to be there?"

He smiled again. "I'd like to claim credit for that, but in fact it was pure happenstance. Alex here—" he gestured minutely toward the man standing over him—"was really only trying to get you out of the way for awhile so that another of my people could examine the device he saw you bring inside after your long day at the hospital."

"I hope he got a good look before the phone call scared him away," I said coldly.

He cocked an eyebrow at me. "Your anger is understandable, Mr. Ravenhall, but totally unnecessary.

He had explicit instructions not to tamper with the device. After all—" he shrugged—"I'd hardly go to all this trouble only to lose my child."

Beside me, Colleen stiffened. "What do you mean, *your* child?" I demanded.

"I mean," he said softly, "that when the baby is born I'll be taking charge of it."

"Like hell you will," I said, a flash of anger hazing my vision with red. "It's Colleen's baby, and whatever arrangements are made will be up to her."

"And her sponsors?" he asked pointedly.

I frowned. "What do her sponsors have to do with it?"

He looked at Colleen. "Your monthly stipend, Miss Isaac; the money without which you would have little or no way of surviving. It comes from the University of Regina, Regina General Hospital, and the Canadian Psychiatric Institute, correct?"

She hesitated, then nodded. "Yes."

His eyes came back to me. "And your funding, Mr. Ravenhall, comes from the Draper Fund for Basic Medical Research and the Iowa State University of Science and Technology. Correct?"

"You're well informed," I told him. "What's the point?"

His face hardened, just a little. "The point is that all of that money—*all* of it—comes from me. Not from some kindly bureaucracy or generous charity or the U.S. and Canadian taxpayers: from *me*. And not just yours, but all of your fellow telepaths' as well."

"What are you saying, then?" Colleen asked quietly. "That you own us?"

For a long moment he gazed thoughtfully at her. "I wanted to own you," he said at last. "And if I'd succeeded it wouldn't have been because I had to fight off the competition. Even before all the initial hype and media attention had died down, all of the hard-headed realists of this world had already come to the conclusion that your talent was far too limited to be useful. You could really only transmit words, which cut out any possibility of sending technical data or drawings cross-country; you had to get within thirty feet of your target before you could do any direct spying; and with the liberals in the legal system screaming about the Fifth Amendment you were reasonably useless for solving crimes." He smiled at me. "At least officially. I daresay John Talbot Myers is still trying to figure out what exactly happened to him." He sobered again. "But the most telling point of all against you was that, at least at the beginning, you were literally internationally known figures. Even now, while that recognition has slipped enough for you, Mr. Ravenhall, to walk anonymously into a night club in Regina, all the truly important people in the world would recognize you in an instant."

And at last it hit me. "And that's why you want Colleen's baby, isn't it?" I said. "Because if you can keep his existence a secret . . ."

"He'll be the Unknown Telepath," he finished for me. "And brought up to be totally loyal to me."

Dimly, I was aware that Colleen was pressing close to me; but at that moment all I wanted to do was wrap my hands around that neck and squeeze the satisfied look off his face. Without even thinking about it I surged to my feet—

"Sit down, Mr. Ravenhall," the man told me, his voice calm but abruptly icy cold. "I don't especially need *you*, you know."

I broke off in mid-stride, enough of my brain functioning again through my rage to see that his stooge Alex had his right hand inside his opened jacket. Just about where the business end of a shoulder holster would be. . . .

And then Colleen's hand darted up to grip mine in an iron vise, and my last thought of resistance evaporated. For now, at least. Taking a deep breath, I sat down again. "You'll never get away with it, you know," I told him. "Colleen and I can't just disappear without someone noticing."

He shrugged, all affability again. "There's no reason why either of you should have to disappear. Miss Isaac can stay here, certainly until her condition begins to show, after which she can take a vacation for a few months and then return. You, of course, will have to eventually head back to Des Moines."

"Oh, certainly," I snorted. "And if I happen to meet with an accident on the way back—well, that's just the way it goes?"

His eyes hardened. "I don't like being called a murderer, Mr. Ravenhall," he said softly. "I like even less being called a fool. Do you think I've spent over four million dollars in the past ten years just to throw it away by killing you?"

Behind the haze of anger and helplessness, a small corner of my mind recognized that that was exactly the attitude I wanted to foster in him; but at the moment I wasn't interested in listening to reason. "If you expect some kind of future cooperation, you can forget it," I told him instead. "Not from me, not from any of the others."

"Perhaps, perhaps not," he said placidly. "You may be surprised—some of them may be more grateful for my assistance over the years than you are. Your late colleague Nelson Follstadt, for instance, was quite willing to assist me with some small experiments before his untimely death."

"Nelson was ill," Colleen said, her tone laced with contempt. "Only a bastard would take advantage of a man like that."

"I never claimed sainthood," the other said with an unconcerned shrug. "And, of course, there may be things you can do that don't require a surplus of cooperation. Sperm donor, for example—as soon as Miss Isaac delivers we can take that telepath suppressor apart and learn how to build others, and at that point the number of potential telepaths is limited only by our imagination."

"It'll be years before you get a return on your investment," Colleen reminded him. She was working hard at keeping her voice calm and reasonable, but the hand I held was stiff with emotion. "None of us developed our telepathy until adolescence; there's no reason why my baby should be otherwise."

He smiled. "I have nothing against long-term investments, Miss Isaac. You and Mr. Ravenhall are living proof of that."

"You won't get away with it," I told him, dimly aware that I'd already said that once this morning. "What's to stop us from calling the police down on you?"

He gave me an innocent look. "Down on whom? You don't even know who I am."

"You said you were funding all of us," I reminded him. "Those connections can be traced."

"Not in a hundred years of trying," he said. "Face it, Mr. Ravenhall, you can't stop me. Not even if you were so foolish as to try."

There was something in his voice that sent a chill up my back. "And what's that supposed to mean? That you're willing to lose some of your investment after all?"

"I'm always willing to do that if necessary," he said coolly. "But I'm actually not referring to myself at all here. All right; assume that you call the Mounties and relate this conversation to them. What do you suppose they'd do?"

"Throw your butt out of the country," I growled.

"Possibly, though I don't know what exactly they'd charge me with. And then?"

"Suppose you tell me," I challenged.

"You know as well as I do," he said. "The first child born to a telepath?—*and* the first known method to dampen telepathic abilities? You and your machine would be in secret custody somewhere in the northern Yukon within six hours. Or in Langley, if the CIA got to you first." He looked speculatively at Colleen. "Your child would disappear as soon as he was born, Miss Isaac; disappear into a Military Intelligence family, probably, so that he'd be properly prepared for the life they'd eventually put him to."

"Which is no different than the life you have planned for him now," she countered, her voice stiff.

He shrugged. "Working for me he would be in the United States, transmitting private messages or testing employees' loyalty or doing a little industrial espionage."

He cocked an eyebrow. "Working for the CIA he would be in Eastern Europe or Iran or the Soviet Union, spying on people who would most certainly torture him to death if they caught him."

Colleen didn't say anything. Neither did I. There didn't seem to be anything left to say.

Apparently, our visitor could tell that, too. "Think about it," he said, getting up from his chair and buttoning his coat. "You either accept what I'm offering, Miss Isaac, or else you suffer through what the government will do to you and your child when they find out—and they *will* find out; don't think for a moment you can hide it from them forever." Stepping to the door, he paused and nodded courteously. "I or one of my people will be in touch. Good day to you." He pulled open the door and stepped outside. Alex locked eyes briefly with each of us, and then he too was gone.

And we were alone.

With an effort I unclenched my jaw. Colleen was still pressed tightly against me; bracing myself, I turned my head to look at her. "I'm sorry, Colleen," I said quietly.

She lifted her eyes to mine . . . and even as I watched, I could see the fear and hopelessness and near-panic in her face began to fade. Into a simmering anger. "He won't get my child, Dale," she said, her voice a flat monotone that I found more unnerving than a scream of rage would have been. "I'll die before I'll let him have my child."

My mind flashed to that horrible scene at Rathbun Lake, the frozen tableau of Colleen facing down Ted Green with a knife pressed against her stomach. "It won't come to that," I told her through suddenly dry lips. "We'll find another way. I promise."

She blinked away tears. "I know," she whispered.

She didn't say it like she believed it, but that was hardly surprising: I didn't really believe it myself. If even half of what our visitor had said was true, we were up against frightening amounts of money and power, and I couldn't even begin to imagine how we could hide Colleen from such power for the next eight months.

But I'd find a way. I had to. More than anyone else I'd ever known, Colleen had a solid sense of what things in this world were worth dying for; and at Rathbun Lake she'd proved she had the courage and will to carry such convictions out.

One way or another, she wouldn't be giving her child up into slavery.

Gordy and Calvin listened silently to my story, but even without words I could feel the anger growing steadily in both of them—in Gordy's case, an anger that was already halfway to full-blown fury. *He can't get away with it*, Calvin said when I'd finished. *If he's really the one funding us, we'll be able to track him down.*

We can try, I agreed. *He didn't seem to think it likely we'd succeed.*

Yeah, well, let's not take his word for it, okay? Gordy said bitterly. *You seem to be taking all this pretty calmly.*

Only because I've had two days to get used to it, I told him shortly. *And because Colleen and I have had time to think and plan. You see—*

I hope you didn't do your planning in the house, Gordy interrupted me. *Your lousy child-snatching-Fagin pal probably had the place bugged.*

Don't worry, we figured that, too, I assured him. *We did all our discussions in writing, most of it at night in bed with a small flashlight. And we burned the papers afterwards and flushed the pieces down the toilet.*

All in the best traditions of TV cop shows, Gordy growled.

You want to listen to this or not? The thing is, we've come to the conclusion that our Fagin pal, as you call him, isn't nearly as all-powerful here as he'd like us to believe. Whatever the size and scope of his business or organization or whatever, he's throwing only a tiny fraction of it our way.

Maybe that's what he wants you to believe, Calvin suggested. *Maybe he's just trying to lull you into a false sense of security.*

Why? Underplaying it makes no sense—he wants us

to knuckle under, remember? To give up and let him have his way.

Then you're reading it wrong, Gordy concluded sourly. *He'd have to be an idiot not to throw in everything he's got.*

Which is exactly my point, I said. *He is throwing in everything he can; but that isn't very much.*

From Calvin came a sudden flash of understanding. *Ah-ha,* he said. *Of course. He can only use the people he can trust completely, because everything turns on his keeping the baby's existence a secret.*

At least until it's born, I agreed. *After that he can spirit the child away, and even if the world finds out there's an unknown telepath on the loose they still won't know what he looks like and he'll be difficult or impossible to track down. But until then, everything's got to be kept secret, or the media will descend on Colleen and he'll have lost his chance.*

Then that solves our problem, Gordy said. *We call a news conference—*

And have Colleen vanish into some secret government stronghold after all the hysteria fades a little?

Gordy's surge of satisfaction faded. *Maybe we can bluff him with it anyway,* he suggested, more doubtfully. *Tell him that he either backs off, or we blow the whistle and the hell with the consequences.*

It wouldn't work, Calvin said. *Dale and Colleen have had two days to do that, and the fact that they didn't will imply to him that they'd rather take their chances with him than with the government.*

That's what we hoped he'd think, I agreed. *Which is why we waited this long for me to leave. To make sure Fagin's watchdogs didn't think I was heading out somewhere to whistle up the Marines.*

For you to—wait a minute, Dale, where are you?

On Trans-Canada One, heading east

There was a moment of stunned silence. *You're leaving her?* Gordy asked, something darkly unpleasant bubbling beneath the surface of the words. *Just like that? Leaving*

*her stuck all alone, with maybe one of Fagin's Neander-
thals watching the house—?*

Oh, I'm sure someone's watching the house, I told him
grimly. *Otherwise, Colleen could just pack up the shield
and make a run for it. As it is, with the thing as bulky
as it is—and with the garage unattached from the
house—anyone watching the house would see her in
plenty of time to go take her by the hand and lead her
back inside.*

Like I said—trapped in the house, Gordy all but
snarled. *Damn it all, Dale—*

And that's where they've finally made a mistake, I cut
him off. *Colleen can leave Regina any time she wants to.
Fagin doesn't know about the second shield.*

Gordy's growing tirade cut off in mid-accusation. *He
doesn't know about it?* he asked, sounding incredulous.
How on God's earth did he miss something like that?

I don't know, exactly, I admitted. *Best guess is that he
simply never thought to look. Presumably his local people
picked up on Colleen's pregnancy while she was undergoing all those tests at the hospital and tailed us home.
They would have seen me haul the line-current model
into the house, but I never got around to taking the
portable one out of Colleen's trunk that night. By morning Fagin was in town and giving us his big pitch, so of
course we just left it where it was.*

And it's still there? Calvin asked.

If it weren't, I wouldn't be having this conversation, I
said, and despite myself felt a shiver run up my back.
*Before I left this morning I took Amos's magic kernels
out of the line-current shield.*

You what? Dale—

Gordy broke off, the texture of his thoughts more confused than anything else. Too many shocks in too short
a time, I decided, and for a few minutes I drove on in
silence, listening to the background clutter and giving
them time to assimilate all of it. *We seem to be running
about two steps behind you, Dale,* Calvin said at last.
Why don't we shut up and let you give us the rest of it.

I sighed. *There's not much more to tell. The day after*

tomorrow—in the late afternoon, around sundown—Colleen will drive off as if going to the little mall around the corner from her house, and will just keep going. By then Rob Peterson will hopefully have had time to put together a new shield with the kernels I scavenged from the old one, and I'll head west to rendezvous with her. We'll hide her someplace where she'll be safe for the next eight months, get Scott and Lisa working on finding an adoption family when the time comes . . . and that will hopefully be that.

Calvin seemed to mull that over; but Gordy's response was far more immediate. *It won't work. Not for long enough. God's sake, Dale, you really think Fagin won't be able to trace her? I mean, her license plates alone—*

If you've got a better idea, let's hear it, I snapped. *We've got between six and nine days now until the new batteries we put in the portable shield run out, and it'll take at least half a day for us to reach our rendezvous point. We simply don't have the time to set up anything more elaborate.*

So we've got until tomorrow night, Gordy said, his tone oddly dark. *Fine. Give me until then to come up with something, okay?*

I suppose I should have expected something like that, but the offer took me by surprise anyway. Calvin, who knew Gordy better than I did, was somewhat faster on the uptake. *We can't risk it, Gordy,* he told the other. *Suppose Fagin is having you watched? Or has access to airline reservation computers?*

I have a friend who's a private pilot, he said stubbornly. *She can fly me up there without anyone knowing where I've gone.*

Fagin could check on the flight plan, I pointed out, feelings of resentment stirring within me. This was *our* war, not his—

She can file a false flight plan, Gordy insisted. *She'll know how to pull something like that off.*

And then she's in the hot seat, too, huh? I growled . . . but I could see now that it was a losing battle. Gordy

was determined to put his oar in here; with our blessing
if possible, without it if necessary.

Calvin saw it, too. *I don't suppose there's really any
way we can stop you,* he conceded. *Just remember that if
you tip Colleen's hand there won't be any second chances.*

Even seven hundred miles away in Spokane I could
feel Gordy's shudder. *I'll remember,* he said softly.

There was little enough time to spare, and I drove
straight through the day, arriving in Des Moines just after
one in the morning. On the way into town I stopped at
a phone booth—I wasn't about to trust my home
phone—and gave Rob Peterson a call. He was great;
didn't ask any questions, just promised to be at my house
at ten with all the equipment he'd need to put together
a new telepath shield.

He was there on time, and I left him working while I
returned the van to the rental agency. One of the
employees drove me home, and on the way I had him do
a leisurely drive around the block. If Fagin had anyone
watching my house, I didn't pick him up. More evidence
that he was running this on a shoestring. . . . if, of course,
I was reading the signs right. Given my recent record, I
wouldn't have bet a lot on it.

It took me only a couple of hours to pack the stuff
Colleen and I would need for our getaway, and after that
I had little to do except worry. A little before noon
Gordy arrived in Regina—apparently unnoticed by
Fagin's friends—and spent the afternoon poking around
town on errands he wouldn't discuss with either Calvin
or me. I tried pressing him for information once or twice,
but it was obvious he wasn't going to give me any, and
by early afternoon I gave up the effort. Leaving Calvin
to keep an eye on him, I settled down to wait, dividing
my attention between worrying and watching Rob work.
The worrying was what I did best.

I'd assumed that it would take at least a day to build
the new shield when I'd set things up with Colleen; but
on that, at least, I'd been overly pessimistic. By five-thirty
that afternoon Rob had the device finished—a briefcase-

sized one, this, instead of the bulkier model I'd scavenged the kernels from. I told Calvin to stand by and flicked the switch.

The background clutter—as well as Calvin's and Rob's thoughts—vanished. Getting into my car, I headed slowly down the street, and within a few minutes had confirmed that it did indeed have the same half-mile range as the model I'd left with Colleen. I reported to Calvin and drove back home, watching for parked cars with Fagin's watchdogs sitting in them. Again, if they were there, I couldn't spot them.

Rob was waiting just inside the door when I pulled up. "Well?" he asked eagerly. "Does it work?"

"Like a champ," I told him, clapping him on the shoulder and stepping over to where the mass of wires and chips and Amos's enigmatic kernels was sitting on the kitchen table. "You did great, Rob. Especially given that you'd never actually done this before."

He shrugged modestly. "Yeah, but remember I examined the stuffing out of the thing last month. Now if I could just figure out how Amos made those kernels we'd be in real business."

I nodded and flipped the off switch—

And an instant later my head filled with a din of shouting. *Dale! Are you there? Dale—!*

I'm here, Calvin, I said, the skin on my neck crawling. There was a note of near-panic in that tone—*What's wrong?*

Gordy's gone in, he said, and behind the words I could visualize clenched teeth. *The minute you confirmed the range and headed back home, he disappeared.*

God in heaven—*He can't do that,* I said, reflexively looking at my watch. It would be just about sundown in Regina, exactly the time we'd planned for her to make her break . . . except that Gordy was twenty-four hours early. *What in hell's name does he think he's doing? Colleen won't be ready yet.*

I don't know, Calvin hesitated. *But I think he may be up to something desperate. He's been . . . really brooding about this.*

Which I'd been too absorbed in my own thoughts to notice? But it was too late to worry about that now. *Did he tell you the name of his pilot friend?*

Yes—Jean Forster. Why?—you think she's involved in some way?

She's at least involved to the extent that she got him there, I reminded him grimly. *It might be a good idea to call the Regina airport and try to warn her about Fagin's goon squad—*

And with a suddenness I wasn't prepared for, Gordy was back. *Calvin, Dale—listen.*

I didn't get a chance to ask what it was he wanted us to listen to ... but an instant later I got the answer anyway. As from deep in a well, I heard an angry voice. *Get out here, you son of a bitch. God damn it—look what you did to my car.*

I sensed Gordy being hauled all but bodily from a vehicle by two men, and I strained to try to see their faces through his eyes. It was no use; the images I could pull in were too weak, and in the dim light of dusk all I could see were silhouettes. But I didn't need to see them to guess who they were. Fagin's stamp was all over them. *Cute, friend—real cute,* the angry man snarled again, his silhouette raising as if on tiptoe to look past Gordy. *What, you figured you'd give her a head start and then catch up? You lousy son of a—*

Knock it off, Billy. The second man's voice was hard and calm and authoritative, and Billy shut up. *There's no real harm done. It was pretty stupid, you know,* he continued, talking to Gordy now. *We had orders to stop anyone we caught trying to take anything big out of the house—and that included garbage men. Take a look in back, Billy—make sure the thing's there.*

Billy's silhouette nodded and headed obediently off to the left, and as Gordy turned to watch him I saw that they were indeed standing beside a small garbage truck. Briefly, I wondered how Gordy had gotten hold of it. *Yeah, it's here,* I heard Billy call. *Uh ... shouldn't we be getting on the phone and getting Harry on the trail?*

What for? the other asked calmly. *She'll be back. Any minute now, probably.*

Yeah, but if she didn't see him crash our car—?

The other man turned to face Billy's returning figure; and once again, Billy shut up. *She probably didn't,* he agreed quietly. *So what?*

Oh. Right. Billy nodded belated understanding. *The headaches'll start up again. That'll tell her he didn't get away.*

And I don't think she'll miss the implications, the other agreed. He turned, and I got the feeling he was peering down the street, looking for Colleen's returning car. *Though on second thought . . . come here; watch this guy for a minute.*

Billy's silhouette replaced his in front of Gordy, and he stepped over to a nearby car and leaned in the open door. He emerged with something in his hand, which he did something to and then held to the side of his head. A cellular phone, probably. *Harry? Warfield. Listen. I want you to cruise south down Albert Street to the highway—see if our pigeon has gone off the road somewhere . . . No, I want you to leave her there—of course you bring her back home, damn it; we can go back and get her car later.*

Warfield reached in and hung up . . . and suddenly I sensed Gordy's mind tensing as he prepared for action. *She'll be back,* Warfield said, straightening up to face Gordy again. *Unconscious, maybe—probably with one hell of a headache—but she'll be back.*

No.

The word seemed to hang in the air, and for a moment I could sense Warfield and Billy staring at him. *What do you mean, no?* Warfield asked, his voice calm but with menace beneath it.

I felt my fingernails digging into my palms as I clenched my fists in agonized helplessness. God, he was going to ruin everything—it was far too soon to spill the fact that Colleen had her own telepath shield. I wanted to scream at him to shut up; but it was too late, he'd already said too much, and sooner or later now they'd have the rest of it. Impotent fury bubbled up inside me, turning my stomach inside out. All my worry and planning . . . and with a single word Gordy had betrayed it all. *I said, what did you mean, 'no,'* Warfield demanded again, taking a step toward Gordy. I braced myself—

And Gordy took a step toward Billy, slammed his fist into the goon's stomach, and ran.

It was probably the sheer unexpectedness of it that let him get away with it; with the telepath shield out of quick reach at the bottom of the garbage truck and with Colleen still well within the close-approach death zone, Gordy had literally nowhere to run, and both his captors surely knew that. But unexpected or not, Warfield clearly had good reflexes. Even before Gordy reached the back of the truck I could hear the sudden scraping of feet on pavement that showed the chase was on. Where the hell did Gordy think he was going—?

An instant later I found out. Gordy skidded to an abrupt stop at the rear of the garbage truck, threw a wild punch to keep Warfield back—

And slammed down the compression lever.

The sudden growl of the motor drowned out Warfield's startled exclamation; but Gordy's reply was only too clear. *I'm taking Colleen the one place your filthy boss can't reach us,* he shouted.

You stupid bastard, Warfield yelled over the grinding of the hydraulic crusher jaws. He leaped forward, grabbing Gordy by the shoulders and trying to force him away from the lever. But Gordy held his ground, wrapping his arms around the other.

And then the crusher hit metal, grinding away against the angle iron holding the telepath shield together . . . and, abruptly, as if by mutual consent, both men stopped their struggling. The grinding stopped, and I could see Warfield's silhouette draw back in confusion. *What the hell?*

Gordy looked slowly back at the garbage truck, as if not believing what he was seeing. *It . . . can't be,* he said, and even through the tunnel effect I could hear the bewilderment in his voice. *We agreed—if I didn't get away—*

He broke off, and I could just hear the electronic warbling of the car phone. Gordy glanced over that way, and I saw Billy reach in for the phone. *Get away from there*, Warfield ordered Gordy abruptly, shoving him away from the lever. *Must not have busted the thing all the way—*

Hey! Billy called, his voice odd. *It's Harry. C'mere—you gotta hear this.*

Warfield took Gordy's arm and marched him toward the car. *What is it?*

Harry found her car, Billy said, and now I could identify the emotion in his voice. Disbelief. *It's down by the lake. Next to a spot where it isn't all frozen.*

For a long moment Warfield just stared at him. Then, taking a long stride forward, he snatched the phone from Billy's hand.

Dale? Calvin? You both listening.

With a conscious effort, I unclenched my teeth. *We're both here, Gordy. What's—where's Colleen?*

On her way out of town in a car I rented and left at the lake, he said. *She'll meet you at the rendezvous you set up.*

Get out of there, Calvin put in, his voice urgent. *Now. Before they remember you're still there.*

Sorry, but I can't. Gordy's voice was calm . . . but beneath it I could feel a tightness. A tightness, and the winding up of courage; and over all of it, a strangely wistful sadness.

And suddenly I realized that Gordy was preparing himself to die.

Calvin's right, I snarled. *Colleen's in the clear—get out of there.*

I can't, he said again, and this time there was an edge to it. *I have to make sure they're convinced that she would rather die than give up her child to that kind of slavery, and that once the game was up that she would commit suicide rather than let me kill both of us. And they're not going to want me around to testify after that.*

I bit hard at my lip, searching frantically for a way to

convince him . . . and then my brain seemed to catch, and I cursed my stupidity. *Calvin—get on the phone*, I ordered. *Call the Regina police, tell them there's a kidnapping in progress. Where are you, Gordy?*

A flicker of hope, the realization that maybe he wouldn't have to sacrifice himself after all—*The corner of Fourteenth Avenue and Rae Street—*

And suddenly Warfield spun around, his brain apparently catching, as well. *God damn it*, he snarled viciously, hand jabbing at Gordy. *Billy—take him out*. Now, *damn it.*

Here it comes, Gordy said, and there was no longer any tension in his tone. Just a quiet acceptance. *Goodbye. Tell Colleen that I love her—*

And then a shadow swung at his head, and the image was gone.

I don't know how long I stood there, staring at nothing and listening to the silence where Gordy had been. Gradually, I became aware that there was a hand on my arm. Blinking my eyes against a painful dryness, I found Rob gazing at me, his thoughts highly worried. "I'm all right," I told him. Even to myself my voice sounded dead.

He didn't believe it, of course. "Anything I can do to help?"

I shook my head. *Calvin?*

Here, Dale. I've got through to the Regina police, and they're sending a car. He hesitated. *I also told them about Colleen's car, and hinted that we suspected suicide.*

Yeah. It felt wrong, somehow, to maintain the lie; but if we didn't, then Gordy's sacrifice would have been for nothing. *You think they realized he was lying?*

I'm sure they didn't, Calvin assured me. *I think it just suddenly penetrated that with the shield supposedly destroyed he could get through to us again. They couldn't afford that.*

It made sense. The game was lost, as far as they knew, and their first priority now would be to cover their tracks. *What the hell's keeping those cops?*

Take it easy, Dale—it's only been a couple of minutes.

I sighed. *I'm sorry. I just. . . .*

I let the sentence trail off. There really wasn't anything left to say. Dimly, through the moisture fogging my vision I felt Rob leading me to a chair, and allowed myself to be sat into it. Fagin would pay, I promised myself. If I had to track him down myself, and kill him with my own two hands—

Dale? The police have arrived on the scene, but there's no one there. Just the garbage truck.

Of course there's no one there, I said savagely. *They wouldn't just leave him there for the cops to—*

I don't know why it clicked just then. But it did . . . and suddenly my grief vanished into a surge of adrenaline. *He's not dead*, I told Calvin. *Of course he's not—what kind of an idiot am I?*

Dale, I know it's hard—

No, listen! I cut him off. *Listen! They wouldn't just kill him like that—Fagin would have their heads on poles. He'd want to question Gordy and make sure he was telling them the truth about Colleen.*

For a long moment Calvin thought about that, and despite his determination not to build up false hope I could sense a growing excitement. *You may be right*, he agreed. *In which case we should send the police to the airport, try and head them off.*

Yes—no. Wait a minute, let me think. Something Fagin had said . . . *He knew Nelson*, I told Calvin. *Probably pretty well—he mentioned once that Nelson had done some experiments for him. Maybe the Las Vegas stuff that Amos caught onto.*

Maybe, Calvin allowed cautiously, wondering with a distinct undercurrent of uneasiness just where I was headed with this. *So what does that tell us?*

I grinned humorlessly, my lips tight enough to hurt. *It tells us*, I told him, *that for the first time since Nelson tried to kill me, he's going to do something useful.*

Calvin said something cautionary sounding, but I didn't wait to hear it. All my thoughts and senses were turned inward as I searched out that part of my personality which had come from my close-approach with Nelson. It was all still there, of course: the greed, the arrogance, the deception, the contempt for mankind in general and his fellow telepaths in particular. Everything I'd fought so hard and for so long to bury was right there, just waiting against the barriers I'd painfully erected against it.

I thought about Gordy and Colleen . . . and let the barriers fall.

And nothing happened. Nothing at all. The Nelson part didn't surge out like poison gas under pressure; didn't flow out like an attacking army bent on destruction; didn't gloat, didn't cheer, didn't rage. It was just there, like nothing more or less than a memory. A dark memory, to be sure, full of pain and anger and terror; but a memory nonetheless.

It was perhaps the greatest surprise of a long day of surprises, that the very thing I'd feared so much for so many months would in fact turn out to be so utterly powerless. Perhaps it was just the healing effects of time; perhaps that deadly confrontation at Rathbun Lake had been the killing blow, only I hadn't realized it.

I was whole again.

There would be cause for quiet celebration later, perhaps, but not now. For now, Gordy's life was hanging by a thread . . . and that thread was somewhere in those memories of Nelson. Bracing myself, I plunged in.

And there it was. *Calvin? I got it. Fagin's name is Lawrence Barringer, and he's based somewhere in the Los Angeles area.*

Got it, Calvin said. His emotions were masked, but it wasn't hard to guess that he was wondering what that information had cost me. *You want to call the LA police, or should I?*

No one's calling any police. Not yet, anyway.

What? Dale, he's got Gordy, remember?

No, he doesn't—and that's the whole point, I told him. *His goons have Gordy; and they're hardly likely to drag him to Barringer's house and dump him on the living room rug. They'll take him to some out-of-the way place and question him there.*

I felt Calvin's shiver. *You think they'll . . . torture him?*

My stomach turned, and for a long moment I dug again into Nelson's memories, searching for more details of Barringer's personality. They were there, all right; but even as I sifted through them it suddenly occurred to me that nothing I found here could be taken at face value. Colored as it all had been by Nelson's own warped mentality, there was no way for me to sort out objective fact from wishful or even malicious fantasy.

But I had to try. *Okay, here it is. From what Nelson knew about Barringer he was an absolute fanatic for secrecy in his activities. He'd rather take extra time and make sure he's not being watched or monitored than rush into something and find out later that the whole thing's been captured on tape. Given that—and given that they'll assume we'll call the cops in—my guess is that they'll sedate Gordy and drive him out of town, contacting Barringer from someplace reasonably distant. He'll send a private plane for them, again rendezvousing somewhere away from Regina, and fly them leisurely down to some quiet spot near Los Angeles where they hopefully won't be disturbed. That make any sense to you?*

Calvin pondered it. *I suppose so,* he agreed, almost reluctantly. *There really isn't any rush, after all—if Colleen's alive he's got eight months to track her down. You think Barringer will want to be in on the questioning?*

Yes. On that score I had no doubt at all. *Absolutely. He wouldn't trust it to anyone else, for one thing. And that's where we're going to nail him.*

Wonderful—except for one small problem, Calvin pointed out heavily. *Namely, we don't know where this quiet spot is that they're going to take him. Unless,* he interrupted himself with a sudden surge of excitement, *your friend Rob can put Amos's old telepath-detector back together. If he can—*

Sorry. I'd already had that idea, and found the flaw in it. *The kernels he would need for that are already being used.*

In the second shield; right, Calvin said, the excitement evaporating. *In that case, I don't see that we have any choices left, Dale. We have to call in the police and ask them to put a tail on Barringer.*

If we do that, I reminded him, *we lose Colleen's baby to the government.*

If we don't, he snarled with uncharacteristic harshness, *we lose him to Barringer. Or don't you think he'll be able to make Gordy talk?*

Yes, I'm sure he will. I took a deep breath. *As a matter of fact . . . I'm rather counting on it.*

It took Calvin nearly an hour of phoning to track down Jean Forster, Gordy's pilot friend, and ask for her help. Five hours later, just after midnight, she called me to announce that she and her twin-engine Beechcraft were at the Des Moines airport. An hour after that, we were airborne.

In many ways it was yet another echo of that desperate race to Regina only a few days earlier, and I found many of the same black thoughts swirling around and through my mind as we flew westward. Suspended between land and sky, the occasional concentration of town and city lights below clumping like distorted fun-house mirror images of the stars above, the sense of unreality was even stronger than it had been then.

As was the sense of desperate danger.

I died a thousand deaths that night. At least that many. I'd put on a good front when selling this whole scheme to Calvin, but I knew all too well that a hundred things could go wrong. If I'd read Barringer wrong—if he broke his pattern and decided that speed was more important than caution—then Gordy would be in Los Angeles and the interrogation over and done with long before we got anywhere near the scene.

And even if everything went exactly according to plan, it could still go bad. Horribly bad.

I was able to doze a couple of those long hours away, but mostly I spent the night wide awake, staring out the window at nothing in particular and wondering if I should just give up and abort this whole crazy plan. Colleen had a good head start; with luck, perhaps we could bury ourselves so deeply that even Barringer couldn't find us. And he surely wouldn't be stupid enough to hurt Gordy, no matter what happened.

It was a private battle I fought over and over again that night; and it was Jean Forster's presence beside me, more than anything else, that helped me push back the temptation each time it surfaced. From the beginning I'd had reservations about bringing her into this, and had given in mainly because there hadn't been any other choice; but ten minutes of sitting next to her in a cramped cockpit had laid every one of those reservations to rest. She was smart, competent, tough, and fiercely loyal to the small and select group of people she named as her friends. Just getting me this far had required her to litter our flight path with a half dozen broken FAA regulations, and she knew full well that her license was the least of what she was putting at risk tonight.

In many ways she reminded me of Colleen ... and it wasn't hard to guess what both of them would say if I suggested abandoning Gordy now.

And so we headed west, swinging a bit northward to avoid getting too close to Calvin in Pueblo. We stopped once for refueling at a field Jean knew outside of Grand Junction ... and finally, with local sunrise still half an hour away, we came in sight of the sea of lights that was Los Angeles.

For a few minutes—a few long, long minutes—there was nothing. I sat watching the city lights, sweating as I strained for a contact and fought back the fears and terrors swirling around me. We'd gambled, and we'd lost. Barringer had held the interrogation in Canada, or had flown Gordy here five hours ago, or had simply killed him to cover his tracks. Jean eased the plane a bit to the left, heading southwest toward the southern edge of the city—

And I felt it. Tenuous, weak, almost imagined; but definitely there. The touch of another telepathic mind.

Gordy.

Calvin? Calvin, wake up.

Here, Dale, Calvin replied with an alertness that showed he hadn't been asleep. *What is it?*

I've got him. And he's still unconscious.

I could feel Calvin's cautious relief. *Which means they haven't started on him yet. I hope.*

Yeah. Me, too. Muscles I hadn't even realized were tight were starting to relax. We'd gambled, and we'd won. Barringer had gone with the leisurely, secure approach, after all, and we'd beaten him to the punch. *Have you heard from Rob yet, by the way?*

Five minutes ago, as a matter of fact, Calvin said. *He made it to Colleen's hideout and gave her the second shield, and she's on her way to wherever it is you two planned for her to go. I didn't want to wake you if you were trying to sleep.*

So Colleen, at least, was safe. One down, one to go. I took a deep breath—

And in a single instant the muscles tightened again. "Oh, my God," I whispered.

At least I thought I'd whispered it. Jean heard anyway. "What?" she snapped.

I forced my teeth to unclench. "He got stronger. Much too strong, much too fast. They're waking him up."

Take it easy, Calvin said, glacially calm. *It's bound to take them a few minutes to bring him up to where he can answer questions for them.*

"You want me to radio the police?" Jean called.

"Can't yet," I told her, willing some of Calvin's calm to flow into me. "We still don't know where he is." *Gordy?* I called. *Gordy, can you hear me?*

There was no response ... but even as I strained I could tell our direction was correct. He was somewhere south of Los Angeles, and we were now heading straight toward him.

Straight toward him. As Nelson had flown straight toward me. . . .

I shook my head to clear it. "We're going in," I called to Jean. "You remember the plan?"

She nodded. "You want belt or arm?"

"Belt," I said, reaching over to hook the fingers of

my left hand into her belt. I'd rather have held her
arm, but I couldn't trust myself not to tug it the
wrong direction at a critical moment. Already I could
feel the pressure building in my mind as we flew
toward Gordy.

Toward Gordy . . . and toward the theoretical twenty-
mile limit that would kill us both. In, at the Beechcraft's
current speed, something like twenty minutes.

The pressure was growing steadily stronger, its edges
becoming tinged with a red haze I remembered all too
vividly. The fuzziness that was Gordy's unconscious mind
was becoming ever clearer, and I could feel the first
wisps of pain as the surfaces of our minds began to
merge. . . .

Dale? Calvin's thought was dim and faraway, a scream
almost lost in a hurricane. *Can you hear me? Dale?*

I could hear him—just barely—but I couldn't answer.
My mind was bending now, molding itself against Gordy's even as his bent against mine. Setting my teeth together, I fought against the pain, hunting amid the din
of two minds clashing for the information I desperately
needed. The darkness in Gordy's mind seemed to be
lifting; with all my strength I tried to reach through it.
To search beyond him—

And with a suddenness that made me gasp, I had it.
Four men stood around him, one of them leaning close
to his face. Reaching through Gordy's mind was a blaze
of pain; fighting it back, I pressed harder. Through the
man's eyes I saw Gordy, lying motionless on an ambu-
lance-type stretcher; through his ears I heard the sounds
of distant surf and even more distant traffic. And through
his mind—

"Oc—Oceanside," I gasped. "They're in . . . Oceanside."

Dimly, I felt a hand shaking my shoulder, heard a
voice shouting in my ear. "—address? Come on, Dale—
give me the address."

I pulled the street and house number from the other's
mind and choked them out; and then the pain was too
much, and I fell back. Gordy's mind was growing clearer
by the minute—

"Gordon Sears," a voice said into my mind—into Gordy's mind. "Can you hear me?"

A moment of silence. I wondered vaguely if Gordy, half asleep as he was, could feel the pain I was feeling. Wondered if it would keep him from answering, or would instead go the other way, sapping any strength he might have to resist them. "Yes," Gordy answered, the word coming first through his mind and then through his ears.

And then through my ears, as I repeated it aloud? Maybe. I couldn't tell for sure.

"Good," the voice came again through Gordy's mind. "Listen to me, Gordon—listen closely. I will ask you some questions and you will answer them. You will tell me the truth; because I'm your friend, and I'm Colleen Isaac's friend, and her life depends on your telling me the truth. Do you understand that?"

"Yes," Gordy said again. His voice was dreamy, just like his mind. I wondered what kind of drug they'd used on him, but I was too afraid of the pain to touch the stranger through Gordy's mind again.

"Excellent, Gordy," the voice said. "Then tell me where Colleen Isaac is."

I could feel Gordy's mind fighting against the drug. "Gordy?" the voice asked again; and this time there was a hard edge to it. "Gordy, where is Colleen Isaac? *Where is she?*"

I could feel his mind weakening. Helpless in the drug's grip. . . .

But Gordy's mind was not his alone anymore . . . and I had none of their poison in my body. "She's dead," I murmured, and heard the echo in my mind as Gordy's mouth obediently repeated the words. "She died . . . in Regina. In the lake. To . . . save me."

"She's not dead!" a new voice shouted. Barringer's voice. "She can't be dead, damn it—she *can't* be. *Where is she?*"

"She's dead," I said again, and an involuntary sob escaped our lips. The pain was a red haze over our mind, and I felt our fingers trembling in Jean's belt. We could let go, and she would pull up and take us away from the pain. But it was still too soon. Still too soon.

Barringer was screaming something else, but we could hardly hear him. All around us was the din of two minds wrenching against each other.... "She's dead," we said once more. "She told me ... she would rather die than lose her baby to ... anyone."

And suddenly the screaming was gone. We tried to listen through the noise, to hear what was going on; but the noise was too loud. The noise, and the pain....

"Dale? Dale!"

I blinked; blinked again as I realized there were tears in my eyes. That voice ... and the pain was almost gone. And it was only me. "Wha—?" I croaked. There was no echo.... "Jean?"

"It's okay, Dale," she said, and I could hear the almost limp relief in her voice. "God, for a while I thought we were going to lose you. To lose both of you."

Abruptly, I realized my fingers were still wedged in her belt. "Where are we? Wait a minute—we can't leave—"

"It's okay—it's okay," she soothed me. "The cops are there. Nailed Barringer and his goons red-handed. Soon as they radioed that they'd got him, I took off." She leaned forward to frown at me, and I heard the question in her mind. "Is—I mean, did it work?"

I took a deep breath. "He should be fine," I told her, answering the question she'd wanted to ask. We were heading east, now, heading back home. Ahead, the sky over the mountains was red with the approaching sunrise.

And the long night was over.

"It's not the Hilton," Colleen said, waving a hand around the two-room cabin, "but it's home."

"For the next few months at least," I agreed, looking out the window at the snow-covered mountains and trying hard not to think of how isolated she was going to be out here. "Certainly a great spot to get away from it all."

"There's room for two," she said.

I turned to see her gazing at me, her forehead wrinkled with concern. "Thanks, but I can't," I told her. "If

I disappeared for too long someone would start to wonder if you really weren't dead, after all. It would be a shame to blow a perfectly good lie like that."

"Certainly not after all the effort you and Gordy put into it." She smiled, but the smile didn't touch her eyes. "I don't think I'll ever be able to thank you for what you did for me. When you risked—"

"Colleen." I turned to face her and took her hands in mine. "It's over. Okay? Over and done with, and both Gordy and I are fine. Really."

"But the flashbacks—"

"Will go away," I reminded her. "Remember, I've been through this once before. Nelson's attack isn't much more than a bad memory now, and he and I got much closer together than Gordy and I did."

She nodded. Squeezing my hands, she let go and stepped over to stare out one of the windows. "I just . . . it's still going to weigh on my conscience, Dale. Neither of you is going to ever be quite the same again, and all because of me. I'm sorry if that sounds silly, but that's how I feel."

"Doesn't sound silly at all," I assured her. "Tell me, Colleen: who is that baby you're carrying?"

She turned to frown at me. "What do you mean?"

"Well, he's part you and part me, right? I mean, that's where he came from."

The frown was still there. "I don't understand what you're driving at."

I sighed. "We're all unique, Colleen, but at the same time most of who we are ultimately comes from other people. Not just our parents' genes—all of us, all our lives, are continually influenced by those around us. Our politics are molded by politicians and commentators, our tastes are influenced by our job or station in life . . . and we're forever exchanging styles and traits and interests and catch phrases with our friends." I shrugged. "It just happened that with Nelson and Gordy I got an accelerated version of the process."

She thought about that for a moment. "What about Barringer?" she asked.

Which meant the subject was closed, at least for now. Which was fine with me. I knew she'd think about it, and eventually realize I was right. "He's going to be far too busy treading legal water to bother us for awhile," I told her. "There are half a dozen charges pending, up to and including kidnapping, and when the locals are done with him Canada's waiting to take their shot."

"But if they know Gordy was taken from Regina—?" She threw me a questioning look.

I nodded, a slightly sour taste in my mouth. "There really wasn't any way to hide the existence of the shield from them any longer. The Regina police retrieved what was left of the one Gordy crushed in the garbage truck, and the simple fact that you two were together proved that you'd had *some* way to beat the close-approach limits."

"Then all this was for nothing."

I put my arm around her shoulders. "Not in the least. We saved you and our child from being snatched away into some form of slavery, didn't we? You call *that* nothing?"

"No, of course not. But—" She shook her head.

"It would have been nice if we could have kept the shield a secret," I conceded gently. "But to be perfectly honest, Gordy and I would have had to be fools to risk our lives for a machine. It's the people in this world that are important, Colleen—don't forget that. Not that a person as caring as you are is ever likely to. Must be why I love you so much."

"And speaking of love and people," I added briskly, squeezing her shoulders and stepping away, "grab your coat. I've got a surprise for you."

She blinked at me, sniffling back some tears. "What kind of surprise?"

"A nice one," I assured her, picking my own coat off the couch. "Something I stumbled on more or less by accident on the way in. Come on—and don't forget your hat and mittens."

We bundled up, and I led the way out into the frosty mountain air. In front of the cabin the snow-packed dirt road sloped gently upward, peaking at a cut in the mountains before sloping down toward the small mountain village a few miles away. I led us along the road for a few minutes; and suddenly Colleen, huffing along a step behind me, grabbed my arm. "Wait a minute, Dale, we can't go any farther. The edge of the shield—"

"Is right there," I pointed at a pair of branches sticking up out of the snow beside the road ten yards ahead. "Just don't pass the sticks there . . . and say hi to Calvin for me."

She stared at me. "What are you talking about? The shield's edge isn't sharp enough for me to do that."

"Agreed," I nodded. "*One* shield's edge isn't that sharp. But if you put two of them in line about a foot apart—we can mark the spots on your floor when we get back—and kind of lean forward, just a little, it turns out that you can stick your head far enough out for you to have limited communication without the baby knowing a thing about it. Go ahead—I tried it on the way in, and Calvin's waiting."

She didn't say anything; just threw her arms around me and hugged me close for a minute. Then, straightening, she walked tentatively toward my markers, head and shoulders hunched slightly forward.

And then, abruptly, she stopped . . . and I thought I'd never seen such a look of pure joy.

There was still a long road ahead of her, and much of it would be hard. But at least now she wouldn't have to travel it alone

For a moment I watched her. Then, shivering with the cold, I turned away. There was, I'd noticed, a pile of boards stacked in the rear of the cabin, as well as a complete tool kit, a spare sleeping pad, and an extra Coleman heater. With a little judicious hammering and some careful positioning, I ought to be able to put together quite a cozy little shelter for her up at the edge of the shield. I had the distinct feeling she'd be spending a lot of time out here over the next few months.

I walked back to the cabin, and got to work.

THE PEACEFUL MAN

Bombshells come in small packages these days. I stared down at the orders in my hand, not believing what I saw, as my head filled with the sound of crumbling plans. "What is this, Colonel? I can't go to Falkwade. I'm due to ship out for the Academy on Friday."

Colonel Lleshi shrugged uncomfortably. "I'm sorry, Lieutenant Hillery, but my own orders were explicit: 'One Enforcer Brigade plus attached alien psychologists to be sent to Falkwade immediately. I've pulled the Eighteenth Enforcers off R and R and scraped together enough men to bring them back up to combat strength, but you're all I've got in the way of psychologists. Besides, I know you've done some reading on the Falki natives. So you're at least familiar with the situation. Anyway, I've relayed your new orders back to Earth; if the Academy wants to get you reassigned back to them, they've got a week to get word back here."

"They won't try. I'm not vitally needed there, and

teaching positions are low on the priority list." I glowered at the orders. "What do they need me on Falkwade for, anyway? The contact team there is bound to have its own A1-psychs."

"I don't know," Lleshi said. "But except for the Enforcer security groups, the contact team is mainly civilian. Perhaps they need a psychologist with a military viewpoint."

"Oh, great. What's happened—the fighting broken into a full-scale brush war?" The very thought made my hands sweat.

"You're the scholar around here, Lieutenant," Lleshi said. I winced slightly. To him, I knew, the word "scholar" also implied passiveness, impractical theories, and lack of fighting spirit—the sort of things he considered most unmilitary. "A list of relevant computer files has been delivered to your quarters—everything we've got available on Falkwade and its natives can be dug out of there. Good thing you're already packed; I'm sure you'll be able to use the extra time. Dismissed."

And that was that—my whole life rotated ninety degrees for at least a year by the stroke of a stylus. Giving Lleshi my most deprecatory salute, I turned and left.

I didn't find out just how hard Lleshi had had to scramble to beef up the Eighteenth Enforcers until we assembled at the transport ship for preflight instructions and I got my first look at the roster. Fully a quarter of the eighty-four officers and men had been transplanted into the brigade to replace those lost in the fighting on Rhodes. That wasn't good; a combat unit, especially one that has been in actual warfare, builds up a hefty camaraderie, and newcomers invariably meet with suspicion or even hostility. With my trained psychologist's eye, I could pick out the new men just by looking at them; their uneasiness was very apparent. I hoped the two-week trip to Falkwade would be long enough for them to be integrated into the group.

Major Tait Eldjarn's preflight talk was nicely designed to ease the fears of men just recently returned from combat. He emphasized the primitive state of Falki culture and weaponry and the fact that the village where they would be stationed was safe from attack. He wound up with a flourish of optimistic platitudes and called for questions.

For a moment there was silence. Then one of the men in the first rank raised his hand. "Corporal Saiko, sir," he said in a heavily accented voice. "I have one, sir."

I'd noticed Saiko right away, of course. On an absolute scale he wasn't particularly small—a little shorter than average height, perhaps, with a slender build—but against the more massive physiques of the rest of the brigade, he seemed almost childlike. His smooth, Oriental face also stood out of the crowd, its lack of racial mix marking him as an Earthman. He was clearly a newcomer, and I could tell the others hadn't quite figured him out yet.

Eldjarn nodded. "Go ahead, Corporal."

"Sir, has anyone tried to negotiate with the Falkwade natives, to find out why they object to our presence?"

Eldjarn blinked in surprise at Saiko's question but recovered quickly. "Not all the Falkren are against us," he said. "The females, who control the villages, accept both the contact team and the mineral exploration groups as friends."

From what I'd read, the Falki females were closer to neutral on the subject, but I didn't say anything. Eldjarn went on. "It's only the neuters out in the hills and woodlands who are trying to kick up a guerrilla war."

"Yes, sir, but has anyone tried talking with *them*?" Saiko persisted. "There may be no need to fight."

In the silence that followed, someone snickered, and I could see both disgust and amusement flicker across the Enforcers' faces. Eldjarn kept his own expression neutral. "We're Enforcers; we fight. Talking is for the feeble and the diplomats. Any other questions, Corporal?"

"No, sir." Saiko's face didn't change, but I felt a stab of pain for him. Enforcers were not noted for sensitivity or compassion, and I knew Saiko would be the butt of some very low humor all the way to Falkwade.

"All right, then," Eldjarn said. "Eighteenth Enforcers: prepare to board."

I wasn't wrong. Before we were even off the ground, Saiko had been given his first Enforcer nickname: *Love-and-kisses*.

Enforcers, the elite policemen of the Starguard, like to keep in fighting trim, and our transport had been furnished with this in mind. One of the cargo holds was equipped as a gym/combat room; another boasted a si-muholographic shooting range where one could hone one's marksmanship without putting needle dents in any bulkheads. Other training and practice equipment was distributed around the passenger areas.

None of this was of any personal interest to me. So I stayed pretty much in my quarters, reading and working from the mountain of material I'd brought with me. It wasn't until the fourth day of the trip that I had my first visitor.

It was Saiko. "Excuse me, Lieutenant Hillery," he said, standing at the door. "I wonder if I might talk to you for a moment."

"Sure, Saiko, come on in," I waited until he was seated before continuing. "How are you doing?"

"Fine, sir. I wanted to ask you a few questions about the Falkren, if I may."

I covered my surprise; I'd expected him to want help on personal problems. "Sure. What do you want to know?"

"Well, sir, I've read the material we were provided, and it seems to have some inconsistencies in it. Are there three Falki sexes or just two?"

I nodded; I'd noted the inadequacy of the official handouts and was working hard to turn out a better set. "Good question, and it depends on how you look at it. While there are really just male and female Falkren, the males periodically undergo hormonal changes that leave them sexless. We call these *neuters*; and while they are, in a gross physiological sense, identical to the males, their emotional and social makeup is completely different.

Whether or not they should count as a third gender is still being debated."

"I see," Saiko said slowly, "I think. But the reports said the males lived in the villages with the females. They only dislike humans in their neuter state?"

"How the males feel about us is really irrelevant because they're completely under the control of the females, who are tolerating us at the moment."

"I'm not sure I understand."

"Okay." I hunched forward slightly in my chair, feeling my professorial side taking over. "Here's the Falki setup. The females all live in the villages that are scattered over the major land masses. With them live the males, who handle all the heavy work—building, hauling, some farming—while the females have babies, do lighter work, and give all the orders. The males are completely subservient—as long as they're male. The minute they change to neuter—and the change apparently only takes minutes—they can't be ordered around any more by the females. They immediately leave the village and join up with the neuters who live in the surrounding area. We don't know the social structure of that group yet, but it's clear that they have one, because things get done. The neuters do all the hunting, fishing, lumbering—anything that needs to be done outside the village proper, delivering the goods to males at a rendezvous point near the village border and getting grain and clothing in return. If the village needs to move, the neuters blaze the trail and act as a moving screen while the males and females travel. And, of course, they do any fighting that needs to be done."

"And when they go back to being male?"

"They return to the village."

Saiko stroked his lip thoughtfully. "Interesting. It makes sense to protect those who are breeding, both female and male, as much as possible. A most unusual expression of oneness, with this periodic changing of roles."

"You mean the way the females dominate the males

but not the neuters? I suppose that does make for a certain symmetry."

He fixed me suddenly with a curious gaze. "Why do you insist on seeing it in terms of domination and submission? Couldn't it simply be that the Falkren recognize their interdependence and take the roles which allow their survival and growth?"

I floundered for a good five seconds on that one. "I suppose I'm anthropomorphizing," I said at last. "Most human societies run along power/authority lines. So I guess we have an automatic tendency to assume aliens behave that way, too."

"I see." There was an odd note of disappointment in Saiko's tone.

"You disagree?" I probed.

"Well . . . I don't think that is the best way for even humans to look at the universe. It leads to unnecessary conflict."

He hesitated, unblinking eyes gauging my reaction. I knew that look and the thoughts behind it; my own rather nonmilitary personality had made me an oddball of sorts even among other Starguard scientists. The search for a kindred spirit could be a long and painful one. "Go ahead," I encouraged him.

"If I think in terms of dominance and submission, then I must consider myself as separate from the rest of the universe," Saiko said. "In other words, if I consider you to be outside of me, then I can try to dominate you. This sets up conflict between us.

"If instead I consider you to be actually another part of *me*, then I won't fight you, because we don't fight ourselves. I'll try to help you, try to let you have your way as much as possible. You see? The conflict is now gone."

"Yes," I said carefully. I'd heard of that philosophy before. Oriental in origin, it was largely in the clutches of various mystical cults these days, at least out in the Colonies. "It's an interesting concept, but I think it's a bit risky. Humanity has certainly had more wars than we've needed, but it may be better sometimes to err on that side than to be too pacifist and get trampled. You see, with your philosophy there's very little you can do in the way of self-defense."

Saiko shrugged. "I could point out that an overly aggressive policy also has its dangers. What if you run into a powerful force which you provoke to an unnecessary conflict, for example?"

"True," I admitted. "But at least you're ready for the war when it comes. If you're unable or unwilling to hit back, you won't survive." I could hardly believe I had wound up on this side of the argument. Saiko must be even less a swashbuckler than I was, I decided.

"There *are* ways to defend yourself without injuring your opponent," Saiko said, smiling faintly.

"Sure—force fields. If you ever invent one let me know. Incidentally, if you don't approve of combat, what are you doing in an Enforcer Brigade?"

"The Eighteenth needed another ordnance tech and I was available. On the other hand, where better to speak against conflict than where the conflict already exists?" His smile vanished and he grew serious. "Tell me, sir, *have* negotiations been tried with the Falkren?"

I waved at my computer terminal and the pile of hardcopy records beside it. "All the information I've got says we've tried talking with all three sexes. The males don't seem to count at all. The females are willing for the mineral exploration teams to poke around in exchange for the gifts we give them, but they have no authority outside the villages. The neuters have flatly refused to let us on their turf, and when armed teams go out anyway, they shoot crossbow bolts at them. Even using their best ambush and guerilla tactics, the casualties are running about twenty to one against them, but they still refuse to even discuss the issue. Although with the Falki social system as genetically based as it is, I'm not sure talk would help anyway."

"Perhaps it's a point of honor," Saiko murmured.

"Perhaps." Honor, I'd heard, was supposed to be important to the Oriental mind. I wondered if Saiko realized how dishonorable it looked to the other Enforcers for him to meekly accept the nickname they'd pinned on him.

Either Saiko was thinking along the same lines or something in my face tipped him off, and he gave me a half-smile. "Honor is an internal quality, Lieutenant. It doesn't rely on the perceptions of others." He stood up and saluted. "Thank you for your time, sir. I must leave now."

"I'm glad you stopped by, Saiko. Feel free to drop back any time."

"Yes, sir." Moving with quiet grace, he left the room.

Down deep, I sensed I'd just flunked a test—but, then again, he wasn't the kindred spirit *I* was seeking, either. Sighing, I got back to my work.

The incident in the Enforcers' mess happened two days later, and it was simple luck that put me there at the right time. I was looking for one of the noncoms and had dropped in on the chance he was having lunch. He wasn't there, but as I turned to leave a bellow from across the room made me spin around. "Hey, Love-and-kisses!" a gravelly voice shouted. "You, Saiko! Get back here!"

Saiko, who had been carrying his tray toward an empty table, turned as a behemoth of a man rose a few paces behind him. I recognized the man instantly: Sergeant Cabral, universally known as Moose. And for good reason. "Yes?" Saiko said.

"You made me spill my drink on my tray," Moose accused.

Saiko shook his head. "I didn't touch you when I passed. It might have been someone else."

"Never mind the excuses. Get over here and clean it up. And then go get me another drink."

Saiko shook his head. "It was not my fault," he said, and turned to go.

Moose was reputed to have a short fuse even at the best of times—and this wasn't one of them. Saiko's blunt refusal was barely out of his mouth when Moose leaped across the intervening distance and caught Saiko's upper arm in a painful-looking grip. "Damn it, I said clean it up!" He yanked, pulling Saiko toward him—

And with a stupendous crash, Moose hit the floor two meters away.

The snickering which had started at Saiko's expense vanished like beer at a picnic, leaving the whole room in stunned silence. Moose rolled to his feet and turned back to face Saiko, his face a dangerous shade of red. "Damn you," he said softly. "You're gonna regret that." And then he charged.

Saiko set down his tray, which had by some miracle survived the first clash, and waited. Moose launched a punch that should have sent Saiko across the room; instead, the smaller man leaned aside, caught the arm and spun around . . . and, somehow, Moose was again on the floor.

Saiko stood aside and waited . . . and Moose proceeded to prove his nickname didn't just refer to his size. He got up and tried again, this time throwing two fast savate kicks and a punch in rapid succession. Saiko evaded both kicks and again caught the punching fist. With a brief intertwining of arms, Moose again hit the deck. This time Saiko went down into a crouch next to him; and, though the tables blocked my view, I could hear Moose swearing and struggling to get up.

Just about then I suddenly broke out of my fascinated paralysis. "Ten-HUT!" I shouted.

There was a loud scramble of chairs as all the Enforcers shot to their feet. The two combatants were a second behind the others and I beckoned them forward. Moose, I noted, was panting somewhat and massaging his right wrist, but was otherwise unmarked. Saiko wasn't even breathing hard.

Technically, I wasn't in the brigade's chain of command. So, short of squealing on them to Major Eldjarn, there was little I could do in way of punishment. So I gave them both a stern warning about saving their strength for the Falkren, told Saiko to report to my quarters later, and let everyone go back to lunch.

Saiko showed up half an hour later. "You wanted to see me, sir?"

"At ease, Saiko, and have a seat."

He did so. "Sir, I must apologize for my part in the fight—"

"Forget it. He deserved what he got. But I wanted to ask you—what the blazes you were using on him?"

"It's called *Aikido*, sir. It's an ancient Japanese martial art which uses an opponent's strength and movements against him."

"Like jujitsu?" I knew that Enforcer training included a smattering of that.

"In some ways. Aikido is—" he hesitated— "*gentler*, I suppose. We don't attempt to block an attack with our own strength, but to evade the blow, allowing it to continue and then joining with the movement and redirecting it. An Aikidoka, you see, seeks to subdue his opponent without harming him. Most other martial arts, including jujitsu, strive to defeat the opponent with more forceful and potentially damaging methods."

A memory clicked. "Is Aikido what you meant when you talked about defense without injury?"

He nodded. "As you pointed out, sir, the philosophy of peace and oneness would quickly die out if its followers could not protect themselves. It is said that a master of Aikido is untouchable, no matter how many men attack him."

"Are *you* a master?"

Saiko dropped his gaze to the floor and smiled faintly. "I have studied the art for seventeen years. The founder of Aikido, Morihei Uyeshiba, spent over forty years in practice and always considered himself merely a student."

The legendary Oriental patience, I thought wryly— something modern man could use a lot more of. A little less hurried impatience might save us a lot of fighting on worlds like Falkwade. "I understand."

"Will that be all, sir?"

"Yes. You can go now."

I saw Saiko off and on during the rest of the trip,

though he never came to my quarters again to talk. He still seemed to have no real friends among the other Enforcers, but their general attitude was considerably more respectful toward him than it had been earlier. Enforcer nicknames, once given, tend to stick. So I noted with some amusement that "Love-and-kisses" Saiko was tacitly changed to the less obviously insulting "L.K." Saiko. It was a small step, but Saiko seemed satisifed.

We landed in groups of twelve, via shuttle, at the edge of the village where the contact team had set up shop two years ago. The landing pad was surrounded by an earthwork barrier manned by heavily armed Enforcers—for protection, I was told, against sniping from the forest that pressed against the village on two sides. Apparently the village itself was off-limits for attack, but the neuters considered the pad itself fair game.

Major Eldjarn and I were in the first shuttle down and were driven immediately to the contact team's prefab, looking out of place among the interwoven-branch huts of the village's four hundred-odd Falkren and the seventy humans who now resided here. Several of the natives—each one the size of Moose Cabral and reasonably human-looking—could be seen working at various tasks.

"I'm glad to have you here," Colonel David Sherwood, the contact team's commander, said when the military formalities were out of the way. "We've lost four men in the past two days alone, all but one from villagers down the coast. Fresh Enforcers should help morale a bit."

"I thought the villages were safe," Edljarn said, frowning.

"The villages are, yes. But we can't sit around all day doing nothing. We send out an average of three survey teams a day via aircar. Almost the minute they land anywhere there are neuters running at them with those long knives of theirs and shooting those damn crossbows. It doesn't matter how far we are from here, either—the word seems to have gotten out to the whole planet. Even clans that usually fight each other are willing to join

forces against us." Sherwood shook his head. "We use
scatterguns, exploders, and even heavy lasers on them,
kill them by the dozens—and they still keep coming.
Don't they understand that they can't beat us, that we
have the whip hand on this planet?"

Saiko's words about dominance and conflict flashed
briefly through my mind. "Perhaps they refuse to be
dominated by us."

Eldjarn snorted. "How do you 'refuse' to be dominated?"

"By fighting back," I told him. "The neuters must
know that you can't kill too many of them without losing
whatever good will you have among the females."

"Lieutenant Hillary is right," Sherwood admitted.
"Killing neuters is eventually equivalent to killing males,
and the females won't put up with too much of that. We
don't dare kill except in self-defense, and even that's
dangerous. The neuters have both time and numbers on
their side."

"Have you tried to find out why the neuters don't want
us around?" I asked.

"They shoot at anyone who tries to go out and talk
to them. About all we can do is talk to the males, try
to get them to take truce offers out there when they
change to neuter. So far it hasn't worked; we don't
know why. Dr. Ariyoshi, our alien psychologist, suggested the memory of what we said to them might not
survive the change. So we've been trying to catch one
of them right after the change, before he can leave the
village, and drum in some instructions. So far they've
gotten out too quickly for us. All of Ariyoshi's notes
will be available to you—I hope you can make something out of them. The doctor himself chose this time
to come down with some viral infection. He was flown
off-planet last week for treatment." Sherwood seemed
to consider it a personal insult that Ariyoshi had gotten
sick. "Corporal Snyder outside will take you to Ariyoshi's hut; you might as well bunk there for now. Study
the stuff he's done and work out some kind of plan to
stop the neuter harassment of us. This has been going

on for almost two years, and I'm getting tired of it. Results, Lieutenant—I want *results*."

"Yes, sir. I'll do what I can."

It took me nearly a week to go through the material Ariyoshi had collected—he hadn't organized it for someone else to use, and I had to do a lot of digging—and while it was interesting, I didn't get any brilliant ideas from it. For obvious reasons most of his studies covered only the males and females and their interrelationship. It was fascinating reading; humanity has few martriarchal cultures left, and none where the females so completely dominate the males. But little if any of it gave me any clues about even the basics of neuter psychology, let alone what sort of threats or inducements might stop their attacks. While Ariyoshi had been convinced that a thread of consciousness ran through the male/neuter change, he'd been unable to determine how much memory or personality was transferred along this thread.

I was mulling over the problem one evening as I sat outside Ariyoshi's hut sipping a native drink that was reminiscent of strong limeade. In front of me was a small open area on the edge of the village where some of the male Falkren liked to relax after their day's labors. Fifty or so were here this particular evening, and the still air was full of both their scent and their quiet conversation. Only one other human was visible. Saiko, sitting cross-legged on the far side of the open space, was talking earnestly to a large male.

I watched with only mild interest. Saiko, I'd heard, was spending much of his off-duty time trying to sell his philosophy to as many of the Falkren males as he could corner. To me it was obvious that he was trying to implant the teachings in the hope that they would survive through the change; to the rest of the Enforcers the whole idea of preaching peace to the peaceful was both amusing and demeaning, and once again Saiko was the butt of jokes and scorn. After what had looked like the first steps back toward peer acceptance on the transport, I was discouraged by this return to pariah status, especially since I saw little hope for his project. Most of the Falkren of this village understood English by now, though they were not properly equipped to speak it, but Ariyoshi's notes made it clear that they were totally uninterested in anything human except for the gifts we gave them.

I suppose that if I'd been paying more attention I would have seen the change coming; certainly Ariyoshi's notes had described the syndrome in sufficient detail. As it was, I was as startled as Saiko when the Falki he was talking to abruptly scooped up a small stool and hurled it straight at the seated Enforcer.

Saiko's reflexes were excellent, but even so the stool caught his left arm as he threw himself to the right. He was on his feet in another second, just in time to catch the—now—neuter Falki's lunge. Ducking under the first swinging arm, he caught the the other arm, twisted—and was hurled to the ground.

I gaped, and even as I jumped to my feet and yanked my scattergun from its holster, I understood what had happened. Saiko's Aikido tricks were designed for human anatomy. Falki muscles, joints, and bodily dimensions were subtly different—enough so, clearly, that Aikido was useless against the natives. And Saiko wasn't wearing his scattergun. Cursing under my breath, I ran forward through the crowd of Falkren who were trying to get out of the way of the fighting. But by the time I had a clear shot it was too late. Saiko was back on his feet and the neuter was grabbing for him—far too close for my mediocre markmanship. By all the rules this shouldn't be happening at all; I was almost sure they were still in the village proper, where the neuters weren't supposed to fight us. But there were no females here to claim authority, or maybe the neuter knew better than I how the zigzag boundary really ran. Whatever the reason, Saiko was in big trouble, and he would have to take one more fall before I could help him.

The neuter caught Saiko's left arm and pulled him close. Saiko reached up with his right hand, dipped slightly and pivoted—and suddenly the neuter was bending forward at the waist, Saiko holding his arm at the

wrist and elbow. The Falki roared and lashed backwards
with a foot; Saiko let go and danced back out of the way.
Spinning around, the neuter leaped again ... and this
time he was the one who hit the ground. He jumped up,
lunged, and was thrown, and I lowered my scattergun.
Apparently, Saiko had figured out how to handle the
Falki anatomy, and if he was performing with less than
his usual grace, the results were no less impressive. All
I had to do now was wait until the neuter had all the
fight knocked out of him and Colonel Sherwood would
have the freshly changed neuter he wanted.

It took another half-dozen throws before the Falki
finally gave up. He lay on his back, his sides working like
bellows, and stared up at Saiko. I stepped forward.
"Good work, Saiko," I said. Shifting my attention to the
neuter, I gestured with my scattergun. "Get up."

"What are you going to do with him, sir?" Saiko asked.

"The colonel wants to try giving a neuter some messages to take out to the others," I explained. "This is the
first one we've been able to catch."

Saiko shook his head. "I don't think he'll sit still for
it, sir. He'll fight if you try to hold him, and he'll either
kill someone or be killed himself. It would be better to
let him leave."

I looked at Saiko, then back down at the neuter. It
was the kind of concern I would have expected from
Saiko, but it also made a certain amount of sense. Already
the Falki was breathing easier, and I doubted that anyone
but Saiko could handle him without killing or maiming
him—a fine messenger he'd make then. One more neuter
out there wouldn't increase our danger noticeably ...
and maybe some of Saiko's message of peace had gotten
through. And, besides, there was one other possibility
that had just occurred to me that made it a fair gamble.
"All right," I said slowly. "He can go."

"Thank you, sir." To the alien: "Leave quickly, before
others come."

His eyes on Saiko, the neuter carefully rose to his feet.
For a moment he stared at the Enforcer ... and then

he was moving into the growing darkness toward the forest.

From the village behind us a group of Enforcers ran up, weapons at the ready. "What's going on here?" their sergeant demanded.

I took a deep breath. "Come on, Saiko, let's go talk to the colonel."

Colonel Sherwood was absolutely furious.

"Damn it, Lieutenant, I should have you court-martialed," he stormed at me. "Letting that Falki go was tantamount to disobeying a direct order. More importantly, it may ultimately cost some of my men their lives."

I kept my eyes fixed directly ahead of me as the verbal flash flood swept around me. I dared not look to see how Saiko, at my side, was taking this. Fortunately—I suppose—most of the flak was directed at me.

Finally, Sherwood ran out of invective. "You have any explanation to give for your irresponsible behavior?" he growled.

"Yes, sir," I said in as calm a voice as I could manage. "It occurred to me that the Falkren neuters may not acknowledge our superiority because we use unfair weapons against them."

"That doesn't make any sense."

"Excuse me, sir, but it does. Our weapons are not *us*; they're merely our tools. Since the Falki society is genetically based, the neuter pecking order is most likely determined by toolless attributes: strength or fighting ability, probably. If the neuters consider an unarmed Falki superior to an unarmed human, they may refuse to submit to us even though *with* our weapons we can cut them to ribbons. This sort of thing has been seen before; in the natives of Bellias, for instance. . . ."

I trailed off as Sherwood stalked to a bookshelf and returned with a labeled cassette. He held it up inches from my face. "Report for the week June 8 through 14," he identified it unnecessarily. "On Thursday of that week an Enforcer karate expert named Sergeant Zawadowski caught and fought with a neuter just outside the village.

In full sight of at least half a dozen neuter snipers he disarmed the Falki and beat him silly. The neuter had to undergo medical treatment in the village for almost a month before he could leave again. He currently seems to be in charge of the northern flank of snipers—our sentries spot him occasionally among the trees. The plastic arm cast we gave him is very distinctive." He tossed the cassette on his desk and glared at me. "Didn't Ariyoshi's notes refer to the incident?"

My mouth felt very dry, and my whole career flashed before my eyes. "I . . . must have missed that," I managed.

"Really. Well, to make sure you have enough time to do your work properly, you're confined to quarters until further notice." The colonel shifted his glare to Saiko. "And for your part in this you're relieved of duty for one day."

"Yes, sir," Saiko said evenly.

"That's all; dismissed."

Ariyoshi's notes did indeed mention that incident, I discovered two hours later; the report covered half a page in a file I'd only skimmed. I felt like a fool—and not least because I'd let Saiko's philosophy of peace influence my decision. Restraint was fine in its place, but my career was on the line here, and I couldn't afford to be trigger-shy any more. I would get Sherwood the newly changed neuter he wanted, one way or another. If Saiko agreed to help, fine; if not, the neuter was going to get hurt. It was that simple.

The alarm klaxons went off just after dawn the next morning, jarring me out of deep sleep. Rolling out of bed, I pulled on my pants and boots and snatched up my tunic and gunbelt. The alarm had meanwhile changed tone and was giving out a steady *dot-dash-dash:* Morse for *W.* Ducking out the hut door, I took a quick glance around me and then headed west.

About half the off-duty personnel were already at the village perimeter when I arrived. Ahead of us was an astounding sight: a hundred meters away, standing just this side of the forest, was a line of armed neuters, cross-bows lowered but ready. Picking their way across the small grain field between us and the forest were three figures: two neuters and a human.

Saiko.

Colonel Sherwood must have been only seconds ahead of me, because one of the Enforcer sentries was still giving his explanation as I approached them.

"—just stood there as the other two came forward. That one—Saiko—has been coming out here before dawn the last few days—meditating, or something—and one of the neuters beckoned to him. He seemed to recognize the Falki, because suddenly he said 'he must have understood what I was telling him!' and handed me his scattergun. Before I realized what he was doing, he'd walked out there to meet them. Garcia hit the alarm about then. We couldn't shoot without hitting Saiko, and—well, the others haven't attacked us."

Sherwood nodded and filled his lungs. "Saiko!" he roared. "Get back here!"

Saiko stopped and turned, his escort doing likewise. "I'm sorry, Colonel, but this is too important. I think they must be willing to speak of peace with me."

"What? Why you?" Sherwood called, but Saiko had already turned his back and resumed walking.

I stepped to the colonel's side. "He believes all life in the universe is interrelated and should try to be at peace with itself," I explained. "He's apparently been talking to the village males about it; one of those walking with him looks like the male that changed yesterday. Maybe you should let him go to them."

"Like hell I'm not going to sit here and let one of my men be kidnapped—even a mystical idiot." Sherwood glanced around him. "Garcia, Daniels—go out there and bring him back."

Two Enforcers started forward—and the crossbows abruptly came up.

I wasn't the first to see it, but I was the first to say something. "Hold it!" I snapped. "Back off. Carefully."

The two men took a step backwards, and once again

the neuters lowered their weapons. Sherwood turned to me, glowering. Strangely enough, he wasn't angry at my countermanding of his orders. "So that's how it is, eh? They want Saiko, and only him—and are ready to start something that'll get them slaughtered if we try anything else."

"You can't open fire, Colonel," Major Eldjarn, standing on Sherwood's other side, said. "I count a hundred twenty-nine neuters out there—that's nearly the village's entire complement. The females would go crazy if we killed all of them."

"I know that!" Sherwood snapped. "Hamedon! Call the pad and have them send up a spotter car. I want Saiko tracked if they take him into the forest."

"Corporal Saiko can take care of himself," Eldjarn murmured. I silently seconded him; nevertheless, my heart was pounding by the time Saiko reached the forest.

I had already noticed that the line of neuters resembled a flattened normal curve; that is, the Falkren on the two ends were the smallest, with the sizes increasing toward the center, where the largest Falki I had ever seen was standing. It was to this neuter that Saiko was led. The neuter stepped forward as the two escorting Falkren moved off to either side, returning to what were evidently their places in the line. Saiko bowed to the large neuter, and through the dead silence that had descended I could just hear his words: "I greet you, honorable sir—"

The neuter handed his crossbow to the Falki next to him and charged.

Saiko had already seen one Falki surprise attack, and he was a lot nimbler when not sitting down. He fell to his right, rolling on a curved but rigid arm back to his feet, easily evading the attack.

"Please stop," he said, his voice controlled but showing signs of agitation. "There is no reason for fighting."

The Falki charged again; again Saiko dodged, still trying to talk peace to his opponent. I expected the Falki to try another charge, but he apparently was out of patience. He bellowed something in his own language, and the next three largest neuters handed off their weapons and stepped forward.

All around me was the soft sound of cloth on flesh as scatterguns were raised. I wasn't aware I'd drawn my own weapon until Colonel Sherwood's hand grasped my arm, forcing the muzzle down. "Hold your fire," he ordered, frigidly calm. "We still can't shoot them."

The four neuters formed a box around Saiko, who had given up talking and now waited silently in an agile-looking stance. At some unseen signal, his attackers moved forward.

Saiko moved, too, stepping away from the center of the square so that the Falkren would not all reach him at the same time. The closest neuter swung at his head; Saiko grabbed the arm, pivoted in a circle, and dropped the Falki on his back. Two others reached him simultaneously; Saiko pushed one into the other and took advantage of their momentary entanglement to send the fourth attacker flying. By then the first Falki was back in the fray. . . .

Sherwood was muttering something incredulous under his breath. Even I, who'd seen Saiko in action twice before, was impressed—I hadn't expected Aikido to be useful against more than one opponent at a time. The fight went on and on . . . and, suddenly, the largest Falki bellowed something.

The other attackers froze. Slowly, they straightened or got to their feet and returned to their places in line. The big one stood facing Saiko in silence for a moment; then he, too, returned to the line. As if on signal, the neuters all turned and disappeared back into the forest.

Saiko watched them go. Then he started back toward the village, a puzzled and worried expression on his face.

Colonel Sherwood turned to me. "All right, Lieutenant, what was *that* all about?"

A growing suspicion was gnawing at me. "I'm not sure, sir," I said. "But I've got an idea. I suggest you send a patrol into the forest in—oh, say an hour or so, with instructions *not* to shoot unless in extreme danger. If they aren't attacked, I think we may have the solution to the neuter trouble for you."

Sherwood gave me a long, measuring look. "Daniels! I want six men ready for patrol duty in one hour."

The patrol was not attacked.

The twelve-passenger shuttle was a speck in the blue Falkwade sky. "One more and then it's our turn," Major Eldjarn remarked, shading his eyes as he watched for one of the other two shuttles to appear. "I still can't believe it. A week ago the neuters were trying to kill anyone who stepped outside the village, and now they're so cooperative Colonel Sherwood doesn't even need us any more. Here comes the shuttle." He lowered his gaze to me. "Are you going to loosen up and tell my why they changed?"

"Didn't the colonel explain it?" I asked, somewhat mechanically; my thoughts were elsewhere.

"No. He said he doesn't like repeating someone else's theories until he's willing to believe them himself. And Saiko's been even less talkative than usual lately; he won't talk about it at all."

"That's because he understands what's happened." And is blaming himself for it, I added silently.

"Great. So how about letting me in on the joke?"

I sighed. "It's anything but a joke, sir. You remember that I suggested the neuters might be refusing to acknowledge our superiority over them? I was right. Shooting them simply brought out their own combat instincts; they saw us as just another kind of threat to be resisted, the same way neuters have fought threats to their villages for millennia.

"And then Saiko came along. He fought one of the neuters, who went and told the others, and Saiko was invited to what amounted to a showdown with the chief neuter."

"And Saiko won," Eldjarn nodded. "But we've been winning fights against the neuters for two years. Was it because Saiko was so much smaller than they were?"

"Not at all. But Saiko was using Aikido, a nondestructive

form of combat. He didn't tear them up with scattergun fire or break bones with karate kicks. He defeated them *without hurting them*."

"So?"

"Don't you see? Dominance *without injury* is precisely the relationship of the females to the males in a Falki village. As males they have to submit to that; apparently they have to do so as neuters, too, if someone is able to take the proper role."

Eldjarn was looking bewildered. "You mean they think we're females?"

"No, of course not. But the *pattern* is the same, and patterns are very important in genetically governed behavior. In this case the pattern is even stronger because it's reinforced every time the neuter changes back to male—he doesn't outgrow or discard it at any point in life. Saiko's triggered whatever instinct or state of mind goes with the pattern, and I don't think the neuters have any real choice in their response. As long as no one shoots at them again, they should remain submissive to us."

That last, at least, Eldjarn understood completely. "Well, that's great. Soon as we can get some more of those martial-arts guys in to show their stuff at some of the other villages, we should have all the territory we need to work with." He chuckled. "It's fitting, you know, that it should be old Love-and-kisses Saiko who wound up finally bringing peace to the planet."

"Yes," I said shortly and turned away. It was no use trying to explain Saiko's feelings to Eldjarn; his dominance-oriented military mind would find Saiko even more incomprehensible than the Falkren. He wouldn't understand that Saiko's goal was peace with dignity and honor for all sides, not the peace of complete capitulation. He wouldn't understand the shame Saiko felt at having used his "gentle" martial art—however unknowingly—to provide a beachhead for human domination over a planetful of intelligent beings. And he would never understand what disgrace and loss of face could mean to Saiko's sense of honor.

And yet, despite all this, Saiko's philosophy of peace remained unshaken. I had talked to him often this past week, and through all his pain I had never seen even a glimpse of cynicism or despair or disbelief in the path he had chosen. A philosophy that strong, it seemed to me, was worth careful study—and my interest was not purely on a professional level. Tomorrow morning, at 0600 sharp, Saiko is going to give me my first training in Aikido.

I am looking forward to it.

THE EVIDENCE OF
THINGS NOT SEEN

Omens.

There are men in space today who'll tell you, in all apparent sincerity, that every major star ship disaster is preceded by an omen of one kind or another. I suppose most of those who say that don't really believe it, but I *have* seen crewers walk off a ship half an hour before launch because they thought a rash of snafus in the countdown checks meant the ship would disappear into a cascade point somewhere in the near future. Superstitious nonsense, of course, and I can prove it—because the day the *Aura Dancer* lifted for the last time was just as smooth and trouble-free as polished teflene.

I mean that; and for a struggling tramp starmer like the *Dancer* that's a minor miracle all in itself. Wilkinson and Sarojis had the cargo stowed away twenty minutes ahead of schedule, Matope ran a complete check of the *Dancer*'s systems without finding a single malfunction that Baroja's overly stuffy tower controllers could frown at; and

Matope's success meant Tobbar was available to welcome our handful of passengers aboard, a task which traditionally falls to a ship's captain but which I've almost always successfully avoided. About the only thing that could remotely have been considered a problem was that Alana Keal, my second-in-command, nearly missed the boat.

She buzzed in about fifteen minutes before our scheduled lift, and I *do* mean buzzed. All the worry and guilt on her face couldn't mask the fact that she'd just been through some very serious celebrating with some old friends and was running a good two points above cruise velocity. "Sorry I'm late, Pall," she apologized with the slight breathlessness of having come from the hatchway to the bridge at a dead run. "Did you have to drop us in the lift pattern?"

"No, I was going to give you another five minutes before I called the tower," I told her as she slid into her chair.

"They'd have had your head," she said, keying for a systems check. "You're supposed to give them twenty minutes' notice of a delay."

"Life is tough all over," I shrugged, watching her fingers skate over the keys. For a moment I considered telling her all the pre-lift checks had been done, but changed my mind. Alana was the serious type who insisted on pulling her own share of the load, and there was no point making her feel any worse about her tardiness. Not that she was really feeling bad now, but it would eventually catch up with her. "So . . . how did the *Angelwing* take the news that they had a new captain?"

She laughed, a sparkling splash of sound we heard all too seldom aboard ship. "The funny thing is that they really *do* have one. Old Captain Azizi's finally retired, and Lenn Grandy's been promoted."

"Ah." The name was vaguely familiar; one of Alana's fellow junior officers during the year she'd been on the *Angelwing*. "I presume you compared notes on which of you got the captaincy first?"

"Oh, we tried, but we ran into the usual simultaneity problems. He probably made it first, though."

"Well, I bet you look better in the captain's uniform than he does."

She glanced a smile up at me. "Why, thank you, Pall. Maybe sometime this trip you can stay with me during a cascade point and see for yourself."

Right then I decided she was unfit to be poking around the *Dancer's* bridge controls. Going through a cascade point alone is about as much fun as an untreated double hangover; doing it with someone else is even worse. "We'll see about that," I told her. "But for now *you* are going to your cabin until whatever Grandy and his fellow clock-watchers were plying you with wears off."

"They're not clock-watchers—Cunard's just very touchy about keeping their liners on schedule," she protested. But she obediently got to her feet and headed for the door. "Just remember, I've got first cascade point duty in four hours."

"We'll see if you're up to it," I called after her, a line that permitted me to be basically honest while still avoiding an argument. Physically, she'd certainly be up to doing the point by then. But emotionally—

Emotionally, she would still be carrying the warm glow of the celebration and the triumph of a "captaincy" which, though purely imaginary, was in another sense very real.

And I had no intention of letting cascade point duty ruin that for her quite so quickly.

Four hours later I was alone on the bridge, and ready for the first cascade point.

The *Dancer* was quiet. All her sensors and control surfaces had been shut down, all electronics including the computer put into neutral/standby mode. The crewers and passengers were shut down, too, the sleepers Katé Epstein had administered guaranteeing they would all doze blissfully unaware through the point. They were ready, the *Dancer* was ready; and postponing the inevitable gained nothing for anyone.

Lifting the safety cover, I twisted the field generator

knob . . . and watched as the cascade pattern began to fill up the room.

Someone early in the Colloton Drive's history, I'd once heard, had described the experience as being like that of watching some exotic and rapid-growing crystal, and there'd been times I could see it myself on almost that high of an intellectual level. The first four images that appeared an arm's length away were quickly joined by the next set, perfectly aligned with them, and then by the third and fourth and so on, until I was at the center of an ever-expanding horizontal cross of images.

Images, of course, of me.

Land-bound philosophers and scientists still had lively arguments as to what the effect "really" was and what the images "really" represented, but most of us who saw them regularly had long since come to our own conclusions, minus the fine details. The Colloton Drive puts us into a different kind of space . . . and somehow it links us through to other realities. The images stretching four ways toward infinity were hints of what I would be doing in each of those universes.

In other words, what my life would be like if each of my major decisions had gone the other way.

I spent a moment looking down the line, focusing on each of the semi-transparent images in turn. Four figures away, conspicuous among the jumpsuits and coveralls on either side of it, was an image of myself in the gold and white of a star liner captain.

I didn't regret the decision I'd made a year earlier that had lost me that universe, but the image still sometimes raised a reflexive lump into my throat. I had the *Dancer*—*my* ship, not some bureaucracy's—and I was satisfied with my position . . . but there was still something siren-song impressive about the idea of being a liner captain.

And if anyone aboard ship had had any doubts about that, the living proof would be taking over for me as soon as this cascade point was past.

Reaching to the small section of control board that still showed lights, I activated the *Dancer*'s flywheel. The

hum was clearly audible in the silence, and I shifted my
gaze to the mirror that showed the long gyroscope needle
set into the ceiling above my head. Slowly, as the flywheel built up speed, the needle began to move. The
computer printout by my elbow told me the *Dancer*
needed a rotation of three point two degrees to make
the four point four light-years we needed for this jump.
It was annoying to have to endure a cascade point for
such relatively small gain—the distance traveled when we
left Colloton space went up rapidly with the size of the
yaw angle the ship had rotated through—but there was
nothing I could do about it. The configuration of masses,
galactic magnetic field, and a dozen other factors meant
that the first leg of the Baroja/Earth run was always this
short. And it *was* accounted for in our—as usual—tight
schedule. So I just leaned back in my chair, did what I
could to ease the induced tension that would turn into a
black depression when we returned to normal space, and
thought about Alana. Alana, and her phantom captaincy.

It had been on the last cascade point coming in to
Baroja that she'd first seen the gold-and-white uniform
in her own cascade image pattern, tucked in there among
the handful of first- and second-officer dress whites that
represented the range of possibilities had she stayed with
the *Angelwing*. She'd caught the significance immediately, and the resulting ego-boost had very nearly gotten
her through the point's aftermath without any depression
at all. She'd left the liner four years back for reasons
she'd apparently never regretted, which put the new
image into the realm of pleasant surprise rather than
that of missed opportunity. A confirmation of her skills;
because had she stayed aboard the liner, *she*, not Lenn
Grandy, would be captain today.

Or so the theory went. None of us who believed it had
ever come up with a way to prove it.

The gyro needle was creeping toward the three-degree
mark now. Another minute and I'd shut the flywheel
down, letting momentum carry the *Dancer* the rest of the
way. A conjugate inversion bilinear conformal mapping
something something, the mathematicians called the

whole thing: a one-to-one mapping between rotational motion in Colloton space and linear translation in normal space. Theorists loved the whole notion—elegant, they called it. Of course, they never had to suffer the drive's side effects.

But then, neither did most anyone else these days. The Aker-Ming Autotorque had replaced the old-fashioned manual approach to cascade maneuvers aboard every ship that could afford the gadgets. The *Angelwing* could do so; the *Dancer* and I could not. I wondered, with the first hint of cascade point depression, whether Alana would spend her own next point regretting her decision to join up with me.

Three point one degrees. I flipped the gyro off and, for no particular reason, turned my attention back to my cascade pattern.

The ship was still rotating, and so the images were still doing their slow dance, a strange kaleidoscopic thing that moved the different images around within each branch of the cross. A shiver went up my back as I watched: that complex interweaving had saved my life once, but the memory served mainly to remind me of how close I'd come to death on that trip. Automatically, my eyes sought out the pattern's blank spots, those half-dozen gaps where no image existed. In those six possible realities I *had* died ... and I would never know what the decision had been that had doomed me.

Or whether I might yet make the same fatal choice in this, the real universe. Shivering again, I turned my eyes resolutely away.

The gyro needle had almost stopped. I watched it closely, feeling afresh the sensation of death quietly waiting by my shoulder. If I brought the *Dancer* out of Colloton space before its rotation had completely stopped, our atoms would wind up spread out over a million kilometers of space.

But the spin lock holding the field switch in place worked with its usual perfection, releasing the switch to my control only when the ship was as close to stationary as made no difference. I flipped the field off and watched my cascade images disappear in reverse order; and then I drew a shuddering breath as my eyes filled with tears and cascade point depression hit like a white-capped breaker, dragging me under. I reactivated the *Dancer*'s systems and, slumping in my seat, settled down to ride out the siege.

By dinnertime two hours later the ship and crew were long back to normal, and the passengers were showing signs of life, as well.

Or at least some of them were. I reached the dining room to find a remarkably small crowd: three of our eight passengers plus Alana, Tobbar, and Matope. They were grouped around one of the two tables, with two seats to spare. "Good evening, all," I said, coming forward.

"Ah—Captain," Alana said, a look of surprise flicking across her face before she could catch it. "I was just explaining that you probably wouldn't be able to make it down here for dinner."

A fair enough assumption, if not entirely true: I usually managed to find a plausible reason to avoid these get-togethers. But a chance comment Tobbar had made when reporting the passengers were all aboard had made me curious, and I'd decided to drop by and see the phenomenon for myself. "I probably won't be able to stay very long," I said aloud to Alana and the table at large. "But I'd hoped at least to be able to personally welcome our passengers aboard." I cocked an eyebrow at Tobbar.

He took the cue. "Captain Pall Durriken, may I present three of our passengers: Mr. Hays Trent, Mr. Kiln Eiser, and Mr. Rollin Orlandis."

Trent and Eiser were youngish men, with what seemed to be very athletic bodies under their business suits and smiles that somehow didn't reach their eyes. I said hello and turned my attention to Orlandis . . . and found that Tobbar had been right.

Orlandis didn't belong on a ship like the *Dancer*.

That much I got in my first quick glance; but as my brain switched to logic mode to try and back up that intuitive impression, I realized it wasn't nearly as obvious a conclusion as I'd thought. His suit, which had seemed too expensively cut for a tramp starmer passenger, turned out to be merely a small jump above the outfits Trent and Eiser were wearing, not much more than twice what I could afford myself. His ring and watch looked new but ordinary enough; his vaguely amused look no worse than others I'd seen directed the *Dancer's* way. But *something* about the man still felt wrong.

I apparently hesitated too long, and the conversational ball was plucked neatly from my hands. "Good evening, Captain Durriken," Orlandis said, giving me an easy, not-quite-condescending smile. His voice was quiet and measured, with the feel of someone used to being listened to. "First Officer Keal has been explaining the ins and outs of the *Aura Dancer* to us, and I must say it sounds like a fascinating craft. Would you be able to spare her a bit later in the journey for a guided tour? Say, tomorrow or the next day?"

The question was put so reasonably it seemed impossible not to simply say *yes*. But my speech center had long-standing orders on this topic. "Actually, Mr. Orlandis, Mr. Leeds and Dr. Epstein usually handle passenger tours. If you'd like—"

"I'd prefer Ms. Keal."

For a moment my tongue tangled around itself with confusion. Orlandis hadn't raised his voice, hadn't so much as cocked an eyebrow, but suddenly I felt like a child . . . or an underling.

And if there was anything guaranteed to pull my control rods it was someone pushing me around who didn't have the right to do so. I was ungluing my tongue to say something approximating that when Alana jumped in. "If you don't mind, Captain," she said, "I have no objections to showing Mr. Orlandis around during my off-duty hours."

I looked away from Orlandis's steady gaze to find Alana staring just as intently at me, a hint of pleading in her expression. *Don't anger the passengers.* With a supreme effort of will I gave in. "Very well," I said, turning back to Mr. Orlandis. "You and Ms. Keal may make your own arrangements on this. Please bear in mind that her work schedule may need to change on short notice; ships like the *Aura Dancer* are almost by definition always short of hands to do the necessary work."

He nodded once, a simple acknowledgment without any detectable trace of triumph to it. He was *used* to being obeyed; pure and simple. "It will be, what, another five days until the next cascade maneuver?"

"About that," I told him, wishing obscurely that I could rattle off the precise time to him, in days, hours, *and* minutes. "You'll have plenty of warning; don't worry."

"I wasn't. Will the food be much longer?"

I glanced at Tobbar, who had presumably been there when they all submitted their orders. "Another minute or two; no more," he told Orlandis. "Our autochef is getting a bit old and sometimes takes its time filling orders."

"These things happen," Orlandis said equably. "Captain, I don't believe you've ordered yet."

An invitation to an entire evening of cat-eat-mouse sparring? Perhaps; but if it was, I was going to take the coward's way out. "I'm sorry; but as I said, I won't be able to stay," I told him, getting to my feet. "There's some work on the bridge I need to attend to. Please enjoy your dinner, and I expect I'll be talking with you all again soon."

"Perhaps under more relaxed conditions," Orlandis said. "Good evening, Captain."

I turned, and as I did so the autochef beeped its announcement that dinner was finally ready. Assured that they all had something more interesting than me to occupy their attention, I made my escape.

I went to the bridge, kicked Pascal out—it was his shift, but he had some maintenance work on the computer he wanted to do anyway—and pulled a copy of the cargo manifest. Just for something to do, actually . . . but when Alana stopped in an hour later I was still studying it. "Dinner over already?" I asked her as she slid into her chair and swiveled it to face me.

"More or less," she said, eying me closely. "Orlandis and Tobbar are going hard at a discussion on governmental theory. I get the impression Orlandis knows a lot about the subject."

"Good—maybe we'll finally find out if *Tobbar* does, then."

She smiled. Tobbar could talk at length on practically any subject, and most of us on the *Dancer* had long since given up trying to figure out which ones he was simply wool-pulling us on. "He'll probably lose whether he does or not," she said. "I also get the impression Orlandis is in the habit of winning his arguments."

I grunted. "You noticed that, did you?"

"Come on, Pall—it's no big deal if I play tour guide for a couple of hours. I've done it before, you know."

"It's the principle of the thing," I told her stiffly. "Passengers don't give a ship's captain orders."

Her eyebrows rose at that. "He never *ordered* you to let me show him around. You could have said no anywhere along the line."

"After you cut the landing skids out from under me?" I retorted. "Come on, now—I couldn't very well fight *both* of you."

"And you shouldn't fight with *passengers* at all," she shot back. "I was trying to give you a dignified way out; if you're hot about that, take it out on me, not him. But bear in mind I was doing you a *big* favor in there."

"How do you figure *that?*"

She flashed an impish smile. "He *could* have asked *you* to show him around."

I held onto my frown for another second before giving up and grudging her a twisted smile in return. "I can't win *any*thing today, can I?" I muttered, only half joking. "Oh, all right, I owe you one. If Orlandis was bound and determined to cause me trouble he missed his biggest chance."

"I don't think that was what he was up to," she demurred thoughtfully. "I think he's just used to the very best of everything."

"Then the change here should do him good," I snorted.

She gave me a *now, now* sort of look and waved at the manifest in front of me. "Trouble with the cargo?"

"Not really." I shook my head, glad to have a change of topic. "Just trying to figure out why we've suddenly attracted new customers."

"What do you mean?"

"Well, I didn't notice it before, but nearly a quarter of our cargo space is being taken up by four large crates coming from two companies we've never done business with."

She got out of her seat and peered over my shoulder. "Huh. Are we the only ship heading between Baroja and Earth at the moment? If they need to get the cargo there right away that might explain it."

And also explain why someone like Orlandis would stoop to our level? "Maybe, but that seems unlikely. Didn't you say the *Angelwing* was even going to Earth this trip?"

"Yes, but by way of Lorraine. They won't arrive until a month after we do."

I sighed. "Well, I suppose it's not impossible. Seems pretty odd, though."

"Maybe I can poke around the question with Orlandis tomorrow," Alana suggested. "He's a businessman; he ought to know about shipping schedules and all."

"What business is he in?"

Her forehead furrowed. "Now that you mention it, I don't think he ever actually said," she told me slowly. "Though I got the impression it was something important."

"He ought to be on a commercial liner if he's that rich," I grumbled.

"Unless," she said quietly, "he's afraid of people."

I looked up at her, feeling my stomach tighten reflexively. Alana had made practically a second career for herself years back as a mender of bruised spirits and broken wings; had overdosed on the loss and pain that nearly always seemed to come with the job; and was only

in the last year or so taking her first tentative steps out
from behind the self-erected barriers. If Orlandis was
aboard because he was psychologically unable to mingle
with the masses of people on a standard liner, then she
probably had enough of a challenge to last her the rest of the
trip. "Well, if he is he's picked a lousy place to hide," I
growled. "Not much real privacy on this albatross."

She touched my shoulder gently. "Don't worry about
me," she said. "Orlandis doesn't scare me."

"Um," I said brilliantly, and for a moment we were
both silent. Then she took a tired-sounding breath and
stepped toward the door.

"I'd better head downstairs and get some sleep," she
said. "You ought to do the same, you know—and it *is*
Pascal's shift."

"In a minute," I told her. "Goodnight."

" 'Night."

She left, and with a sigh I called back to the computer
room and told Pascal to finish whatever he was doing
and get back to the bridge. It wasn't any business of
mine if Alana wanted to play emotional counselor on her
own time. It wasn't my business *whatever* she did with
her own time. She was all grown up and fully in charge
of her life.

Pascal arrived, and I headed down to my cabin. Eventually, I went to sleep.

I spent the next five days walking around on mental
tiptoe, waiting for trouble of one type or another to spark
between Alana and Orlandis. But all I got for my trouble
was the mental equivalent of strained arches. I saw them
only once myself as they passed through the engine
room, and to all appearances their relationship was running on a strictly proper crewer/passenger level. Certainly
Alana was well on top of things; I had ample opportunity
to chat with her between our bridge shifts and at occasional meals in the duty mess, and she showed no strain
that I could detect.

I also got to meet the rest of the passengers as they
found their space legs and dribbled one by one out of

their cabins. No big deal, as usual; they ran the *Dancer*'s usual range of semi-scruffy to reasonably respectable, their occupations mainly in the academic or lower-middle business sectors. I suppose my major reaction to the whole bunch was relief that there weren't any more like Orlandis among them.

Meanwhile, with the ship largely running itself, I spent a couple of duty periods trying to make some sense out of the mysterious first-time clients represented so heavily in our cargo holds. But our computer records had limited information on business and financial arcana, and my attempts to trace through parent firms, holding companies, managing directorates, and so forth all ended quickly with zero results. Eventually, I concluded that word of mouth must have been kinder to the *Dancer* than I realized. Either that, or we really *were* the only ship that had been heading straight to Earth.

And then the *Dancer* came up on its second scheduled cascade maneuver out from Baroja . . . a maneuver I will never forget as long as I live.

It was Alana's turn to handle the point; and I wasn't yet entirely out of the mind-numbing sleeper state when I pried my eyes open to find her sitting on the edge of my bed, one hand shaking my arm as tears rolled down her cheeks. "Wha's wron'?" I slurred, trying to at least sit up but finding my body in worse shape than even my brain was. "Lana—wha's *wron'*?"

Her face was filled with horror and pain and hopelessness as she fixed blurry eyes on me—a cascade depression times a thousand. "Oh, Pall," she managed to get out between sobs. "It's gone—the *Angelwing* is gone. And—and *I died with it.*"

And with that the storm broke again . . . and she buried her face in my shoulder, sobbing like she would never stop.

I held her close to me for nearly an hour, until her mind and body were simply too exhausted to cry any more. And only then did I finally find out exactly what had happened . . . and if it wasn't quite as nerve-chilling as her seeing her own death, it was plenty bad enough.

"I'd started the *Dancer*'s rotation," she said, her voice trembling with emotional fatigue and the echoes of her horror. "I was watching the cascade images, thinking about Aker-Ming Autotorques and wondering whether I'd trust one even if we had it . . . and I was looking at the image of me as the *Angelwing*'s captain when it—when it just disappeared. There's nothing there now but another gap."

In my mind's eye I watched it happen . . . and nearly started crying myself. I'd known people who'd been forced to watch helplessly as a loved one died; had seen the way a trauma like that could make a person a bag of broken glass. And to see it, in effect, happen to *yourself* . . .

I tried to find words of comfort to say, but without success. So I just continued to hold her, and after a minute she spoke again. "They *are* dead, aren't they? All the people aboard the *Angelwing*?"

"I don't know," I said honestly. "Maybe not. Maybe it just means you would have made some mistake if you'd been in command. I mean—maybe your friend Lenn did something else and the ship's okay."

"I've been trying to think of some way a captain could get killed without the rest of the ship dying, too," she said, still talking into my shoulder. "But the *Angelwing*'s a *liner*— Cunard liner, yet. It's got failsafes on the failsafes, the best medical facilities you can get—"

She trailed off. Unfortunately, she was right. I was plenty familiar with liner facilities myself, and there were damn few accidents that could conceivably happen that the medics aboard couldn't handle. "Could you tell what your image was doing?" I asked her. "I mean . . . did it look in pain or sick or anything?"

"I don't think so. It was just . . . there . . . like all the others." She took a deep breath and finally pulled away from me. Her face looked terrible, all red eyes and pain. "I guess I'd better get back upstairs. I haven't computed position or—"

"Never mind all that," I told her. "I can do it after we get you in bed and have Kate give you a sedative."

"No, I'm okay." She attempted a smile that didn't even come close and got to her feet. "Really. Thanks for the listening ear."

I stood up, too. "I'll help you to your cabin."

She tried to argue, but her heart clearly wasn't up to even that much effort. Five minutes later Kate Epstein was tucking a blanket under her chin and making the soothing sort of sounds doctors traditionally make while waiting for their potions to take effect. I hung around in the background until Alana's eyes began to glaze over, and then headed to the bridge. By the time I'd finished the position check and cleaned up the various odds and ends of the maneuver the rest of the crewers were starting to call in to find out what the hell had happened to Alana. I told the story twice, then just gave up and pulled everyone in on the crew intercom hookup for one final rendition. They were as shocked as I'd been, and equally at a loss as to anything we could do to help her. I got two offers to relieve me on the bridge, turned down both of them, and sent them all back to whatever they'd been doing.

We all sort of limped along at half speed for a couple of days after that. Alana spent the first one alone in her cabin before venturing out to return to duty, claiming she was recovered enough to function as first officer again. I pretended to believe her and juggled her back into the shift schedule . . . and as I kept a close eye on her, I decided she really *was* up to it. In retrospect, I suppose, I shouldn't have been all that surprised; anyone who mended other people's traumas for a hobby would have to come equipped with a high degree of emotional toughness.

I wasn't nearly so tough, though; and if I'd thought I was, I found out otherwise when I came off the bridge on the third day to find Orlandis waiting for me on the command deck.

"Good afternoon, Captain," he said smoothly. "I wonder if I might speak to you for a moment."

"Mr. Orlandis," I nodded, staying civil with a supreme effort. "This area is off-limits to passengers."

"Yes, I know. As I said, though, I wanted to have a quiet word with you."

I glanced down the hall. Near the spiral stair leading down to the passenger deck I could see either Eiser or Trent—I couldn't tell which of the two passengers it was—reading the little cartoons Pascal liked to put up by the computer room door. It never failed, I thought with a flash of disgust: let one passenger wander where he wasn't supposed to, and pretty soon you'd find the rest following. Two-legged sheep, the whole lot of them. "We can talk down in the lounge," I told Orlandis shortly.

"Or perhaps as we walk," he said, starting leisurely toward the stairway.

I took two long strides and settled into step beside him, already wondering if there was some legal or at least practical way to block off that stair. "If there's a problem with service or accomodations—"

"Then Leeds is the man to see. No, Captain, this is something quite different. I was wondering about the rumors circulating about something happening to Ms. Keal during the last cascade maneuver."

My murderous thoughts toward the passengers switched to murderous thoughts toward the crew. The one single order I'd issued on this was that the passengers were *not* to get even a whiff of what had happened. "I'm not sure what you're referring to," I said carefully. "Ms. Keal had a slightly more traumatic reaction than usual to the cascade point, but she's certainly up and about now."

Facing forward with my eyes locked on Eiser ahead, I could still tell Orlandis was smiling. "Come now, Captain, we don't have to play these games. I assure you anything you tell me will go no further."

A great confidence-builder, if I'd ever heard one. Still, even walking slowly, we were getting within earshot of Eiser, and if one person with a rumor was bad, two would be even worse. "Suppose you tell me what exactly you've heard," I suggested, for lack of a better idea.

"I heard she saw something terrible in her cascade images," Orlandis said. "Something that indicated a ship—possibly even the *Aura Dancer*—was going to be destroyed."

I groaned inwardly, making a note to personally strangle whoever had let this mangled version slip. "The *Aura Dancer* is in no danger whatsoever," I told Orlandis. "Another liner *may* have suffered damage—"

"Or been destroyed?"

"*Or* even been destroyed," I snarled. "But that's all strictly conjecture. Do you know anything about cascade images?"

"Some of the theory, but I've never seen them myself."

"Well, then you at least know that the images represent *possibilities*, not realities. What Ms. Keal saw may or may not have anything to do with the real universe."

"But regardless, the *Aura Dancer* itself is not in danger?"

"None at all."

Orlandis nodded. "I see. Thank you for putting my mind at ease."

The idea of his mind being any more at ease than it always seemed to be anyway was faintly ludicrous, but I wasn't in the mood to appreciate the irony. We'd reached Eiser now and I told him briefly that he didn't belong up here. His immediate and highly embarrassed apology nearly made up for Orlandis's lack of same, and I felt a little better as I watched the two of them go down the stairway. Following, I made sure the "Off Limits to Passengers" sign was indeed still prominently posted, and then headed back upstairs to the bridge.

Alana still didn't have all of her fire back, but she was as firm and adamant as she could be without it. "No, I certainly did *not* tell Orlandis anything," she said when I'd described my little confrontation with the man. "I was told you'd given orders not to spread it about."

"I did," I growled, already making a mental list of the next likely suspects. Orlandis didn't have the same access to most of them that he had to Alana, but obviously that hadn't mattered to someone. Sarojis, possibly—he talked as much as any other two aboard. Leeds and Kate Epstein? They were reasonably discreet, but they worked most directly with the passengers and Orlandis could be pretty overwhelming—

"Just forget it, Pall," Alana sighed.

"Forget what?"

"Raining fire on anyone's head. So the passengers know—big deal. As long as there's no panic, I can handle any extra stares and whispers. Whoever spilled probably feels bad enough as it is."

I took a deep breath, let it out slowly. She was right, of course. As usual. "Oh, all right." I tried another breath and was more or less back to normal. "You going to do a check of my calculations for the next point?"

"Already started." She licked her lips and looked up at me. "I'd like to do this one, Pall, if you don't mind."

"Just to prove you can handle it?" I shook my head. "Thanks, but it's my turn."

"But I still owe you one—"

"Then we'll settle things later in the trip," I told her firmly. "You're not up to it yet."

"If I'm not up to it *now*, when will I be?"

"All right, then; *I'm* not up to letting you do it. Okay?"

She glared at me for a minute, but then the brief spark faded. "Okay," she sighed. "If you're going to make it an order."

"I am," I nodded, knowing at that point that I had indeed made the correct decision. If she wasn't strong enough to argue with me, she almost certainly wasn't strong enough to handle a cascade maneuver. "Just make sure I got all the numbers entered properly. Talk to you later."

I left, trying not to feel like an overprotective mother. I *would* handle the next cascade maneuver, whether it bothered her pride or not.

And as it turned out, it was probably a good thing I did.

*   *   *

Below me the flywheel was humming its familiar drone, and in four directions the cascade images had begun their intricate saraband. Among them, like departed dance partners whose places no one had dared to take, the six dark gaps wove in and out as well. Always, their presence was noticeable; today, it was almost overwhelming. Gaps ... flaws ... voids—mortality underlined. I wondered how I would feel to see one of my own images wink out like Alana had ... wondered if I'd be able to handle the shock as well as she had.

I doubted it. I'd had my share of nightmares about losing the *Dancer*; had come close to actually doing so on at least one occasion. To know that, even in another reality, I was capable of killing myself, my crew, and my passengers through some foolish decision wasn't something I was prepared to face.

And right about then all the relays in my brain went click together, and I stared at the gaps in the pattern as suddenly everything that had made sense five days ago ceased to do so.

I finished the maneuver on sheer brain stem reflex, and five minutes afterward was in Alana's cabin. It took me another fifteen to shake her adequately awake, by which time most of my depression had passed.

"Pall?" she asked, concern beginning to show through the fog.

"Relax," I told her. "I think I may have good news for you. Maybe. Tell me, was it *only* your captain's image that vanished? None of the ones around it?"

"Uh-huh. Why?"

She would have gotten it in a minute, but I was too impatient to wait for her to wake up all the way. "Because the two or three on either side of the captain's image were of you as a subordinate officer on the *Angelwing*. You see? If the ship had died *those* should have disappeared, too."

Her eyes widened as it finally penetrated. "Then ... the *Angelwing*'s still all right?"

"It *has* to be. Look, consecutive cascade images are usually pretty similar, right? So whatever happened to the captain should *also* have happened to the first officer next to it in the pattern. Only it didn't, because the captain's gone but the first officer's still there. With you not in command, apparently, the ship comes out okay—and you're *not* in command. QED."

She closed her eyes and seemed to slump into her mattress. "It's all right," she murmured.

I squeezed her hand and got to my feet. "Just thought you'd like to know. Got to get back to the bridge now, check our position. See you later."

I didn't wait for the rumor mill this time, but went ahead and broadcast the news on the crew intercom as soon as the sleepers wore off. I can't say that there was any great jubilation, but the easing of the general tension level was almost immediately evident. They stopped tip-toeing in Alana's presence and got a little of their usual vigor back, and within a day I'd even heard an off-handed reference to the shortest captaincy on record. I came down a bit on that one—it was still a traumatic experience from Alana's perspective, after all—but in general I was satisfied with the results of my surprise insight. Little things like that were what made a captain feel he was doing his job.

I got to bask in that self-generated glow for two days more . . . and then the whole thing started to unravel.

It was Pascal, predictably, who was first to tug on the thread. I was relieving him on the bridge, and he had given me the normal no-changes report, when suddenly his eyes took on an all-too-familiar faraway look. "Captain, I've been thinking about the *Angelwing*," he announced.

"Yes?" I said with quiet resignation.

"Yes, sir. I've been trying to think of an accident that could possibly occur that could kill the captain and no one else."

I suppressed the un-captainly urge to tell him to shut up. Pascal was famous for coming up with the most thoroughly bug-brained theories imaginable . . . and I *really* didn't want to hear anything more about the *Angelwing*.

But if I could let Alana cry on my shoulder, I figured I could at least hear Pascal out. "We don't *know* no one else would have been killed," I reminded him, choosing my tenses carefully. It *had not happened*, after all. "Just that if Alana hadn't been in command *she* wouldn't have been killed."

He waved the distinction aside. "Regardless, sir, the point remains that liners are almost as obsessive about safety as they are about staying on schedule. In the three hundred or so years of commercial star travel there've been only six hundred single deaths aboard commercial carriers; and ninety-five percent of those have been due to personal health failings—coronaries, apoplexy; that sort of thing. Almost all of those were passengers, of course."

I nodded: liner companies keep their employees' health under embarrassingly tight scrutiny. "What about the other thirty-odd deaths?"

"Direct violence. Murder, in one degree or another."

I thought about the politics you get in any large company, and the fact we were still talking abstract might-have-beens didn't affect the shiver that went down my back. "Are you suggesting she would have been *murdered* if she'd been made captain?"

Pascal shrugged. "Possibly, but I don't think it was that. Statistically, it's much more likely that she would have died from one of the two multiple-death causes. Quite a few thousand have gone that way. Now—"

"Where'd you get all these figures, anyway?" I interrupted. "You're not wasting library space with this stuff, are you?"

He looked surprised. "It's all from the *Worlds' Standard Deluxe* you bought for us last year."

I ground my teeth. I'd picked up the encyclopedia originally as a tool for settling shipboard arguments. Obviously, I hadn't been thinking about Pascal at the time. "All right, then, let's have the rest of it. What are these two multiple-death causes?"

"One is the complete destruction or disappearance of the ship," Pascal said. "Usually disappearance, presumably from failure of the Colloton field generator during cascade maneuver. Seldom proved, of course."

"Right." Whether a ship disappeared completely down some unknown galactic rabbit hole or spread itself over a few million kilometers of its path weren't results you could readily distinguish. "And number two?"

"Large-scale accident. Engine room plasma explosion, flywheel breakup—things like that."

I gnawed at the inside of my cheek. "Neither of those ought to affect the captain," I pointed out, with more enthusiasm than I felt. The logical corner this conversation was directing us toward had a lot of unpleasant thoughts lurking in it. "What sort of accident could affect a liner's bridge?"

Pascal sighed. "I don't know, yet. That's the part I'm still working on."

"Well, work on it down below," I grunted. "And let's not spring this one on anyone else for a while."

He shrugged. "Yes, sir. If you insist."

I forced my brain and fingers to go through my standard check-out routine after he left, confirming that the *Dancer* and her systems were functioning properly. But when that task was over there was little left to do but sit back, watch the displays and status boards, and think.

Mostly, I thought about Pascal's theory.

The figures themselves could be checked out easily enough, but I had no reason to doubt them. Pascal's research was usually good; it was in the conclusions that he usually clarnked up. So assuming his numbers, I was left with three possible cases.

Case One: a freak accident or sickness. I didn't really believe in the first and definitely didn't believe in the second. I watched my crewers' health as closely as the commercial lines did, and it was virtually impossible for a life-threatening condition to slip through a full examination without making at least a hint of its presence known. Alana was in far too good a shape simply to drop over dead. Regardless, my duty in response to Case One: no action. The *Angelwing* was proceeding on its way with its first officer in command, and we'd eventually learn the details.

Case Two: Colloton field failure. Maybe *only* if Alana had been captain, though that was also a hard scenario to set up. Case Two response: again, no action. If the *Angelwing*'s field had gone, it was far too late to do anything now.

And Case Three: a major accident that had killed the captain and possibly crippled the ship. My response . . . ?

My response should be to turn tail, make hell-bent back for Baroja, and raise the alarm. With an early enough jump, the ship might be saved.

I ran through the logic five times, and got stuck at that same spot each time. Returning to Baroja would throw the *Dancer*'s own schedule completely out the lock, and the resulting flurry of penalty-clause claims could bring us flaming out of orbit for good. For the guarantee I'd save some lives it would probably be worth the risk. But without any such certainty . . . and here I found Case Four staring me in the face: an unexplained cascade point event and Pascal's fertile imagination teaming up to create a giant wad of nothing.

The more I thought about it, the more Case Four seemed the likeliest. To get information like Pascal was assuming out of the cascade images you had to assume that they were able to couple to the real universe *and* that they were able to respond to changes in the universe instantaneously *and* that Alana's captaincy was the only significant difference between us and that particular might-have-been. None of those assumptions sounded likely, let alone orthodox. If I bankrupted the *Dancer* and made a fool of myself for nothing, never forgiving myself would be the kindest of possible responses.

But if Case Three *was*, in fact, correct . . .

It took me an hour to conclude finally that there was no logical way out of the deadlock, and another half-hour to decide that, as matters stood, the evidence was too frothy to justify risking our financial integrity. At that point, it took a mere five minutes to decide it would be best if no one else even heard about the theory.

A good, rational decision, and one I probably could have lived with. Unfortunately, as it turned out, I made it nearly an hour too late.

I'd put the *Angelwing* out of my mind—with some difficulty, I'll admit—and was looking over the plots for our three upcoming cascade points when Alana came charging onto the bridge. "Pascal tells me the *Angelwing* may be crippled," she said without preamble. "What are we going to do?"

"Wring Pascal's neck, for starters," I growled. "I ordered him not to tell anyone."

"He didn't—well, not really," she said, coming to stand next to my chair. "I picked up on an under-the-breath comment he made and forced it out of him."

"Like forcing a star to give off light. He's worse than Sarojis when he locks onto something."

"I told him it would be all right, Pall—please don't make a legal action out of it. So now what are we going to do about the *Angelwing*?"

"What do you suggest?" I asked.

She seemed taken aback. "That we head to the nearest port and get a patrol rescue squad out there, of course."

"And what do we tell them when they ask how we know the ship's in trouble?"

"We tell them—" She broke off, suddenly recognizing the problem. "Well, we tell them the truth, I guess."

"You think they'll listen?"

Her uncertainties began to edge into anger. "Pall, what's the matter with you? There may be people out there who'll *die* if they don't get help right away."

"*Or* who may *not* die; or who may not be out there at all. And before you get mad, just listen to me a minute."

I gave her a condensed version of the mental gymnastics I'd gone through earlier. Somehow, the arguments didn't sound nearly as persuasive when listed aloud. Not to me, and certainly not to her. "And what if you're wrong?" she asked quietly when I'd finished. "You could be, you know. Maybe this is a perfectly normal aspect of the Colloton Drive that's just never been noticed before."

"And what if it was really just wishful thinking?"

That was *not* what I had meant to say, or at least not the way I'd meant to say it. But all the good intentions in the universe couldn't soften the shock that appeared on Alana's face like a handprint after a slap. "Pall ... you think I *want* the *Angelwing* to die?"

"No, of course not," I told her, wishing I could bite off my tongue. "I just meant that maybe as a—oh, I don't know; a justification, I suppose—that maybe to justify giving up your position there your subconscious might have ... done some editing."

Her smile had an edge of permafrost to it. "*You're* the one who's always had problems with cascade images, not me. If the mind could edit them out at will, don't you think yours would have done so long ago?" She didn't wait for an answer, but headed back to the door. "If proof is what you're looking for, then that's damn well what you're going to get," she said over her shoulder.

"Alana—" I called. But too late; she was already out the door. For a long minute I stared at the displays, swearing whole-heartedly under my breath. Suddenly, with a few badly arranged words, I'd changed the whole character of this issue. No longer was it simply a theoretical question of whether there was a ship in danger out there; now it'd become a test of Alana's psychological health and my trust in her.

And that meant the option of simply dropping the whole thing was no longer available. I'd seen Alana in this kind of mood before, and she wouldn't rest until she'd dug up some proof, real or otherwise, to show both of us that she wasn't imagining things. As a strongly empathic and emotionally-oriented person, she apparently needed to prove occasionally that her brain worked as well as anyone else's.

Which very likely meant that whatever she came up with, I was going to have to pretend to believe her.

I swore again and punched up a list of our current cargo contracts, keying for the penalty clause sections. It was as bad as I'd expected it to be—if we hit Earth that late the *Dancer* would be years paying off the penalties. Assuming our creditors let us fly again at all.

I was about a third through when I hit the first anomaly, and by that time my mood had deteriorated so far that I did what I would normally have found impossible to do: I called Wilkinson up on the crew intercom and actually yelled at him.

Good old solid unflappable Wilkinson, he just sat there quietly and absorbed it for the two minutes it took me to run down, never so much as raising his voice in protest. I wished afterwards that he had; I might have felt less like a fool if he'd cut me off sooner. "There's nothing missing from that contract, Cap'n," he said calmly when I finally gave him a chance to respond. "That's exactly how it came aboard."

"That's ridiculous," I snorted. "No penalty clause, no secondary routing or credit arrangements—this thing looks like it was thrown together over someone's lunch hour."

"Yeah, I noticed that," Wilkinson nodded. "All the crates from our two first-timer clients are the same way."

"You're kidding." I hadn't reached the others yet, but now I called up their listings, to find that Wilkinson had actually understated the case a bit. Not only were all the contracts deficient, they were deficient in exactly the same areas. "Are you *sure* you were really dealing with people from these companies?" I asked. "Harmax Industries practically invented Baroja's electronics business— you can't tell me they don't know how to write a shipping contract."

"The papers had the proper letterheads and ID grain. And the fund transfers were done properly."

"But you didn't run a full confirmation check?"

"Didn't think it was necessary, with the shipping fee already in our account. Besides, with the deals cut as late as they were I probably wouldn't have been able to get a check through the hierarchy and back in time."

I remembered now Wilkinson's telling me our cargo space had finally been filled, barely two days before our scheduled lift. What I *hadn't* realized— "All *four* of those big crates were contracted the same day?"

"Plus one small one that's in the Ming-metal shield. That one's Harmax, too."

With, I quickly discovered, the same amateur contract . . . and by now my anger and frustration had given way to another emotion entirely. A cold, unpleasant one . . . "You, uh—you have any idea what's inside any of them?" I asked carefully.

"Industrial equipment, the manifest says."

Which told us exactly nothing. As it was probably meant to.

And suddenly I began to feel nervous. Nervous enough to try something both unethical and highly illegal. "Wilkinson," I said slowly, "do you think you could get those crates opened enough for us to take a look inside? And then seal them again undetectably?"

"Well . . . I could open them, sure. But closing them up, probably not."

"It doesn't matter that much. Meet me in the number three hold right away, with whatever tools you'll need."

"Yes, sir," he said. Breaking the connection, I gave the status boards one last check and headed out the door, trying not to show the anxiety I felt. Pascal hadn't been able to come up with any reasonable accident on the bridge that could result in the captain's death, and in my own hours of thinking about it I hadn't found any possibilities, either. But there *was* one scenario that could easily explain it.

Sabotage.

We opened the first of the huge crates as carefully as if it were loaded with loose eggs . . . and to my great relief found nothing resembling a bomb inside. What we *did* find was far more unlikely.

"What the *hell*?" I growled as we peered down through the plastic slatting Wilkinson had opened. "What's Harmax doing shipping space yachts around?"

"It's just the nose, Cap'n," Wilkinson pointed out, playing his light around the back of the vaguely conical shape. "Maybe 'bout—oh, 'bout a third of a ship."

"A third?" There were *four* crates, plus the one inside

the shield ... and my stomach was starting to churn again. "Let's take a look inside the others."

He turned out to be correct. Two of the other crates contained the mid and aft sections of the yacht, with what looked to me like a complete quick-connect system at the edges. The fourth crate contained an impressive set of tools, including welding equipment and several SkyHook gravetic hoists.

It also contained a small, flat flywheel.

The implications of the latter were clear, but neither Wilkinson nor I really believed it. We had to open the box in the Ming-metal shield to confirm that it did, indeed, contain two Aker-Ming Autotorques before either of us would admit out loud that we had a miniature star ship aboard the *Dancer*.

"It's crazy," Wilkinson grunted as we set about resealing the crates. "No one builds ships that size for interstellar travel. Costs too much to put a Colloton Drive aboard, for starters."

"Could it be a new design lifeboat?" I suggested. "You could probably squeeze ten or twelve people aboard the thing if you really worked at it. Lord knows the passenger lines have been begging for a Colloton-equipped lifeboat long enough."

"And they'll continue to beg for one," he said. "Matope could tell you why you get the size constraints you do, but I know this much." He rapped the plastic we were working on with his hammer for emphasis. "This little boat here probably cost as much as a top-of-the-line passenger ship."

I glared down at the plastic, trying to make sense of it. "Could it be a new, cheaper design Harmax is sending to Earth as a demonstrator model? For contract bids?"

"Why send a whole boat?" Wilkinson countered. "The specs or computer trials would be adequate. Besides— sent it with *us*?"

I sighed and gave up. "Okay, so there *isn't* a logical explanation. We'll write Harmax a letter when we get to Earth and ask them about it."

Wilkinson cleared his throat. "Speaking of unexplained

phenomena . . . I understand we may be diverting back to Baroja soon."

I clenched my jaw momentarily. "I get one guess as to where *that* idea came from?"

"She talked to me for a couple of minutes about the *Angelwing* maybe being in trouble, just before you called with your questions about these shipments," Wilkinson said, looking as close to embarrassed as I'd ever seen him. "And since *you* were asking about penalty clauses, I assumed you'd decided she was right."

"What do *you* think?" I asked him.

He shrugged. "I never was good at that kind of decision, Cap'n. Maybe you should ask one of the others if you want advice. They've probably heard about it by now."

Sometimes I wondered why I ever bothered with the crew intercom. "Thanks, but a vote won't be necessary. If you'll finish up here, I need to get back to the bridge."

I started the computer calculating the run back to Baroja and then used the main intercom to set up a meeting with the passengers in half an hour. I expected Alana would check in with me before then, and I was right.

"We're going back?" she asked quietly, again coming over to stand beside my chair instead of sitting down.

"Yeah," I told her, keeping my voice as matter-of-fact as possible. "It looks like we might possibly be carrying some stolen property aboard, and I think it's worth looking into." I explained about the sectioned yacht and the oddly deficient papers on it. "Whether it's some rich man's toy or a breakthrough prototype, it doesn't belong on a tramp starmer," I concluded.

"Unless there's some perfectly reasonable possibility we've overlooked," she said. "Though . . . I suppose it still gives you a good enough excuse to go back."

Her unspoken sentence hung heavy in the air for a moment, and eventually I gave in and answered it. "It's not that I doubt your belief in what you saw," I told her. "It's just that . . . I don't want to look like a fool, Alana. And I especially don't want to lose my ship while looking like a fool."

"I understand. Dignity is very important to you." She touched my shoulder gently. "Thanks for . . . indulging me on this. What can I do to help?"

I glanced at my watch. "You can start by remembering everything you can about the *Angelwing*—her routines, her facilities, her crew, and especially everything you know about Lenn Grandy. We're going to have to present the patrol rescue squad with a plausible accident scenario if we want to get them moving."

"I haven't been thinking about much else lately," she said dryly. "When do you want to listen?"

"In about fifteen minutes," I said, unstrapping and getting to my feet. "I've got to go to the lounge and give the passengers the exciting news. I'm sure they'll be just thrilled."

Stunned would have been a closer prediction. Stunned, followed by worried and angry in about equal proportions. For no particular reason I skipped the whole thing about the yacht in our hold, giving them instead the ship-in-danger reason for our course change. Fortunately, I suppose, no one seemed to know enough about interstellar communication to ask embarrassing questions about how we knew the *Angelwing* was in trouble, though I *was* kept busy answering more mundane questions of scheduling, delays, fuel and provision reserves, and so forth. The whole thing took nearly twice the fifteen minutes I'd promised Alana, and it was with a wet-noodle kind of relief that I finally bid them good day and escaped from the lounge.

Or almost escaped. I'd made it barely ten meters down the hallway when Orlandis caught up. "A word with you, Captain?" he said, falling into step beside me.

I kept walking. "If it's brief. There's a lot of work to be done in rerouting the ship."

"I understand. Tell me, do you really believe this *Angelwing* is in trouble?"

"I wouldn't be disrupting all of our lives like this if I didn't," I told him shortly. It was a pretty stupid question.

"Um. Captain . . . I need to get to Earth as soon as possible. It's why I chose the *Aura Dancer*, in fact; you were the most direct carrier. It seems to me that we're very near the midpoint of our trip right now—is that correct?"

"More or less. In time, at least, which I presume is what you care about."

"Yes. All right, then, why can't we simply continue on to Earth and alert the patrol there?"

"That should be obvious." *Even to you*, I added silently. "The *Angelwing* will be within a very few light-years of Baroja. Getting the message from Earth back to Baroja would add a minimum of three more weeks to the two it'll take us to get things going anyway."

We took a couple more steps in silence, and then Orlandis cleared his throat. "I understand liners are legally required to keep a three months' emergency-ration supply of food on hand. Three extra weeks shouldn't be fatal to them . . . and I *could* make it worth your while to continue on to Earth."

I snorted. "I doubt that very much, Mr. Orlandis."

"No? The *Aura Dancer* is currently running several sizeable debts—"

He overshot a step as I abruptly stopped and turned smoothly to face him. "How the hell do you have access to the *Dancer*'s finances?" I snarled. "That's legally privileged information—"

"Except to the companies handling those finances," he put in calmly.

The rest of my speech evaporated. "And what one do you work for?"

"I don't *work* for any of them," he said with a faint tinge of disdain. "But I have extensive financial interests in various companies and institutions, including four to whom you owe money. Shall I quote you names and account numbers?"

"Uh . . . yeah, why not."

He proceeded to do so, and I felt the universe tilt gently around me. Even getting such information *il*legally required a lot of money, and it slowly dawned on me that I was facing a man who could probably buy Cunard Lines a new *Angelwing* if he wanted to without unduly straining his resources. "And you're offering to cancel my debts if we get you to Earth right away?" I asked him carefully.

He smiled. "When you're talking potential millions, a few thousands to get you out of debt aren't really significant. Yes, I'm offering that ... and perhaps some extra compensation besides."

Out of debt. The words echoed through my brain. To be finally out of our slowly deepening hole ...

Which would be of no comfort at all to the *Angelwing*'s dead. Or to Alana.

I took a deep breath. "I can't morally justify those extra three weeks of delay," I told Orlandis. "But maybe we can compromise. Have you ever heard of Shlomo Pass?"

He frowned slightly. "I don't think so."

"Well, it's sort of an in-joke among star ship pilots. It's just a section of space between Earth and Cetiki that happens to be very 'smooth'—that is, easy to calculate cascade maneuvers from. A lot of ships use it, and not only for that particular run.

"Now, it'll take us three cascade maneuvers to get back to Baroja anyway, and we can probably make the first of those to Shlomo Pass. Getting in position for the next one would take a couple of days; and *if* during that time we get within communication distance of a ship bound for Baroja, I can have *them* report on the *Angelwing* while we turn around and make for Earth. You'd lose— oh, a maximum of five days, probably closer to three. Would that be enough to salvage whatever deal you need to get back for?"

Orlandis pursed his lips and then nodded. "Yes, I believe it would. And if you *don't* find such a ship—?"

"We continue to Baroja."

His eyes searched my face, and I had the sudden, uncomfortable feeling of being a side of beef up for appraisal. But if he'd been planning to raise his offer, he apparently changed his mind. "Very well. I certainly understand your position. Let's both hope you find a cooperative ship. Good day."

He nodded and stepped past me, heading back toward the passenger areas. I continued on toward the bridge, resisting the urge to turn and watch him go. Whether he realized it or not, in five minutes of conversation the man had just about doubled the confusion level surrounding this whole affair. The confusion and, with his bribe offer, the pressure I was feeling. Grumbling under my breath, I tried not to stomp and wished I'd followed my original coward's inclination to let Alana or Tobbar give the passengers the news.

And yet . . .

I've been told more than once that I work best under pressure. Work *and* think. And it was as I was climbing the circular stair to the command deck that the first pieces finally started falling tentatively together. . . .

Alana was still waiting when I reached the bridge. "I was wondering if you'd gotten lost," she greeted me, searching my face unobtrusively as if for fresh traumatic scars. "Someone make a fuss?"

"It was actually more of an offer." I gave her a sketch of Orlandis's proposal and my counter to it, watching the emotions shift across her eyes as I did so.

"And what are you going to do when Shlomo Pass turns out to be empty?" she asked when I'd finished.

"Pessimist."

"Realist. I know Shlomo as well as you do—it isn't exactly the grand switching station you make it sound like."

"In that case we go back to Baroja ourselves," I growled. "How many times today am I going to have to say that?"

"Sorry." She shook her head. "Sorry for everything, Pall—this whole mess is my fault."

"Let's worry about assigning blame after the fallout's decayed about a half-life, okay? For now let's concentrate on the *Angelwing*."

"Yeah." She took a deep breath. "Where do you want me to begin?"

The intercom beeped before I could answer: Kate

Epstein, down in the passenger section. "Captain, do you know were Alana is?"

"I'm right here, Kate," Alana spoke up. "It's Mr. Orlandis, right?"

"Yes. He says you'd promised him a chess rematch this afternoon."

"I know; I'd completely forgotten. Listen, would you make apologies for me, and—"

"No, go ahead," I interrupted her. "This talk isn't all *that* urgent—we're a solid day away from even the first cascade point back."

"But—"

"No buts about it," I said firmly. Another piece of the puzzle had clicked into place—maybe—and suddenly it was highly desirable to have Alana and Orlandis off in a quiet corner. Away from the rest of us. "Look, tell you what I'll do: I'll stay here with you through the first part of your shift and we can talk about the *Angelwing* then. Fair enough?"

She hesitated a second, as if seeing there was something hidden behind my words. But then she nodded. "All right. That's ... uh ... about two hours. If I can beat Orlandis fast enough I'll be here sooner."

"Fine. Have fun."

I watched her leave, and gave her enough time to meet Orlandis and get into their game. Then I got on the crew intercom. It took a few minutes, but eventually I had the seven other crewers tied into the circuit with me. "I suppose you've heard rumors by now about a course change back to Baroja," I told them. "I want to open the floor to discussion ... but before I do, one *very* important question." I took a deep breath. "After Alana saw her cascade image captain disappear, I asked you all to keep what had happened away from the passengers. If one of you let it slip anyway, I need to know that. I have no interest in placing blame or in punishment, but that information is *vital* to what we do next. Understand? All right, then: anyone?"

My crewers have their fair share of problems, but I'll give them this much: every last one of them is unflinch-

ingly honest. And one by one, they thought it through
and declared themselves innocent of even discussing it
within passenger earshot.

I turned them to the Baroja issue then, and for awhile
the pros and cons, facts and figures flew back and forth
freely. But I didn't really hear most of it. My mind was
on another subject entirely . . . one that was slowly beginning to twist my guts.

Orlandis had accosted me three days after the event
with clear knowledge of Alana's cascade point vision. But
he *hadn't* found out about it from anyone aboard. Was
he telepathic? Hardly. A good guesser and judge of body
language? That could have given him only a reading on
the crewers' tension level, not any of the details.

Then had he somehow known the *Angelwing* was
headed for disaster?

Sabotage. The word repeated itself over and over in
my head. A man who could *buy* a ship if he needed to
get to Earth in a hurry, and yet he'd chosen instead to
travel on the *Dancer.* Whose first officer just *happened*
to have once been an officer on the *Angelwing.*

Had he known what would happen to Alana's cascade
pattern? Known, or guessed, or intuited? And if he had,
what did confirmation of the *Angelwing's* disaster gain
him?

I couldn't imagine. But I knew it was necessary for
him to go to Earth to make it worth his while. He'd as
much as admitted that when he risked exposing himself
as wealthy enough to make his bribe offer believable.

Wealthy enough to afford the pocket star ship down
in our hold?

Perhaps . . . and that thought sent a fresh shiver down
my back. If that *was* Orlandis's, then he didn't actually
need the *Dancer* to get where he needed to go.

Abruptly, I realized conversation had ceased. "Any
other comments?" I asked. "All right, then. Again, this
issue is *not* to be discussed with the passengers. You
get any questions or complaints, you buck them to me.
Understood?"

They assured me they did, and we broke the multiple

connection. I went back to thinking; and when Alana arrived ninety minutes later I was still at it. "You beat him?" I asked as she settled into her seat.

"Uh-huh. Shall we get started?"

"Whenever you're ready."

"Okay. Let's start with Lenn Grandy. He's a lot like me in many ways—an old-fashioned type who doesn't really trust wizard gadgetry like the Aker-Ming Auto-torque . . ."

She talked nonstop for over an hour, and I listened in silence the entire time. More than once I considered telling her my suspicions about Orlandis, but each time I fought down the urge. Alana was smart and capable . . . but she was also a mender of bruised souls, a woman who empathized with and cared for people. What would her reaction be to finding out she'd been associating with a possible murderer?

I couldn't risk it. For once, I was on my own.

Shlomo Pass was, from a theoretical viewpoint, a fascinating anomaly in the sky: and, from a practical viewpoint, a boon for calculation-weary travelers. For nearly a quarter light-year in any direction the magnetic, gravitational, and ion vector fields were extremely flat, which meant you could calculate a cascade maneuver several hours ahead of time without worrying too much about fluctuation errors sending you to hell and gone off your intended target point. There also wasn't a single sizeable body for five light-years to clarnk you up, and on top of that it was a convenient spot for at least fifteen interstellar runs. All in all, if there was any spot in deep space you were halfway likely to run into another ship, Shlomo was it.

Unless, apparently, you were the *Aura Dancer*.

We spent two days traversing a section of the Pass, and never once picked up signs of anyone else.

"I've got the calculations for the next point," Pascal announced as I came onto the bridge on that final day. "That is, if you still want to head out in three hours."

I nodded and took the printout in silence. A full sixteen light-years back toward Baroja—Pascal had taken good advantage of Shlomo's benevolence. "Looks fine," I said. "Okay, I'll take over now."

"Yes, sir. Uh ... Captain? I've been thinking some more about the *Angelwing*. I think I may have an idea of what could have happened."

Think, may, could. With qualifiers like that, this one ought to be a real gem. "Let's hear it," I grunted.

He waved his hand in the general direction of the Colloton field switch. "Even with an Aker-Ming actually doing the work, a liner's supposed to have an officer on the bridge during cascade maneuvers. Right?"

"Right. He's usually in light sleep state, but he *is* there."

"Okay, then. Suppose the Colloton generator somehow created an electrical feedback along the control cable to the bridge—shorted out, maybe, and sent line current along the wires as it was shutting down. An Aker-Ming couldn't take that—it'd likely vaporize its global lattice and explode."

And sitting right next to it would have been the sleeping captain? "Have you talked to Sarojis about this?" I asked.

"Well ... *he* says it isn't possible to get line current to the control cable," Pascal admitted. "But who knows about freak accidents like that? And he *did* say an Aker-Ming *will* explode if you put that much power to it."

"Um. Okay, well, you head below and work out the details. If you come up with a plausible feedback mechanism we'll talk some more about it."

"Sure. See you later, Captain."

I settled down into my seat and ran through the checkout routine ... but even as my fingers kept themselves busy, my eyes kept straying to the Colloton field switch. In some ways Pascal was a curiously naive man; he could theorize an incredible tangle of assumptions about the universe at large while missing entirely the factor of simple, human evil.

You didn't need line current across the Aker-Ming Autotorque when a bomb would work equally well.

I reached over to the crew intercom, keyed for the engine room where Tobbar had just come on duty. "Everything normal back there?" I asked when he answered.

"Yes, sir. No problems at all."

"Good. Tobbar, you once told me that Orlandis didn't belong on the *Dancer*. Why not?"

"He's too rich and important," was the prompt reply. "Probably rich enough to own his own ship; at least rich enough to charter a decent one."

"But how do you *know*?"

"Because he talks too slowly."

I blinked. "Say again?"

"He talks too slowly. You see, Captain, when you're important enough you don't *have* to talk fast—people will take whatever time's necessary to hear you out. It's those of us at the *bottom* of the social heap who have to get our thoughts out quickly before everyone walks away."

I thought back over the few brief conversations I'd had with Orlandis, and damned if Tobbar wasn't right. Precise, carefully measured speech—and a very clear sense that you *would* stand patiently by until he'd finished. "Any chance he could be faking it?" I asked Tobbar.

He shrugged. "I doubt it. If he were trying to pass himself off as the original nabob of borscht he should have put some more money into his clothes and jewelry. If he were smart enough to change his speech pattern, he should have been smart enough to think of obvious details like that."

I gritted my teeth. "Yeah. Okay, thanks. We'll be doing our next point in about three hours, so you can start securing things whenever you're ready."

"Yes, sir."

I broke the connection and scowled at the Colloton field switch for a few minutes. Okay: so Orlandis *was* rich. And the yacht in our hold was certainly expensive; it was hard to avoid the inference that the two went together. So let's see: Orlandis had sabotaged the *Angelwing* by unknown means and for unknown purpose, then signed aboard the *Dancer* in hopes of getting confirmation of his success. A sudden thought occurred to me, and I called up the passenger manifest. Yes: Orlandis had booked passage four days after our arrival on Baroja; two days after Alana's first get-together with her old *Angelwing* friends. With a good enough information network, then, he would have had enough time to hear about her cascade point "captaincy" and make his plans.

So far, so good ... except that none of that yet explained the yacht. Unless Orlandis didn't want word of the *Angelwing*'s distress getting out until it was too late. Which meant eliminating the *Dancer*.

Steady, Durriken, steady, I told myself as a lump rose to about the middle of my windpipe. *Think it out*.

Would getting rid of us really do the trick? If *we* didn't raise the alarm the first hint of trouble would be when the *Angelwing* failed to show up at Lorraine. Twenty-eight days after her departure from Baroja; nearly that since her accident. I hadn't been joking earlier about Cunard's clock-watching reputation: on a given run their ships always took the exact same number of cascade points, each of an exactly specified length, with the real-space intervals between them equally well defined. Given that, the Lorraine office probably wouldn't let the ship be more than two or three days overdue before sounding the alarm ... and when they did, they would have only those four precisely demarcated real-space areas to search.

Except that from the timing of Alana's cascade point event we knew that the disaster had occurred on one end or the other of the *Angelwing*'s first maneuver ... which meant it was either a few hours out from Baroja— and presumably already rescued—or else nine point two light-years out toward Lorraine. To reach *that* spot, the Lorraine searchers would require another three weeks. Total time: less than eight weeks. Easily within the three months the *Angelwing* should be able to survive.

I shook my head, trying to clear it. The more I tried to track through the logic, the more confused I became and the more the loose ends threatened to grow up my sleeves. If Orlandis was trying to destroy the *Angelwing*, he was doing a lousy job of it. If he *wasn't*, then none of this made any sense at all.

Unless the accident itself was what he needed, fatalities or lack of them being irrelevant. The accident, and getting quickly to Earth. Well, if *that* was what it took to make him feel happy, then I was perfectly happy to oblige. Keying the main intercom to general broadcast, I flipped it on. "Good morning, everyone, this is Captain Durriken," I said into the mike. "In just under three hours Dr. Epstein will be administering your sleepers for the *Aura Dancer's* next cascade maneuver. You will be pleased to know that we've changed course once again and *will* be continuing on to Earth as scheduled. A few minutes ago I was able to contact another ship bound for Baroja, and so the rescue mission I told you about will be handled without any need for us to go back. Thank you for your patience, and I'm glad things have worked out this way. Enjoy your day; Captain out."

I switched off the intercom and picked up the printout Pascal had left me. If Orlandis wanted to play games, fine. I could play games, too. Maybe sometime in the next few days I'd figure out what exactly was going on here. Preferably before we actually arrived at Baroja.

Death and taxes are still the only two items universally acknowledged as inevitable; but on my own personal list a post-cascade visit from Orlandis was running a pretty close third. Correctly, as it turned out; and as I came down the spiral stair to the passenger deck at the end of my shift I found him waiting. At least this time he'd had the grace to stay where he belonged.

"I just wanted to thank you for your assistance and cooperation, Captain," he said as I stepped around the stairway railing. "And I wanted also to assure you that my end of the arrangement will be carried out as soon as we reach Earth."

"Thank you, Mr. Orlandis," I said gravely. "I hope your own business deal will be successful."

"It should be," he nodded. "In fact, if you could allow me access to the ship's communication equipment once we're within range, I could practically guarantee it."

"Well . . . we'll see, but it should be all right. I don't suppose this deal is anything I could get in on?"

His smile wasn't *quite* condescending, but it was pretty damn close. "I'm afraid not, Captain. Not unless you have a hundred million in investment capital available to you. Tell me, what do you think happened to the *Angelwing*?"

The abrupt change in subject threw me off guard. "The—uh—what do you mean?" I stammered at last.

"You know—the accident you believe happened to it. What do you think went wrong?"

My mind went blank. With my suspicions about Orlandis, I'd been fighting to avoid even *thinking* about the *Angelwing* in his presence, lest he pick up something odd in my attitude. To have him ask such a point-blank question was the last thing I'd expected . . . and with no plausible story prepared I had only one recourse. "Well, I'm not sure. But my computer expert thinks it may have been a field generator feedback . . ."

I spun out Pascal's whole theory for him, working hard to make it sound plausible. I must have succeeded, because when I finished he nodded. "I see. Interesting. Would a blast of that sort actually be enough to disable a ship that big?"

I shrugged. "The exploding Autotorque, probably not. But remember that the field generator would also have been ruined, and if the damage was extensive enough it might be beyond repair."

"Leaving the ship helpless somewhere out in deep space," he nodded.

"Exactly nine point two light-years out, if they were on Cunard Lines' standard Baroja/Lorraine run," I said, obscurely glad I could quote him the exact number. "And of course they would have blown out a cloud of high-speed distress buoys as soon as they knew they were in trouble, so the rescue ships won't have to get closer than maybe five light-hours to find them."

"Sounds like you've worked all of this through quite well," Orlandis said. "I trust the patrol rescue squads will be equally astute. How long now before we land?"

"Uh—" I tried to remember how long it usually took from Shlomo Pass to Earth. "Should take three more cascade maneuvers, unless conditions have changed drastically in the past year or so. Which it may have—the Barnard's Star system can be a pain. Say, ten or eleven more days.

"I see. Thank you, Captain; I'll let you get on with your business now."

"Thank you," I said automatically as he turned and walked away. Scowling to myself, I headed the other way and escaped to the solitude of my cabin. There I threw myself down on my bed and roundly cursed Orlandis and the power he had to make me feel like one of his menials. For a long moment I seriously considered going to the man and telling him that *we* were headed for Baroja, and that if *he* wanted to go to Earth he could jolly well put together his fancy yacht, load his two Autotorques aboard, and leave.

Two Autotorques?

I stared at the ceiling for a long, chilling moment. Then I got back up and left, forcing myself not to run.

Matope was lounging in front of the main engine room status board when I got there a few minutes later with the canvas duffel bag I'd brought up from One Hold. "Everything under control and quiet, Captain," he reported, eying the bag.

"Good," I told him, "because I've got work for you. Come here."

He followed me back to the work table; and even with my peripheral vision I clearly saw his mouth fall open as I carefully withdrew the first of the two Aker-Ming Autotorques. "Captain! Where'd *that* come from?"

"Same place this one did," I said as calmly as I could. "A box marked Harmax Industries in our Ming-metal shield."

He looked at me with the kind of expression he usually reserved for sudden, unexpected problems with the *Dancer's* engines. "Captain—"

"I want you to take them apart," I interrupted him

brusquely. "I think one of them might be rigged to destroy a Colloton generator."

He stared at me for a long minute, gradually getting his face back together. Then, without a word, he picked up the two Autotorques and carried them over to the scale. One, it turned out, weighed nearly a hundred grams more than the other. Taking the heavier one back to the bench, he spread out his tools and got to work.

I'd never seen the inside of an Autotorque before, and it was only as Matope slowly moved down the table, leaving a neat line of components and fasteners in his path, that I began to understand exactly why the things were so damned expensive. About halfway into the disassembly it suddenly occurred to me that we would probably have to take *both* Autotorques apart in order to find out why the first was heavier, because whatever the extra component was it could probably crawl out and bite either of us without our recognizing it as spurious. The thought added one more twist to the wringer around my stomach: we were in plenty of trouble right now without having two Autotorques belonging to someone else that we couldn't put back together again.

But that worry, at least, turned out to be unnecessary. Five minutes later, Matope carefully slid out the delicate global lattice and there, wedged in where it obviously didn't belong, was our culprit: a tiny mechanical timer and a heavy-duty sodium-bromine battery with attached capacitor.

"Well?" I asked after Matope had spent a few minutes poking around the battery and its environs. "What does it do?"

He fingered his screwdriver thoughtfully. "Hard to say exactly, Captain, but it looks like it's supposed to feed extra current into the lattice. Contact points here and here—see?"

I thought about Pascal's theory. "Which would vaporize it and make it explode?"

He gave me an odd look. "I doubt it. Even with the capacitor the power surge should warp or melt the lattice instead of flash-vaporizing it. Even at mid-maneuver, when the lattice is already as hot as it ever normally gets."

My eyes drifted to the timer. "Mid-maneuver. And what happens if the lattice melts?"

He ran some numbers on his calculator. "Hard to say. If the voltage peak is strong enough, it could discharge across the safeties into the Colloton generator control cable here. No, wait a minute—there must surely be a surge protector to ground out dangerous pulses like that."

"Show me."

He poked around for another half hour before finally giving up. If there'd ever been a surge ground line, it wasn't there now. And at that point there didn't seem to be any conclusion available except the one I'd already come to: this Autotorque had been designed to kill its ship.

"If the control circuitry gets hit with that kind of voltage spike, you'll probably lose at least a couple of the major coils before it can be drained off to ground," Matope explained. His voice was as calm and dry as always, but the hand gripping his screwdriver showed white knuckles. "There's a feedback line that would kick in the emergency braking system for the flywheel, though, and even with the generator ruined there's enough hysteresis to hold the ship in Colloton space for at least a few seconds."

"Long enough for the ship to stop?"

He hesitated, then shook his head. "Not if the flywheel and ship were already rotating at top speed. A liner just has too much inertia to stop that fast."

And an instant later, both it and the device that had killed it would be disassociated atoms. I thought about that for a long minute, until I suddenly realized Matope was looking at me with an air of expectation. "All right," I said slowly. "Let's take the batteries and timer out and put the rest back together."

"And after that?"

"I'll put them back in their box in the shield and ... figure out then what to do."

It took longer to reassemble the Autotorque than it had taken to pull it apart, and I was feeling extremely nervous by the time I headed back to the hold. But my temporary theft had apparently gone unnoticed, and within a few minutes everything was back to normal. Five minutes after that, I was flat on my back on my bed, staring at the cabin ceiling and wondering what the hell I *was* going to do.

Because suddenly the whole game had changed. Again. It'd started out as a freak event, moved on to become a logical puzzle, and then to a question of financial risk versus Good Samaritanship and the need to back Alana up in her fears about the *Angelwing*. But now the stakes had abruptly gone up . . . because there was only one reason I could think of for that gimmicked Autotorque to be aboard.

Orlandis was planning the same fate for the *Dancer* as he'd planned for the *Angelwing*.

And I was out of my depth. Completely. Logical problems I could tackle; equipment problems I could turn Matope and Tobbar loose on . . . but this was a situation of human invention, and I didn't have a handle on any of it. What did Orlandis ultimately hope to gain, for starters? Had the *Dancer* been doomed from the start, or was that decision still open?—and if so, what action of mine was likely to push it the wrong way? Orlandis thought we were going to Earth . . . or had he seen through my simple stratagem? And if I couldn't figure out the answers to any of those, how could I possibly save all of our lives?

Alana. I needed Alana—needed her insight, her knowledge of people, her sensitivity—

Her sensitivity.

Slowly, I withdrew the hand that had been reaching for the intercom. Through design or accident, Orlandis had continued to spend a fair amount of time with her even after he'd gotten his confirmation of the *Angelwing* disaster. I didn't know how Alana was starting to view him, but even if she were merely being friendly as part of a crewer's normal duty toward the passengers I still couldn't risk it. What learning the truth would do to her . . .

"All right, damn it," I snarled abruptly at the ceiling. "I'll figure it all out by myself."

And for starters, I'd figure out what exactly—*exactly*—had happened to the *Angelwing*. Because if she'd been fitted with a doomsday Autotorque like the one in our hold, it was clear the thing had failed in its task. *Only* the captain in Alana's cascade pattern had died, which meant the *Angelwing hadn't* disintegrated. So . . . why?

The timer had malfunctioned. If the generator had been fried too soon or too late, the ship could have possibly stopped rotating in time. Which would have left it disabled near one end or the other of its real-space translation.

But why then would the captain have died?

The overload device in toto *had failed.* Not enough power to ruin the generator at all, though possibly enough to change the lattice voltage balance and consequently foul that particular maneuver. Again, though, the captain should have come out of it alive.

I thought about everything Alana had told me about Lenn Grandy. From the old school, she'd described him, uncomfortable with wizard gadgets like the Autotorque. Could he have positioned himself close enough to the device during the maneuver to have somehow taken a lethal shock from it while he slept?

Or could he even have been awake?

Awake.

It was as if someone had suddenly turned on the air-conditioning to my overheated brain. Of *course*—Grandy had elected to remain awake during the maneuver, trading the pain of cascade point depression for the assurance his Autotorque was indeed performing properly. It was something I could easily visualize Alana doing in that position, especially with her captain's gold barely out of its box.

So I now had a key piece to what had at least partially thwarted Orlandis's sabotage . . . a piece that Orlandis very possibly did *not* have.

Did that really help me? At the moment I couldn't think how, but it was a good feeling regardless to be a step ahead of Orlandis in at least one aspect of this mess. Whatever theoretical knowledge he had about the Colloton Drive and cascade points, he had no first-hand experience with them. If there was any further information about the *Angelwing*'s fate to be squeezed out of Alana's cascade pattern, I had a better shot of getting it than he did.

Useful information from cascade images. With all the other thoughts crowding my mind these days I hadn't really paid much attention to the shock wave this was going to send through the academic brain trusts. The idea that the cascade images were imaginary or purely psychological was going to die on its feet, and all of us who'd always known better could finally thumb our collective lip at them. And yet, the sheer *scope* of it was staggering. I'd heard once that collapsing stars sent out adjusting ripples into the general gravitational field; what we had here was the same sort of effect, but on an apparently *instantaneous* time scale. Even granted the obvious limitations of what sort of information could be conveyed, someone *somewhere* would find a way to take advantage of it.

Assuming we stayed alive to report it.

Gritting my teeth, I brought my mind back to the immediate problem at hand. So Lenn Grandy had been awake during the fatal cascade maneuver; had figured out what had happened and interrupted proceedings in time to save his ship. Possibly by unintentionally replacing the Autotorque's missing voltage surge drain, drawing enough of the extra current through his own body to slow the Colloton generator destruction those extra few critical seconds. In which case ... the *Angelwing* could be literally anywhere along a line nine point two light-years long.

Hell in a bubble-pack.

No wonder Orlandis had been so phlegmatic about the idea of sending a rescue mission out after the *Angelwing*. Even if the searchers thought to look in the space that would normally have been bypassed, their chances of finding anything there would be virtually non-existent. Even a single light-year—hell, a single light-*month*—was just too much territory to cover, Colloton Drive or no. Somehow, we had to narrow that range down to something manageable.

And all we had to do that with were Alana's cascade images.

Or . . . perhaps Alana herself.

I thought about it for several minutes, and the longer I looked at the idea the nuttier it sounded. Aside from the fact that its chances of proving anything were slimmer than my credit rating, it might very well drive a wedge between Alana and me, might finally precipitate her departure from the *Dancer*.

I didn't want that. I'd grown accustomed to having someone with Alana's competence beside me in all the big and little emergencies that are part of a tramp starmer's life. To lose both her presence and her friendship— and I'd lose both if I lost either. Were the lives of a bunch of rich strangers I'd never met worth the risk?

They would be worth it to Alana. *That* much I knew for sure . . . and I was willing to defer to her better judgment on such matters.

Rolling onto my side, I poked at the intercom. It took a few seconds, but eventually Pascal woke up and answered. "Yes?" he said, yawning audibly.

"I need you to work up a special program for the astrogate," I told him. "One that'll show our position as what it would be if we were on our way to Earth."

"What do you mean, 'if'?" he asked. "I thought we *were* headed for Earth."

'We're going to Baroja," I said. "The passengers weren't—*aren't*—supposed to know, and to make sure not even a hint leaks out I don't want the other crewers to know, either."

"Not even Alana?"

"Especially not her. That's who the trick astrogate's for."

There was a long pause, and I could just about hear

his wheels spinning as he tried to come up with a theory to explain this one. Well, he could just stew; I wasn't in much of an explaining mood. "I'll do the calculations for the next maneuver," I continued, "but since she'll be the one actually doing the point she'll undoubtedly want to double-check the numbers. I want the computer gimicked so that hers come out identical to mine, even though her input will be different. Can you do that?"

"Uh . . . yessir, I guess so. Uh . . ."

"You'll get a full explanation after it's all over," I sighed. "For now, just do it. And do *not* let anyone know. *Anyone.* Clear?"

He cleared his throat. "Yes, Captain."

"All right. Your next shift's early enough to start, I guess, so go ahead back to bed. Sorry I woke you."

"S'all right. Good night; or whatever."

For a wonder, he *did* manage to keep it quiet. By the end of his next shift he had the fake astrogate program in place, and he spent the first few minutes of mine showing me how to bypass the facade to get back to the computer. Twenty-eight hours after that, Matope and I had the rest of the props in place.

And then there was nothing left to do but worry.

Six hours later, it was time.

"Kate reports all the passengers have had their sleepers," Alana reported as she came onto the bridge. "What's this I hear about the airconditioning up here not working?"

"Matope's fiddling with the electrostatic precipitators in the vents again," I told her, striving for calm. "I've got all the doors locked open, though, so you shouldn't have any problems with stuffiness."

"Okay." She peered at me as she sat down. "You all right?"

"Sure. Why?"

"You seem jumpy." She scanned the printout I'd made for the upcoming maneuver, then activated the computer for her own check. I held my breath . . . but Pascal had done his job right. Alana watched the numbers come up, compared them carefully to mine, and nodded. "Looks good," she announced. "Shouldn't you be getting below? There's only about fifteen minutes to go."

"I've got my sleeper right here," I told her, patting a pocket. I did, too, though I didn't intend to take it. "See you later."

I left the bridge and headed aft toward the spiral stair ... but I didn't go down it. Pascal's computer room branched off to my left; I slipped inside and squeezed into the console chair. Two objects awaited me there: a multi-event mechanical stopwatch, and a strap-on eyepiece connected to an optical fiber bundle snaking into the air system vent. Putting the strap over my head. I adjusted the eyepiece ... and there, seated just as I'd left her, was Alana.

She was already shutting down the ship's systems, protecting everything electronic against the enhanced electron tunneling effects Colloton space created. Feeling uncomfortably like a voyeur, I watched her count down the seconds ... and with an abrupt, almost angry gesture, she turned on the field.

My first four cascade images appeared, but I paid no attention to them. Finger ready on the stopwatch button, I kept my eyes on Alana. For a moment she gazed down the line of images, her face unreadable but—I thought— oddly calm. Then, straightening up, she turned on the *Dancer*'s flywheel. Beneath me, I felt the rumble begin as I pushed the stopwatch button. Its ticking was soft, but clearly audible over the flywheel's hum. Mechanical clock devices are like that—*all* of them, including the one Matope and I had taken from the lethal Autotorque and hidden in the bridge control panel. The big question was, was it loud enough? Holding my breath, I watched Alana.

And it was clear within a handful of seconds that she did, indeed, hear it. Her head turned back and forth, a frown of concentration spreading across her face as she tried to locate the unfamiliar sound. For a moment her eyes paused on the proper section of the panel two meters away—the same distance, according to her layout of the *Angelwing*'s bridge, that the Autotorque mounting socket would be from the duty officer's chair. Her lips compressed to a tight line, she stood up—

And nearly fell on her face.

I winced in sympathetic pain, remembering the last time *I'd* tried to move around with a Colloton field on. Even while sitting still, vertigo was a normal cascade point side effect; actually trying to go somewhere just about tripled the sensation. Alana pulled herself to her knees, staggered almost to the floor again ... and with a hissed word I was glad I couldn't hear, she grabbed the edge of the control panel, raised herself up again, and slapped at the flywheel switch.

And there it was, the whole explanation: simple, yet so contrary to a captain's normal ingrained preoccupation with staying on schedule that I hadn't really considered it. Aborting a cascade maneuver could add several days to a ship's trip time—a delay that would cause confusion and anger at every stop for at least the rest of its run. But Lenn Grandy had reportedly been a lot like Alana ... and unlike me, she had little fear of looking foolish. Grandy had heard an out-of-place sound, had been unable to hunt it down through the Colloton field's effect ... and so had simply turned the damned generator off and to hell with the consequences.

And with those facts in hand I knew where to look for the *Angelwing*.

I almost forgot to key my stopwatch, but I did so without losing more than a second or two. The amount of time Alana had taken to react to the timer's ticking ... though I now realized that number was only useful, not absolutely vital. The flywheel hum faded into silence, and Alana waited with hand poised above the generator switch, eyes darting back and forth between the mirrored gyroscope needle and the area where the Autotorque's timer was hidden. Around me, the cascade images' interweaving slowed ... came to a stop ...

Alana hit the switch, and our patterns began disappearing. Pulling off the eyepiece, I forced myself to my feet and staggered to the door. By the time the last four images were gone I was halfway down the hallway

She had the proper panel cover open and was reaching inside when I stumbled in. "Pall?" she croaked, cascade depression already beginning to etch lines in her face. "Pall, there's a strange sound coming from—" She stopped abruptly, jerking her hand back, as the timer gave the *snap* of a spring-loaded switch and then fell silent.

I clicked my stopwatch; and with the booby-trap's total time setting, I had the last number I needed. "It's all right," I told Alana, stepping forward and putting my arms awkwardly around her. "It's all right. The *Dancer*'s not in danger. I'm sorry, Alana—I'm *sorry*. But it was the only way I could think of—"

And then our tears began to flow, and we sat down together, letting our tension and emotional pain drain away.

And a half hour later, feeling like the lowest form of vermin on twenty planets, I told her what I'd done. And why.

The bridge door slid open, and I turned as Orlandis stepped inside. "Captain," he nodded, looking a bit woozy still from the after-effects of his sleeper. "You asked to see me?"

"Yes." Leeds was still standing in the doorway; I caught his eye and nodded, and he disappeared. "We've got just one more cascade maneuver until planetfall," I continued as Orlandis stepped to the other console chair and sank into it. "You'd said you wanted to send a message when we were within range, and I thought this would be a good time to talk about it."

"I understood the next maneuver was several days away," he said.

"Actually, we'll probably be ready within twenty-four hours or less," I told him. "Though that may put you on a rather tight schedule. Reassembling your little star ship, I mean."

Orlandis was good, all right. No jerking of the head; no widening of mouth or eyes; just a slight hardening of his entire expression to show that all my suspicions about him had indeed been right. "What star ship is that?" he asked gently.

"The one you smuggled aboard under falsified contract papers—papers you apparently made up yourself, and you should have risked hiring an expert to do them for you. The one that's in five boxes below, counting the two Aker-Ming Autotorques in our Ming-metal shield. The one you plan to escape on after killing all of us and then setting up the *Dancer* to disintegrate itself. *That* star ship."

He pursed his lips. "You seem to know a great deal about the private cargo in your hold," he said, "which I'm sure various port authorities would be rather upset by. But your accusations are completely ludicrous."

"Are they?" I countered, fighting hard against Orlandis's aura of authority. "Well, perhaps we should leave those for later then, and move onto more technical ground. Do you want to know why your sabotage of the *Angelwing* failed?"

"I had nothing to do with the *Angelwing*'s sabotage," he said. I remained silent, and after a moment he snorted. "All right. As a matter of intellectual curiosity, go ahead and tell me what happened."

"It's very simple. The captain chose to stay awake through the ship's first cascade point out of Baroja, which left him able to hear the ticking of the timer in their rigged Autotorque. He aborted the maneuver, which meant the ship was no longer rotating when the power surge tried to fry the Colloton generator. Which in turn left the ship stranded somewhere out in space where no one would think to look."

"Except you, of course."

I nodded, swallowing. "Except us, yes. Is that why you're planning to kill all of us? Because we know where the *Angelwing* is and can link it to you?"

"I told you before, I had nothing to do with the *Angelwing*'s sabotage."

"Then how did you know enough to ask about Alana's cascade images?" I shot back.

"Oh, I *knew* the sabotage was being planned," he said with a slight shrug. "It was set up as an assassination attempt by an underworld group against one of the ship's passengers."

"If you *knew*—?"

"Why didn't I tell anyone? Why should I? I'm not in charge of Cunard Lines' security. *My* job is the making of money—and it occurred to me that there would be a distinct dip in Cunard's stock if and when the *Angelwing* was indeed lost."

"You *knew*, did you," I snarled, some of my anger venting itself in heavy sarcasm. "You knew about the attempt, you knew how it was going to be done, you knew where and how to get hold of a killer Autotorque yourself. You didn't just *know*—you were an accessory before the fact."

Again, he shrugged. "A legal distinction only. Impossible to prove, of course."

I stared at him. The man was even more cold-blooded than I'd imagined. "That's it, then. You'd let an entire shipload of people die for a lousy bit of pocket money."

"It's hardly that," he said coolly. "By selling my stock in Cunard—slowly, of course, over the next couple of months—I'll make enough to buy back a controlling share in the line when prices fall."

"And to get those two months' head start you bought passage on the *Dancer*."

He smiled. "It was easily the most ridiculous thing I'd ever heard in my life, and I nearly fired one of my idea people just for suggesting it. But everyone agreed it would be worth a try, and I began to be intrigued by the possibilities. Besides, with fate having put you and Ms. Keal in my path at the right time, how could I resist? After all, all it would cost would be a few weeks aboard this flying slum."

I bristled. "Plus the chance of having your whole scheme unraveled."

His smile remained as he locked eyes with me. "It was for *that* possibility," he said softly, "that I brought my own ship."

A shiver went up my back. In his own, quietly confident way, Orlandis had just sentenced the *Dancer* to death. "Well, I hope you enjoy the trip," I said as casually as I could. "Going to be a rather long haul for you, though. Unless you just want to hop down to Baroja and start the whole trip over."

His smile vanished. "What are you talking about?"

"Oh, didn't I mention it? The planetfall we'll be making with the next point will be back to Baroja. We're currently sitting just about point zero eight light-years out. About a light-month, if you care."

His lip curled. "So you *didn't* find anyone in Shlomo Pass to send a message with. I suspected as much when Ms. Keal began avoiding me right after the last cascade point. I'd hoped you weren't actually foolish enough to leap on your white horse and come out looking for the *Angelwing*."

"Not *looking*, Orlandis," I corrected. "*Finding*."

He stared at me in disbelief, and in the momentary silence I leaned forward and flipped on the radio speaker. Clearly audible over the background static came the *zhu-UUP zhuUUP zhuUUP* of a distress buoy. "We picked up the first signal right after we turned off the Colloton field an hour ago," I told him quietly. "Our estimate of their position turns out to have been no more than a light-hour or two off, and we hit our target position pretty accurately, too. Another fifteen minutes or so and we'll be close enough to raise them with our comm laser."

He glanced quickly at the bridge viewport, as if he thought he'd actually be able to see the liner. "But ... how—?"

"How did we know? Simple. There was really only one place they could be." I reached over and turned off the radio, then hit the switches that put the control systems and computer into neutral/standby. "You see," I continued, "we had your duplicate of the rigged Autotorque to study and we knew quite a lot about the *Angelwing*. *And* we had Alana."

Orlandis's eyes swung back to me, and I could see by their expression that he'd suddenly realized what our being in communication with the *Angelwing* would mean. His right hand dipped into his tunic pocket, emerging with a tiny summoner. "I'm afraid I can't allow you to talk with them," he said softly. "You understand."

"Of course," I nodded. "You're welcome to try and stop me." And with that, I flipped open the Colloton generator safety cover and twisted the knob.

Orlandis actually gasped as the first cascade images appeared around us. "What the *hell*—?"

"Oh, we're not going anywhere," I assured him. "As long as the *Dancer* doesn't rotate we'll come back out in more or less the same position we left. But I was telling you how we found the *Angelwing*. Your assassin friends didn't reckon on Captain Grandy's being awake during the maneuver—and they certainly didn't expect him to shut down the flywheel before the Autotorque had time to blow the generator. We knew Alana would have been killed if she'd been there instead of Grandy, so we set up a similar test last cascade point to see how she'd react, and she did so exactly as I've just said. QED."

"Pretty far-fetched assumption," Orlandis said with some difficulty. He threw a quick glance at the bridge door, then resumed his apprehensive gaze at his cascade pattern.

"Perhaps," I admitted. "But he *had* to have brought the ship to a halt before the timer wound down, else *all* of Alana's *Angelwing* cascade images would have vanished. You following all this?"

He nodded, a short jerk of his head. Again, his eyes darted to the door.

"And finally, the really critical factor: we found out how the Autotorque was supposed to destroy the Colloton generator and how long its timer was set for. Once we knew the ship itself was safe, there were only two possibilities: one, that Grandy had gotten the Autotorque out of the circuit in time to protect the generator— possibly being electrocuted himself in the process, as Alana would have been—or two, that he'd started to take it out, got electrocuted, and still lost the generator. Only in the second case would the *Angelwing* be stranded. So all we had to do then was figure out how far the ship would have rotated in the time available, remembering that Grandy had to rev the flywheel up, rev it back down, *and* get the Colloton field shut off just before the time ran out. That's a pretty tight scenario, and with the relatively small distances you get with small rotation angles it let us calculate precisely how far the *Angelwing* had gotten. Turns out we were right."

Orlandis was starting to breathe heavily as the claustrophobic effect of a roomful of cascade images finally appeared to be getting to him. "You've been very clever," he said, looking again at the door. "But you can't talk to the *Angelwing* from Colloton space."

"True, but there'll be enough time for that later." I waved toward the door. "And incidentally, I wouldn't expect your two bodyguards to show up any time soon. They'll be lucky if they don't break their necks falling down the stairs. If they manage to get that far."

Orlandis stared at me, the uneasiness on his face giving way rapidly to fury. "What—?"

"Eiser and Trent, of course. Once we realized how rich you were, we noticed that one or the other of them always seemed to be hanging around you somewhere in the background. No, cascade point vertigo will have them well out of the game by now. If you want to stop me, you'll have to do it yourself."

"*Damn you*—" Orlandis thrust himself out of his seat toward me, hands outstretched like killing weapons even as he piled headfirst into the floor. He staggered to his knees, lunged another half meter before falling again. I stayed where I was as he gathered himself for another try . . . and as he rose up and crawled forward I let my anger boil up within me; my anger at what he'd done to the *Angelwing* and planned to do to the *Dancer*. He reached out an unsteady hand, clutched at my left knee . . . and with my right foot I kicked him as hard as I could. He flipped over backwards, hitting his head on the padded seat he'd just left, and lay still.

Fifteen minutes later, when I judged it was safe

enough, I turned off the Colloton generator and went out hunting. Eiser and Trent were easy to find, lying unconscious on the floor halfway from the stairs to the bridge. Close, but not too bad: their tiny guns were still at the bottom of the stairs, where they'd apparently been dropped.

And a half hour later I was talking to an extremely relieved duty officer on the *Angelwing*.

What with all the electronic equipment that got singed by my unscheduled cascade point, the *Dancer* was in pretty poor shape by the time we rendezvoused with the *Angelwing*. But Matope and Tobbar were able to make running repairs, and with the computer intact none of us was especially worried about making the short trip back to Baroja. If worse came to worst, we still had that little backup in our hold.

The passengers were somewhat more troubled. They started out furious at having had to actually experience a cascade point; shifted to astonished and only slightly less angry to find we were nowhere near Earth; and finally turned to shock at finding out the truth about Orlandis and company. I decided not to strain them further with pessimistic reports of the *Dancer*'s spaceworthiness, but dropped our three prisoners off with the *Angelwing* for safekeeping and headed to Baroja to whistle up the cavalry.

Through all of it Alana was very professional, never bringing up her feelings about the whole incident and my handling of it, but doing her part to ensure that the *Dancer* made it through in one piece. But her underlying tension was plain; and I therefore wasn't really surprised when she came to my cabin two hours after we were safely down on Baroja to discuss her resignation.

"It won't be the *Dancer* without you," I told her when she'd explained her errand. I tried to keep my voice steady and emotionless; just another bit of business, however unpleasant and depressing, that I had to handle. I didn't succeed very well.

"That's a . . . a nice compliment," she said, no better than I'd been at hiding her emotions on this. "I've enjoyed working with you, Pall—with all of you. But it seems to be time to move on."

I sighed, wondering what I should do. Offer her some inducement—*any* inducement—to stay? Get down on my knees and beg? Or should I simply acknowledge that she was capable of making her own decisions and let her walk out with our individual dignities intact? "You'll be badly missed," I said at last. Even now, I realized, with such a loss staring me in the face, I couldn't take the risk of losing my dignity in front of her. Of looking foolish. "You know more about dealing with people than I ever will. I don't suppose . . . don't suppose there's anything I can say that would change your mind?"

She shook her head minutely, tears glistening in her eyes. "It's a matter of trust, Pall. Trust, and a realistic evaluation of my strengths as well as my weaknesses. If you can't make that evaluation by now, then I don't think you'll ever be able to."

I took a deep breath. "Alana, look . . . I'm sorry I put you through the hoop—I really am. I suppose if I'd thought it out a little better I might have been able to piece together what had happened without having you reenact it. But I was stuck, and we were running out of time."

"You could have come to me." Her voice was quietly accusing. "You didn't know from the beginning that you'd need to reenact things, so there wasn't any good reason to keep me in the dark about Orlandis. Trust, Pall—you trusted Wilkinson with part of it, and Matope, and even Pascal. But me you completely cut out."

"But I *had* to. You were spending time with Orlandis—*lots* of time—"

"And you didn't think I could handle the knowledge that he might have killed Lenn Grandy? What did you think you were going to do, keep me in the dark forever? Just because I'm able to get close to people doesn't mean I lack emotional strength—"

"Who said it did?" I interrupted, frowning. "Good God, Alana—you've got more deep-down toughness than the rest of us put together. *I* know that."

It was her turn to frown. "Then . . . why didn't you tell me?"

"Because you were close to Orlandis, like I said . . . and all your other qualities aside, you're a *lousy* actress."

Her mouth fell open a crack. "You mean . . . *all* you were worried about was Orlandis getting tipped off?"

"Of course."

She licked her lips. "Oh. Well. Uh—" She stopped, looking acutely uncomfortable.

With our individual dignities intact, I reminded myself. "If you'd like to join up," I said, as casually as I could around the lump in my throat, "we just happen to have an opening in the first officer's position."

It was an old, old line . . . but for all that, it worked. "Sold," she said with the first smile I'd seen on her in days. "Thank you, sir. I hear the *Aura Dancer*'s a good ship to serve on."

But of course it wasn't the *Dancer* we shipped out on three months later. There'd been just too much ship-wide damage to be worth repairing, at least in the opinion of the Cunard Lines officials assigned to handle our reward for saving the *Angelwing*. Like so many people spending other people's money, they opted for the simpler if more expensive approach.

Certainly *I'm* not complaining. The *Daydreamer* is a beauty of a ship, with the most up-to-date equipment Cunard's money could buy . . . including the necessary mounting socket for an Aker-Ming Autotorque.

An Autotorque which is currently still in its shipping box in our Ming-metal shield. I figure we'll haul it out and use it one of these days, but strangely enough, neither Alana nor I is in any particular hurry to do so. For all the stress and trouble cascade images have brought into our lives . . . well, I guess it just wouldn't be like the old *Dancer* without them.

GUARDIAN ANGEL

Seldom in the history of the world had there been a success story like that of J. Thaddeus Draut. Born in the middle of the twenty-first century in the Cleveland slums—which had resisted a century's worth of eradication efforts—he had fought and struggled his way to the very top. Not an inventive or even particularly brilliant man by nature, he had instead the rare ability to inspire those who were so gifted.

The "overnight" success of his modest engineering firm came after twelve years of work and sweat on what came to be known as the Kuntz-Sinn force beam. The force beam had applications in every field from medicine to construction to aeronautics, and it put Draut Enterprises in the top ten of the *Fortune 1000*. When Draut's scientists came up with *phased* force beams, which could deliver all their power to a single point, the industrial world went crazy; and when the initial dust settled the corporation was number one. Draut himself was widely considered to be the richest man on Earth, a statement which ranked with that of the world being round: not strictly true, but close enough for practical purposes.

Unlike many wealthy men, Draut had no desire to amass money for its own sake, and he quickly found he could not spend all his income by himself. Thus, much of his money went back into the corporation, spent on a variety of projects. Most were of the borderline screwball type, which meant a large percentage of the funds invested vanished without a ripple. Occasionally, one would work out properly, sometimes even making money.

And once in a great while, there was a truly major brainstorm.

The Public Information room at the Draut Building, the three-hundred-floor headquarters of Draut Enterprises, was crammed with reporters when Draut arrived and made his way to the lectern.

"Ladies and gentlemen of the press," he said when things had quieted down and the cameras were humming, "thank you for coming here today. It is my pleasure to announce a new division of Draut Enterprises, and a scientific breakthrough that must be considered one of the greatest discoveries of our time."

He paused, and in the middle of the room Craig Petrie took the opportunity to get a better grip on his camera, held precariously but steadily above the heads of those in front of him. As a feature writer for *International* magazine, he didn't really *need* good film of Draut's announcement—his work began after the headlines had faded. But he'd once been a news filmer himself and still had some leftover professional pride.

"We have, as you know," Draut went on, "been studying applications of the mathematics which gave us the phased force beam. Our latest triumph in this work has been the perfection of a technique to make a man . . . invisible."

An audible gasp swept the room and a dozen hands shot into the air, waving like an instant wheat field. "I'll answer a few questions when I'm finished," Draut said.

"We are also today setting up Guardian Angels, Incorporated, a business which will lease invisible bodyguards to members of the public. Each person employing one of our Angels, as our guards will be called, will need only to wear a lightweight communicator-sensor device—" he held up a dark-green choker-like neckband—"and our Angel will do the rest. Naturally, we'll begin our operation with an extensive trial period before any leasing is done. For this test we'll be providing five hundred Angels, free of charge, to selected residents of New York City. Those people will be contacted in a few days and will have a week to decide whether or not to participate. Now—questions?"

Petrie's hand went up with the others. Draut chose someone else. "Mr. Draut, how can such a thing as real invisibility be possible? I thought it'd been proven *im*possible?"

"So did I," Draut agreed gravely, drawing a chuckle from the crowd. "As explained to me, it's somewhat akin to the way a phased force beam can carry energy and force through solid objects without affecting them, only delivering its energy when it intersects another properly phased beam. The beams are still *there* the rest of the time, but they simply don't interact with matter. I suspect something similar is being done with the light which would normally have reflected from the Angel, sending it right through him or something. That's the reason for the neckband, by the way. I'm told it's very hard to see when you're invisible because of what's being done with that light. Relaying the images from the neckband sensors to the appropriate Angel will help to alleviate this problem. I'm afraid that's the best explanation I can give; anything further would have to be in mathematics, which I don't speak. Next question? Yes, you."

"I realize there's a lot of danger in the world these days, but do you think there's a market for invisible bodyguards? Will the public accept something that radical?"

"If not, I've just lost a lot of money," Draut replied with a slight smile. "Obviously, I think the market *is* there. Yes. You in the middle."

Petrie chose his words carefully. "It seems to me, Mr. Draut, that workable invisibility opens a large box of snakes with regards to such activities as espionage, terrorism, and crime, to name just three. What are you doing to safeguard this discovery against possible misuse?"

"I'm sure you'll understand that I can't discuss our security arrangements with you." Draut's face was suddenly expressionless. "But I assure you there is *no* way for the invisibility secret to slip out. Very few people know the details, and even their names are highly classified information."

"Then what are you doing to make sure your own people don't abuse their knowledge?" Petrie persisted.

"All I can say is that there is no danger of that," Draut said. "Period; end of file. Next question?"

Draut answered a few more questions, but Petrie wasn't really listening. He'd spent years watching people's faces, and there was something in Draut's expression he didn't like. Studying the lined, middle-aged face, he tried to figure out what it was. Humor? Mockery? Whatever it was, Petrie had a solid gut-level sense that there was more to this project than met the eye. Draut hadn't seemed very happy with his question about security. Did he have some industrial espionage applications in mind?

Or did he have even greater ambitions?

The news conference ended a few minutes later, and the reporters scrambled from the room, looking for quiet corners from which they could call in the story. Petrie lingered, hoping for another look at Draut's face, but the older man left immediately, presumably returning to his office. For a moment Petrie was tempted to follow, to try and badger a few more answers out of him. But Security would probably run a slalom course down his back if he tried it. Besides, confrontations were more fun when both sides had a few facts on hand.

Turning, Petrie strode from the room. The first step, obviously, was to dig up his share of those facts.

Mrs. Irma Lieberman had just settled into her favorite easy chair—the one by the window—and had begun her afternoon's knitting when a knock rattled her door. She looked up, gnarled face wrinkling with surprise and more than a touch of apprehension. Only Mrs. Finch next door visited her these days, and Mrs. Lieberman could always hear her door open and close before she came over. Were the gangs of pre-teenage children becoming bold enough to come right into the senior citizen housing complexes? The thought made her shiver.

The knock came again. "Who's there?" she called.

"Mrs. Lieberman?" a strange voice said. "I'm Alex Horne of Draut Enterprises. I'd like to talk to you about a new service we're starting."

Whatever it was, she knew she couldn't afford it. But it might be nice to talk to someone for a while, even if it meant enduring a sales pitch. Carefully standing up, she walked to the door and warily cracked it open.

The man standing there certainly looked like he belonged to Draut Enterprises. Young, neat, clean, and dressed in a suit that had probably cost half her yearly stipend, he was all smiles as he held out an ID card for her perusal. She hesitated only a moment, then closed the door, removed the chains, and opened it wide. Still smiling, he stepped into her apartment.

"Mrs. Lieberman," he said when they were seated, "my company is beginning a new type of bodyguard service called Guardian Angels. Have you heard of it?"

Was the Pope a Catholic? Facts, speculations, and rumors about Guardian Angels had dominated the news for days now. "That's the one with invisible people, isn't it?"

"Right," he nodded. "As part of our test program, we would like you to accept one of our Angels, free of charge, for the duration of the study."

For a moment she just stared at him, so unexpected was his offer. "Why, I . . . well, that's very generous of you, young man . . . uh, I . . ."

Horne came to her rescue. "You don't have to make a decision today," he said, pulling a colorful brochure from an inside pocket. "Here's some more information about Guardian Angels. Please read it and give us your answer by next Tuesday. There's a number in the brochure for you to call; just give the person your name and we'll set up an appointment for you. Do you have any questions?"

She was still off-balance, but she'd recovered enough to at least hold on to her dignity. "Not just now. If I do later, I'll call."

"Please do. And I would really encourage you to accept an Angel, Mrs. Lieberman. I think it would be rewarding for you, as well as helpful for us. Well, I have many other calls to make this afternoon, so I'd better be going. Thank you for your time."

He left. Alone again, door securely locked and chained behind her, Mrs. Lieberman sat back down and carefully read the brochure. The idea that someone would actually offer such a thing to *her* took some getting used to, and she had to continually remind herself this was really happening. Still . . . there were some disturbing aspects to this whole thing. Having someone dogging your every step was strange enough, but for it to be someone you couldn't even see was downright spooky. Would the bodyguard want to come into her apartment with her? And if she refused permission would he do so anyway? She could see no way of stopping him.

Closing the brochure with more force than necessary, she stood up and began to pace—a slower and more cautious motion than in her youth, but still an effective way to drain off nervous energy. She kept at it for quite a while, but her conflicting thoughts refused to sort themselves out. Pros and cons, wishes, fears, and questions came and went, adding to her confusion instead of dispelling it.

With a start, she noticed the sunlight was coming directly through the window. It was almost four-fifteen; too late now to go to the store as she'd intended. The rush-hour crowds were already beginning to move, and after that was all over . . . well, it would mean coming home in the dark. That was something she knew far better than to do. For people her age, the day ended at sunset, if not sooner. Such things were like arthritis or broken elevators—they could be hated but not changed.

Or could they?

Seating herself by the window once more, she picked up the brochure and began to reread it.

The executive secretary in the Draut Building's public relations office was in her thirties. She was also personable, charming, and stubborn as a lobbyist. "I'm sorry, Mr. Petrie," she said for the sixth time, in response to his sixth phrasing of the same question. "We simply cannot release the names of test subjects in our Guardian Angel program. We've promised them privacy, and we intend for them to have it. I'm sure you can see that."

"Yes, I can," Petrie said, feeling his patience giving out. He'd tried sweet talk, reason, and simple persistence, to no avail. It was time to bring up the artillery. "And I'm sure *you* can see that the Freedom of Information Act XVII entitles any citizen—including reporters—to information that may bear on the dealings of corporations with the public well-being. Gratuities and gifts, such as free bodyguard service, given to government officials or the like could conceivably allow Draut Enterprises to influence their actions—"

"Oh?" Her smile was still in place but her tone had frosted over. "Well, if that's all you're worried about, you may rest easy. All the test subjects are either senior citizens or state-supported persons, and the Justice Department has already ruled that we aren't in violation of F.I. XVII by withholding their names. Now, may I have you shown out?"

The artillery had fizzled . . . and for the moment Petrie was out of ammo. "I know the way," he told her. "Thanks for your time."

He left, more confused than ever as to what was going on. Guardian Angels, Inc., was so tailor-made for industrial or governmental espionage that it was hard to believe Draut wasn't using it that way. But accusing the corporation of spying on the elderly and the poor was too ridiculous a charge even for the sleazoids. Was Draut saving the spy potential for later, lulling the government and public with an aboveboard test?

Maybe he was working this story from the wrong direction. It might be more profitable to concentrate on the Angels themselves, the men—and women—who would actually be invisible. Their personalities, training, and backgrounds might provide a clue as to their ultimate mission.

He was almost to the building's main exit and the security guard there was eying him. Best not to push his luck, Petrie decided; the PR secretary may have alerted the guard to make sure he left, and he didn't want to get himself barred from the building by becoming too much of a nuisance. Smiling pleasantly at the guard, he went out.

The neckband was a wide strip of soft, dark-green plastic embedded with dime-sized bits of glass—the sensors, the technician had told her. It fastened snugly around her neck.

"How does it feel, Mrs. Lieberman?" the technician asked. A courteous young man in a white lab coat, he reminded her of a boy she'd known in college.

She moved her head a few times before answering. The neckband didn't impede her motion, really, but neither did it allow her to forget she was wearing it. "It's all right," she told the other. "Rather like a stiff turtleneck."

"Okay. Now here—" he touched a spot to the left of her throat "—is your on-off switch; turn it to the left for on, right for off. It activates the sensor network that your Angel will need to see and hear well, and also the speaker that he'll talk to you through. You should avoid covering the neckband with anything heavy, but a sheer scarf won't interfere much with the operation. Your Angel will tell you if there's any problem, of course."

She nodded. "When do I meet him?"

"Whenever you're ready. He's already here."

She jumped and looked around her, the muscles in her neck tightening. "Where is he?"

"Why not ask him yourself?"

She looked at the boy sharply, but he didn't seem to be laughing at her. "All right," she told him. If this was some kind of test, she was determined to pass it. "I will." Reaching up, she found the "on" switch and turned it. "Hello?"

"Hello, Mrs. Lieberman." A soft, soothing voice came from just below her right ear. She realized it came from the neckband, but not soon enough to keep from jumping again. "My name is Michael," the voice continued, "and I'll be your Angel for as long as you wish."

"Pleased to meet you," she said. "Uh . . . where are you?"

"In front of you, just to the left of the door."

She squinted hard. More imagined than really visible, she thought she could just barely see a slight wavering in the air.

"You're looking right at me now," Michael confirmed.

She nodded and looked questioningly at the technician. "Unless you have any more questions, you can leave whenever you wish, Mrs. Lieberman," he said. "You're all set up now."

"Thank you." Taking a deep breath, she turned to the patch of wavering air. "Shall we go, Michael?"

"Whenever you're ready."

The first two hours were the hardest. Mrs. Lieberman had purposely scheduled a shopping trip after her appointment at the Draut Building so that she wouldn't be caught in the awkward position of having to make small talk with a stranger. The plan was only partially effective, though, and several times she'd had to pretend to be studying some random piece of merchandise simply because she'd run out of things to say.

Surprisingly, though—at least to her—Michael turned out to be excellent company. As courteous as the technician had been, he was also witty, intelligent, and well-informed. What with TV and movies, she'd come to associate the word "bodyguard" with a beetle-browed hulk of a man whose IQ equalled his chest measurement. Without even seeming to try, Michael left that stereotype in shreds.

At noon they had lunch—or Mrs. Lieberman did; Michael said he couldn't eat on duty—and spent the early afternoon window-shopping on Fifth Avenue, something she hadn't done in thirty years. She and Michael, they discovered, had similar tastes in jewelry and clothing, though her enthusiasm for hats seemed to baffle him. She drew many a confused stare from passers-by who thought she was talking to herself and then heard the second voice.

All too soon it was three-thirty, and time to head home. "We don't have to go yet, you know," Michael told her.

"I don't want to get caught in rush hour, and I don't suppose you do, either," she said. "You've been remarkably good at sneaking through doors and keeping from getting walked on, but I think a rush-hour bus might be more than even you can handle."

He chuckled. "Very likely. However, you could continue shopping or go to a movie if you wanted to and we could go home when the traffic thins out again."

She shook her head. "No, it'll get dark before we could get home that way. I know you're here, but—I just don't want to today."

"Okay; no problem. Let's find a bus, shall we?"

They reached her complex well ahead of the vehicular flash flood, and Michael escorted her to her apartment door. "Thank you for a wonderful day," she said to him, blushing suddenly as she realized how much she sounded like a teenager on a date.

"The pleasure was mine," Michael responded smoothly.

"Would you like to come in for some tea?"

"Not while I'm on duty, I'm afraid."

"Oh, that's right. Will I see you tomorrow? I mean—well, you know what I mean."

"Call me if you want to go out," he told her. "I won't be right outside your door, but I'll be available on a few minutes' notice. If you need any help at night, by the way, just turn on your neckband. I won't be around, but another Angel is nearby and can come to your aid very quickly."

"All right. Good night, Michael."

"Good night, Mrs. Lieberman. Have a good evening."

It took twelve phone calls just to find someone who knew where Guardian Angels, Inc., was actually located in the Draut Building, and once there Petrie ran into a receptionist who made the PR executive secretary look like a pushover. "I'm sorry, Mr. Petrie, but my instructions are very clear. No names or personal data are to be given out; no interviews with Angels or the technical staff are to be allowed; no tours; nothing. Period."

"Not even a phone interview?"

"Not even. Sorry." She didn't look all that sorry, actually.

"Can you give me even a 'typical Angel' profile or something? Have a heart—my editor will flay me if I don't come back with *something*."

She shook her head. "I can't give you anything but sympathy."

He snorted. "Thanks."

Back in the hallway, Petrie pondered his next move. Obviously, the direct approach was well guarded. But maybe there was a back door. Strolling semi-aimlessly, he soon found a temporarily deserted corridor. Pulling out his phone, he dialed a number.

"Hello?"

"Hi, Boyd; Craig Petrie. You busy?"

"Aw, come on, Petrie, de-access me already. Every time you call I wind up in trouble with somebody."

"Easy, Boyd, this won't ruffle anyone's pinfeathers. All I want is something on Guardian Angels."

"You and everyone else in the world. Sorry, but we've got strict instructions on Angel data; it all stays *here*."

"Hold it a second. All I want is some idea how many Angels Draut's hired, just so I know how big an operation Guardian Angels is going to be. Draut's got good business instincts; I want to see how much he's putting into this."

There was a long pause. "Well ... not for publication?"

"My own personal use only. Guaranteed."

"Double the usual price?"

Petrie grimaced. "Okay."

"All right, I'll see what the personnel records say. Round numbers only, though, and absolutely no names."

"Fine. Call me back."

The return call came a few minutes later. "You're out of luck, Petrie. I can't find any records of anyone being hired as an Angel. Either they're being internally transferred to the job from other parts of the corporation or their hiring is being kept completely separate from our records here. Or both."

"Odd. Where else in Draut Enterprises would you get trained bodyguards to use as Angels?"

"Security men would be the closest thing I can think of, but I couldn't find any record of large numbers of them being hired or transferred. I checked," he added, obviously pleased he'd anticipated Petrie's question.

Petrie gnawed at his cheek. "Any major hiring going on *anywhere*?"

"Oh, sure. Research people, mostly. The Force Beam Applications Division is really burning RAM, I know, but that group's still raking in patents and money, so there's no surprise there. Computer Division's adding staff, too. That tell you anything?"

"Not really. Well, thanks anyway, Boyd."

"Thank me in cash," was Boyd's closing remark.

So Draut wasn't hiring his Angels through his own personnel department. Where in blazes, then, were they coming from? Overseas, perhaps? If Draut was planning some sort of action against the government, there were lots of countries that would be only too willing to help. Or perhaps he was hiring from the ranks of illegal aliens. But then how was he finagling the payroll records, which Personnel should have? Or maybe—

Or maybe there were no Angels at all.

Petrie stopped dead as that thought struck him. It sounded insane ... but why not, really? No one outside the corporation had ever claimed to have touched an invisible Angel, or even to have watched one become invisible. With all communication handled through the neckbands, moreover, it would be easy to simply set up a bunch of men with radios and sensor screens pretending to be Angels—ordinary men, without any special combat training or licenses, who could be hidden almost anywhere among Personnel's files.

But why would Draut do something that crazy?

Petrie couldn't guess the answer to that one, but for the moment he didn't need to. All he needed to do was to make the accusation in his next article. If true, Draut would have a lot of explaining to do. If not, it should at least force the old man to cough up some useful information, something that might give Petrie a clue as to what he was *really* up to. All in all, a fair gamble.

Grinning tightly, Petrie headed for an exit. Charlie, his editor, was going to flip over this one.

"We'd better start for home," Mrs. Lieberman remarked with some regret. It was a lovely afternoon, sunny and warm, and she hated the thought of being cooped up in her apartment all evening.

Michael's sigh was just barely audible. "Mrs. Lieberman, I wish I could convince you that you really don't have to go home this early when I'm with you. I realize you have half a lifetime of habit to overcome, but you really *are* safe with me. I'd hoped that nearly two weeks together would have convinced you of that."

"I know, Michael, I know, and I don't mean to insult you or anything. It's just . . . well, sometimes it's hard to believe you're really *here*. You walk so quietly, never bump into anybody, never touch me on the arm. I guess deep down I'm scared you're just a figment of my imagination."

"I'm sorry," Michael said after a short pause. "I wish I could let you touch me, but I have orders against that."

"Orders?" She'd been assuming he was merely shy. "Why, for heaven's sake?"

"Well," he said, lowering his voice confidentially, "for

all I know you could be a lovely and dangerous Russian spy in disguise, plotting to steal the secret of invisibility. If I let you touch me, you might suddenly spring into action, wrestling me to the ground and beating me into unconsciousness. Then you would spirit me back to Russia where you'd receive a medal and a plush Moscow apartment."

She couldn't help it. The picture that evoked was so absurd that she threw back her head and laughed until she was gasping for breath. "Michael, you're a gem," she said when she got her wind back. "All right, I give up. Let's go to a movie. There's one playing near here that I've been wanting to see for ages."

The sun was low in the sky and the last remnants of rush hour traffic were beginning to clear out when they emerged from the theater. "Where is everybody?" Mrs. Lieberman asked, more to hear herself speak than for information. She had never seen the streets and sidewalks so quiet and it suddenly made her very nervous.

"It's dinner time; most people are eating. Are you hungry?"

"A little, but I'd rather eat at home." Where she could feel safe.

"Okay. Let's go. We can catch a bus a couple of blocks from here."

She had gone almost a block when the muggers came up behind her, and they came so silently she never knew they were there until her arm was suddenly grabbed and her purse torn from her grasp. She turned, pulled off-balance by the hand on her arm, and saw her attackers: two weasel-faced teenaged boys. One was clutching her purse like a prize, but she saw him only with peripheral vision—her full attention was on the boy still holding her arm. His eyes smoldered with hate, and even as she shrank from that glare he raised his free hand to strike her.

The blow never fell. Without warning, his head snapped backward and his grip on her arm was broken. He staggered back and doubled over as something jabbed him in the stomach. The second boy gasped, swore, and turned to run, but he got less than two steps before his legs shot out from under him and he made a painful-sounding landing on the pavement, the purse still in his hand.

It was an amazing sight, so much so that Mrs. Lieberman forgot she was frightened. "Why, Michael," she said. "You really *are* here."

"Of course. I—"

He broke off, and she turned just in time to see the first boy lurching forward, a wicked-looking knife gleaming in his hand. "Call him off, bitch," he gasped, his eyes on her neckband. "Call him off or I'll kill you." The knife slashed upward—

And froze in midair.

She watched in fascination as, against all his strength, the boy's hand was slowly forced down. With a clatter, the knife fell to the ground and flew, as if kicked, a few feet away. In the near distance a siren could be heard.

"I alerted the police," Michael explained. "I'm afraid we'll have to wait here until they arrive. Are you hurt?"

"No, I'm fine. And I don't mind waiting." Mrs. Lieberman retrieved her hat, which had fallen off during the attack. Dusting it off, she took a moment to glance at the sky. Some of the clouds were already turning pink; it was going to be a glorious sunset. "I'm not in any hurry," she added.

Hands jammed into pockets not really designed for such abuse, Petrie strode along in the late-morning sunshine, heading back from his latest defeat at the Draut Building and glowering at the world. He hated making a fool of himself—and four weeks after the fact, he still hadn't forgiven Draut's Angels for their rotten timing. Of all possible days for them to grab the headlines, they had *had* to pick the day he was submitting his story about them for Charlie's approval. No fewer than three separate attacks within a twenty-four-hour period had been stopped by the Angels, their elderly charges escaping unscathed. Naturally, this had had the side effect of turning Petrie's story into instant scrap paper, and an angry

Charlie had hauled him onto the carpet the next morning for a canned lecture on proper research methods. He'd then shredded the story, of course.

Petrie had jumped the gun, obviously; he admitted as much, and had tried for a month now to rectify the error. But every approach still ended at either a dead end or a locked door. It was as if Guardian Angels, Inc., had brought Daedalus in as consultant on its corporate structure planning.

Which did nothing to ease Petrie's suspicions. Draut hadn't built this hermetically sealed labyrinth for the fun of it. The apparent proof that invisible Angels actually existed simply looped things back to the original question: what was Draut really up to?

He was picking at the issue for the twelve millionth time when he happened to glance down a cross street he was passing. Halfway down the block a well-dressed young man was talking earnestly with an elderly woman. In the man's hand was an object that looked suspiciously like a Guardian Angel neckband.

Without a pause, Petrie turned down the street toward them. Waiting until he was just within earshot he dropped his comb, and spent a few seconds retrieving it. The man and woman kept their voices low, but Petrie's hearing was good.

"But it doesn't really work, does it?" the woman asked in an asthmatic voice.

"Course not: not for five bucks. But who's to know? It's like a 'beware of the dog' sign without a dog."

Picking up his comb, Petrie continued on his way until he reached the corner. He looked back then and saw both people heading toward the street he had just come from. The man was the faster and had already nearly reached the corner. Petrie hurried after him, afraid of losing him in the crowds. The old woman, he noted in passing, was wearing the neckband.

Petrie followed the man for nearly two hours as he traced a winding path through the city's streets. During that time he accosted nearly a score of old people, six of whom stopped to listen to him. Two of those bought neckbands.

Finally, just before one-thirty, the man's pace quickened and the aimlessness of his direction vanished. Walking a few blocks, he disappeared into one of the side doors of the Draut Building.

Petrie halted across the street, head spinning. It was, almost literally, the last place in the state he would have guessed the man was heading for. And he wasn't just a casual visitor, either; from experience Petrie knew those side doors admitted only authorized personnel. But why would Draut's people be peddling fake Angel neckbands on the streets? As a private black-market scheme it was petty in the extreme; as official corporation practice it made no sense whatsoever.

Unless. . . .

The faintest hint of an ugly thought began to touch Petrie's mind. It was almost ludicrous, but it fit all the facts . . . and if true, it was a blockbuster.

Except that at the moment he had nothing to back up his suspicions. And if he touched the wrong nerves digging that proof out, he could find himself inhabiting a deep hole in the ground.

The thought was both sobering and infuriating, and it made his decision for him. He wouldn't give the corporation time to react, but would confront Draut himself and try to force a confession from him. Prying himself from the wall where he'd been leaning, Petrie set off down the street, glancing once at his watch. There would be just enough time.

It was nearly five when he returned to the Draut Building, and this time he didn't allow secretaries or receptionists to stop him, much to their collective consternation. He was barely one jump ahead of Security when he strode into Draut's outer office.

The secretary there was surprised but unflustered. "Yes?" she asked coolly.

"I want to see Draut," Petrie told her. "Tell him I know about Guardian Angels and the twin fraud he's running with it, and that I'd like to talk with him before I blow it up in his face."

Four burly security guards came charging in before the secretary could reply. One of them had grabbed Petrie in a no-nonsense aikido hold and was marching him toward the door when a voice came from the intercom. "Ms. Smith, please ask the young man to step into my office."

The guards froze in disbelief but, at a nod from Ms. Smith, reluctantly released him. Taking a deep breath, Petrie pushed open the heavy mahogany doors and entered Draut's private office.

The room was roughly the size of a miniature golf course, and was all leather, oriental tapestry, deep-pile rug, and dark wood. One entire wall was floor-to-ceiling windows with a spectacular view of the city below. In the center of the room, standing next to a huge desk, was Draut. "Good afternoon," he said as Petrie hesitated. "You wished to see me?"

Petrie stepped forward, determined not to be intimidated by the surroundings. "My name is Petrie, Mr. Draut. Before I begin I want to warn you that I've given sealed letters to five friends which outline the accusations I'm about to make. If I don't retrieve those letters by eight this evening their contents will be made public."

Draut smiled faintly. "Not very original, but certainly melodramatic."

Petrie ignored the comment. "I've wondered for several weeks about your motives and purposes in setting up Guardian Angels, and I've come to the conclusion that the whole thing is a fraud. Not only are there *no* invisible people for you to rent out, but you have the colossal gall to peddle fake neckbands to old people who think there's really somebody around to protect them."

"Of course there're no invisible men," Draut shrugged. "The concept was proved impossible decades ago."

Petrie had expected a denial. Draut's casual admission threw him off his stride, and he fumbled a bit in getting out his next words. "You've got people somewhere in the city using phased force beams, right? Using the neckband sensors to aim the things?"

Draut nodded. "They operate from a handful of centers scattered throughout the area. With sophisticated military targeting equipment, of course, the beams can be most effective in simulating the actions of an 'invisible man.'" Something in Petrie's face must have mirrored his thoughts, because Draut's mouth twitched in another faint smile. "I'm not telling you all this because I have a trusting soul and you have honest eyes, Mr. Craig Arnold Petrie of Wynne, Arkansas," he said. "You've been buzzing around this building like a hornet for almost two months now and I've had you thoroughly checked out. You seem to me like a man who can probably be trusted with the whole story but not half of it."

"If you're trusting me to keep quiet about this chicanery, you're a lousy judge of character. I'm writing the story, and the minute it breaks you and Guardian Angels will be finished." All of Petrie's anger had evaporated in the past few moments, leaving only disgust in its place. He'd had visions of a diabolical plot against nations and had found, instead, a petty con game. He'd expected more from J. Thaddeus Draut.

"Finished?" Draut shook his head. "No. In fact, we've hardly started. Next week we're beginning new testing operations in Chicago, Pittsburgh, Detroit, and Cleveland."

"What are you talking about? You try leasing 'invisible' bodyguards now and the FTC will—"

"Who said anything about leasing anything to anybody? Those test centers will be just like the one here, giving free Angel service to some of the poor and elderly."

Petrie blinked. "*What?*"

"As I said, you need the whole story. The so-called 'testing phase' is all there is to Guardian Angels, Inc. The rest of the noise we've been making about it was just for publicity purposes, to make sure everyone knew about it."

An uncomfortable suspicion was beginning to creep up on Petrie. "Wait a minute. Are you trying to tell me you're running some sort of charity protection racket? What on Earth for?"

Draut looked him in the eye for a long moment, then dropped his gaze. "I could tell you about my childhood in Cleveland, I suppose. Or about the time my mother and sister had their purses stolen—but I'll just say I'm doing it because it needs to be done. For decades the poor and elderly have been at the mercy of both criminals and those who simply want to take out their frustrations on someone else. No one's done anything about the problem because the government can't afford it and there's no profit in it for anyone else. So okay. I've got money I don't need, and I'm taking a crack at it. Maybe it won't work, but maybe it will. I think it's worth a try, anyway."

Petrie thought about that for a moment. "Why the fiction about invisible men? Why not the truth?"

"Partly publicity, as I said earlier. We needed to make sure potential muggers were aware of us and could associate the neckbands with our Angels. That's the main reason we made the neckbands so big and obvious."

"A deterrent."

"Of course. And secondly, there's a strong psychological kick this way. You tell your average punk that someone two miles away is fiddling knobs on a pair of phased force beam generators and he might take his chances. But tell him there's an invisible man waiting to clobber him?" Draut shook his head.

"Yeah. And the fake neckbands—additional deterrent?"

"Sure. You can't tell them from the working ones, and nobody knows where those are—we made sure of that. And we'll be adding real ones every so often and shifting others around, just to keep things uncertain."

Petrie nodded. Taking a deep breath, he expelled it in an audible sigh. "It won't last, you know, even if you convince me to sit on the story. One of your own people will leak it, or another reporter will figure it out eventually."

"I know that. But the longer we maintain the facade and the more attacks are beaten off, the more confidence people will have in us. I'm hoping that when the lid comes off it won't matter much because we'll have proved we can do the job. My people won't talk; they're all carefully screened, highly idealistic young people who believe in what they're doing. So I guess it's up to you and your colleagues."

"I'll have to think about it."

"Do so." Draut urged. "And while you're deciding I suggest you take a walk through Central Park. Count the number of people there—*real* people, not just muggers. Observe how already they cluster near someone wearing an Angel neckband, and remember that even two months ago none of those people would have dared to go near the place. Good evening, Mr. Petrie."

The trip through the halls and down the elevators took several minutes, and once outside the range of Draut's personality Petrie again began to have doubts. Good motives or not, Draut *was* lying to the public. Didn't they have a right to know that?

He left the building, and as he did so an old woman in a strange-looking hat and an Angel neckband caught his eye. She was walking toward him, her lips moving as if talking to someone, though he couldn't hear her words through the din of traffic. She was nearly abreast of him when she noticed him watching her. Smiling pleasantly at him as she passed, she continued her conversation, and he caught a few of the words: ". . . and I promised Mrs. Finch we'd take her along to the park, Michael— don't let me forget . . ."

Petrie made his decision. The hell with Draut's suggested stroll through Central Park; he had work to do. There were five envelopes he had to pick up before eight o'clock. Turning, he hurried down the street.

EXPANDED CHARTER

The summons to the Secret Service chief's office had come with the kind of low-key urgency Alex Cord had long since learned to recognize, and from the look on Hale's face he knew the problem was indeed a big one. "Assassin?" he hazarded as he slid into a chair.

Hale nodded grimly. "The FBI called it in five minutes ago—CRIMESTOP gives it a ninety-eight percent probability. The full data pack should be—ah; here it comes."

One of the screens on his desk had lit up with a photo of a scrawny-looking man in his late twenties. Joe Crowly, the ID read. Cord raised his left wrist, pushed a button on the tiny computer strapped there, and felt the answering vibration as the device began recording the data the desktop unit was feeding it. "We know where and when this guy Crowly's going to try it?"

"Pretty sure." Hale pushed a button and Crowly's face was replaced by some names and numbers. "He was in Seattle this morning and somehow got access to the

239

Bounzer Tube there. I guess he didn't realize the thing keeps records."

"Or didn't give a damn." Cord frowned. "Kansas City. The President's old school?"

"Bingo," Hale said heavily. "Some kind of big ceremony—not a dedication; I forget what it's called. The mayor will be there and I think the governor of Missouri, too."

"Election-year politicking."

"By any other name," Hale agreed. "CRIMESTOP thinks Crowly's going to claim he was actually aiming for the mayor and hit the President by mistake."

"You're sure he *is* after the President? That computer's been wrong before."

"I think it's pretty clear. That Welfare Reform Act he signed yesterday? Crowly's been fighting passionately against it for the past two years. We have a witness who says Crowly was acting like a madman last night, and was still going strong when he left her this morning."

Cord grimaced. "Great. Got a team in place?"

"Yes, but I want you to go there and take charge. You're one of the best there is at this kind of operation."

"Okay." Why, Cord thought, did the compliments *always* come glued to the real chestnut-roasters? "I'll do my best."

He stopped at the locker room to change and then picked up a gun from the armory on his way downstairs to the Bounzer Tube facilities. The techs there had already been given the proper coordinates, and he was able to step into the giant steel test-tube without delay. Three minutes later the curved wall vanished and he found himself across the street from a modest three-story brick building that was already beginning to collect a fair-sized crowd.

"Cord?"

Cord turned to see a sloppy-looking man leaning against a street light a few feet away. "Right," he acknowledged, stepping closer.

"Dietrich. You bring us any good pictures?"

"Complete set." Cord held his wrist up and displayed

the face he'd seen in Hale's office. "Didn't they send you any?"

"Yeah, but the transmission was lousy and I didn't want to trust it." The other reached down and tapped the record key on his own computer. "You cut things a little fine—we've got maybe five minutes before the motorcade arrives."

"I didn't have much of a choice," Cord glanced at the still-growing crowd. "Crowly's taking a chance on getting torn apart with that smokescreen about aiming for the mayor."

"Better than going up on a federal assassination charge." Dietrich nodded past the school building. "I've got my men positioned where they can theoretically see everywhere in the crowd and also watch all approaches. There's a robot scanner on the school roof keeping watch on the windows in the surrounding buildings. Two men are on the President directly, of course."

Cord nodded. "I think I'll start mingling, then; see if our man isn't standing quietly behind someone taller in the crowd. See you later—and make sure your men get that clearer picture."

"Already sent it. Beep if you need help."

Cord set off across the street, eyes giving the edges of the crowd a quick check. It was too bad that robot scanners weren't capable of good identification in crowds this densely packed; but they weren't, and there wasn't anything he could do about it. Pausing once, he surreptitiously raised his computer and had it rotate Crowly's picture for him, letting him see what the potential assassin looked like from all directions. Then, conscious of the pistol nestled beneath his left arm, he continued on.

Ahead, a car pulled to a rapid halt in front of the school building. Cord looked up, but it was just a TV crew, running ahead of the main cars to get their minicams in position. He kept moving, forcing his eyes to maintain their methodical sweep. Panicking was the worst thing that an agent could do at a time like this.

There was a swell of anticipation from the crowd and a long black limousine pulled smoothly to the curb.

The mayor got out first, waving and smiling at the people as his bodyguards took positions flanking the door. Behind him the governor wriggled out of the seat, his bulk making the operation look awkward. From the school's front door a group of children appeared—an honor guard of sorts, Cord decided—and walked two by two toward the waiting dignitaries. Cord craned his neck for one last sweep . . . and spotted Crowly.

He was, almost exactly as Cord had predicted, peering out from behind a taller, bulkier bystander on the far side of the crowd. His right hand was buried in a side coat pocket, his face a mask of hatred and fear. He leaned out a bit further, edging between two others for a clearer view.

Cord fired.

Nothing spectacular happened at his end, of course; Secret Service weapons were totally silent and flashless. At Crowly's end . . . well, someone paying close attention might have noticed the slight jerk caused by the impacting capsule, or the look of pure terror that erupted on the young man's face and was quickly frozen in place. The tiny jerking motions as he tried to tear free of the "living plastic" film that was rapidly overgrowing him were too small even to bother those standing beside him.

He was just starting to lose his balance when Dietrich's men appeared on either side of him and carried him quietly out of the crowd.

"Well, chalk up another one for the good guys," Dietrich commented as they watched Crowly being loaded into a car a hundred feet away from the unnoticing crowd. The plastic over Crowly's nose and around his rib cage had been removed to let him breathe, but even at their distance Cord could see that the terrified expression was still plastered across his face.

"I suppose so," he told Dietrich. "We got Crowly without causing any fuss, if that's what you mean. But if we were doing our jobs *really* properly he'd never have gotten to the Bounzer Tube in the first place."

Dietrich shrugged. "You can't hold back the tide with

your hands," he said philosophically. "Progress is progress and you can't stop it. Who knows? If they ever get the fine-tune bugs worked out of the method, the Bounzer Tube might actually make our jobs easier."

Cord shrugged, and his eyes strayed to the ceremonies still taking place on the school's front walk. The mayor was shaking hands with each of the children in the honor guard now, and Cord couldn't help but notice the natural dignity one of the boys displayed, the ease with which he faced the politicians. *Even at the age of nine he looks presidential*, he thought. *I wonder if he's decided yet on his life's ambition.* "Maybe it will, someday," he said aloud to Dietrich. "But it'll never be as easy as in the old days, when we only had to protect a President *after* he was elected." He shook his head. "I wish to hell Bounzer had never invented his damn time-travel machine."

FINAL SOLUTION

Narda Jalal had finished her solitary dinner and was starting go load the dishes into the sonic cleaner when the kitchen radio reached its five-thirty timer setting and switched on.

"... Five-thirty world news survey. The Hasar Council of Ministers has officially rejected the demand by the Lorikhan Nation that the minerals of the Enhoav Basin be divided evenly among all the nations of Kohinoor. Supreme Minister Zagro has said repeatedly that, since Hasar provided ninety percent of the technology and funding used to crack the mantle fault three years ago, the bulk of the project's rewards should be ours. Lorikhan's threat of war over this issue is dismissed by the government as mere bluff. The Prima of Missai, meanwhile, has offered his nation's good services as mediator—"

"Radio control: off," Narda called. Obediently, the radio fell silent. Brushing a strand of hair from her face,

Narda stared through the dishes by the sink, her teeth clenched with abnormal tightness. So that was it. Three years of negotiation had ended without anyone budging a single centimeter, and once more the threat of war hung like a weapons satellite over Kohinoor, circling and waiting to drop. And this time it wouldn't be just a local flare-up over borders or water rights. The Enhoav Basin, that tremendous treasure house of minerals torn forcibly from Kohinoor's molten insides, was a potential Juggernaut in a world economy where even copper was selling for over a hundred ryal per kilo. For the riches of Enhoav all the nations would fight. *All* of them.

"Oh, God, please," Narda half-groaned, half-prayed. "Not another world war. Please."

It seemed impossible to her that a single world could have so much war, especially a world with Kohinoor's history. Its founders had left Earth for the express purpose of *escaping* warfare and conflict. They'd been men and women of peace, if the history disks could be believed; visionaries who believed there was a better way. What had gone wrong?

A motion across the street caught her eye. Looking through the window, she saw their neighbor Mehlid step from his door, easel and paints in tow, and head toward the row of hills a few hundred meters behind his house. He was a large man, surprisingly well-built for an artist. Narda watched him as he walked away, thinking of the long, sensitive fingers that seemed so out of place with those broad shoulders—

With a sharp shake of her head she tore her eyes away, a hot rush of guilt flooding her face with blood. She had never been unfaithful to her husband, and she knew with absolute certainty that she never would. Why then did she find herself watching Mehlid so often, and with such interest? It was wrong—wrong and uncomfortably juvenile—and yet she couldn't stop.

A surge of anger flowed in to cover the guilt. It was Pahli's fault, she told herself blackly; Pahli's and the military's. If they would just let the *Susa* stay on patrol around Kohinoor instead of sending it out on so many deep-space surveys, she would have a man around the house more often. Pahli didn't *have* to keep accepting these assignments, either.

No. She was being unfair, and she knew it. At least some of the tension on Kohinoor was due to the lack of new frontiers, to the general feeling that there was nowhere else to go. None of the other twenty-eight bodies in Kohinoor's system was habitable, and the grand experiment with orbiting space colonies had been horribly and tragically ended two wars ago. If Pahli and his crew ever found a suitable world out there, the results would be well worth one woman's minor inconvenience. On the heels of that thought came another, more sobering one: if world war broke out the first battles would be fought in space . . . and even small ships like the *Susa* would be prime targets.

With an effort, Narda pushed her fears from her mind. The news survey would be over now, and some music would help her mood. "Radio control: on," she called. she was in luck; they were playing something soft and peaceful. Picking up one of the dirty dishes, she sent an involuntary glance through the window. Good; Mehlid was out of sight. He was easy to ignore when not visible. Placing the dish in the cleaner's rack, she thought about Pahli. What was he doing now, she wondered . . . and was he thinking of her?

Pahli Jalal's thoughts were, in fact, a dozen light-years from his wife. Specifically, they were on the massive object some fifty thousand kilometers off the *Susa*'s starboard bow.

"No chance that it belongs to Lorikhan or any of the others, is there?" he asked Ahmar, his aide, as he studied the image on the telescope screens.

"None, sir." Peering at his bank of displays, Ahmar touched a button and then shook his head. "Completely unknown configuration and space-normal drive spectrum. Scanner Section reports their star drive probably works on the same principles as ours, but it's definitely not a standard Burke system." He glanced at the commander. "Are we going to make contact?"

Before Pahli could answer, the helmsman spoke up. "Commander, it's changing course—coming toward us!"

"Looks like the decision's been made," Pahli said to Ahmar.

"We could attack, sir, or even run," First Office Cyrilis pointed out. "Or both; we could fire a torpedo salvo and be gone before they even knew the missiles were on the way."

Pahli and Ahmar exchanged glances, and Pahli felt his jaw tighten momentarily. Fight or run—it was always the same reaction to every problem. When, he wondered, would humanity learn to solve conflicts with understanding and mutual respect instead of with animal reflexes? "Recommendation noted, Lieutenant. We'll hold orbit here and see what they want."

"Yes, sir. Recommend we put weapons stations on full alert anyway, Commander. Just in case."

Eyes still on the screens, Pahli waved an impatient hand. "All right. See to it."

Cyrilis saluted and floated across to the main intercom board. *Sotto voce*, Ahmar said, "I hope he doesn't blow them out of the sky before they even have a chance to say hello."

Pahli shrugged. "I wouldn't worry about that. He's got better combat nerves than either of us."

"Commander!" the scanner chief reported suddenly. "UV laser hitting us; coming from the other ship. Low-power, too diffuse to be a weapon. It seems to be frequency-modulated."

Pahli threw a tight smile at Ahmar. "I think they've said hello. Get a recorder on that laser and turn Cryptography's computers loose on it. I think there's also a package of basic language instruction on file, isn't there?"

Ahmar nodded. "Disk file Ninety-three something, for opening communication in case another Earth ship ever came out here."

"Start beaming it across with one of our own communication lasers. It'll prove we're interested in talking, even if they can't understand any of the tape."

The unknown ship took up a parallel course some five hundred kilometers from the *Susa*; and for six hours the two ships did a slow promenade as the lasers continued their information exchange. And it was the unknown, not the *Susa*, that solved its puzzle first.

"I greet you, Human," the bridge speaker boomed out in a voice like flat gray paint. "I am called Drymnu."

The words seemed to echo through Pahli's head. It was indeed as he'd half-expected: no tenth-generation human ship, but a truly alien craft. Kohinoor's first contact with another race ... With as much poise as he could manage, he touched the proper button on his board. "Drymnu ship, greetings," he said, his mouth dry. "This is Commander Pahli Jalal of the starship *Susa*, servant to the Hasar Nation. Have I the privilege of addressing your captain?"

"This concept is one of many I do not understand," came the reply. "Your language does not follow a familiar pattern, and I am surely making grave errors in my interpretation."

The alien's abruptness took Pahli aback somewhat. "Well, we'll be happy to assist as much as possible," he said, motioning to Ahmar. The aide had anticipated him, and was already tying Cryptography into the conversation. "Please explain the problem."

"First, I appear to have found more than one way to address you: *Human*, *Commander Pahli Jalal*, and *Hasar Nation*. Which is correct, or do I misread? In a congruent manner, which reference word is correct: *you*, *him*, or *her*? And how do *I* and *we* correspond?"

Pahli frowned. "All the words are correct in different contexts. 'You' refers to a person being addressed or spoken to, while 'him' and 'her' are used when speaking of a third person."

There was a pause as the other seemed to digest that. "But does third person not refer to a separate entity not part of oneself? Surely there is insufficient space in your craft for two of you to exist."

Pahli cut himself out of the circuit and turned to Cyrilis, who was peering over the scanner chief's shoulder. "Just how big *is* this alien, anyway?" he asked.

The other hunched his shoulders. "Several thousand of us could fit comfortably aboard that ship. He can't be *that* big—square-cube laws would never have let him evolve. We've got to be misunderstanding him."

Pahli nodded and touched the switch again. "We also seem to be misreading," he said. "We are all of one *species*, but there are over one hundred eighty *persons* aboard this craft. Does that help?"

"This is not po*sheliz-scsit-khe-fzeee*—" The speaker squealed unintelligibly for a second and then cut off sharply.

"What was *that*?" Ahmar whispered.

"I don't know. I must have said something wrong," Pahli answered. "Cyrilis, put all defense systems on full alert." The other nodded, and a tense silence descended on the bridge.

When the break came it was almost an anticlimax. "You are a fragmented race," the speaker said, once again in a flat monotone. "Each of your members is distinct from the others. Is this true?"

A strange shiver ran down Pahli's spine. The implications of such a question . . . "Yes, that's true. I, uh, take it you're different?"

"I am one. Aboard this craft is a single mind, a single purpose, with eighteen thousand two hundred twenty-six physiologically distinct units. Never before has a fragmented race survived its intraspecies warfare to reach the stars. That has always been impossible. Where are you from, and how have you accomplished this?"

A surrealistic picture flashed across Pahli's mind: the alien ship transformed into a giant beehive, its corridors filled with buzzing insects. He shook the vision out of his mind and again cut off the link. "Ahmar, do we have a mistranslation here?"

"Doesn't look like it, sir. Cryptography reports that the grammatical structure of the Drymnu language seems compatible with this sort of hive mind thing they're describing." He shook his head. "A hive mind. I've read about such things, but only in fiction. To actually *find* one . . ." He trailed off, still shaking his head.

"Commander," Cyrilis called from across the bridge, "the Drymnu's last question is a potentially dangerous one. I don't think we should tell them—it—anything about Kohinoor."

Pahli nodded slowly. That burst of emotion when the alien realized the nature of humanity could have been surprise, fear, or hatred. Best to err on the cautious side. "No problem. I'll tell him about Earth. Even if he could find it, it's too far away to bother with." If it hadn't blown itself out of existence by now and saved any hostile aliens the trouble, he added silently. On Earth, even more than on Kohinoor, problems were solved with animal reflexes.

Thumbing the switch, he settled more comfortably into his chair and began telling the strange creature called Drymnu about the equally strange creature called Man.

The sun was just setting behind the tall buildings of Missai Gem when the formation of six fighter jets streaked by overhead, heading south toward the Missai-Baijan border. A handful of grain still clutched in his hand, Shapur Nain looked up as they were briefly framed by the city park's trees. He twisted his head to follow them with his eyes, feeling the initial tension drain from his old body. Only a single wing, and not climbing with anything near attack speed, unless his eyes were failing as fast as his legs. That meant it was only a routine patrol, or perhaps that the border forces were being beefed up. The war with Baijan hadn't started. Not yet, anyway.

He watched the jets vanish into the distance and then turned back to the birds and small animals milling around his bench. Tossing them the grain, he watched with interest as members of the different species jockeyed for position. The scavenger rusinh, armed with needle-sharp ridges on beak and wing coverts, had all the obvious physical advantages over the relatively defenseless tree-mice. To compensate, the furry mammals had developed a strategy where two of them would distract a rusinh with lightning-fast feints while a third made off with some of the grain. Each threesome worked in rotation, giving all its members a chance at the food.

Cooperation—that was the secret of survival. Tossing out another handful, Shapur wondered if mankind would ever learn that lesson. He tended to doubt it. Kohinoor had started with the cleanest sheet humanity had ever had—and what had they done with it? The legends said Earth had been worse, but Shapur no longer really believed that. Three wars in his lifetime alone, including one world war . . . his left leg throbbed with the memory. And now this Enhoav Basin problem could close the books on the whole thing permanently. Emotions and rhetoric were running high and hot, especially between Hasar and Lorikhan, and there were no signs that either side was ready to back down.

Shapur shook his head in frustration. Even he, who'd been pretty well cured of foolish nationalistic sentiments by his wartime experiences, had found himself being caught up by the polarizing forces around him. Logically, he could agree that Hasar was entitled to the rewards of its billion-ryal gamble—but the Hasarans were so damned *insolent* about it! And as for Missai playing mediator, that was laughable in the extreme. With the water-rights issue at the southern border on the verge of boiling over again, Prima Simin had little credibility as a peacemaker even among his own people, let alone the rest of Kohinoor.

The shadows of evening had fallen across him, and Shapur shivered with the sudden chill. His bag of grain was nearly empty now; scattering the remaining kernels, he waited until the birds and animals had finished their feeding. Then, grasping the cane that rested against the bench beside him, he got carefully to his feet. For a moment he stood there, waiting stoically for the sudden agony in his leg to subside. Then, keeping the use of the cane to a minimum, he began the slow walk to the edge of the park and his apartment a block away. Someday, he thought, they'd come up with a genuine pain-regulating prosthesis and he wouldn't have to go through this every time he wanted to stand up.

Glancing south, he again shivered. Prosthesis research was always strong during wars.

The preliminary reports were all in, and most of the senior officers had left the *Susa*'s briefing room to continue their work. Only First Officer Cyrilis remained behind, seated quietly at the small table. "Something else on your mind?" Pahli asked, collecting the report disks into a neat pile in front of him.

"Yes, sir. I want to know why you refused my suggestion earlier that we disable the alien ship when we had the chance. We had the drive units pinpointed; a single seeker torpedo in each would have—"

"Would have been a totally unwarranted act of aggression," Pahli interrupted him stiffly. "What did you want to do, start an interplanetary war? Don't we have enough trouble on Kohinoor as it is?"

"It's precisely because of our problems on Kohinoor that I made the suggestion. It may or may not have occurred to you, Commander, but the Drymnu ship presents us with a rare opportunity. Even a partial mastery of an alien technology could give the Hasar Nation a vital military edge over our enemies."

"I don't recall the Drymnu offering us any of their technology. In fact, it seemed to me that they were inordinately eager to get away from us, and weren't in any mood to open trade relations."

Cyrilis shook his head impatiently. "I wasn't suggesting we beg or barter for the items we could use."

"I know what you were suggesting. Ignoring the moral issue for a moment, suppose we'd attacked and found them better armed than we thought?"

"The *Susa*'s a warship. It's our job to take risks when necessary."

Pahli was suddenly tired of this conversation. "Well, the subject's academic now, anyway. The Drymnu's gone, and we can't follow him."

"Yes, we can." Standing up, Cyrilis walked over to

Pahli, moving with practiced ease in the tenth-gee the *Susa*'s rotation was providing. "I took the liberty of launching two sensor drones a few hours before the alien left. We got his para-Cerenkov rainbow from three directions." He handed Pahli a disk. "Here are his course and speed figures."

Pahli took the disk mechanically, looking up at the lieutenant with new eyes. To do something like that without Pahli's permission skated uncomfortably close to insubordination.

"I'd guess we have no more than a couple of hours to give chase before he gets too far ahead of us," Cyrilis continued. For a moment he locked eyes with his commander. "The decision is yours, of course. I trust you won't take too long about it." Saluting, he left the room.

Pahli was still seated at the table, fingering the disk, when Ahmar came in. "I just saw Lieutenant Cyrilis heading toward the bridge, looking like an angry jinn. What did you say to him?"

Pahli brought his gaze back from infinity and focused on his aide. "Actually, he did most of the talking. He thinks we should go after the Drymnu, blow him to bits, and then take any of his equipment that's still in one piece."

Ahmar shook his head. "Thank God he's not in charge. And how does he expect to find the Drymnu again? It's a big universe, you know."

"Not big enough," Pahli displayed the disk. "He got the specs for the Drymnu's first flight segment."

Ahmar blinked in surprise. "Did you authorize that, sir?"

"Of course not." Pahli tossed the disk onto the table. "Unfortunately, he's got a good point. Command *will* want to know why we didn't at least try to barter for some of the Drymnu's technology."

"And why didn't you?"

"Same reason Cyrilis wants the stuff, only in reverse. Kohinoor's poised on a knife edge already. I don't want to be the one to push it off by introducing more weapons into the equation."

Ahmar nodded agreement. "But I suppose rational thought like that would be lost on a fire-breather like the lieutenant."

"Oh, don't be too hard on him. He's a man of war, and from his viewpoint I probably *am* an inferior commander. On top of that, I suspect he's suddenly realized why the *Susa* spends so much time away on these planetary search missions."

Ahmar cocked his head slightly. "Because you're a man of peace?"

Pahli grimaced. "I'm sure Command thinks more in terms of 'lost nerve.' But you're right; I don't think they really trust me too close to the Kohinoor war zone. Cyrilis probably thinks serving under me will reflect badly on his record because of that."

For a moment Ahmar was silent. Then, nodding at the disk, he asked, "So what are you going to do?"

Slowly, Pahli picked up the disk. "I've been thinking, Ahmar. Maybe Cyrilis is right—maybe the Drymnu *does* have something we can use back on Kohinoor. I think we should have another talk together."

Ahmar's jaw sagged slightly. "You're not *serious*. Commander, you don't have to give in to any of this pressure—"

"No, my mind's made up." Abruptly, Pahli got to his feet and handed his aide the disk. "Take this to the bridge and feed the data into the helm. Cyrilis will be up there; tell him to kill the spin and secure for hyperspace. I want the Burke drive firing in fifteen minutes."

Ahmar tried twice before he could get the words out. "As you command, sir." He backed a few steps toward the door, his eyes never leaving Pahli's face. "Sir, are you sure—?"

"Fifteen minutes."

Turning, Ahmar fled the room.

Pahli permitted himself a tight smile as he moved more leisurely toward the door. So Cyrilis wanted technological treasures from the Drymnu, did he? Well, perhaps he would get more treasure than he'd bargained for. A *lot* more.

*   *   *

Flat on his stomach in the dirt, Ruhl Tras poked his head cautiously over the crest of the hill. "There they are!" he whispered to the crop-haired girl beside him. "Must be a zillion Hasar-devils out there!"

"You think we got enough soldiers?" she whispered back, raising the snout of her Flash-Back rifle to point at the imaginary army below.

"Sure," he told her confidently as he brought his own weapon to bear. His wasn't nearly as neat as hers—it was at least two years old and the batteries were running low—but his initial embarrassment over it always disappeared once the game got going. Raising his head higher, he looked to either side and gave the signal. Instantly the hills erupted with a cacophony of whistles, screams, and clicks as a half dozen different guns began going off, accompanied by enthusiastic shouts and yells. Jumping to his feet, his own machine gun clacking away, Ruhl gave a war-whoop and charged down the hill, blasting away enemies as he ran. The others weren't far behind him, but his head start got him to the enemy camp first, and it was Ruhl who raised his gun high and brought it sweeping down to kill the last enemy soldier. "Death to Hasar!" he shouted.

And then all the others charged together behind and into him, laughing and shooting into the air and raining curses down upon the Hasar-devils. In the midst of it all a clear voice intruded, carried on the light breeze: "Ru-u-uhl! Lunchtime!"

"Aw," Ruhl groaned reflexively. Raising his voice, he called, "Okay, Mom!"

"I'd better go, too," one of the others said.

"Yeah, me too," someone else seconded. "Can everybody come back after lunch?"

"I gotta go to the doctor's," the girl with the Flash-Back said disgustedly. "Maybe I'll get back early, though."

"Can I borrow your gun while you're there?" Ruhl asked eagerly, before anyone else could get the same idea.

"Well . . . okay." She handed it over. "But you be careful with it, or else."

"Ruhl!" the clear voice came again.

"Coming! See you guys later."

Clutching the Flash-Back rifle tightly, Ruhl trotted over the hill again, heading for home. He couldn't remember ever having such a fun summer vacation. There was an excitement in the air, both at home and in the village streets, with the news playing marching music and showing warjets and even spaceships flying by in formation. He just wished Lorikhan would hurry up and attack Hasar, so they could get back the Enhoav Basin that the Hasar-devils had stolen. *Then* he'd get to see some *really* neat stuff.

Grinning, he bounded up the steps of his house and barreled through the door. If he ate fast he could be back on the battlefield in half an hour.

Cyrilis's numbers gave the speed and direction the Drymnu had taken when it entered hyperspace, but of course there was no way to predict how far the alien ship would go before dropping back to normal space. Working on the assumption the alien would be more interested in the solar systems along or near its path than in the emptiness of interplanetary space, Pahli brought the *Susa* out of hyperspace at the first system along the projected path.

They were in luck. "Para-Cerenkov radiation, Commander," the scanner chief reported within minutes of their arrival. "Intensity indicates we're only an hour or two behind him."

Which was practically on top of him, considering it had been a ten-day trip. "Full-region scan," Pahli ordered. "I want that ship located as soon as possible."

"If it's still here," Cyrilis said.

It was. The search took three hours, but they finally found the alien's space-normal drive spectrum near a gas giant in the outer system. Five hours after that the *Susa* was in close-communication range.

"Why have you followed me?" the Drymnu asked after

Pahli had identified himself. "I wish no contact with you."

"Why not?" Pahli asked. "We have no hostile intentions toward you."

"That is a logical contradiction. You are a fragmented species—by definition you are hostile toward all other forms of life. You are a blight upon the universe, and unfit to commune with the other intelligences."

"So you consider us violent, do you?" Pahli asked interestedly, his eyes on one of his displays. "I take it you are more peaceful?"

"I am at peace with myself, and do not make war upon other species."

A light flashed on Pahli's display; the torpedo room was ready. "That's good, because it gives me hope that you can help solve our problem. Our world is currently threatened with war—"

"Then perhaps you will yet correct the error that has occurred," the Drymnu said. "Your self-extermination should have taken place long before you reached the stars. This conversation can serve no purpose. Do not attempt to follow me again."

"You will at least listen to my request," Pahli's tone made it clear it wasn't a question. "If you attempt to energize your drive we will destroy it. Our torpedoes are already locked on target."

There was a long silence, and when the Drymnu spoke again its flat voice was infused with bitterness. "As I said—a hostile and violent species."

"True. It's for this reason we need your help."

"I will die, and all the other segments of the Drymnu too, before I help you in your destructive path."

"That's not the sort of help I want." Pahli braced himself mentally and took the plunge. "I want you to help us become a hive mind like you yourself are."

Ahmar spun around, his face a mirror of surprise. Across the bridge Cyrilis's expression was similar, but shading rapidly toward alarm. Keeping an eye on his first officer, Pahli said, "Drymnu? Did you hear me?"

"Please repeat. I think I have made a translation error."

"No, you heard correctly," Pahli assured him. "I want you to help us find a way to become a single mind."

"Why?"

"As you said, we're a violent race. We've come close to destroying ourselves far too many times, and now we're on the brink again. Trying to resolve disputes with force never works. We need to learn cooperation and mutual understanding, and I think this may be the only way we'll ever do so."

"What makes you think I can help you reach this goal? Or would wish to?"

"You're clearly more advanced than we are in some ways; certainly you've had more experience with other races." Pahli shrugged. "And if you hate the idea so much of sharing the stars with a fragmented race you should be happy to help."

There was a long pause. "I must consider this," the Drymnu said at last.

"Fine, take your time. We'll be waiting for your answer."

He tapped the switch as Cyrilis left his station and floated over. "A word with you, Commander?" he asked, his stiff tone belying the politeness of his words.

Pahli looked up calmly. "Certainly."

Cyrilis's eyes flickered around the bridge, and when he spoke it was with lowered volume. "With all due respect, sir, what the hell are you trying to do?"

"Find a solution to war on Kohinoor. Anything wrong with that?"

"The idea, no. The method, yes." He ticked off points on his fingers. "First of all, you have no idea whether this—this hive mind thing is even possible for humans to achieve. Secondly, even if it is, what makes you think that an alien creature who's never even *seen* men before can come up with a way to do it? And thirdly, he's already said he'd like to see us all dead. What's to stop him from just seeding Kohinoor with some sort of plague once we bring him there?"

"The fact that he's never going to come anywhere near Kohinoor. There are one hundred eighty-six men and women aboard the *Susa*; we can supply whatever test subjects are needed. For the rest, I think it's a worthwhile gamble."

Cyrilis's eyes widened momentarily. "You're going to let him experiment on your own crew?"

"As you said earlier, it's our job to take risks. Your concerns are noted; you may return to your post."

For a second it looked like he would refuse. Then his cheek twitched, and he pushed off of Pahli's chair. His back was unnaturally stiff as he drifted back across the bridge.

There was a delicate cough at Pahli's side. "Commander . . . are you sure you know what you're doing?"

"You have objections, too, Ahmar?"

"Yes—the same ones Lieutenant Cyrilis has, as a matter of fact. Plus one more: some of his fears are going to make a lot of sense to the crew."

The unspoken implication hung heavy in the air. "Are you suggesting Cyrilis might lead a mutiny?" Pahli asked, dropping his voice to a bare whisper.

"I think his reaction would depend on whether he sees this as a threat to Hasar. Don't forget, sir, that *his* loyalties aren't to nebulous concepts like world peace, but strictly to his nation."

"True." Pahli thought for a moment. "All right, try it this way. If we succeed in uniting the *Susa*'s crew into a single mind, consider what kind of warship she'd become. Instant communication between spotters and gunners, wounded and medics, officers and crew—half of all ECM equipment is designed to disrupt either scanners or intraship communication, you know. The *Susa* would be unbeatable by anything even twice her size."

Slowly, Ahmar nodded. "Makes sense. Yes. Yes, I think that's the way to sell it."

"Okay. Get busy and come up with a list of advantages that'll satisfy even the diehards. I want the whole crew behind me by the time the Drymnu gives us his answer. And get someone busy figuring out what sort of safeguards we'll need on computer files, navigation equipment, and such to make sure the Drymnu doesn't get even a hint of Kohinoor's location."

Ahmar smiled wryly. "Good idea. The diehards will insist on that."

"Diehards be damned—*I* insist on it."

Ahmar sobered. "Yes, sir." Turning back to his board, he got to work.

Twenty minutes later, the Drymnu agreed to the experiment.

"I'm sorry, Madame Jalal, but you understand we can't give out information on the activities of our ships," the young junior lieutenant said, his face as glacially impersonal as his words.

Out of the phone's vision range Narda made a fist of frustration. "I realize that, Lieutenant," she said in her calmest available voice. "But my husband's never been so overdue before and I'm beginning to get worried. Can you at least tell me whether or not you've been in contact with the *Susa* in the past two months?"

"I'm sorry, but all military communications of that sort are classified."

This was getting her nowhere. "I see. Thank you," she said, and broke the connection.

For a minute she just sat there as ghosts and unnamed fears swirled up around her. The "classified communications" fable didn't fool her for a minute—Command didn't know where the *Susa* was, either.

The world wavered as tears came to her eyes. If Pahli were lost, it would be her own fault. Those thoughts she'd had, and all those surreptitious glances at Mehlid the artist—she was being punished for them now.

Abruptly, she brought her fist down hard on the table. "Stop it!" she snapped aloud to herself, breaking the circle of fear and self-reproach. The universe didn't work that way, she knew—cause and effect were seldom so neatly tied together. The *Susa* was simply behind schedule; having mechanical trouble, perhaps. Pahli would come back home soon, and when he did all her fears would seem silly. In the meantime, she might as well put all this nervous energy to work. The house needed a thorough cleaning, for starters.

Still, as she worked, she took care not to look out any of the windows that faced Mehlid's house.

Pahli finished the latest report and turned off the reader. Rubbing his eyes tiredly, he asked, "How are they this morning?"

"Davaran's still fine, though not showing any measurable telepathic or empathic abilities," Ahmar told him. "Tavousi's still hemorrhaging, but he's stable and occasionally conscious."

"Still telepathic?"

"Yes. The drug's effect seems permanent."

Pahli grunted. "Then we're back to square one again: too little of the drug doesn't do anything, and too much starts the brain bleeding."

"Well . . . the Drymnu hasn't quite given up on this one yet. There's a modification he and the medics are working on—replacing a section of one of the amino chains with a different one, I think. If the Drymnu's right it'll give the drug an extra anti-hemorrhagic effect; I don't know how. It should be ready to try this afternoon."

"I don't know." Pahli traced the edge of the disk reader control panel with his finger. "Maybe we should just give up and go home. We've lost four men already, and all we've gotten in exchange is proof that the human brain has latent telepathic abilities. And we learned *that* in the first three weeks. The past three months have been a complete bust."

Amazingly, Ahmar chuckled. Frowning, Pahli looked up. "What's so funny?"

"You are, sir. You're starting to think in hive mind types of timeframes, as if we could already work at top efficiency. Four months and we've *only* proved man is telepathic?"

Pahli had to smile. "I see what you mean. I guess things went so fast right at the beginning that I lost perspective. All right, we'll take another shot with this drug. Let me know when there are any results."

The commander would later liken that day to the first punch-through in an enemy battle front, the stroke which enables unraveling maneuvers to be started in all directions. By mid-afternoon the modified drug had been synthesized and given to the first two volunteers; three hours later the dosage was doubled, and soon afterward tripled. The telepathic ability showed up in late evening, and by morning of the next day both test subjects could pick up surface thoughts at will from anyone on the *Susa*. Twenty-four hours later the telepathy was still present and none of the usual cerebral hemorrhaging had begun. The dosage was increased still further, and within another ten hours the drug had reached saturation level, at which point further injections were simply excreted. No physiological problems whatsoever could be detected . . . and the two subjects behaved increasingly like two parts of the same person. Four more volunteers were started on the treatment; then six, then ten. By the time Pahli felt ready to try the final test a foolproof delivery system had been developed. Foolproof but with a slightly delayed effect—it took sixteen hours for the rest of the *Susa*'s crew to begin to feel the incredible experience that was the fledgling hive mind. But it worked . . . it *worked!*

Thirty hours later the *Susa* was on its way home.

It was a novel and curious experience to view the blue-and-white globe of Kohinoor simultaneously from every viewscreen and scanner on the ship. *Home*, Pahli thought, and through his mind flashed images from one-hundred-plus home towns and cities that the word evoked—a kaleidoscope of faces and sounds from the *Susa*-mind's collective past. A ripple of mild nervousness accompanied it, a last vestige of the emotional shock everyone had felt to one degree or another back at the beginning as all their dark thoughts and secret dislikes suddenly became public knowledge. It had been a sobering and painful experience, and it had taken several hours for the new strains to be worked out. But they'd managed

it, and had adapted to their new relationship with a
strength of will that had surprised all of them. Without
a doubt, Pahli thought, he had the best crew in the universe ... and a whisper of pleasure echoed through the
ship at the compliment.

The feeling faded into a kind of comfortable background as the mind turned its attention to more immediate matters. In their tubes, ready to fire, were a score of
modified seeker torpedoes, their warheads replaced with
flasks of the bacteria the Drymnu had developed to
deliver the "brotherhood drug." Once inhaled, the bacteria would travel through the bloodstream until it reached
the brain, where the high concentration of certain hor-
mones would release the drug from its hiding place just
under the cell wall.

I sense the people of Kohinoor, part of the mind—one
of the first who had used the drug, in fact—reported,
and an instant later the sensation flowed from him to the
rest of them. Pahli nodded in satisfaction. That had been
the only part of the plan they'd been unsure of: whether
or not the drug would make the telepathic melding
strong enough to stretch between countries. But if they
could detect the planet's untreated minds from space
then there would be no problem. The new hive mind
would encompass all of Kohinoor.

It also implies the power grows stronger with time,
Cyrilis pointed out. Pahli saw the first officer's logic instantly—if he hadn't, of course, he would have caught on
almost as fast through someone else—and for a moment
he wondered if that was cause for worry. *No, it'll merely
draw us all closer*, someone said, his thought accompanied by general agreement from the others. Pahli relaxed.
They were right, of course. One of the *Susa*-mind's first
major conflicts had been between those who wanted to
keep the advantages of the hive mind for the Hasar
Nation and those who wanted all Kohinoor to join in,
and it had been only as the interaction deepened that
the issue had been resolved. Even the most militant
among them, it was discovered, saw strength of arms as
a means to insuring peace—and once that common goal

was established consensus in the method followed quickly. Only by extending the hive mind to all nations would there be a lasting solution to war. And the stronger the telepathic ties between people, the better the mind would function.

Through a scannerman's eyes Pahli saw the indication that a laser beam was focusing on the *Susa*'s hull; through the signal officer's ears he heard the words riding that beam: "Hasar Military Command to the *Susa*; come in, please."

Open the circuit, Pahli commanded, clearing his throat. "This is the *Susa*," he said, startled a bit by the sound of his own voice—a sound he hadn't heard for over a month. "Commander Jalal here."

A new voice came on, and as the laser steadied on its target a picture swam into view as well. "Commander, this is General Amindari. Are you all right up there?"

We're in position now, the *Susa*-mind reported.

Fire the first five missiles. "Perfectly, sir. I'm sorry we're so late, but we had some equipment malfunctions on our way back. Nothing serious, but time-consuming."

"All right, we'll wait until you're down to debrief you— what?" The general disappeared off camera for a moment, and when he returned he was frowning. "*Susa*, scanners indicate you're firing seeker torpedoes over Hasar territory. What's going on?"

Pahli had thought about this moment for days and had all the proper expressions and words ready. "What?" He pretended to study his telltales in consternation. "Damn! Part of the malfunction—I thought we had it fixed. Gunner control!—lock onto torpedoes and destroy." *Wait a few seconds first, to give them more distance.*

Of course. Already locked on.

"Do you need assistance?" Amindari asked. "Our ground-based lasers are ready and tracking."

"Unnecessary, sir." *Fire.* "I'm sure we can—ah, there we go. Got them all, sir." All of them properly shattered by the *Susa*'s lasers, releasing the bacteria to drift down onto the people of Hasar.

"*Susa*, your braking orbit is projected to take you very

near to Lorikhan territory," the general said. He sounded a little worried. "If you're having trouble with your tubes maybe you'd better hold in space until we can get a tender alongside to off-load your torpedoes."

"Negative, Command; we're all right," Pahli said. This whole subterfuge was a little silly, but releasing missiles near Lorikhan air space was bound to make the defense people there nervous, and it might help if their spy equipment had seen the same thing happen over Hasar first. They would certainly send scoop drones to test for the presence of dangerous microorganisms, but the bacterium the Drymnu had used was only a slight variation of a harmless strain already on Kohinoor. By the time anyone found out differently, it would be too late.

A hundred kilometers past its closest approach to Lorikhan, the *Susa* fired and then destroyed six more of its missiles; the remaining nine were exploded in wind patterns that would take their contents over Missai, Baijan, the Enhoav Basin, the Urm District, and the tiny republics of the Ihrahil Mountains.

It's done, the *Susa*-mind said. *Let's go home.*

As it had on the *Susa*, the drug's effect appeared only slowly; the ship had landed and its crew—still in contact with each other—were undergoing debriefing and medical checks before the first wisps of contact began to be felt by the people of Kohinoor. At first it was thought to be individual hallucinations; then mass hallucinations; and then a new type of enemy attack. The Last War could have started right then, with launchings of doomsday missiles that would have ended war on Kohinoor in their own ghastly way. But the missiles remained in their silos, satellites, and submarines for the simple reason that by the time the brotherhood drug was perceived to be an attack the generals were not the only ones with their fingers on the buttons. The people near the various command centers, fearful though they might be, did not want to fight back that way.

So the bacteria multiplied and the telepathic unity grew, uniting families and cities as the physical boundaries of mountains, rivers, and borders ceased to exist.

Like a tapestry woven in fast motion the web of awareness and communication spread. The handful of spaceships still in orbit were ordered down to join in the change, before their unaffected crews could misinterpret what was happening and use their weapons rashly.

Within hours the *Susa*-mind's mission was accomplished. War on Kohinoor was forever ended.

It came to Shapur Nain as a curious feeling of lightness and almost-forgotten youth, and he nearly lost his balance as the word *senility* flashed through his mind. A few dozen meters to his right a group of children had been playing steal-ball, but even as he turned to face them the game ground to a halt, the players looking at each other with wide eyes. One of them glanced at Shapur, and he caught an incredibly sharp sense of wonder and fear. He thought to tell the boy it was all right, but before he even opened his mouth he felt a ripple of reassurance from the group. His own surprise and confusion at this premature result somehow struck them as funny, and as their laughter echoed through his mind he felt their fear evaporate completely. Recovering from his surprise, Shapur joined in the hilarity. *Anything one can laugh at can't be all evil*, he thought, and the children accepted the nugget of wisdom readily and without question. It had been a long time since anyone had listened to anything Shapur had to say, and it felt good.

New tendrils of awareness were beginning to creep into his mind, both from the buildings surrounding the park and the cars on the streets bordering it. He could hear the screech of brakes as startled drivers slammed to a halt, snarling traffic and adding to the confusion and growing panic. Instinctively, Shapur threw himself against the fear, even as he'd done with the children. *Don't panic! It's all right, we'll be all right. Together we can handle whatever is happening. Fear and panic will gain you nothing.* The children joined with him, adding their strength to his assault. The wave of fear poised for a moment against their island of reason . . . and then, slowly, the wave's strength began to decay. True, there was nothing like tranquility or joy yet in the growing web, but the cautious wait-and-see attitude that was rapidly smothering the panic was a big improvement.

So engrossed had Shapur become in the happenings around him that someone else first noticed that his left leg was hurting. Getting a new grip on his cane, the old man began to move again toward the bench he'd originally been aiming for. He sensed and then saw two of the children detach themselves from their group and move alongside him. With their added support he reached the bench in—for him—record time. He thanked them mentally as he sat down, and was pleased to find that happy smiles had their mental equivalent. The two ran back to their friends, and after a brief mental conference got back to their game. Though the rules were clearly different now.

Resting back against his bench, with one part of his mind enjoying the children's game, Shapur reached out to the growing consciousness around him. Whatever was happening, he knew he'd want to stay alert and be an active part of it.

It was nighttime in eastern Lorikhan, and Ruhl Tras was fast asleep when it happened there. For him it began as a dream which, though strange, was not as nightmarish as some he'd had. Once, in the middle of the night, he woke up with his heart pounding and the taste of fear in his mouth, and he almost cried out. But, somehow, he could feel that his parents were with him, and with that strange but warm presence to calm him he rolled over and went contentedly back to sleep.

By morning he had grown reasonably accustomed to the whole thing. What all the panic was about he couldn't really understand.

Narda Jalal thought she was going insane.

"Oh, no," she gasped, clutching her head with both hands as the whispers of—what?—grew stronger. "No! I can't—I mustn't!" She began to talk to herself, louder and louder, trying to drown out the voices invading her head. But it was no use. Louder and clearer they became, voices of fear and confusion that mirrored her own feelings. "Pahli!" she gasped in hopeless anguish. But he was lost somewhere in deep space. . . .

Narda? Narda, can you hear me? Relax, darling, it's all right.

Pahli? No, that was impossible. A cruel trick of her dementia—

No, it's not, the voice in her head assured her. *It really is happening. We're making Kohinoor over, making it so there will never again be war on our world.*

For a moment she forgot the other voices. *How can that be possible?*

You're feeling it already. All our people are being melded into a single vast consciousness that'll span the planet. Never mind how for the moment—you'll learn soon enough. I'll be home soon, but until then we can talk telepathically as much as you like.

The voices—minds—around her had listened to the entire exchange, Narda realized, and it seemed to have relieved some of their own fears. That it *was* a true conversation and not something self-generated she no longer doubted, somehow. *All right. But please hurry. I don't like being away from you.*

His chuckle echoed through her mind. *We'll never be apart again, darling. I promise.*

They talked only sporadically after that. Narda had always preferred face-to-face communication over the long-distance variety, and she still couldn't see this telepathy as anything more than an elaborate wireless phone network. Still, now that she could watch what was happening without fear for her sanity, she began to get a glimmer of what Pahli had been talking about. Already she could see that this wasn't going to be just a new sort of town meeting. The more distant thoughts came, like Pahli's, as a normal spoken conversation would, but she could feel a deeper melding taking place with those people nearby. As if she could see through their eyes or feel what they were feeling—

She jerked, physically, as if she'd grabbed a live wire.

For a second she'd touched Mehlid—had seen his current painting, his palette and brushes—had been as close to him as she ever was with her husband. And had enjoyed it. . . .

Had anyone noticed? She hoped not, but knew down deep that even if she'd escaped this time it was only a temporary reprieve. All the contacts were growing stronger, and soon she wouldn't be able to avoid Mehlid's mind no matter how she tried. And then he'd learn about her silly thoughts, as would all the neighbors . . . and Pahli.

Oh, Pahli, she groaned, already feeling the shame that would come.

Narda? Hang on, I'm on my way home now. I'll be there soon.

She'd forgotten how near he was. *Please hurry.* Perhaps having him near would distract her from— Gritting her teeth, she forced herself to think of other things.

He was there within fifteen minutes, and for the last hundred meters she was able to follow his progress through his own eyes and mind. She was standing in the doorway as he brought his car to a halt and bounded up the steps, smiling all over. *Narda!* his thought came, wrapping itself around her like some exotic fur.

And then she was in his arms, clinging tightly to him. His mental presence, incredibly strong at this range, was almost frightening in its intensity. It was as if her six years as his wife had only let her scratch the surface of who he really was. Suddenly she could see that he was far more complex a person than she'd ever realized. It was exhilarating, but she knew they'd need a lot of quiet time together to adapt to this newly deepened relationship.

Pahli, however, had been in space for a long time, and he had other things on his mind. Under his caresses, both physical and mental, she felt herself responding with unexpected passion as his impatient desire both fed and drew from hers. Together they moved toward the bedroom, undressing each other as they went. At the side of the bed he lifted her tenderly and laid her on the softly swaying mattress. Sitting down on the edge, he reached out—

And in the space of a single heartbeat her passion turned to ice as a horrifying truth stabbed like lightning through her mind.

Even in the old days, Pahli wouldn't have missed the abrupt change, and he certainly didn't now. *Darling, what's wrong?*

She could hardly even bring herself to form the thought. *There are . . . people watching. They're watching us!*

He frowned at her, confusion uppermost in his mind. *But . . . they're not really watching. They don't especially care what we're doing. We ran into this a little on the Susa but once the initial shock wears off you won't even notice the rest of the mind. Trust me.*

She couldn't. She'd always been too private a person to change so quickly into . . . into an exhibitionist. And among those who'd be watching—

It's not like that, Pahli protested. Abruptly, the texture of his thoughts shifted. *What's this about Mehlid?*

Nothing! she thought, too quickly. Even to herself it rang false.

His face hardened, and she felt his mind probing hers, searching—she knew—for evidence of infidelity. She endured the inquisition without protest, her thoughts dark with shame . . . and this, too, was being watched.

It seemed like a long time before he pulled back. *I'm sorry,* his thought came, and she sensed his own shame at his suspicions. *I'm sorry. I shouldn't have done that.*

It's all right. She tried to really mean it, but knew she didn't fool him. Steeling herself, she asked, *Do you want to continue?*

I guess not, he answered, and she realized his lust had drained away in the past few minutes. For a moment he sat on the edge of the bed and looked at her, and she felt his love and concern. Standing up, he found his pants and began to get into them. *It'll be okay,* he assured her as he dressed. *It'll take a while to get used to this, but it'll be better for all of us—you'll see.*

I hope so, she answered, reaching for her own clothes. But the other minds were still there. Watching.

There was much to be done.
What shall we do with all these weapons?
Destroy them, of course. Electrical components and motors can be reclaimed; the other metal parts can be melted down and reformed.

Melting is costly, but we have an experimental process that uses a series of electrocatalyst reactions to separate out the different metals of an alloy. The system's not yet ready for general use, but we think it shows promise.

The Kohinoor-mind took a moment to give directions. The process *had* been a Lorikhan military secret, but now all interested scientists and technicians would be traveling there to help develop it for practical use. Already similar joint efforts were under way to improve crop yields in Baijan, public health in the Urm District, and housing in slums all over the planet.

And what of the doomsday missiles? Should we keep such weapons as safeguards against invasion from outside our system?

Unnecessary, the elements which had once been the *Susa*-mind argued. *Only other hive minds travel the stars, and they're uniformly peaceful.*

So says the Drymnu, was one skeptical reply. *And even if true, at least one fragmented race travels space as well.*

Yes, the mind agreed. *We must decide how we can bring our brother humans to share our unity. Until then—*

The debate was long, but the issue was eventually resolved. The doomsday missiles were removed from the planet and placed for safekeeping at Kohinoor's trailing Lagrange point. There were no hard feelings about the decision, but the very fact that debate was needed showed that the Kohinoor-mind was not yet functioning as capably as the Drymnu had. *But our hive mind is still young*, Pahli and some of the others pointed out. *We must give ourselves time to adjust.*

On this too the mind agreed. But an underlying strain remained, a tension that the elimination of war had not relieved. *A more equitable sharing of resources is necessary*, part of the mind said, and steps were taken to correct the disparity. *Will the powerful still deny justice to the weak?* another part asked. But the telepathic contacts were becoming ever deeper with time, and it was clear that soon the "powerful" and the "weak" would effectively merge. At that point justice and self-interest became identical motivations. The weak saw, and were satisfied.

But the tension remained.

Give it time, was the only answer the mind could offer. *Give it time*.

As had been anticipated, the telepathic contact between people grew stronger as the weeks went by. But far from relieving the tension, it seemed to make it worse. . . .

Ruhl Tras trudged outside to the empty field near his home, fingering his ball restlessly. It was almost the only toy he could play with these days that didn't bring a flood of disapproval from one part of the Kohinoor-mind or another. Some of his playthings were too dangerous, to someone's way of thinking; others were considered a bad influence—especially his guns—and others were simply deemed "childish," with an accompanying sense of guilt he couldn't understand. His parents had tried to help him, pointing out again and again to both him and the mind that he *was* a child and should be allowed to enjoy that part of his life without interference. But it was hard to ignore the constant presence and instruction of so many adults, especially when he'd always been taught to respect his elders. Some of them, to be fair, were now bending almost backwards in trying not to influence him . . . but for the closer ones that was an impossible task. And even worse, his parents' own resolve was beginning to give way under the conflicting views on child rearing that continually buffeted them. Ruhl had always thought his parents were doing a good job of raising him, and their growing uncertainties about that made him very uneasy. Many of his friends, especially those whose parents had been pretty unsure of themselves to begin with, were a lot worse off than he was. Their fears and growing mental chaos were a permanent spot of pain in his mind.

Pain. That, probably, was the thing he feared most about what had happened. Pain was no longer limited to something in your body that hurt, and that rubbing or spraying with salve would end. Now, he could feel—had no choice but feel—every pain in his whole village. Some of it could be blocked, and some of it could be drained off—somehow—by the people around him. But some of it always got through, always lasted until the person who was actually hurt got treated. Pain could come from farther away, too, carried like a ripple in a pond by intermediate minds, but that kind could be blocked more easily.

Even as he thought about it a sharp twinge shot through his leg. Automatically, he blocked it out. He'd felt this one before—an old man in Missai Gem with a hurt leg. Shuddering, he remembered the first time the pain had come to him. It had been accompanied by a horrible vision of a damaged warjet sweeping in to the pitted deck of a carrier, where the impact shattered its hydrogen tanks and turned it into a hailstorm of shrapnel and a terrible fireball—

Ruhl slapped the side of his head to clear it, even as he felt the pain of that memory spread out among the people around him. For now he could still do that, could drive such thoughts and feelings away with simple tricks of distraction. But what would happen, he wondered bleakly, when the region around him grew to include the old man and his memories? And it would . . . he knew it would.

It wasn't something he could afford to think about.

He'd reached the field now, and for a moment looked around him, wishing for the days when he and his friends had played here together. But wishing for the past was childish . . . or so someone had told him. Hesitantly, half-expecting to incur disapproval, he began to play with his ball.

Shapur Nain leaned against the wall of his apartment as the pain quickly subsided and was replaced by the lightheadedness of the capsule he'd taken. He hated drugs—hated them with a passion—and left to himself he would rather have gritted his teeth and waited out the discomfort. But such decisions could no longer be made with only his own preferences in mind. The hive mind was broadening, and pain had become a problem for the community as a whole. Shapur had lived with intermittent pain for many years now, and he knew there were limits to how much the human psyche could take. Whatever the cost to himself, it was his duty not to add more pain than necessary to the people of Missai Gem.

The first wave of dizziness passed, but for a moment he remained against the wall, staring at his last thought. *The people of Missai Gem.* Once, he would have referred to them as his countrymen or his neighbors; in the first days of the Kohinoor-mind he would have called them friends or comrades. *The people of Missai Gem.* The expression damned with nonexistent praise. What had changed?

The answer came instantly, as if it had been waiting to ambush him. *You're the one that's changed. You've become hypercritical of everyone around you.*

Not true, he shot back, but even as he said it he knew they were right. He'd always had a touch of the judgmental in him—in the Missai Air Defenses he'd made a fair number of enemies that way. His usual solution in the past had been to simply avoid people whose quirks and shortcomings irritated him. But now—

Now he could see deeply into the minds and souls of literally millions of people. And there was no avoiding any of them.

You conveniently forget your own faults, of course, don't you? You've raised more hell than a lot of those

*you criticize. You're no better than anyone else on Kohi-
noor. Maybe worse—hypocrites are usually worse.*

Clenching his jaw, Shapur pushed off from the wall
and made his stiff way to a chair by the window. To hell
with all of it—the hive mind and everything else. He
couldn't change the way he was made, and he was too
old to try.

From the window he could look out on the park.
Drenched with sunlight, its full contingent of rusinh and
treemice milling about in uncaring ignorance of mankind's new condition, the square of greenery looked even
more inviting than usual. But Shapur wouldn't be going
there today, as he hadn't gone yesterday or the day
before. Nowhere on Kohinoor could he have solitude any
more, but at least within his own four walls he could
have the illusion of privacy.

Illusion! The thought was scornful, and only part of the
contempt came from outside him. *And you look down on
the rest of us!*

Shapur ignored the slur. Propping his cane by the window, he placed his vial of pain pills on the sill within
easy reach and settled back to survive another day.

Pahli woke with a start, heart racing, and for a long
moment he lay staring into the darkness in groggy confusion as the thoughts from a million other minds complicated his effort to remember where he was. Then the
figure beside him moaned and stirred restlessly, and
things came back into focus. He was home with his wife
. . . and it was she who was having the nightmare that
had awakened him.

Rubbing his temples tiredly, he gazed at Narda, his
mood a mixture of irritation and concern. He'd tried to
be patient with her, recognizing that she needed time to
adjust to the Kohinoor-mind. But it had been six months
now, and in many ways she was no better off than she'd
been at the beginning. Her fear of the voyeuristic potential of the hive mind remained especially strong; she
showered and dressed alone these days, her eyes either

closed or rigidly fixed on something harmless. And their sex life—

Pahli's irritation shaded into anger. They'd made love exactly twice since his return, and both times she'd been so tense it had been a waste of effort for both of them. For a short time desperation had goaded him into considering an affair, but the misery that had caused Narda had made him drop the idea completely. It was no comfort that the problem was becoming chronic all over the planet, as only those with a touch of the exhibitionist seemed still able to perform. Those who deliberately watched did so enviously.

Narda's dream was becoming darker, and Pahli realized his irritation with her was influencing it. With an effort he fought the mood, feeling her nightmare's texture change as he did so. They were trapped in a no-win situation, he thought dully; he couldn't conceal his dissatisfaction even long enough to encourage her efforts; and she, in response, had effectively given up in despair.

Turning over on his side, Pahli closed his eyes. He was tired, but sleep was going to be hard to recapture now that he was awake. Around him the Kohinoor-mind swirled its kaleidoscope of thoughts, almost as many now as in the middle of the day. The ever-growing number of minds impinging on each person had driven many to search for a semblance of privacy in the traditional hours of sleep. The first few to take up nocturnal habits had indeed found relative quiet; now, with a third or more people doing it, the advantages had become illusory. Like standing up at the stadium, in the days when there were such things as games.

A myriad of thoughts echoed through his mind, giving him the feeling of living in a crowded auditorium with perfect acoustics. He wasn't the type that needed even moderate amounts of privacy—he could never have survived conditions on the *Susa* if he had—but lately he had felt strangely oppressed by the gaze of this eye that never blinked. Had he changed so much in the past months? Or—

Or was he absorbing the characters of those around

him, losing himself to the greatest leveling force humanity had ever known?

Were all men finally to be made truly equal?

The thought jolted him like nothing else ever had. Somehow, he'd never considered all the hive mind's implications on such an intensely personal level before. *I've been blinding myself*, the thought came. Was that his own opinion, or the Kohinoor-mind's?

Does it matter any more?

Something inside him snapped. *Get out of my mind!* he roared, shocking even himself with the virulence of his sudden hatred. The hive mind recoiled, but it didn't—it couldn't—do as he demanded. And as it settled back around him he saw his anger sweep outward like a tsunami, adding its contribution to the growing blackness. How long, he wondered, before the darkness overwhelmed them all?

Give it time, came the mocking, hopeless reply.

And finally it was finished. The hive mind encompassed all of Kohinoor, linking each mind directly with all the others.

Shapur Nain locked his apartment door behind him— an unnecessary precaution, since the Kohinoor-mind already knew full well what he planned. It could have stopped him long before now if it had cared to. But after the first few it had given up the use of physical force and now limited itself to a—to him—pathetic effort at moral persuasion.

We still need you, Pahli Jalal said; but the appeal lacked conviction. Shapur knew that the former commander of the *Susa* felt each of these deaths strongly— more so, perhaps, than the average person—but even he had bowed to the inevitable. And Shapur's motives, unlike those of the others, were not purely selfish. To him, if to no one else, it was an important distinction.

Please don't do this just because of me, Ruhl Tras pleaded as Shapur drew the vial of pain pills from his pocket. Of all of them, the young boy felt the only genuine concern, and for a moment Shapur savored the feeling, as he had once enjoyed the beauty of flowers in the park. *I must*, he told Ruhl gently. *I don't know why my wartime memories strike you with such strong horror; but they do, and there's no other way I can stop that from continuing. Please don't feel guilty—this will be better for both of us.*

The boy sobbed once, and Shapur felt the mind reaching out with what little comfort it could still muster. Taking the cap off the vial, he swallowed the contents quickly. A few minutes would be all it would take. A bottle of his favorite whiskey—a close friend these last few weeks—awaited him by his window seat. Sitting down, he uncorked it and took a last, long drink. Then, setting it down carefully—*mustn't spill on the rug*—he sat back and gazed out at the park. Quietly, gently, he drifted off to sleep. . . .

Pahli sighed as the distinctively acrid tang of another · death flowed like factory waste into the hive mind. Shapur was not the first suicide Kohinoor had experienced, but somehow his death was the final straw, as if with the old man had died Pahli's last desperate hope for Kohinoor's future. *It's over*, he admitted to himself, knowing as he did so that it was something the hive mind itself had already accepted. *As surely as if we'd fought the Last War, I've destroyed our world.*

The blame must be shared, Ahmar and Cyrilis said together. *All of us aboard the* Susa *made the same assumption, that the hive mind on Kohinoor would exactly mirror our own experience. You had no way of knowing what a million-fold increase in the size of the mind would do—or of knowing how people who had never lived in the confines of a starship would react.* The words did not console Pahli; consolation no longer existed on Kohinoor.

Laying blame is a useless exercise. We've attempted to remake Man in our own way, and have paid the price for our arrogance. I wish we'd never met the Drymnu, or that the Susa *had been lost forever in deep space. Death is now the only escape for any of us from this poison-filled prison we've built.*

Perhaps not, the mind suddenly said. *Perhaps there is one other way.*

Within seconds the idea had been fully considered, its scientific, technical, and logistic ramifications examined in detail. It was desperate and probably a hopeless waste of effort . . . but only probably. For a world without any hope at all, the odds were good enough.

So for the first—and last—time the Kohinoor-mind began to work at its full capacity, throwing the combined power of two hundred million people into this final project. The results were staggering—a true echo, Pahli thought wistfully, of the efficiency and cooperation he'd once hoped to give his world. For such power to be used to complete the mind's own destruction was just one last irony.

They began to build starships. Hundreds a week at first, but within six months over a hundred thousand a day. Small and cramped, they were little more than shuttles with sleeper and recycling facilities, Burke stardrives, and planet-scanning equipment. But they would fly . . . and they would carry just one person each.

It took over two years to build ships enough for everyone, and the project left Kohinoor gutted of metals and other materials. In a way, it was fortunate that many of the weaker people were unable to stand the long wait and chose instead the easier escape. For them, of course, no starships were needed. . . .

For Pahli, it ended as it had begun, in the eternal darkness of space. Through his tiny viewport he watched as Kohinoor fell behind his ship. He was one of the last to leave—his sense of honor had demanded that—and within a day or two Kohinoor would be deserted.

Pahli, can you still hear me? the last remnant of the hive mind touched his. He didn't answer, but it knew he heard. *We don't blame you for what happened, Pahli. Please don't blame yourself.*

How can I not? I failed my world, and good motives are no excuse for the destruction I brought upon us. I've

*already accepted your forgiveness; allow me the privilege
of withholding my own.*

The mind seemed to sigh. *Very well, if that's truly
your wish. But note that your self-imposed martyrdom is
not without its irony. Indeed, you did* not *fail at the task
you set for yourself.*

The contact was fading, and Pahli had to ask the question twice before it got through. *What do you mean?*

Through the growing silence he heard the faint
answer: *You found a final solution to war.*

The contact broke, and for the first time in three years
Pahli was truly alone. Taking a deep, clean breath, he
shifted his gaze from Kohinoor's disk and scanned the
rest of the sky. A hundred or more ships were still visible,
their drives showing like tiny blue stars. Their passengers,
too, were alone now as they prepared for the long voyage
ahead. Perhaps—perhaps—a few years of solitude would
break the hive mind forever, and bits of this mass exodus
would someday be able to come together again safely.
But Pahli doubted that would ever happen. Individual
survival was all that was left to them now; on new worlds
if they were lucky, aboard their cramped ships if they
were not. Their cramped, one-man ships . . . and Pahli
forced a bitter smile. Yes, the mind had been right; he
had found a final solution.

It takes at least two people to have a war.

Behind him the sleeper tank chimed its readiness.
With one last look at Kohinoor, Pahli went to strap in.
He'd be entering hyperspace soon.

PAWN'S GAMBIT

To: *Office of Director Rodau 248700, Alien Research Bureau, Clars*

From: *Office of Director Eftis 379214, Games Studies, Var-4*

Subject: *30th annual report, submitted 12 Tai 3829.*

Date: *4 Mras 3829*

Dear Rodau,

I know how you hate getting addenda after a report has been processed, but I hope you will make an exception in this case. Our most recently discovered race—the Humans—was mentioned only briefly in our last annual report, but I feel that the data we have since obtained is important enough to bring to your attention right away.

The complete results are given in the enclosed film, but the crux of the problem is a disturbing lack of consistency with standard patterns. In many ways they are unsophisticated, even primitive; most of the subjects reacted with terror and even hysteria when first brought here via Transphere. And yet, unlike most primitives, there is a mental and emotional resilience to the species which frankly surprises me. Nearly all of them recovered from their fear and went on to play the Stage-I game against their fellows. And the imagination, skill, and sheer aggressiveness used in the playing have been inordinately high for such a young species, prompting more than one off-the-record comparison between Humans and the Chanis. I suppose it's that, more than anything else, that made me unwilling to let this data ride until our next report. Confined as they are to their home planet, the Humans are certainly no threat now; but if they prove to be even a twelfth as dangerous as the Chanis they will need to be dealt with swiftly.

Accordingly, I am asking permission to take the extraordinary step of moving immediately to Phase III (the complete proposal is attached to my report). I know this is generally forbidden with non-spacing races, but I feel it is vital that we test Humans against races of established ability. Please give me a decision on this as soon as possible.

Regards,
Eftis

* * *

To: *Office of Director Eftis 379214, Game Studies,
Var-4*

From: *Office of Director Rodau 248700, A.R.B.,
Clars*

Subject: *Addendum to 30th annual report.*

Date: *34 Forma 3829*

Dear Eftis,

Thank you for your recent addenda. You were
quite right to bring these Humans to our attention;
that is, after all, what you're out there for.

I find myself, as do you, both interested and
alarmed by this race, and I agree totally with your
proposal to initiate Phase III. As usual, the authori-
zation tapes will be a few more weeks in coming,
but—unofficially—I'm giving you the go-ahead to
start your preparations. I also agree with your suggestion that a star-going race be pitted against your
Human: an Olyt or Fiwalic, perhaps. I see by your
reports that the Olyts are beginning to resent our
testing, but don't let that bother you; your results
clearly show they are no threat to us.

Do keep us informed, especially if you uncover
more evidence of Chanilike qualities in these aliens.

Sincerely,
Rodau

*   *   *

The glowing, impenetrable sphere of white mist that
had surrounded him for the last five minutes dissolved
as suddenly as it had formed, and Kelly McClain found
himself in a room he had never seen in his life.

Slowly, carefully, he looked around him, heart pounding painfully in his ears. He'd screamed most of the panic
out of his system within the first three minutes of his
imprisonment, but he could feel the terror welling up
into his throat again. He forced it down as best he could.

He was clearly no longer in his office at the university's reactor lab, but losing his head wasn't going to get him back again.

He was sitting in a semicircular alcove facing into a small room, his chair and about three-quarters of his desk having made the trip with him. The room's walls, ceiling, and floor were made of a bronze-colored metal and were devoid of any ornamentation. At the right and left ends of the room he could see panels that looked like sliding doors.

There didn't seem to be a lot to be gained by sitting quietly and hoping everything out there would go away. His legs felt like they might be ready to hold him up again, so he stood up and squeezed his way through the six-inch gap between his desk and the alcove wall. The desk, he noted, had been sheared smoothly, presumably by the white mist or something in it. He went first to the panel in the right-hand wall; but if it *was*, in fact, a door, he could find no way to open it. The left-hand panel yielded identical results. "Hello?" he called tentatively into the air around him. "Can anyone hear me?"

The flat voice came back at him so suddenly it made him jump. "Good day to you, Human," it said. "Welcome to the Stryfkar Game Studies Center on Var-4. I trust you suffered no ill effects from your journey?"

A *game* studies center?

Memories flashed across Kelly's mind, bits of articles he'd seen in various magazines and tabloids over the past few months telling of people kidnapped to a game center by extraterrestrial beings. He'd skimmed some of them for amusement, and had noted the similarity between the stories; humans taken two at a time and made to play a strange board game against one another before being sent home. Typical tabloid tripe, Kelly had thought at the time.

Which made this an elaborate practical joke, obviously.

So how had they made that white mist?

For the moment, it seemed best to play along. "Oh, the trip was fine. A little boring, though."

"You have adjusted to your situation very quickly," the

voice said, and Kelly thought he could detect a touch of surprise in it. "My name is Slaich; what is yours?"

"Kelly McClain. You speak English pretty well for an alien—what kind are you, again?"

"I am a Stryf. Our computer-translator is very efficient, and we have had data from several of your fellow Humans."

"Yes, I've heard about them. How come you drag them all the way out here—wherever *here* is—just to play games? Or is it a state secret?"

"Not really. We wish to learn about your race. Games are one of the psychological tools we use."

"Why can't you just talk to us? Or, better still, why not drop in for a visit?" Much as he still wanted to believe this was a practical joke, Kelly was finding that theory harder and harder to support. That voice—like no computer speech he'd ever heard, but nothing like a human voice, either—had an uncomfortable ring of casual truth to it. He could feel sweat gathering on his forehead.

"Talking is inefficient for the factors we wish to study," Slaich explained offhandedly. "As to visiting Earth, the Transphere has only limited capacity and we have no long-range ships at our disposal. I would not like to go to Earth alone."

"Why not?" The tension had risen within Kelly to the breaking point, generating a reckless courage. "You can't look *that* bad. Show yourself to me—*right now*."

There was no hesitation. "Very well," the voice said, and a section of the shiny wall in front of Kelly faded to black. Abruptly, a three-dimensional image appeared in front of it—an image of a two-legged, two-armed nightmare. Kelly gasped, head spinning, as the misshapen head turned to face him. An x-shaped opening began to move. "What do you think, Kelly? Would I pass as a Human?"

"I—I—I—" Kelly was stuttering, but he couldn't help it; all his strength was going to control his suddenly rebellious stomach. The creature before him was *real*—no make-up job in the world could turn a man into *that*.

And multicolor hologram movies of such size and clarity were years or decades away . . . on Earth.

"I am sorry; I seem to have startled you," Slaich said, reaching for a small control panel Kelly hadn't noticed. The muscles moved visibly under his six-fingered hand as he touched a button. The image vanished and the wall regained its color. "Perhaps you would like to rest and eat," the flat voice went on. The door at Kelly's left slid open, revealing a furnished room about the size of an efficiency apartment. "It will be several hours before we will be ready to begin. You will be called."

Kelly nodded, not trusting his voice, and walked into the room. The door closed behind him. A normal-looking bed sat next to the wall halfway across the room, and Kelly managed to get there before his knees gave out.

He lay face-downward for a long time, his whole body trembling as he cried silently into his pillow. The emotional outburst was embarrassing—he'd always tried to be the strong, unflappable type—but efforts to choke off the display only made it worse. Eventually, he gave up and let it run its course.

By and by, the sobs stopped coming and he found himself more or less rational once more. Rolling onto his side, unconsciously curling into a fetal position, he stared at the bronze wall and tried to think.

For the moment, at least, he seemed to be in no immediate physical danger. From what he remembered of the tabloid articles, the aliens here seemed truly intent on simply doing their psychological study and then sending the participants home. Everything they'd done so far could certainly be seen in that light; no doubt they had monitored his reactions to both their words and Slaich's abrupt appearance. He shuddered at the memory of that alien face, feeling a touch of anger. Psychological test or not, he wasn't going to forgive Slaich very quickly for not giving him some kind of warning before showing himself like that.

The important thing, then, was for him to stay calm and be a good little test subject so he could get home with a minimum of trouble. And if he could do it with a little dignity, so much the better.

He didn't realize he'd dozed off until a soft tone startled him awake. "Yes?"

"It is time," the computerized voice told him. "Please leave your rest chamber and proceed to the test chamber."

Kelly sat up, glancing around him. The room's only door was the one he'd entered by; the test chamber must be out the other door of the room with the alcove. "Where's the other player from?" he asked, swinging his feet onto the floor and heading for the exit. "Or do you just snatch people from Earth at random?"

"We generally set the Transphere to take from the vicinity of concentrated energy sources, preferably fission or fusion reactors when such exist," Slaich said. "However, you have made one false assumption. Your opponent is not a Human."

Kelly's feet froze halfway through the door, and he had to grab the jamb to keep his balance. This was a new twist. "I see. Thanks for the warning, anyway. Uh . . . what *is* he?"

"An Olyt. His race is somewhat more advanced than yours; the Olyts have already built an empire of eight planets in seven stellar systems. They have been studied extensively by us, though their closest world is nearly thirty light-years from here."

Kelly forced his legs to start walking again. "Does that make us neighbors? You never said how far Earth is from here."

"You are approximately forty-eight light-years from here and thirty-six from the Olyt home world. Not very far, as distances go."

The door on the far side of the room opened as Kelly approached. Getting a firm grip on his nerves, he stepped through.

The game room was small and relatively dark, the only illumination coming from a set of dimly glowing red panels. In the center of the room, and taking up a good deal of its floor space, was a complex-looking gameboard on a table. Two chairs—one strangely contoured—completed the furnishings. Across the room was another door, and standing in front of it was an alien.

Kelly was better prepared for the shock this time, and as he stepped toward the table he found his predominant feeling was curiosity. The Olyt was half a head shorter than he, his slender body covered by what looked like large white scales. He was bipedal with two arms, each of his limbs ending in four clawed digits. His snout was long and seemed to have lots of teeth; his eyes were black and set back in a bettle-browed skull. Picture a tailless albino alligator wearing a wide sporran, Sam Browne belt, and a beret. . . .

Kelly and the Olyt reached their respective sides of the game table at about the same time. The board was smaller than it had first looked; the alien was little more than a double arm-length away: Carefully, Kelly raised his open hand, hoping the gesture would be properly interpreted. "Hello. I'm Kelly McClain; human."

The alien didn't flinch or dive down Kelly's throat. He extended both arms, crossed at the wrists, and Kelly discovered the claws were retractable. His mouth moved, generating strange noises; seconds later the computer's translation came over an invisible speaker. "I greet you. I am Tlaymasy of the Olyt race."

"Please sit down," Slaich's disembodied voice instructed. "You may begin when you have decided on the rules."

Kelly blinked. "How's that?"

"This game has no fixed rules. You must decide between you as to the objective and method of play before you begin."

Tlaymasy was speaking again. "What is the purpose of this?"

"The purpose is to study an interaction between Olyt and Human," Slaich said. "Surely you have heard of this experiment from others of your race."

Kelly frowned across the table. "You've been through this before?"

"Over one hundred twenty-eight members of my race

have been temporarily taken over the last sixteen years,"
the Olyt said. Kelly wished he could read the alien's
expression. The computer's tone was neutral, but the
words themselves sounded a little resentful. "Some have
spoken of this game with no rules. However, my question
referred to the stakes."

"Oh. They are as usual for this study: the winner is
allowed to return home."

Kelly's heart skipped a beat. "*Wait* a minute. Where
did *that* rule come from?"

"The rules and stakes are chosen by us," Slaich said
flatly.

"Yes, but ... What happens to the loser?"

"He remains to play against a new opponent."

"What if I refuse to play at all?"

"That is equivalent to losing."

Kelly snorted, but there wasn't much he could do
about it. *With dignity*, he thought dryly, and began to
study the game board.

It looked like it had been designed to handle at least
a dozen widely differing games. It was square, with two
five-color bands of squares running along its edge; one
with a repeating pattern, the other apparently random.
Inside this was a checkerboard-type design with sets of
concentric circles and radial lines superimposed on it. To
one side of the board itself sat a stack of transparent
plates, similarly marked, and a set of supporting legs for
them; to the other side were various sizes, shapes, and
colors of playing pieces, plus cards, multisided dice, and
a gadget with a small display screen. "Looks like we're
well equipped," he remarked to the Olyt, who seemed
also to be studying their equipment. "I guess we could
start by choosing which set of spaces to use. I suggest
the red and—is that color blue?—the square ones." He
indicated the checkerboard.

"Very well," Tlaymasy said. "Now we must decide on
a game. Are you familiar with *Four-Ply*?"

"I doubt it, but my people may have something similar.
Describe the rules."

Tlaymasy proceeded to do so. It sounded a little like

go, but with the added feature of limited mobility for the pieces once on the board. "Sounds like something I'd have a shot at," Kelly said after the alien had demonstrated some of the moves with a butterfly-shaped playing piece. "Of course, you've got a big advantage, since you've played it before. I'll go along on two conditions: first, that a third-level or fourth-level attack must be announced one move before the attack is actually launched."

"That eliminates the possibility of surprise attacks," Tlaymasy objected.

"Exactly. Come on, now, you know the game well enough to let me have that, don't you?"

"Very well. Your second condition?"

"That we play a practice game first. In other words, the *second* game we play will determine who gets to go home. Is that permissible?" he added, looking up at one of the room's corners.

"Whatever is decided between you is binding," Slaich replied.

Kelly cocked an eyebrow at his opponent. "Tlaymasy?"

"Very well. Let us begin."

It wasn't such a hard game to learn, Kelly decided, though he got off to a bad start and spent most of their practice game on the defensive. The strategy Tlaymasy was using was not hard to pick up, and by the time they finished he found he could often anticipate the Olyt's next move.

"An interesting game," Kelly commented as they retrieved their playing pieces from the board and prepared to play again. "Is it popular on your world?"

"Somewhat. The ancients used it for training in logic. Are you ready to begin?"

"I guess so," Kelly said. His mouth felt dry.

This time Kelly avoided the errors he'd made at the beginning of the practice game, and as the board filled up with pieces he found himself in a position nearly as strong as Tlaymasy's. Hunching over the board, agonizing over each move, he fought to maintain his strength.

And then Tlaymasy made a major mistake, exposing

an arm of his force to a twin attack. Kelly pounced, and when the dust of the next four moves settled he had taken six of his opponent's pieces—a devastating blow.

A sudden, loud hiss made Kelly jump. He looked up, triumphant grin vanishing. The Olyt was staring at him, mouth open just enough to show rows of sharp teeth. Both hands were on the table, and Kelly could see the claws sliding in and out of their sheaths. "Uh . . . anything wrong?" he asked cautiously, muscles tensing for emergency action.

For a moment there was silence. Then Tlaymasy closed his mouth and his claws retracted completely. "I was upset by the stupidity of my play. It has passed. Let us continue."

Kelly nodded and returned his gaze to the board, but in a far more subdued state of mind. In the heat of the game, he had almost forgotten he was playing for a ticket home. Now, suddenly, it looked as if he might be playing for his life as well. Tlaymasy's outburst had carried a not-so-subtle message: the Olyt did not intend to accept defeat graciously.

The play continued. Kelly did the best he could, but his concentration was shot all to hell. Within ten moves Tlaymasy had made up his earlier loss. Kelly sneaked glances at the alien as they played, wondering if that had been Tlaymasy's plan all along. Surely he wouldn't physically attack Kelly while he himself was a prisoner on an unknown world . . . would he? Suppose, for example, that honor was more important to him than even his own life, and that honor precluded losing to an alien?

A trickle of sweat ran down the middle of Kelly's back. He had no evidence that Tlaymasy thought that way . . . but on the other hand he couldn't come up with any reasons why it shouldn't be possible. And that reaction had looked *very* unfriendly.

The decision was not difficult. Discretion being the better part and all that—and a few extra days here wouldn't hurt him. Deliberately, he launched a bold assault against Tlaymasy's forces, an attack which would require dumb luck to succeed.

Dumb luck, as usual, wasn't with him. Seven moves later, Tlaymasy had won.

"The game is over," Slaich's voice boomed. "Tlaymasy, return to your Transphere chamber and prepare to leave. Kelly McClain, return to your rest chamber."

The Olyt stood and again gave Kelly his crossed-wrists salute before turning and disappearing through his sliding door. Kelly sighed with relief and emotional fatigue and headed back toward his room. "You played well for a learner," Slaich's voice followed him.

"Thanks," Kelly grunted. Now, with Tlaymasy's teeth and claws no longer a few feet in front of him, he was starting to wonder if maybe he shouldn't have thrown the game. "When do I play next?"

"In approximately twenty hours. The Transphere must be reset after the Olyt is returned to his world."

Kelly had been about to step into his rest chamber. "Twenty hours?" he echoed, stopping. "Just a second." He turned toward the alcove where his desk was sitting— but had barely taken two steps when a flash of red light burst in front of him. "Hey!" he yelped, jumping backwards as heat from the blast washed over him. "What was *that* for?"

"You may not approach the Transphere apparatus." Slaich's voice had abruptly taken on a whiplash bite.

"Nuts! If I'm being left to twiddle my thumbs for a day I want the books that are in my desk."

There was a momentary silence, and when Slaich spoke again his tone had moderated. "I see. I suppose that is all right. You may proceed."

Kelly snorted and walked forward warily. No more bursts of light came. Squeezing around to the front of his desk, he opened the bottom drawer and extracted three paperbacks, normally kept there for idle moments. From another drawer came a half-dozen journals that he'd been meaning to read; and finally, as an after-thought, he scooped up a couple of pens and a yellow legal pad. Stepping back to the center of the room, he held out his booty. "See? Perfectly harmless. Not a single neutron bomb in the lot."

"Return to your rest chamber." Slaich did not sound amused.

With the concentration needed during the game, Kelly had temporarily forgotten he'd missed both lunch and dinner. Now, though, his growling stomach was demanding attention. Following Slaich's instructions, he requested and obtained a meal from the automat-type slots in one wall of his cubicle. The food was bland but comfortably filling, and Kelly felt his spirits rising as he ate. Afterwards, he chose one of his paperbacks and stretched out on the bed. But instead of immediately beginning to read, he stared at the ceiling and thought.

Obviously, there could be no further question that what was happening to him was real. Similarly, there was no reasonable hope that he could escape his captors. There were no apparent exits from the small complex of rooms except via the Transphere, whose machinery was hidden behind metal walls and was probably incomprehensible anyway. He had only Slaich's word that the Stryfkar intended to send him home, but since they apparently had made—and kept—similar promises to other humans, he had no real reason to doubt them. True, the game rules this time seemed to be different, but Tlaymasy had implied the Stryfkar had pulled this on several of his own race and had released them on schedule. So the big question, then, was whether or not Kelly could win the next game he would have to play.

He frowned. He'd never been any great shakes as a games player, winning frequently at chess but only occasionally at the other games in his limited repertoire. And yet, he'd come surprisingly close today to beating an alien in his own game. An alien, be it noted, whose race held an empire of eight worlds. The near-victory could be meaningless, of course—Tlaymasy might have been the equivalent of a fourth-grader playing chess, for instance. But the Olyt would have had to be a complete idiot to suggest a game he wasn't good at. And there was also Slaich's reaction after the game; it was pretty clear the Stryf hadn't expected Kelly to do that well.

Did that mean that Kelly, average strategist that he was, was still better than the run-of-the-mill alien?

If that was true, his problems were essentially over. Whoever his next opponent was, it should be relatively easy to beat him, especially if they picked a game neither player had had much experience with. Four-Ply might be a good choice if the new tester wasn't another Olyt; the game was an interesting one and easy enough to learn, at least superficially. As a matter of fact, it might be worth his while to try marketing it when he got home. The game market was booming these days, and while Four-Ply wasn't likely to make him rich, it could conceivably bring in a little pocket change.

On the other hand . . . what was his hurry?

Kelly squirmed slightly on the bed as a rather audacious idea struck him. If he really *was* better than most other aliens, then it followed that he could go home most any time he wanted, simply by winning whichever game he was on at the moment. And if *that* were true, why not stick around for another week or so and learn a few more alien games?

The more he thought about it, the more he liked the idea. True, there was an element of risk involved, but that was true of any money-making scheme. And it couldn't be *that* risky—this was a *psychology* experiment, for crying out loud! "Slaich?" he called at the metallic ceiling.

"Yes?"

"If I lose my next game, what happens?"

"You will remain here until you have won or until the test is over."

So it didn't sound like he got punished or anything if he kept losing. The Stryfkar had set up a pretty simple-minded experiment here, to his way of thinking. Human psychologits would probably have put together something more complicated. Did that imply humans were better strategists than even the Stryfkar?

An interesting question, but for the moment Kelly didn't care. He'd found a tiny bit of maneuvering space in the controlled environment they'd set up, and it felt very satisfying. Rules like these, in his book, were made to be bent.

And speaking of rules . . . Putting aside his paperback, Kelly rolled off the bed and went over to the cubicle's folding table. Business before pleasure, he told himself firmly. Picking up a pen and his legal pad, he began to sketch the Four-Ply playing board and to list the game's rules.

* * *

To: *Office of Director Rodau 248700, A.R.B., Clars*

From: *Office of Director Eftis 379214, Game Studies, Var-4*

Subject: *Studies of Humans*

Date: *3 Lysmo 3829*

Dear Rodau,

The Human problem is taking on some frightening aspects, and we are increasingly convinced that we have stumbled upon another race of Chanis. Details will be transmitted when all analyses are complete, but I wanted to send you this note first to give you as much time as possible to recommend an assault force, should you deem this necessary.

As authorized, we initiated a Phase III study eight days ago. Our Human has played games against members of four races: an Olyt, a Fiwalic, a Spromsa, and a Thim-fra-chee. In each case the game agreed upon has been one from the non-Human player's world, with slight modifications suggested by the Human. As would be expected, the Human has consistently lost—but in each case he has clearly been winning until the last few moves. Our contact specialist, Slaich 898661, suggested early on that the Human might be *deliberately* losing; but with both his honor and his freedom at stake Slaich could offer no motive for such behavior. However, in a conversation of 1

Lysmo (tape enclosed) the Human freely confirmed our suspicions and indicated the motive was material gain. He is using the testing sessions to study his opponents' games, expecting to introduce them for profit on returning to his world.

I'm sure you will notice the similarities to Chani psychology: the desire for profit, even at the casual risk of his safety, and the implicit belief that his skills are adequate to bring release whenever he wishes. History shows us that, along with their basic tactical skills, it was just these characteristics that drove the Chanis in their most unlikely conquests. It must also be emphasized that the Human shows no signs of military or other tactical training and must therefore be considered representative of his race.

Unless further study uncovers flaws in their character which would preclude an eventual Chani-like expansion, I personally feel we must consider annihilation for this race as soon as possible. Since we obviously need to discover the race's full strategic capabilities—and since our subject refuses to cooperate—we are being forced to provide a stronger incentive. The results should be enlightening, and will be sent as soon as they are available.

Regards,
Eftis

* * *

The door slid back and Kelly stepped into the test chamber, looking across the room eagerly to see what sort of creature he'd be competing against this time. The dim red lights were back on in the room, indicating someone from a world with a red sun, and as Kelly's eyes adjusted to the relative darkness he saw another of the alligator-like Olyts approaching the table. "I greet you," Kelly said, making the crossed-wrist gesture he'd seen at his first game here. "I am Kelly McClain of the human race."

The Olyt repeated the salute. "I am *ulur* Achranae of the Olyt race."

"Pleased to meet you. What does *ulur* mean?"

"It is a title of respect for my position. I command a war-force of seven spacecraft."

Kelly swallowed. A trained military man. Good thing he wasn't in a hurry to win and go home. "Interesting. Well, shall we begin?"

Achranae sat down. "Let us make an end to this charade quickly."

"What do you mean, 'charade'?" Kelly asked cautiously as he took his seat. He was by no means an expert on Olyt expressions and emotions, but he could swear this one was angry.

"Do not deny your part," the alien snapped. "I recognize your name from the reports, and know how you played this game for the Stryfkar against another of my people, studying him like a laboratory specimen before allowing him to win and depart. We do not appreciate the way you take our people like this—"

"Whoa! Wait a second; I'm not with them. They've been taking *my* people, too. It's some sort of psychology experiment, I guess."

The Olyt glared at him in silence for a long moment. "If you truly believe that, you are a fool," he said at last, sounding calmer. "Very well; let us begin."

"Before you do so we must inform you of an important change in the rules," Slaich's voice cut in. "You shall play *three* different games, instead of one, agreeing on the rules before beginning each. The one who wins two or more shall be returned home. The other will lose his life."

It took a second for that to sink in. "*What?*" Kelly yelped. "You can't do that!" Across the table Achranae gave a soft, untranslatable hiss. His claws, fully extended, scratched lightly on the game board.

"It is done," Slaich said flatly. "You will proceed now."

Kelly shot a frustrated glance at Achranae, looked up again. "We will not play for our lives. That sort of thing is barbarous, and we are both civilized beings."

"Civilized." Slaich's voice was thick with sudden contempt. "You, who can barely send craft outside your own atmosphere; you consider yourself *civilized?* And your opponent is little better."

"We govern a sphere fifteen light-years across," Achranae reminded Slaich calmly, his outburst of temper apparently over. For all their short fuses, Kelly decided, Olyts didn't seem to stay mad long.

"Your eight worlds are nothing against our forty."

"It is said the Chanis had only five when they challenged you."

The silence from the speaker was impressively ominous. "What are the Chanis?" Kelly asked, fighting the urge to whisper.

"It is rumored they were a numerically small but brutally aggressive race who nearly conquered the Stryfkar many generations ago. We have heard these stories from traders, but do not know how true they are."

"True or not, you sure hit a nerve," Kelly commented. "How about it, Slaich? Is he right?"

"You will proceed now," Slaich ordered, ignoring Kelly's question.

Kelly glanced at Achranae, wishing he could read the other's face. Did Olyts understand the art of bluffing? "I said we wouldn't play for our lives."

In answer a well-remembered flash of red light exploded inches from his face. Instinctively, he pushed hard on the table, toppling himself and his chair backwards. He hit hard enough to see stars, somersaulted out of the chair, and wound up lying on his stomach on the floor. Raising his head cautiously, he saw the red fireball wink out and, after a moment, got warily to his feet. Achranae, he noted, was also several feet back from the table, crouching in what Kelly decided was probably a fighting stance of some kind.

"If you do not play, both of you will lose your lives." Slaich's voice was mild, almost emotionless, but it sent a shiver down Kelly's spine. Achranae had been right: this was no simple psychology experiment. The Stryfkar were searching for potential enemies—and somehow both humans and Olyts had made it onto their list. And there was *still* no way to escape. Looking across at Achranae, Kelly shrugged helplessly. "Doesn't look like we have much choice, does it?"

The Olyt straightened up slowly. "For the moment, no."

"Since this contest is so important to both of us," Kelly said when they were seated again, "I suggest that you choose the first game, allowing me to offer changes that will take away some of your advantage—changes we both have to agree on, of course. I'll choose the second game; you'll suggest changes on that one."

"That seems honorable. And the third?"

"I don't know. Let's discuss that one when we get there, okay?"

It took nearly an hour for the first game, plus amendments, to be agreed upon. Achranae used three of the extra transparencies and their supports to create a three-dimensional playing area; the game itself was a sort of 3-D "Battleship," but with elements of chess, Monopoly, and even poker mixed in. Surprisingly enough, the mixture worked, and if the stakes hadn't been so high Kelly thought he would have enjoyed playing it. His own contributions to the rules were a slight adjustment to the shape of the playing region—which Kelly guessed would change the usual positional strategies—and the introduction of a "wild card" concept to the play. "I also suggest a practice game before we play for keeps," he told Achranae.

The Olyt's dark eyes bored into his. "Why?"

"Why not? I've never played this before, and you've never played with these rules. It would make the actual game fairer. More honorable. We'll do the same with the second and third games."

"Ah—it is a point of honor?" The alien cocked his head to the right. A nod? "Very well. Let us begin."

Even with the changes, the game—Skymarch, Achranae called it—was still very much an Olyt one, and Achranae won the practice game handily. Kelly strongly suspected Skymarch was a required course of the aliens' space academy; it looked too much like space warfare to be anything else.

"Did the Stryf speak the truth when he said you were not starfarers?" Achranae asked as they set up the board again.

"Hm? Oh, yes." Kelly replied distractedly, his mind on strategy for the coming game. "We've hardly even got simple spacecraft yet."

"Surprising, since you learn space warfare tactics so quickly." He waved his sheathed claws over the board. "A pity, too, since you will not be able to resist if the Stryfkar decide to destroy you."

"I suppose not, but why would they want to? We can't be any threat to them."

Again Achranae indicated the playing board. "If you are representative, your race is unusually gifted with both tactical skill and aggressiveness. Such abilities would make you valuable allies or dangerous adversaries to my starfaring race."

Kelly shrugged. "You'd think they'd try to recruit us, then."

"Unlikely. The Stryfkar are reputed to be a proud race who have little use for allies. This harassment of both our peoples should indicate their attitude toward other races."

The Olyt seemed to be on the verge of getting angry again, Kelly noted uneasily. A change in subject seemed in order. "Uh, yes. Shall we begin our game?"

Achranae let out a long hiss. "Very well."

From the very beginning it was no contest. Kelly did his best, but it was clear that the Olyt was able to *think* three-dimensionally better than he could. Several times he lost a piece simply because he missed some perfectly obvious move it could have made. Sweating, he tried to make himself slow down, to spend more time on each move. But it did no good. Inexorably, Achranae tightened the noose; and, too quickly, it was all over.

Kelly leaned back in his chair, expelling a long breath. It was all right, he told himself—he had to expect to lose a game where the alien had all the advantages. The next game would be different, though; Kelly would be on his own turf, with *his* choice of weapons—

"Have you chosen the game we shall play next?" Achranae asked, interrupting Kelly's thoughts.

"Idle down, will you?" Kelly snapped, glaring at the alien. "Give me a minute to think."

It wasn't an easy question. Chess was far and away Kelly's best game, but Achranae had already showed himself a skilled strategist, at least with warfare-type games. That probably made chess a somewhat risky bet. Card games involved too much in the way of chance, for this second game Kelly needed as much advantage as he could get. Word games like Scrabble were obviously out. Checkers or Dots were too simple. Backgammon? That was a pretty nonmilitary game, but Kelly was a virtual novice at it himself. How about—

How about a *physical* game?

"Slaich? Could I get some extra equipment in here? I'd like a longer table, a couple of paddles, a sort of light, bouncy ball—"

"Games requiring specific physical talents are by their nature unfair for such a competition as this," Slaich said. "They are not permitted."

"I do not object," Achranae spoke up unexpectedly, and Kelly looked at him in surprise. "You stated we could choose the games and the rules, and it is Kelly McClain's choice this time."

"We are concerned with psychological studies," Slaich said. "We are not interested in the relative abilities of your joints and muscles. You will choose a game that can be played with the equipment provided."

"It is dishonorable—"

"No, it's okay, Achranae," Kelly interrupted, ashamed at himself for even suggesting such a thing. "Slaich is right; it would've been completely unfair. It was dishonorable for me to suggest it. Please accept my apology."

"You are blameless," the Olyt said. "The dishonor is in those who brought us here."

"Yes," Kelly agreed, glancing balefully at the ceiling. The point was well taken. Achranae wasn't Kelly's enemy; merely his opponent. The Stryfkar were the real enemy.

For all the good that knowledge did him.

He cleared his throat. "Okay, Achranae, I guess I'm ready. This game's called *chess*. . . ."

The Olyt picked up the rules and movements quickly, enough so that Kelly wondered if the aliens had a similar game on their own world. Fortunately, the knight's move seemed to be a new one on him, and Kelly hoped it would offset the other's tactical training. As his contribution, Achranae suggested the pawns be allowed to move backwards as well as forwards. Kelly agreed, and they settled into their practice game.

It was far harder than Kelly had expected. The "reversible pawn" rule caused him tremendous trouble, mainly because his logic center kept editing it out of his strategy. Within fifteen moves he'd lost both bishops and one of his precious knights, and Achranae's queen was breathing down his neck.

"An interesting game," the Olyt commented a few moves later, after Kelly had managed to get out from under a powerful attack. "Have you had training in its technique?"

"Not really," Kelly said, glad to take a breather. "I just play for enjoyment with my friends. Why?"

"The test of skill at a game is the ability to escape what appears to be certain defeat. By that criterion you have a great deal of skill."

Kelly shrugged. "Just native ability, I guess."

"Interesting. On my world such skills must be learned over a long period of time." Achranae indicated the board. "We have a game similar in some ways to this one; if I had not studied it I would have lost to you within a few moves."

"Yeah," Kelly muttered. He'd been pretty sure Achranae wasn't running on beginner's luck, but he'd sort of hoped he was wrong. "Let's get back to the game, huh?"

In the end Kelly won, but only because Achranae lost his queen to Kelly's remaining knight and Kelly managed to take advantage of the error without any major goofs of his own.

"Are you ready to begin the actual game?" Achranae asked when the board had been cleared.

Kelly nodded, feeling a tightness in his throat. This was for all the marbles. "I suppose so. Let's get it over with."

Using one of the multifaced dice they determined the Olyt would have the white pieces. Achranae opened with his king's pawn, and Kelly responded with something he dimly remembered being called a Sicilian defense. Both played cautiously and defensively; only two pawns were taken in the first twenty moves. Sweating even in the air-conditioned room, Kelly watched his opponent gradually bring his pieces into attacking positions as he himself set his defense as best he could.

When the assault came it was devastating in its slaughter. By the time the captures and recaptures were done, eight more pieces were gone . . . and Kelly was a rook down.

Brushing a strand of hair out of his eyes with a trembling hand, Kelly swallowed hard as he studied the board. Without a doubt, he was in trouble. Achranae controlled the center of the board now and his king was better defended than Kelly's. Worse yet, he seemed to have mastered the knight's move, while Kelly was still having trouble with his pawns. And if the Olyt won this one . . .

"Are you distressed?"

Kelly started, looked up at his opponent. "Just a—" His voice cracked and he tried again. "Just nervous."

"Perhaps we should cease play for a time, until you are better able to concentrate," Achranae suggested.

The last thing Kelly wanted at the moment was the alien's charity. "I'm all right," he said irritably.

Achranae's eyes were unblinking. "In that case, I would like to take a few minutes of rest myself. Is this permissible?"

Kelly stared back as understanding slowly came. Clearly, Achranae didn't need a break; he was a game and a half toward going home. Besides which, Kelly *knew* what an upset Olyt looked like, and Achranae showed none of the symptoms. No, giving Kelly the chance to calm down could only benefit the human . . . and as he gazed at the alien's face, Kelly knew the Olyt was perfectly aware of that.

"Yes," Kelly said at last. "Let's take a break. How about returning in a half-hour or so?"

"Acceptable." Achranae stood and crossed his wrists. "I shall be ready whenever you also are."

The ceiling over Kelly's bed was perfectly flat, without even so much as a ripple to mar it. Nonetheless, it reflected images far more poorly than Kelly would have expected. He wondered about it, but not very hard. There were more important things to worry about.

Pulling his left arm from behind his head; he checked the time. Five more minutes and Slaich would sound the little bell that would call them back to the arena. Kelly sighed.

What was he going to *do?*

Strangely enough, the chess game was no longer his major concern. True, he was still in trouble there, but the rest period had done wonders for his composure, and he had already come up with two or three promising lines of attack. As long as he kept his wits around him, he had a fair chance of pulling a win out of his current position. And that was Kelly's real problem ... because if he did, in fact, win, there would have to be a third game. A game either he or Achranae would have to lose.

Kelly didn't want to die. He had lots of high-sounding reasons why he ought to stay alive—at least one of which, the fact that no one else on Earth knew of the threat lurking behind these "games," was actually valid—but the plain fact was that he simply didn't *want* to die. Whatever the third game was chosen to be, he knew he would play just as hard and as well as he possibly could.

And yet ...

Kelly squirmed uncomfortably. Achranae didn't deserve to die, either. Not only was he also an unwilling participant in this crazy arena, but he had deliberately thrown away his best chance to win the contest. Perhaps it was less a spirit of fairness than one of obedience to a rigid code of honor that had kept him from capitalizing on his opponent's momentary panic; Kelly would probably never know one way or the other. But it really didn't matter. If Kelly went on to win the chess game he would owe his victory to Achranae.

The third game . . .

What would be the fairest way to do it? Invent a game together that neither had played before? That would pit Kelly's natural tactical abilities against Achranae's trained ones and would probably be pretty fair. On the other hand, it would give the Stryfkar another chance to study them in action, and Kelly was in no mood to cooperate with his captors any more than necessary. Achranae, Kelly had already decided, seemed to feel the same way. He wondered fleetingly how long the Stryfkar had been snatching Achranae's people, and why they hadn't retaliated. Probably had no idea where this game studies center was, he decided; the Transphere's operations would, by design, be difficult to trace. But if he and Achranae didn't want to give the Stryfkar any more data, their only alternative was to make the rubber game one of pure chance, and Kelly rebelled against staking his life on the toss of a coin.

The tone, expected though it was, startled him. "It is time," Slaich's flat voice announced. "You will return to the test chamber."

Grimacing, Kelly got to his feet and headed for the door. Maybe Achranae would have some ideas.

"Are you better prepared to play now?" the Olyt asked when they again faced each other over the board.

"Yes," Kelly nodded. "Thanks for suggesting a break. I really *did* need it."

"I sensed that your honor did not permit you to make the request." The alien gestured at the board. "I believe it is your move."

Sure enough, now that his nerves were under control, Kelly began to chip away at Achranae's position, gradually making up his losses and taking the offensive once more. Gambling on the excessive value the Olyt seemed to place in his queen, Kelly laid a trap, with his own queen as the bait. Achranae bit . . . and five moves later Kelly had won.

"Excellent play," the Olyt said, with what Kelly took to be admiration. "I was completely unprepared for that attack. I was not wrong; you have an uncanny tactical ability. Your race will indeed be glorious starfarers someday."

"Assuming we ever get off our own world, of course," Kelly said as he cleared the board. "At the moment we're more like pawns ourselves in this game."

"You have each won once," Slaich spoke up. "It is time now to choose the rules for the final game."

Kelly swallowed and looked up to find Achranae looking back at him. "Any idea?" he asked.

"None that is useful. A game of chance would perhaps be fastest. Beyond that, I have not determined what my duty requires."

"What are the possibilities?"

"That I should survive in order to return to my people, or that I should not, to allow you that privilege."

"A pity we can't individually challenge the Stryfkar to duels," Kelly said wryly.

"That would be satisfying," Achranae agreed. "But I do not expect they would accept."

There was a long silence . . . and an idea popped into Kelly's mind, practically full-blown. A risky idea—one that could conceivably get them *both* killed. But it might just work . . . and otherwise one of them would certainly die. Gritting his teeth, Kelly took the plunge. "Achranae," he said carefully, "I believe I have a game we can play. Will you trust me enough to accept it *now*, before I explain the rules, and to play it without a practice game?"

The Olyt's snout quivered slightly as he stared across the table in silence. For a long moment the only sound Kelly could hear was his own heartbeat. Then, slowly, Achranae cocked his head to the right. "Very well. I believe you to be honorable. I will agree to your conditions."

"Slaich? You still holding to the rules you set up?" Kelly called.

"Of course."

"Okay." Kelly took a deep breath. "This game involves two rival kingdoms and a fire-breathing creature who harasses them both. Here's the creature's underground chamber." He placed a black marker on the playing board, then picked up three of the transparent plates and their supports and set them up. "The two kingdoms are called the Mountain Kingdom and the Land City. The Mountain Kingdom is bigger; here's its center and edge." He placed a large red marker on the top plate and added a ring of six smaller ones around it, two squares away. Moving the black marker slightly so that it was directly under one edge of the ring, he picked up a large yellow marker. "This is the Land City," he identified it, moving it slowly over the middle transparency as his eyes flickered over the board. Ten centimeters between levels, approximately; four per square . . . he put the yellow marker eight squares from the red one and four squares to one side. It wasn't perfect, but it was close and would have to do. "Finally, here are our forces." He scattered a dozen each red and yellow butterfly-shaped pieces in the space between the two kingdoms. "The conditions for victory are twofold: the creature must be dead, and there can be no forces from the opposing side threatening your kingdom. Okay?"

"Very well," Achranae said slowly, studying the board carefully. Once again Kelly wished he had a better grasp of Olyt expressions. "How are combat results decided?"

"By the number of forces involved plus a throw of the die." Making up the rules as he went along, Kelly set up a system that allowed combat between any two of the three sides—and that would require nearly all of both kingdoms' forces combined to defeat the creature with any certainty. "Movement is two squares or one level per turn, and you can move all your forces each turn," he concluded. "Any questions?"

Achranae's eyes bored unblinkingly into his, as if trying to read Kelly's mind. "No. Which of us moves first?"

"I will, if you don't mind." Starting with the pieces closest to the Olyt's kingdom, Kelly began moving them

away from the red marker and toward the black one.
Achranae hesitated somewhat when it was his turn, but
he followed Kelly's example in moving his forces down-
ward. Two of them landed within striking range of some
of Kelly's; but the human ignored them, continuing on-
ward instead. Within a few more moves the yellow and
red pieces had formed a single mass converging on the
black marker.

The fire-breathing creature never had a chance.

"And now . . . ?" Achranae sat stiffly in his chair, his
claws about halfway out of their sheaths. The creature
had been eliminated on the Olyt's turn, making it Kelly's
move . . . and Achranae's forces were still intermixed with
the human's. A more vulnerable position was hard to
imagine, and Achranae clearly knew it.

Kelly gave him a tight smile and leaned back in his
seat. "Well, the creature's dead—and in their present
positions none of your forces can threaten my kingdom.
So I guess I've won."

There was a soft hiss from the other side of the table,
and Achranae's claws slid all the way out. Kelly held his
breath and tensed himself to leap. Surely Achranae was
smart enough to see it . . . and, abruptly, the claws disappeared. "But my kingdom is *also* not threatened," the
Olyt said. "Therefore I, too, have won."

"Really?" Kelly pretended great amazement. "I'll be
darned. You're *right*. Congratulations." He looked at the
ceiling. "Slaich? By a remarkable coincidence we've both
won the third game, so I guess we both get to go home.
Ready any time you are."

"No." The Stryf's flat voice was firm.

A golfball-sized lump rose into Kelly's throat. "Why
not? You said anyone who won two games would be sent
home. You set up that rule yourself."

"Then the rule is changed. Only one of you can be
allowed to leave. You will choose a new game."

Slaich's words seemed to hang in the air like a death
sentence . . . and Kelly felt his fingernails digging into
his palms. He really hadn't expected the aliens to let him
twist their rules to his advantage—he already knew this

was no game to them. But he'd still hoped . . . and now he had no choice but to gamble his last card. "I won't play any more games," he said bluntly. "I'm sick of being a pawn in this boogeyman hunt of yours. You can all just take a flying leap at yourselves."

"If you do not play you will lose by forfeit," Slaich reminded him.

"Big deal," Kelly snorted. "You're going to wipe out earth eventually anyway, aren't you? What the hell difference does it make where I die?"

There was a short pause. "Very well. You yourself have chosen. Achranae, return to your Transphere chamber."

Slowly, the alien rose to his feet. Kelly half expected him to speak up in protest, or to otherwise plead for the human's life. But he remained silent. For a moment he regarded Kelly through the transparent game boards, as Kelly held his breath. Then, still without a word, the alien crossed his wrists in salute and vanished behind the sliding door. "You will return to your rest chamber now," Slaich ordered.

Letting out his breath in a long sigh, Kelly stood up and disassembled the playing board, storing the pieces and plates away in their proper places. So it had indeed come down to a toss of a coin, he thought, suddenly very tired. The coin was in the air, and there was nothing to do now but wait . . . and hope that Achranae had understood.

* * *

To: *Office of Director Rodau 248700, A.R.B.: Clars*

From: *Office of Director Eftis 379214, Games Studies, Var-4*

Date: *21 Lysmo 3829*

XXXXX URGENT XXXXX

Dear Rodau,

It is even worse than we expected and I hereby make formal recommendation that the Humans be completely obliterated. The enclosed records should be studied carefully, particularly those concerning the third game that was played. By using his tactical skills to create a game he and his opponent could jointly win, the Human clearly demonstrated both the ability to cooperate with others, and also the rare trait of mercy. Although these characteristics gained him nothing in this particular instance—and, in fact, can be argued to have been liabilities—we cannot assume this will always be the case. The danger that their cooperative nature will lead the Humans into a successful alliance instead of betraying them to their destruction cannot be ignored. If the Chanis had been capable of building alliances they might well have never been stopped.

It is anticipated that a full psycho-physiological dissection of our Human subject will be necessary to facilitate the assault fleet's strategy. We request that the proper experts and equipment be sent as soon as they become available. Please do not delay overlong; I cannot guarantee our Human can be kept alive more than a year at the most.

Eftis

* * *

Kelly's first indication that the long wait had ended was a faint grinding sound transmitted through the metal walls of his rest chamber. It startled him from a deep sleep—but he hardly even had time to wonder about it before the room's door suddenly flashed white and collapsed outward. Instantly, there was a minor hurricane in the room, and Kelly's ears popped as the air pressure dropped drastically. But even as he tumbled off the bed three figures in long-snouted spacesuits fought their way in through the gale, and before he knew it he'd been stuffed in a giant ribbed balloon with a hissing tank at the bottom. "Kelly McClain?" a tinny, static-distorted voice came from a box by the air tank as the balloon inflated. "Are you safe?"

Kelly's ears popped again as his three rescuers tipped him onto his back and carried him carefully toward the ruined door. "I'm fine," he said toward the box. "Is that you, Achranae?"

It was almost fifteen seconds before the voice spoke again; clearly, the Olyt's translator wasn't as good as the Stryfkar's. "Yes. I am pleased you are still alive."

Kelly's grin was wide enough to hurt, and was probably even visible through his beard. "Me too. *Damn*, but I'm glad you got my message. I wasn't at all sure you'd caught it."

They were out in the Transphere chamber before the response came, and Kelly had a chance to look around. In the ceiling, stretching upwards through at least two stories' worth of rock, was a jagged hole. Moving purposefully through the chamber itself were a dozen more Olyts in the white, armor-like suits. "It was ingenious. I feared that I would not be allowed to leave, though, once I had seen the board."

"Me too—but it looks like we had nothing to worry about." Kelly grinned again—it was so good to talk to a friend again! "I'll lay you any odds that the Stryfkar haven't *yet* noticed what I did. It's the old can't-see-the-forest-for-the-trees problem; they'd seen that four-tiered board used for so many different games that it never occurred to them that you and I would automatically associate it with Skymarch, the only game we'd ever played on it. So while they took my kingdoms-and-dragon setup at face value, you were able to see the markers as a group of objects in space. I gambled that you'd realize they represented our home worlds and this one, and that you'd take note of the relative distances I'd laid out. I guess the gamble paid off."

Kelly was beneath the ceiling hole now, and a pair of dangling cables were being attached to his balloon's upper handholds. "We shall hope that winning such risks is characteristic of your race," Achranae said. "We have destroyed the Stryfkar base and have captured records that show a large force will soon be coming here. We have opened communication with your race, but they have not yet agreed to a tactical alliance. Perhaps your testimony will help persuade them. It is hoped that you, at least, will agree to aid us in our tactical planning."

The ropes pulled taut and Kelly began moving upward. "I'm almost certain we can find some extra help on Earth," Kelly told the Olyt grimly. "And as for me, it'll be a pleasure. The Stryfkar have a lot to learn about us pawns."